Blood of the Dragon

MARCUS ROBINSON

authorHOUSE®

AuthorHouse™
1663 Liberty Drive
Bloomington, IN 47403
www.authorhouse.com
Phone: 1-800-839-8640

First published by AuthorHouse 9/7/2011

ISBN: 978-1-4634-3596-7 (sc)
ISBN: 978-1-4634-3595-0 (e)

Library of Congress Control Number: 2011912807

Printed in the United States of America

Table of Contents

Prologue:

Perfect Night for a Revival

San Antonio Texas, Present day

The evening air was cool enough for people to be comfortable. It was a special tent revival for the San Antonio Church of Christ. The large big top tent was filled to capacity with the celebration of the praise and worship portion of the church service; a thousand disciples stood beneath the big top, singing and clapping to Christian songs, whose lyrics were displayed on a large-screen so that everyone might be able to read along.

The leader of the church, Pastor Willis Ware, was a large black man built like a cross between Vin Diesel and Michael Clarke Duncan. He was clean-shaven and wore glasses. The fifty-seven year old pastor was in remarkable shape and appeared years younger than he was. From the front of the stage he mouthed the words, while checking on the rear side exits behind him, and glancing around at the security team stationed at every entrance to the permanent big top structure. Although the pastor was distracted, anxious, and frightened, he still managed to pull himself together and focus on praise and worship.

The pastor's twenty-seven year old daughter turned heads as she parted through the crowd of Christians and visitors on her way to the stage. She was indeed a very attractive woman, as though Rihanna and Rosalyn Sanchez had been amalgamated to create a single woman. Megan.

"I'm sorry I'm late," said Megan. She hugged her father and then took a seat beside him. "We just landed and came straight here, but there was loads of traffic on 85."

The pastor put his arm around her. "I'm just glad you're here," he said.

"Are the kids alright?"

The pastor nodded and told her they were in class.

When the song ended, the congregation sat down for the greetings portion of the service. On cue, the assistant pastor, Bruce Lawson, approached the podium. He was a young African American in his early thirties; short and stocky, his hair was wavy and he wore rectangle glasses. Bruce delivered a powerful thought provoking welcoming service.

Megan noticed that her father was distracted. She wrapped her arm around him and smiled at him, reassuringly. "Daddy, it's all over. The culprits have been caught, and besides, Agents Navaro and Phelps have assured us that it's really over."

"Then, why are *they* here?" the pastor said, nodding towards the guards.

"It's just a precaution. And I'm glad they're here. Aren't you?"

"You're right. I'm being silly. If it wasn't safe, the revival would not be taking place here and now." The pastor gestured at the empty chair to his right. "He's not coming is he?"

Megan raised her brow and shrugged.

Bruce was done with his welcoming message and excused

himself in time for the song ministry to take the stage and sing one more song to prepare everyone for communion.

The pastor said under his breath, "Jubei, I hope you come tonight."

Undercover security guards patrolled the perimeter around the special event's grounds. The ministry's children and teenagers met in their own tents. And both tents were flanked with armed security guards. Every car that pulled into the parking lot was searched. Drivers and their passengers were required to present their ID, and their names were required to be on the official guest list. Only after the security guards had patted each person down and had thoroughly gone through their belongings were they granted permission to proceed on to the big top.

On the outer perimeter of the grounds, snipers were perched in trees, several hundred yards from the church; their rifles pointed toward the big top.

A voice in their earpieces articulated, *Snipers, report.*

"Alpha dog, all clear." The sniper lifted his right sleeve, which was covering a night vision watch as well as a small tattoo on his hand, of a golden gate with angel wings. He peered into the night scope, switched it to thermal vision, and scanned the west field where he detected shapes hiding amid the tall grass. Before he could react, an arrow flew through the air and penetrated the sniper's scope, eye and brain. He dropped to the ground.

From within the darkness, a shadow descended upon the perch and confirmed that the sniper was dead.

Another sniper faced the parking lot and was checking his assigned section. A shadow swept in from above, on a hang glider, and as it angled in, the shadowy figure released himself from his harness and landed quietly on the perch, where he swiftly pulled out a sword and drove it through the sniper's neck before he was able to call for help.

Three other ninjas detached from their hang gliders and landed in the field. They slaughtered the security guards that were stationed around the perimeter, and then remained in place until receiving orders to proceed.

A military family had been cleared to proceed to the big top, where a lanky candy vendor was passing out free cotton candy and candy green apples at the entry. Two of the teenagers selected green candy apples and then hurried into the tent, followed by the father and his eldest son, each with a cone of cotton candy.

The tithe and offering portion of the service was already over and Pastor Willis walked over to the steps of the stage with his bible in hand.

Megan glanced at the empty chair and sighed. She bowed her head in prayer.

Outside, a white minivan pulled up to the gate. The security team searched the black driver and his Asian passenger, both men in their twenties. The Asian man grumbled about the excess of security for a church revival. The guards remained professional, said nothing and did their job, allowing them both through.

At the entrance of the big top, the Asian man helped himself to cotton candy and his friend chose the green candy apple, before heading in and being led to their seats by an elderly usher.

Meanwhile

Riding across a zip line over the crowd of Christians and visitors alike, a single ninja assassin in a Navy blue uniform landed at the very top of the tent; a sword strapped to his back and metal gauntlets on his arms, his shins, and calves. The ninja crept unnoticed into the big top and hid high above the crowd and over the make shift stage in the center of the ring. Once in position, the lone ninja waited.

As the communion service ended the pastor climbed the steps; the song ministry had taken to the stage for one last song before the pastor's sermon.

The father of the military family took the cone the cotton candy had been on and rolled it up. The oldest child took the candy off and threw it on the ground. The stick the apple was on was a sharpened wooden stick, he gave the stick to the father who then placed it in the tube of the makeshift blowgun. Across the big top, seated in exactly the same position, were the other two teenagers. They had also prepared their makeshift weapons. All of them aimed at Pastor Willis who was taking the stage.

"Amen!" the pastor said excitedly. "I'd like to welcome everyone, members and visitors to the new and improved San Antonio Church of Christ! For too long have we been silent, due to the horrors that affected churches and mosques across our nation. Well, here we are. Back to do doing what needs to be done. We have a mission and we can't let the darkness hold us back an longer." Pastor Willis was pacing, which made it challenging for the assassins to aim with accuracy.

From above, Jubei scanned the audience with enhanced ninja vision. He could make out the makeshift blowguns pointed at Pastor Willis. Jubei had to act fast. He pulled out three Shuriken knives and jumped through the top of the tent, catching the attention of the crowd as he came down;

people hollered as he dropped. Jubei flipped in the air before landing unharmed on his feet. Right away he took hold of the pastor, pressed a button, and before anyone could figure out what was happening, Jubei and the pastor were whisked into the air. Just as Jubei moved, blow darts, which had been aimed towards where the two men had been standing, struck and killed innocent targets—a little boy and his father. A mass panic erupted. People began to trample one another to as they tried to flee the scene.

At the top of the tent, Jubei tried to steady the pastor. "If you wish to live, do exactly as I say," he said.

"My daughter," Pastor Willis pleaded. "Save my daughter first."

Megan frantically scanned the crowd for her father as she scrambled to the closest exit. She was knocked to the ground, tried to stand back up but was knocked off balance again. Jubei located her and jumped down, landing on hysterical people headed toward Megan. He threw multiple kicks, knocking a few others out of the way. He grabbed the pastor's stunned daughter around the waist, launched another rope and pressed his button and they ascended with Megan holding onto Jubei for dear life; her nails dug into his biceps all the way to the top of the tent where the pastor awaited his daughter and embraced her.

Across the big top Jubei spotted another pole that might safely help them back to the ground. He shot a zip line to the pole and then, from his concealed pouch, he pulled a handle and hooked it to the zip line.

Ninjas approached the threesome. They drew their swords and charged at them. Jubei was ready and brandished his sword. He cut down the ninjas who surrounded him, like a tornado of spinning blades.

A couple of ninjas swept in on hang gliders, aiming at the pastor with poison-tipped arrows. Jubei shoved the pastor to the side, caught the arrows in mid-flight and hurled it into the heart of the ninja that had shot it at them.

Jubei pulled out incendiary Shuriken knives and, upon pressing a button, their tips began to glow. He threw the Shurikens, which exploded on impact, blowing off a ninja's hand and blowing melon-sized holes in the chests of two others.

The blasts startled Pastor Willis. He tripped. Jubei rolled and grabbed the pastor's hand before he could fall. Megan comforted her father while Jubei finished setting up the zip line, which he then used to send her down and the pastor followed her.

The ninjas lurking in the field finally received orders to move in. They slaughtered disciples as they crept in.

Jubei leapt from the top of the tent, flipped in mid-air and landed steadily on his feet. He gestured for Pastor Willis and Megan to follow him.

Megan shouted, "We can't leave without the children!"

Jubei told her there wasn't enough time but Pastor Willis pleaded with him, "Whoever you are, please save them. Save the children, please."

Jubei could not deny them.

A ninja closed in on a hang glider, released himself and rolled to his feet, and then threw Shuriken after Shuriken. The first few Jubei managed to deflect and then a slashing star sunk into Jubei's shoulder, another in his upper thigh, but none could have guessed he was struck because he fought on, as though unfazed by his wounds.

Jubei tossed a smoke bomb, and, while the screen of smoke disoriented the ninja, Jubei swept in on the ninja like a ghost, decapitating him. Megan never did see the arterial spray or the head roll off. Like a hit-and-run in the fog, the smoke had veiled the gruesome gesture.

Jubei took hold of the pastor's sleeve and Megan's hand.

Hurriedly he led them through the circus grounds where other ninjas had been awaiting. But Jubei, a near-perfect weapon, left a trail of corpses in his path.

From atop a tree, a sniper ninja shot a poisonous arrow at Jubei. Jubei attempted to deflect the arrow but it hit him in the side. Jubei dropped to his knees. Still he was able to use his ninja focus to slow the trajectory of another arrow headed toward the pastor and his daughter. Jubei tossed a Shuriken to deflect the arrow.

He clenched his teeth and yanked out the arrow. The ninja shot another arrow, which Jubei kicked. It went off-course and struck a ninja in the neck.

Jubei activated his night vision goggles. He could make out the outline of a sniper crouched in a nearby tree. From a small backpack, Jubei pulled out a miniature crossbow and fired a dart, hitting the sniper between the eyes.

Jubei scanned their surroundings to see whether the coast was clear. "Hide in the hay," Jubei loud-whispered. "Hurry!"

The pastor and Megan crawled into the wagon and covered themselves with hay. They did not notice that Jubei had run off toward the children's tent.

The children were cowering and screaming as they watched the tips of swords and knives slash into their tent. The instructors made a valiant effort to protect the children, running forth to try to hold back the intruders. However they were no match for armed ninjas. The adults were stabbed. The children hollered; you couldn't tell the shrill cries of the boys apart from those of the girls.

The ninjas pushed through the herd of terrified children. Huddled behind them all were the boy and girl the ninjas had been tracking down. Ignoring the other children who were scattering about, the men grabbed the terrified boy and girl by their arms.

Bruce witnessed it all. He could hardly stand and held onto his sides, having been wounded by a ninja during an earlier rescue attempt. "Mara! James!" he yelled out, powerless as he watched the ninjas lead the young captives down an overgrown path into the woods toward the point of extraction.

Sirens wailed in the distance.

When Jubei reached the children's tent, they were no longer running around like chickens without their heads. They stood frozen among the corpses of their instructors and guards. Jubei sheathed his sword and scanned the horrified little faces for those of James and Marie, although he sensed they were no longer there.

He knelt down to eye-height of a chubby boy who looked like he had just woken from a nightmare. "The bad men," said Jubei, "where did they take James and Marie?" he asked, as calmly as he could.

The horror-struck boy only blinked. The pale girl beside him pointed towards the woods.

Outside, the SWAT team trucks and a caravan of police, FBI, County Sheriffs, and National Guard, were congregating.

Jubei rushed toward the woods before anyone might try to stop him and waste both their times with an endless interrogation.

As he neared the tree line he came upon Bruce, who was moaning in the grass. He held out his hand to assist him to his feet, but, in a panic, Bruce tried to crawl away, in vain. His injury knocked him on his back.

"I'm trying to protect the pastor and his family," Jubei said. "Do you know where they are?"

As the girl had, Bruce pointed into the woods. Jubei ran down the darkened path.

He began to feel the poison coursing through him. He stumbled.

A ninja stepped out from behind a tree and charged at Jubei, but he punched him, knocking him out cold. Several other ninjas stepped out from behind surrounding trees. Jubei had nowhere to turn. The ninjas moved in.

Jubei leaped and backflipped off a tree. He ran. The ninjas followed close behind, so close that he could hear them breathe. Jubei pulled two silver boomerangs from his bag, turned, and hurled them toward the approaching ninjas. The boomerangs opened in mid-air, revealing three long razor sharp blades that he used to slice his pursuants at the knees. Jubei grabbed two more swords and fought his way through another squad of ninjas closing in from the front. Swiftly he cut them down as well.

And then he reached behind and caught the returning boomerangs.

Jubei could sense the presence of sniper ninjas in the treetops. They were aiming their arrows at Jubei when his boomerangs sliced through the leaves. They toppled and Jubei ran, ignoring his pain; he concentrated on the poison coursing through his body and slowed it down.

He came upon a clearing. Marie and James were being lifted into an unmarked black helicopter. Ninjas sprung from the ground and Jubei drew his sword.

A ninja moved in. Jubei blocked the attack. Once more, Jubei felt the poison burn through him. He dropped to his knees. The ninja raised his sword and readied to slash Jubei, but Jubei grabbed a tiny knife he kept in a nylon sheath strapped to the back of his boot and with it he sliced the ninja behind the knee before he could bring the sword down on his head. The ninja knelt in agony. Jubei grabbed the man's sword.

Another ninja ran towards him. Jubei shielded himself

with the injured ninja's body, still twitching in pain. The ninja ran his sword through his comrade's body.

Jubei vaulted into the air and landed behind one ninja and sliced him in half.

Another ninja moved in. Jubei stabbed him in the stomach and yanked the sword out just in time to deflect another attack.

Jubei shot a bunch of spikes into one ninja's face. He dropped his sword and Jubei cut him down.

Jubei spun around shooting spikes, cutting down the remaining foes.

Jubei was reloading the spikes when the helicopter began to take off. Jubei shot a grappling hook at the helicopter's landing gear. He climbed the rope.

The ninjas in the helicopter shot at Jubei, but he had vanished. Jubei was beneath the helicopter, holding on with magnetic ninja claws. To those in the aircraft it appeared that Jubei had fallen.

Jubei crawled back up to the landing gear and he pulled out a smoke bomb, tossed it into the helicopter. The smoky explosion caused a commotion during which Jubei climbed into the cabin and slaughtered all the adults, including the pilot. And, although the helicopter began to drop, Jubei did not lose his composure. He pulled the dead pilot from his seat and took the controls, steadied the helicopter, and managed to land it in the field, where the FBI had already arrived and were examining the corpses.

Jubei cut the engines as the agents surrounded the helicopter with their guns drawn.

An agent shouted, "Get out of the helicopter with your hands up. Do it, now!"

James yelled out, "We're in here."

The FBI agents waited for the propeller to stop spinning

before cautiously approaching the helicopter, peaking into the cabin where the children sat amid dead ninjas.

"All clear!" the agent said. "We're gonna need body bags." He surveyed the field. "Lots of them."

Jubei ran down the small trail, back to the circus' grounds, where ninjas and law enforcement were at war; innocent people caught in the crossfire—collateral damage. Ninjas killed law enforcement agents and law enforcement agents killed ninjas.

Additional ninjas had been called in as reinforcements to battle law enforcement and continue to hunt down Pastor Willis.

Jubei moved through the circus' grounds undetected, until an FBI agent caught sight of him and open fire. Jubei dodged the bullets. Another agent flanked Jubei and fired shots. FBI agents surrounded Jubei.

"Get down on the ground!" they yelled. "Down on the ground, now!"

Jubei obeyed. The agents kept their guns on him as a couple of agents moved in to restrain him. Jubei shot small needles from under his sleeve, which hit the agents in the neck. Jubei leaped in the air and drop kicked the first two agents. Jubei landed on his back and tossed Shurikens to disarm the agents. Then he sprang to his feet and spin kicked one agent as another tried to punch Jubei. He parried the attack and grabbed the agent by the wrist, twisting his arm until it broke, and then hit the agent in the neck, knocking him out.

A Shuriken sailed through the darkness and struck Jubei in the back. He slumped forward. More Shurikens came at him. Jubei rolled on the ground and deflected them with his gauntlets.

Ninjas leaped down. Jubei sprang to his feet and blocked

an attack; he pivoted around to get behind a ninja, striking him in the back. Jubei spun around to kick the second ninja in the face. A third ninja moved in with his sword drawn. Jubei vaulted over the second ninja and kicked the sword from his hand. The third ninja pulled out a knife and slashed at Jubei. Jubei dodged the strikes.

An unexpected sharp pain tore through Jubei's body and he fell to his knees. The ninja brought the knife down over Jubei's head and Jubei X blocked the attack. The blade stopped an inch from Jubei's face. Jubei overpowered the ninja, disarmed him and sliced his throat.

The ninjas had been decimated. The FBI agents had been incapacitated. Finally, Jubei could return to the haystack where he had left Pastor Willis and Megan.

"We got to move quickly," he said.

"Not so fast," said a woman's voice, which did not sound familiar. "Turn around slowly."

Jubei raised his hands and turned. The woman holding a gun on him was a beautiful Latino woman in FBI gear.

The pastor and his daughter recognized agent Navaro and climbed out of the wagon.

"Don't shoot him," said Pastor Willis. "He saved us."

Navaro kept the gun aimed at Jubei but before she knew it, Jubei had dashed toward her and easily disarmed her, turning her own gun on her.

"They're not safe here," Jubei said. "Get them out of here, alive."

Jubei turned to leave.

Megan grabbed his arm. "The children," she began to say, but Jubei interrupted her.

"They are safe," Jubei said. He returned Navaro's gun to her. She was about to say something when Jubei suddenly shoved her to the side, simultaneously hurling a knife that stabbed a ninja in the chest. Navaro was startled. She had not even noticed the ninja creep up on them. On the other hand, Jubei had not only spotted him but also taken him down before she could even thank him for returning her gun.

Jubei shouted, "Move!" He led the way through the circus' grounds.

Jubei and Navaro fought off ninjas along the way.

As they were about to get into an unmarked van they were surrounded by ninjas. Gunfire erupted and the ninjas dropped dead. The shots had come from within the unmarked van. Commando-like soldiers in black uniforms spilled out from the van. Two of the gunmen had a small patch on their chest embroidered with a golden gate spreading angel-like wings. Pastor Willis, Megan, and Navaro got in the van and, as agent Phelps lowered his head to get in, an arrow hit him through the neck. He died instantly.

More arrows were shot and Jubei deflected them. "Get out of here now!" he shouted and pushed Megan into the van. She attired to get his attention before the van door closed, but Jubei had already turned his back and pulled out his sword. The van drove off.

The ninjas were discombobulated. As they tried to get back up, Jubei slaughtered them, one after another. By the time he was done, the ninjas were nothing more than intermingled body parts.

A ninja hiding nearby had witnessed Pastor Willis and Megan enter the van and signaled a comrade on the ground. As the van drove off, Jubei followed in the stolen police car. The van turned a sharp corner. Jubei followed, all the while glancing in the rearview mirror, to make sure that no one was following them.

A ninja perched on a rooftop aimed a rocket launcher at the police car. As he readied to fire the rocket launcher he received orders not to: "The device has been planted. Fall back."

Tearing through the streets, the mysterious van ran through traffic lights and sped through downtown until it reached the interstate. Jubei bobbed and weaved through the traffic so that he could keep up with the van. Jubei listened to police dispatch. The police was headed his way. He took a sharp turn and veered away from the van. As he turned down the street he came head to head with the police, and swerved, turning onto Interstate 10, heading west toward Lackland Air Force Base. Police helicopters were now tracking Jubei and ignored the black van. The highway patrol joined the car chase. One of the officers leaned out the window and aimed at the tires of the stolen police car. Jubei swerved to dodge the bullets. The police closed in from both sides. Bullets flew and Jubei's rear tires were shot out. He lost control of the car. The car flipped and landed on its side in a ditch, passenger side down. Police officers rushed to surround the stolen sedan and aimed their guns. Slowly, Jubei climbed out from the car window.

Officers yelled, "Down on the ground!"

Jubei pulled out a needle and readied to inject himself. The police officers fired their tasers. His resistance to the tasers stunned the officers. They kept raising the volts until Jubei passed out. It took longer, much longer than anyone had expected.

They lifted his unconscious body and hauled it to a police van.

A policeman picked up Jubei's needle with latex gloves, dropped it in a clear bag, sealed and tagged it.

Half-a-mile from where Jubei had been captured, the black van veered off the interstate and down a county road. The paved road turned into a dirt road. The van's headlights cracked through the pitch-black night.

"Where are we going?" Pastor Willis asked. "And what about the children?"

Navaro got off the phone and, without looking at the pastor, she said, "The children are alright. They'll be at headquarters."

Pastor Willis and Megan sighed deeply.

Megan was watching the commandos from the corner of her eye, and yet she couldn't help thinking about the ninja who had selflessly saved them.

"Who was he?" Megan asked out loud.

"Who was who?" asked Navaro.

"The man who saved us."

"We think he was the one that had been trying to warn you of what was going to happen."

"You mean, he may have been the man who gave me the journal?"

"We think so," Navaro said."Whoever he was, he saved our life. And that's all I need to know."

She turned off the dirt road into a gravel driveway.

"Where are we going?" Megan asked.

"To a safe house," Navaro replied. "It's the only place where you'll be safe until we figure out our next move."

Navaro followed the winding dirt road until they came upon a boarded up dilapidated plantation home.

"It's a safe house," said Navaro.

Suddenly the grass, trees and bushes became alive. You could hear the rustling and crackling before you even saw the soldiers come out from their hiding places, camouflaged in shrubbery and dark green and black face paint, so that you couldn't even tell whether they were man or woman, black or white or anything in between. They approached the car. Navaro rolled down her window and without a word she presented her ID. A soldier checked it carefully, handed it back and waved them through. With a hand signal he ordered his men to withdraw and the guards stepped back into the darkness, vanishing as instantaneously as they had emerged.

The car slowly proceeded up the driveway and parked in front of the boarded up front door.

Navaro swiped her ID card alongside the mailbox and the board slid away, revealing a lovely wooden door that opened onto further darkness. She stepped in first, followed by the pastor and Megan. The door shut automatically behind them and once more the boards slid into place, sealing the house up. The lights turned on and the inside was not like the outside at all. The interior was a beautifully restored plantation mansion with its magnificent old world furniture.

"Welcome to the Narrow Gate," said Navaro.

Megan whispered, "Never judge a book by its cover."

An elderly man entered the foyer with his head bowed, reading the bible as he walked. Navaro cleared her throat and he looked up from his book, seemingly not surprised to see the newcomers. However he was, he was happy to see Navaro and shut the bible so that he could greet her with open arms. They embraced.

"Welcome home, agent Navaro," he said, in a thick Middle Eastern accent. "I see you brought company."

"Al Kazim," Navaro said, "this is Pastor Willis, and his daughter, Megan."

Al Kazim held out his hand. "My name is Al Kazim. You are most welcome here. Follow me, please." He led the group into the living room where a couple of muscle-bound ex special force marines were watching American Idol's audition show on an oversized television. They glared at the pastor and Megan as they walked across the living room.

"Don't mind them," Al Kazim said. "They're teddy bears."

Al Kazim showed the pastor and Megan into the library

where he invited them to sit on the couch. He pulled sat on a chair across from them. "Did agent Navaro fill you in on the Narrow Gate?"

"Not really," the pastor said, "but I'm beginning to understand. It's from the biblical description of the narrow path into Heaven, Matthew 7:13-14. *"Enter through the narrow gate. For wide is the gate and broad is the road that leads to destruction, and many may enter it. But small is the gate and narrow is the road that leads to life.""*

Jubei woke up in the back of a paddy wagon. He was restrained; his mask and hood had been removed. His African and Asian mixed descent features were strikingly handsome. His face was chiseled and his complexion copperish.

He was sitting between armored officers and a couple other officers sat across from them. His hands, feet, and head were restrained, magnetically sealed to the seat.

"Well, look who woke up," an officer said in a taunting manner. "It's Ninja Gaiden."

The officers laughed.

"So, you're da one running around, killing those ninjas."

One man was holding up a clear evidence bag that held Jubei's needle. "And what's this, your suicide needle in case you get captured?"

Jubei ignored the questions and remained silent. All he could move were his eyes and with them he scanned the carriage searching the panel for the controls to the electro-magnetic restraints. His tongue roamed around his mouth for a dart he kept beneath a fake molar, and popped the molar out, slid a dart in place, swallowed the fake tooth, aimed for the appropriate button on the control panel and spat the dart, which hit the target, turning the power indicator from green to red. Before the SWAT officers could react, Jubei struck one in the throat with his elbow and the other in the neck. The SWAT officer locked up, as if he were catatonic. The third SWAT officer sitting across from Jubei reached for his gun and shot. Jubei caught the taser dart and stabbed the fourth SWAT officer in the leg. He kicked the third officer with such force that he smashed the glass shield and cracked the man's helmet in half. The fourth SWAT officer convulsed as hundreds of volts surged through his body. Jubei removed the taser dart and punched the SWAT officer through the helmet's glass shield.

After grabbing his sword, mask, and hood, Jubei swung open the Paddy Wagon door and saw that it was being escorted by another squad car. Jubei leaped onto the hood of the squad car, flipped in the air and landed on the sidewalk, then ran across the street towards the exit ramp and leaped off the overpass.

The squad cars switched their sirens on. An announcement of Jubei's escape was dispatched.

The lights of the police sirens were close behind Jubei as he reached an alley. An officer shot him through the right shoulder, but Jubei ignored the wretched pain and kept running at top speed.

Within moments the police regrouped and resumed pursuing Jubei, whose heart was throbbing a mile a minute in his chest. He stopped to rest in a back alley. His shoulder bled profusely and he was trying to bandage the wound when a police car turned the corner, sirens blaring, red and blue lights flashing.

"Police. Freeze!"

Jubei ran up the side of the wall and backflipped onto a fire escape.

A police officer shot a taser dart at Jubei. Jubei climbed on up the fire escape to the roof, from which he could see multiple police cars heading in his direction. A police helicopter approached from the east. Jubei leaped across one rooftop and onto another. Another police helicopter approached from the west. Jubei kept leaping from rooftop to rooftop trying to flee the helicopters.

He came upon a locked rooftop door, which he shattered with a side kick and went in.

Police cars encircled the building. A SWAT van pulled up. Residents from the apartment complex ventured into the street, most in their pajamas, curious as to the cause of the commotion outside. The police instructed them to return to their apartment and remain there with the windows shut tight and the doors locked.

"Suspect was last seen on the roof," a SWAT officer said over the radio. "We've got the building's exits covered."

Jubei heard the SWAT team in the stairway as it rushed up the stairs to sweep the roof.

"Stairway to the roof, clear," a SWAT officer reported into his communicator.

"Stay in position, just in case the suspect tries to go back to the roof."

Jubei was on the ceiling using his ninja climbing claws for grip. Blood from his wound dripped onto a SWAT officer. The man looked up. "On the ceiling!" he shouted.

Taser darts flew out. Jubei leaped down like a lightning streak, knocking most SWAT officers unconscious; others crawled around in confusion while Jubei took off down the stairwell.

He paused long enough to peer through a stairwell window. Police officers were going door to door, asking residents whether they had seen anything unusual or suspicious.

Jubei pulled out a ball from his bag, cracked open the stairwell door and rolled the ball toward the police officers. He pressed a button and the ball exploded, releasing a thick cloud of smoke into which he slipped and then stealthily headed down the smoky hallway at the end of which he reached a garbage chute. He hopped into it, just as the smoke dissipated. The dazed police officers had their guns drawn and were leaning against the wall as they tried to regain composure. One officer initiated a role call but was interrupted by a young officer who was pointing at the garbage chute. The young man yelled, "The chute. He went down the chute."

Word was sent out to the SWAT team and other personnel, and right away the officers covered all exit points to the chute, guarding them in the expectation that Jubei was headed their way. They had no idea that Jubei had only slid down the chute for a bit and had then held himself in place.

The basement

The cops gathered around the large dumpster the chute emptied out into.

Over the communicator, the SWAT leader asked, "Anything yet?"

"No, sir,"

"He must still be in the chute. Smoke him out."

One of the officers that had remained besides the top floor chute dropped a tear gas canister down the chute. Jubei shut his eyes and held his breath, let go of the sides and as he slid down he dropped a smoke bomb, which preceded Jubei and exploded in the dumpster, an instant before Jubei landed in it.

The police began to dig through the trash, but were blinded by the smoke and had to wait for it to clear, only to realize that Jubei wasn't there.

"What do you mean he's not in there?" the commander shouted over the communicator.

"He hit the dumpster. I know he did because we all heard him. But now he's not in there. Who is this guy?"

"Search the entire basement. He can't have gotten far. It's just one man, for crying out loud."

The officers scattered to search the premises, leaving behind a single officer to guard the chute.

Jubei had cut a hole at the bottom of the plastic dumpster. Silently he crawled out from beneath and snuck up behind the officer; pressed his blade against the officer's back.

"Take off the uniform," Jubei whispered, as though talking to a lover.

The police officer acquiesced. The men hastily switched clothing.

Jubei seemed pleased that they were both similar in size and inspected how well the officer wore his ninja garb. Jubei nevertheless kept a straight face and whispered, "Run."

The officer ran for his life. He ran toward the exit, into the alley, his hands waving in the air to signal his fellow officers, but they shot him down with taser darts before he was close enough for them to hear what it was that he had been yelling out to them. He lay immobile, flat on his face. The officers had to roll him over so that they could remove his ninja mask and hood.

"It's Lazarus."

By the time word of the uniform swap got back to command, Jubei had easily crossed the police perimeter. The hunt was on again.

Jubei came upon an old homeless man asleep in an alley. He shook him awake with some effort. The man reeked of booze. He was disoriented and seemed not to understand that this policeman wanted to buy his worn clothing. What he did understand was that the gold coin Jubei was offering was worth a small fortune, a veritable treasure. He was mesmerized and no longer seemed to hear what Jubei was saying. Jubei placed the gold coin in the old man's withered hand and proceeded to undress him. The old man held the gold coin tight and allowed himself to be disrobed without protesting.

Jubei tossed the police uniform and by the time he had slipped into the dirty clothes, the old man had left the alley in nothing more than his underpants and a gold coin concealed in his cheek.

A police car turned into the alley and slowed as he passed Jubei who was pushing the empty shopping cart the old man had left behind.

The driver asked. "Did you see a policeman around here within the last 15 minutes?"

Jubei pointed in the direction of the road the police car had come from, and then he shook his head, scratched it, and pointed in the opposite direction. Then, he corrected himself again and kept at it until the cops in the car exchanged amused looks. They drove on.

Jubei knocked out a businessman as he was unlocking the door to his 2010 black Jaguar parked in front of his apartment complex. Jubei picked up the keys and took off in the businessman's car.

He went to a public storage facility where he opened a storage unit in which he had been keeping his gear, including an armory that contained hundreds of weapons, from swords to grenades.

Jubei hastily changed into a new ninja uniform. He helped himself to a Blackberry and loaded up on weapons.

Back in the car, Jubei activated the Blackberry, which was connected to the ninja's network, and he could follow conversations among the members of the ninja hit squad. Through them he learned that the ninjas had placed a tracking device on the arrow that had killed agent Phelps.

Jubei immediately changed directions and began to head

towards the coordinates indicated on his Blackberry. It was a race as to who would be the first to reach Pastor Willis and his family.

A doctor was brought in to remove the arrow lodged in Phelps' neck. While extracting the arrow tip, it opened up, revealing a blinking light within. The doctor removed the miniature device and asked his assistant what it could be.

"A poison dispenser?"

Navaro snatched the device from the doctor's hand. "This is a homing device. They killed Phelps only to plant a tracking device on us." She ran off to find Pastor Willis and Megan.

Navaro shouted out, "We've been compromised! We got to move. Now!"

The pastor and his daughter followed Navaro through the house without asking any questions. She opened the door to the garage, which housed multiple vehicles, high to low end, of which he chose an armored Escalade with the bulletproof glass.

The security detail spotted two unmarked dark vans speeding down the gravel driveway. They fired relentlessly at the vehicles as approached the house, riddling the vans with holes. The vans slowed to a stop and the shooting died down. The soldiers cautiously approached the vans, which blew up. Several guards were killed in the massive blast.

A shower of arrows, fitted with explosive tips, followed the explosion. The guards were bewildered.

Within the house, self-destruct protocols were activated, and the safe house was evacuated.

Ninjas finally managed to infiltrate the headquarters, only to find an empty house. Bombs went off, destroying the house and incinerating all those inside.

The Escalade sped from the garage and weaved around

the debris of the decoy vans. Navaro turned the wheel hard, crossing the lawn and down the dirt road, into the woods. The SUV passed over spike strips. The front and back tires blew out. Navaro gripped the steering wheel, trying her best to keep the vehicle under control. She hit the center button on the steering wheel and the four flat tires automatically inflated.

There was a ninja blockade a few hundred feet down the road.

Navaro flipped the handle off the gearshift, uncovering a red button. Pressed it. Missiles shot out from the headlights. The vans that had been blocking the road blew up.

Navaro shouted, "Hold on!" She drove through the debris and kept going. Suddenly the Escalade hit a land mine. The car flipped over, on its roof, and slid a few hundred feet on the dirt.

Ninjas surrounded the vehicle. Pastor Willis, Megan, and Navaro were dragged out of the car and forced to kneel. A ninja unsheathed his sword.

Jubei was driving towards them with his headlights off, to conceal his approach. He opened the sunroof, placed something heavy on the gas pedal, and then leaped out the sunroof, flipping in the air. The Jaguar crashed into the Escalade and both were engulfed in flames.

Jubei drew his sword in mid-air and came down with a slash, cutting the ninja in half. He cut down the other ninjas, but more of them descended. One of them launched a chain around Jubei's sword and yanked it from his hands. Another ninja's chain wrapped around Jubei's leg and knocked him on his back. He shattered the chain and sprang to his feet, dashed toward the ninja and punched his chest so hard that the man died instantly. Jubei pulled out his second sword and with it he slashed down the ninjas. A cloud of smoke rose behind Jubei as his back was slashed. He staggered but was quick to regain his footing. A blade popped out from the toe of his tabi boots as he spin kicked and raked the blade across the ninja's neck. Blood spurted. The man was dead before he dropped to the ground.

Jubei sliced another ninja's throat while deflecting Shurikens with his sword. He pointed his blade at one ninja and pressed a button concealed within the handle. The blade extended, impaled the ninja, and, when Jubei yanked the blade out, it returned to its regular size.

Jubei was being attacked from above. He knelt and blocked the downward slash, swiftly turning the handle upwards so that the blade pointed downward and pressed another button and spikes shot into the ninjas chin. Jubei stood up. With a single swing of his sword he decapitated his attacker, and then kicked the bloody head into the face of a ninja, who was charging at him, knocking the man out cold.

A ninja appeared, seemingly out of nowhere. He cut Jubei across the stomach. Jubei staggered back and his stomach was sliced again, but Jubei would not fall. Instead he ran and tackled the ninja and snapped the man's neck.

Jubei sensed a presence behind him. He backflipped over a ninja landed behind him and grabbed the man around the chest with one arm and cut his throat with his free hand. The man went limp in Jubei's arms. He lifted the dead man's body up over his head and threw it at two ninjas who were attacking Pastor Willis. Both ninjas were toppled over, and, in an instant, Jubei was standing over the men and finished them off.

Armed with razor sharp ninja claws, two more ninjas charged at Jubei. But he easily parried the first attack and evaded the second one. He pivoted around and, in an upward slash, he cut off a ninja's arm, which he caught and used to clobber the second man's face. The ninja fell back. Jubei cut off the man's arm before dropping to his knees, due to his own injuries. The one-armed ninja charged at Jubei in a fury. Jubei overcame his moment of weakness and chopped off the man's other arm and snapped his neck.

A couple of ninjas stepped out of a cloud of smoke, startling Jubei. They managed to disarm him by kicking Jubei's swords out of his reach.

Another three ninjas appeared, as if out of nowhere, and grabbed Jubei by the arms. They still had the ninja claws attached to them. Although Jubei was dizzy with exhaustion, he summoned enough strength and wits to take the ninjas down, brutally bludgeoning them to death with the arms. Then Jubei tossed the arms and, as he bent over to retrieve his swords, ninja after ninja emerged from the surrounding darkness, as though from the womb of the woods.

With his swords in hand, Jubei readied himself. He had already killed dozens of ninjas and now faced countless more faceless men. He knew he would have to kill them all. He cracked his neck and dropped his shoulders, regulated his breathing, heartbeat; he felt the muscles in his face relax and a soothing feeling ran through his body and, suddenly, it was as if he had stepped outside his own body and had nothing to lose.

The ninjas moved in, stepping over their comrades' mutilated corpses. Jubei carved his way through the onslaught of ninjas, one after the other. Limbs, still warm, littered the ground in bloody puddles that shimmered under the glow of the moon. The dirt road itself had been stained crimson. Thick drops of blood dripped from Jubei's blade. He shook the blood off his sword and kept killing. It was as though he were placing bodies in a wood chipper.

Although Jubei's exploits seemed supernatural, he did not escape unscathed, having sustained numerous cuts and stab wounds over his entire body. And after cutting off the legs of yet one more ninja, Jubei collapsed. It was as if someone had switched a button and turned him off.

One ninja remained standing, though barely. He limped toward Jubei with his sword raised. Navaro shot him in the head.

Pastor Willis and Megan hurried over to Jubei's side and tried to revive him, but Jubei did not respond. After calling for help on her cell phone, Navaro bent down and began to perform CPR on Jubei. She asked Megan to help her and remove his mask.

Megan removed both Jubei's mask and hood. She gasped. "Jubei?"

Megan and her father exchanged astounded looks. They could not believe that this one ninja who had left a trail of bodies of ninja assassins in an effort to protect them, was their dear friend, Jubei.

Chapter One:
The Art of Killing

Taipei, Taiwan, six months earlier

The ghost danced across the rooftops with ease and grace, moving silently through the dark sky, undetectable and invisible. Its fluid motion was eerie as it glided from one building to another. The lights of the penthouse and the sounds of the party were getting closer and louder. A couple more ghosts glided with a similar unearthly finesse toward the brightly lit penthouse. The three ghost-like figures came together on the last rooftop, before reaching the penthouse, appearing like shapeless shadows without any distinguishing marks.

Penthouse

Taiwanese girls, no older than fourteen, were being forced to undress. The youngest must have being eight years old. The lustful men and women surrounding them not only ogled the children, but also reached out to touch their smooth skin.

One by one, the girls were escorted off the stage and taken to their new owners. One girl struggled to get away from her owner's grip. She was shot, sending out a firm message to the other weeping girls.

Once the Taiwanese girls had been cleared from the auction stage, three more girls were brought on. They were slightly older, at least seventeen, all Americans, also forced to strip at gunpoint.

The auctioneer began to take bids on the new girls. Two of them were bawling; their faces distorted with fear. The other girl stared ahead blankly. She flinched when an elderly man began to fondle her. She tried to back away but a gun was placed against her temple and before the gunman could pull the trigger, an arrow pierced through his head.

The crowd panicked. Chaos erupted. Guards armed with automatic weapons fired randomly, without a clue as to where the arrow might have come from.

The American teenagers were removed from the stage and ushered inside the penthouse, where sinful acts were being committed, young girls forced to give up their purity to perverted men and women alike.

Outside, guards on the rooftop deck ceased to fire and scanned the surrounding rooftops. Arrows hummed through the air and struck them down.

A ninja, dressed head to toe in black, swung down to the deck and kicked through the thick plate glass doors in pursuit of the American girls. Guards shot at him and he rolled on the floor. The bullets whizzed over his head. He jumped up, hurling Shurikens, hitting the guards between the eyes. With his sword, the ninja finished the guards off.

A guard aimed at the ninja and the ninja jumped through the air, with blinding speed, and spin kicked to the guard's jaw; the force of the kick so powerful that the man's neck broke.

The second ninja pursued the auctioneer into a bedroom, where a businessman was molesting a teen-aged girl who was tied up. The auctioneer leapt from the window, down the fire escape, busted through yet another window a few stories below that led into an apartment where a family was watching a black and white ninja movie.

In the bedroom, the ninja killed the businessman and then cut the ropes from teenager's wrist. "Go home," he said, and before she could thank him he had vanished out the window, after the auctioneer, entering the apartment below in the midst of a scene in the movie in which a ninja was chasing an enemy through an apartment.

The auctioneer had grabbed one of the children on the couch and pressed a gun to the side of the little boy's head. Using the child as a shield, he began to shoot the ninja, but the ninja dodged the bullets with ease. He swiftly released a high-powered mechanical chain that wrapped around the child's wrist, and he yanked the boy away from the auctioneer. And then, as he deflected the bullets with his sword, the ninja charged the auctioneer. The auctioneer's headless body fell to the floor. The children covered their eyes while their parents rushed to their youngest brother, whom the ninja had saved from the man now lying dead on their living room floor.

The ninja took his leave as quickly as he had appeared.

The American girls were forced into an unmarked van.

The third ninja caught sight of the van as it thundered through the alley toward the road. With supernatural speed he pursued the speeding van and, as he approached the ledge, he realized that he was running out of room to run and that the gap was too wide for him to jump. Yet he kept running at full speed, keeping the van in sight, and took a leap of faith off the roof, pulled out his sword as he fell fast and flipped in the air before driving his sword through the roof of the van, impaling the driver's head. The ninja pulled his sword back out and jumped off the van in a fluid motion, but staggered upon landing due to the speed of his fall. The van crashed into a dumpster.

The three surviving guards stumbled out from the van and began shooting. The ninja took cover behind a steel dumpster.

Police sirens drew closer.

The ninja rolled out from behind the dumpster and flung three Shurikens, which disarmed the guards, and the ninja hurried towards them and struck them down. One guard was split in half. The others lost their head.

The ninja wiped the blood on his sword on the dead men before sheathing it.

He found the American girls cowering in the back of the van. "You're safe now," he said softly.

A couple other ninjas joined him and together they helped the girls out.

From a nearby rooftop the three ninjas watched the police and ambulances swarm in on the scene.

One gloated, "A successful mission."

"You call this successful?" said the lead ninja. "You two were too slow. If it hadn't been for my having anticipated their escape, these American girls would've been lost. And besides, there's more perversion taking place in that penthouse as we speak."

"We've been sent to save the American girls," said the second ninja. "Nothing more."

The lead ninja back punched the second ninja and sent him flying onto the ground. The second ninja stood back up and drew this sword.

"This mission was a failure. Your mission was to rescue the Americans and bring them home safely. Now they are in the hands of the police. Failure in your training is no less than your failure as a ninja. The two of you must die."

The third ninja also drew his sword and positioned himself besides his comrade.

"I won't even use my sword. And if you strike me down you will redeem yourselves. However, if you don't, I will kill you and then I'll to go back there and end the perversion and the suffering of those young girls."

The ninjas moved in. The lead ninja dodged and blocked the strikes. The second ninja lunged at him, readying to stab him, while the third ninja slashed downward. The lead ninja pivoted to the side and did a fluid block that broke the blade of the second ninja's attack. With a quick finger strike to the neck, the second ninja was paralyzed. The third ninja came around with a horizontal slash. The lead ninja ducked beneath the blade and jabbed the third ninja's knee, yet the third ninja continued to attack despite his broken knee. In a swift motion the lead ninja broke the second ninja's neck. He flipped over the crippled third ninja and palm punched the ninja in the back, shattering his back, and then he finished the third ninja off by cutting his throat.

The ninjas were dead now, and the lead ninja piled their bodies and lit them on fire.

Yakima Mountains, 350 miles from Nagano, Tokyo

Within the mystical beauty of the Yakima Mountains, a vast village lies peacefully isolated from the rest of the world. Its inhabitants were unlike most of the Japanese population. These residents had a blend of Japanese and African features. Their complexion ranged in hues of brown and their hair from silky to nappy. These were the descendants of Japan's first Shogun, an African who lived in Japan during the Heian period, evidence of the existence of a strong African presence in ancient Japan.

The palace was the tallest building in the village. It was home to Ukyo Tamuramaro, a handsome middle-aged man with high cheekbones and mocha brown skin. His eyes were almond-shaped, and his hair was cut low and skin-tight on the sides. Three ninjas in uniform stood guard as Ukyo was reading a Taiwanese newspaper that related the events of the previous night.

A young man entered the chamber and whispered something to Ukyo.

"Show him in," Ukyo said, in a commanding tone.

A younger man who resembled Ukyo, with exception of his having silky hair, entered the room. The young man was Jubei Tamuramaro, Ukyo's son.

Jubei knelt down before his father, his face buried to the floor.

"Two unidentified bodies were found burned on a rooftop adjacent the Yung-Wu Penthouse. Authorities are unable to confirm if the bodies are connected to the penthouse murders."

"Surely that is not all the article says," Jubei said.

"The rest, I am not concerned with. The Americans were returned safely to their father, so why kill Sato and Tashi?"

"They failed. They stormed into the penthouse and allowed themselves to be seen. They were slow and clumsy. The orders were quite specific: rescue the American girls and bring them home. Had I not intervened, their mission would have failed. The price for failure has already been set, father. I was merely collecting their debt."

Ukyo handed the newspaper to a servant.

"Your report is satisfactory," Ukyo said dismissively. He pressed a button on his chair and a secret compartment underneath the chair opened. A scroll rolled on the floor to Jubei's feet. Its seal was marked by a black symbol. Jubei scrutinized the ink mark and nodded.

Five years ago

Jubei knelt before his father, his hood and mask clasped in his hand. A beautiful woman in her mid to late forties was sitting beside Ukyo. Matsumi was her name. She was Jubei's mother. Jubei glanced at her and then turned his gaze to the floor, not daring to look his father in the eyes.

"You have proven yourself thus far, Jubei. One more test remains, to prove your readiness to join the Dragon ninja ranks."

Ukyo released a scroll from the secret compartment in the chair. The scroll was sealed with a black symbol. Jubei unrolled the scroll and, after reading it, he rolled the scroll back up and bowed. His eyes revealed no emotion, as though he were soulless, inhuman. He bowed once more and took his leave.

After Jubei had left the chambers, the ninja guards were dismissed, leaving Ukyo and Matsumi alone.

"He is ready," Ukyo said. "The successful completion of this mission will prove that he has indeed become a Dragon ninja."

"What name was on that scroll?" Matsumi asked.

"You do not need to know the name on the scroll, just that the outcome must be death."

Ukyo waved his hand and three ninjas appeared. Another scroll rolled out from beneath the chair. Matsumi quickly intercepted the scroll. The ninja backed away and bowed. Matsumi ripped open the scroll and on it she read the name. She glared at Ukyo. "You know the rules by which we live.

Failure is not something a Dragon ninja can afford. Jubei is no exception. He has accepted his fate."

Matsumi threw the scroll to the ground and stormed off.

Maki Takanonsune was a head-turning beauty in the Tamuramaro village. Her long silky black hair stretched down her back; her green eyes shimmered in the moonlight.

She was walking home from the village schoolhouse, carrying schoolbooks and a variety of other useful items in a wheeled cart. A small boy, no older than three, accompanied her. It was her little brother Hanzo. He was pulling a cart of his own.

On the rooftop, Jubei was invisible. He held a compound bow and took out two arrows. He placed the first arrow and drew back on the bow, ready to release the arrow as he aimed at an empty target and waited.

Three ninjas also pointed their arrows at Jubei from different locations.

Jubei waited until Maki and Hanzo were in plain view and, as soon as they were, he was overcome with memories of the love he had shared with her. Maki's beautiful face seemed so clear in his mind, and, in a stream of consciousness, their life together unraveled. Jubei had put the bow down without being aware of it when he realized that his targets were nearly out of range. Jubei came to his senses, picked the bow back up, drew and released the first arrow. Hanzo fell. Maki let out a blood-curdling scream. Jubei felt like it cut through him.

Lights from nearby homes turned on.

Maki's father was nearby. He had been putting some tools back in the shed when her scream echoed in the silent night. He dropped a rake and ran. An arrow struck his neck before he could reach his daughter. No one came to help. No one dared open his or her door.

Maki left her dying brother with the carts and ran. Jubei aimed again but Maki was out of range. He was relieved and yet still he took after her with his bow in hand. Maki reached home, covered in Hanzo's blood. Her mother collapsed at the sight of her bloodied daughter. "They're dead, they're both dead," Maki said in one breath. Before she could reach for her mother, Jubei busted through the front door. From the doorway he shot Maki's mother. Maki tried to get away but Jubei slashed her down the back. She fell to the ground, lifted herself enough to try crawling away. He stabbed her in the back. He knew he wasn't done yet. He then turned his sword on all the relatives he found hidden within the house. Not a soul was spared.

Two hours later

Jubei entered Ukyo's chambers dragging two large bags, which he dropped at his father's feet. Ukyo could see the blood splatters on Jubei's uniform and still he wanted to examine the contents of both bags while Jubei stood by, as still as a statue. Once satisfied, Ukyo gestured at his servants to toss the bags into the fire. Then he nodded and dismissed Jubei without saying a word. Jubei left the chambers as the stench of burned flesh wafted into the room. When the doors closed behind him a tear rolled down his cheek. Jubei hurriedly made his way out the palace through the secret tunnels that led into the forest and he ran, as far from the palace as he could, until he was nearly disoriented and fell on his hands and knees, sobbing and screaming and wishing he were dead.

"Maki!" he screamed, again and again.

Five years later

Jubei was handed a scroll; this one marked with the symbol of betrayal. He knew what had to be done, what only a Dragon ninja could do. Jubei bowed his head and with this gesture he accepted the mission as he had accepted every mission, every single one of them. Ukyo dismissed him and Jubei vanished amid black smoke.

"May God have mercy on the traitor," Matsumi said, as she entered the chamber, "because Jubei will not."

"He has become the best of the Dragon ninjas. His ability to follow through on all missions is uncanny. I have created the master weapon."

"You speak of him as if he were a thing to be used, like he isn't your son."

"He *is* a thing to be used. He is a living weapon and will one day bring world power to the Tamuramaro clan ." Ukyo left the chambers, and Matsumi alone to ponder his words.

"Ukyo, you're a fool," she murmured. "Jubei's destiny is not to take the Tamuramaro clan to the heights of power. He is destined to be something so much more, and I will not allow him to become like you."

Tinton Falls, New Jersey, the next night

Shinza Tanaka, a Japanese expatriate in his mid-thirties, was closing up his florist shop in the Tinton Falls Plaza, a quaint Ikebana flower shop, the only one in the New Jersey that specialized in the art of Japanese flower arrangement. He had just pulled down the metal gate and crouched to pick up a few petals on the sidewalk, when an armor-piercing arrow struck the spot where his head had been. Another arrow was headed toward him but Shinza rolled out of its way.

About fifty yards separated him from his car. The plaza

was empty; Shinza's car was the only one left in the parking lot. With the metal gate already lowered, there was no way to get back inside the shop. Shinza scrambled to take cover behind his car, deflecting arrows with his briefcase along the way.

A black cloud materialized in front of Shinza and out lunged Jubei with his sword raised. Shinza block the sword with his briefcase. The sword slashed right through it and the tip of the blade nicked Shinza in the neck. Jubei twisted his sword to disarm Shinza, and the briefcase flew off the blade. Jubei jumped up and kicked the briefcase, which hit Shinza in the chest, catapulting him onto his back. Grimacing in pain, Shinza was able to roll back to his feet.

Jubei moved in with blinding speed, but Shinza did a leg sweep on Jubei who backflipped out of the fall. Jubei threw small explosives to disorient Shinza with an explosion of smoke. Shinza leaped into the air, grabbed onto the awning of Luciano's Italian restaurant and climbed onto the awning. Jubei jumped up and cut down the awning before Shinza could hop onto the roof.

Shinza kicked at Jubei, but Jubei blocked the kick, grabbed Shinza's foot and spun him around. Shinza tried to backflip out the leg grab but Jubei punched him while he was in the air. Shinza went through the glass window, tripping the silent alarm, and landed flat on a table. Jubei entered. A visor slid over his eyes and enabled night vision. Shinza was not hiding in the dinning room.

Shinza had taken cover in the cooler, in the kitchen. His cell phone had been broken during the fight. Shinza looked for something he might be able to use as a weapon. He knew Jubei would not stop until he was dead. Shinza found a broom that had been stored in the cooler. He broke it to make a staff.

In the kitchen, Jubei could not find any sign of Shinza.

The back door was ajar, which Shinza had expected would mislead Jubei into thinking that he had fled out the back door. Instead, Jubei turned toward the cooler. Shinza powerfully side kicked the cooler door off its hinges and it flew at Jubei. Jubei cut it in half. Shinza attacked Jubei with the staff, which Jubei not only deflected but cut in half, leaving Shinza to fight with a couple of sticks. Jubei matched every one of Shinza's desperate moves, but Shinza did manage to kick Jubei, who fell backwards and dropped his sword, which Shinza was quick to retrieve and pointed at Jubei. Suddenly, Shinza was electrocuted. He released the sword and rushed toward the back door.

Jubei threw a few Shurikens at him. Shinza ducked just in time, and then grabbed kitchen knives, which he used to deflect the ninja stars while running towards the back door. And he managed to deflect all but one, which lodged into Shinza's shoulder. Jubei tossed another ninja star and it struck the other shoulder. Both of the Shurikens were impaled in pressure points, disabling Shinza's arms, however, his legs were fine and he ran as fast as his short legs could take him. Nevertheless, Jubei easily caught up with him and kicked out one of his legs. As Shinza was falling, Jubei kicked him into the dumpster, shattering Shinza's back. He could no longer move.

"Ten years," Shinza Said. "I had ten good years of freedom. I know you cannot spare my life. I know that it's too late to ask mercy for my family. Just tell me whether their deaths were swift."

"They did die quickly," Jubei said. "No one suffered."

"Allow me to see the face of my killer before I die."

Jubei was hesitant, but he removed his mask.

"I know you," said Shinza. "You were a child back then, Jubei, son of Ukyo. Even as a child you followed the code of our clan with blind loyalty. The trouble with blind loyalty is that you do not see the real purpose behind actions. We are not idealists killing only the bad guys, Jubei. Many innocent people have died at our hands, and many continue to die. That is why I defected, although I knew that my fellow Dragon ninjas would never stop hunting me. However, I am the first ninja to have survived this long without being discovered. Do you want to know how I did that? After you kill me, examine my body and you will find a scar. That is where I cut out my tracking device."

Jubei could not disguise his surprise.

"That's right. They were implanted in all of us. Every one in a different area. Sometimes more than one."

From his pocket, Shinza pulled out a bloodstained photograph and took one last lingering look at it. Tears welled up in his eyes and he nodded before he could cry.

Once Jubei had killed Shinza, he examined his body and located the scar Shinza had mentioned. Suddenly he felt chocked up with uncertainty. Suspicion.

The break into Luciano's had tripped the silent alarm. Now the sirens could be heard approaching. Jubei bowed to Shinza and vanished into the night before the Tinton Falls police found Shinza's corpse in the back alley.

Tamuramaro village

Deep below the palace of the isolated mountain village was the clan's intelligence sector—a room filled with advanced technology and computers the world had yet to see. A computer was downloading hundreds of dossiers within seconds, thousands of images flashed on the screen.

An Intel agent noticed an incoming message blinking in corner of the monitor. He clicked on the icon, opening a complete profile on Pastor Willis Ware. He printed out the file and handed it over to another agent who walked it over to a vault, flanked by Dragon ninjas, lasers, and traps.

The guards allowed the agent through and, as soon as he stepped into the vault, it automatically locked behind him. Poison gas filled the small space. The agent had no way out and knew it. He kneeled and died before he could regret any of the choices he had made during his lifetime.

As the poison dissipated through concealed vents, a robotic arm retrieved the profile, which vanished by use of a cloaking device. A trap door on the floor swung open and engulfed the body.

In the Intel room, all workers stopped what they were doing to bow respectfully as a scroll was carried through the room, on a golden tray, to an elevator in which the scroll was vacuumed up.

Fanned by a pretty young servant girl, Ukyo sipped on rice wine as he observed the students' training session in the gardens. Two young men in uniforms were called to the center of the ring. The y bowed to Ukyo, and, with his consent, they bowed to each other, took their positions, and began sparring.

A servant handed the scroll to Ukyo. He read it, and said, "Summon Jubei to the chambers, at once."

Chapter Two:
Man of Faith

San Antonio, Texas, four months ago

The Church of Christ was alive with singing and clapping and dancing along to the upbeat song , *I don't know what you came to do*. Ushers also clapped as they shimmied down the aisle and assisted late arrivals to find a seat in the crowded auditorium. The congregation's rhythmic enthusiasm echoed onto the streets of downtown San Antonio. Strollers along the famous San Antonio Riverwalk could hear echoes of the religious jubilation.

When the song finally died down, Megan Ware stepped up to the microphone with her notes in hand. "Amen, church! I don't know what happened here today, but the singing was awesome. Let's give a hand to the music ministry. They were off the chain today."

Megan paused, to allow the congregation to clap. "Okay. We have a couple of announcements…"

From the backstage Pastor Ware observed, with pride, as his beloved daughter read out the announcements for the very first time. To the pastor's delight, she had recently been appointed to the ministry.

He felt a buzzing against his left leg and checked his pocket for his cell phone. Its screen read: 911. He answered the call.

"Pastor," said a man. "It's Grayson. He's gone and locked himself in the bathroom, and he's got a gun. He's gonna shoot himself! He's gonna kill himself, Pastor."

"Jeffrey, calm down," the pastor said, calmly. "Did you call the police?"

"No. I went ahead and called you. You've got to help us. Please."

"I'm on my way." The pastor hung up and walked onto the stage as Megan was finishing the announcements, and the singers prepared to deliver the communion song.

"I have to go. Tell Bruce he will need to fill in for me."

Megan nodded and did not question him.

New Braunfels, Texas, 15 minutes later

A young man awaited Pastor Willis at the entry of the mid-sized ranch house. His face was red and wet with tears. "Help him, Pastor. Help him, please!" He hurriedly led the pastor through the house, down the hallway at the end of which was a closed bathroom door. It was locked from within.

"Jeffrey," the pastor said. "I want you to go to your neighbors and stay there. I need you to pray for your brother. Can you do that?"

Jeffrey agreed but he did not move. The pastor took the young man in his arms and noticed that he was shaking.

"Don't let him kill himself," Jeffrey begged in a small voice.

"You go pray, Jeffrey. And stay there until I come for

you." The pastor walked Jeffrey out, to make sure that he would leave the house, and doubled back to the bathroom. He knocked.

"Leave me alone!"

"Grayson, it's me, Willis."

"Leave me alone or I'll shoot myself. I swear, I will."

"I can't do that. You've got Jeffrey scared to death. I had to send him away. He doesn't need to hear you threatening to pull the trigger."

"Good. I don't want him here. And I don't want you here either. I don't want to hear dozens of reasons why I shouldn't do it."

"So let's talk about the reasons why you should. Your wife left you. You lost your job. You lost your house. You hardly have any friends left. I guess, if I were you, I would have blown my brains out a long time ago, so you're much stronger than you give yourself credit for."

Police sirens approached. A crowd had begun to gather. A couple of police vehicles pulled up. The officers drew their guns.

"The situation's getting bad, Grayson. Now the police is here."

Pastor Willis heard a muffled clicking sound.

Grayson yelled, "Tell them to back away. Tell them to back away, now."

"Okay. I'll go do that. But you better still be here when I get back. "

Outside, a police officer recognized Pastor Willis.

"We got a call from a neighbor. Were you first on the scene, Pastor?"

"Yes."

"Alright. We'll take it from here."

"That's the last thing you're gonna do," the pastor said boldly. "I'm a retired police officer and have of the right experience, and besides, he knows me well. I've been reaching out to this man for a few months and he trusts me. You send go sending someone in who doesn't know him, and they say the wrong thing, and that's the end of that."

"It's against protocol, retired or not."

"I understand your protocol, but let me try God's protocol. All these guns, and someone else may set him off. Give me ten minutes."

The officer hesitated, and then said, "Okay. Three minutes."

Pastor Willis agreed. The men shook hands and the pastor returned inside.

"Grayson, they've agreed to back away, for now. But in three minutes they're gonna take over. They'll try and talk you out of it and, if that doesn't work, they might come in here by force."

There was silence on the other side of the door.

"Grayson?"

"Relax. I'm still here."

"Do you have your cell phone on you?" asked the pastor.

"Why?"

"I want to send something to you. When you get it, I want you to take a moment to think about what you really want to do. And then, if you still want to kill yourself, I'll just walk away. But you'll have to give me a few minutes to pick up some things for Jeffrey. And before you off yourself, maybe you can give me an idea as to where I should take Jeffrey. He'll be needing a place to live after you've gone on and killed yourself."

"Fine. Go ahead and send whatever it is that you want to send me."

In the bathroom

Grayson was a Latino man in his mid-thirties. He sat on the closed toilet lid with the barrel of a 12- gauge shotgun impressed into his chin. His finger held the trigger lightly. His cell phone was resting on top of the sink. It buzzed. Grayson had to take his hand off the trigger to access his text message: a photograph of arms, each with a long scars stretching from the wrists all the way to the elbows.

"Those are my arms," Pastor Willis said through the door. "I had plenty of reasons to off myself too. I was as good as dead. I shouldn't even be here right now, but God had a plan for me. I never thought the suffering would ease, and that I could be where I'm at now. At the time, all I could see was my pain, but God had a purpose for me and I was saved. I do know what you're going through. These scars on my arms are proof that I know what I'm talking about. If you kill yourself, you take away any hope of escaping the pain and suffering. In fact, that would be when the real pain and suffering would start. You know where I'm going with this. I had to learn to see myself as God sees me. And love myself the way God loves me. At the time though, I couldn't think about what my committing suicide would do to Megan. I did not love her like God calls us to love one another, just like you're not thinking about what your killing yourself would do to Jeffrey."

"But if God really does loves us, then why do we have to suffer so much? I was doing the right thing, studying the bible. I was even about to get baptized when all this stuff happened."

"There was someone who suffered more than you. And he would do it again to save you, to save all of us. Being a child of God does not mean we get a free pass, and that we won't suffer. Sometimes it means that we suffer more. But in the end we persevere. The bible says in James 1:2-3, *consider it pure joy when you face trials of many kinds, because you know that the testing of your faith develops perseverance.* Once you come up from that water you have the Holy Spirit in you and you're on Satan's most wanted list. But he can't have you. However, if you do kill yourself, then you're handing him all rights to your soul. That's what I had to come to terms with, as I was lying in that tub bleeding to death."

"Well. I just don't see the point."

"Pull the trigger and you won't have to. But if you trust in God, then you will."

There was a moment of silence. The pastor held his ear to the door and thought he heard movement of some kind. The doorknob turned and the door swung open. Grayson handed the shotgun to Pastor Willis, who hurried to unload it, but it wasn't loaded. Grayson placed two shotgun shells in the pastor's hand. He thanked the pastor. "Another five minutes and I would have loaded that gun."

The pastor put the gun down and embraced Grayson as if he were a long lost son. Tears streamed down Grayson's face and he collapsed. Pastor Willis helped him up, Grayson steadied himself, and arm in arm the men walked down the hallway and out the front door.

Before getting into the police car Grayson smiled at the pastor. In the man's face Pastor Willis could tell he was grateful.

Jeffrey ran from the house next door as the police car pulled off with Grayson in the back seat. He tried catching up with the car. The pastor's heart tightened. He sat down on the bench and watched Jeffrey give up as the police car sped away.

"Where are they taking Grayson?" Jeffrey asked the pastor.

"It's gonna be okay. He's going to a place where he will get all the help he needs.

"But, his bible is still in the room."

The pastor smiled kindly. "Why don't you pack up some things? You might have to stay with me for a while."

Later on that night

Megan greeted her father and Jeffrey at the entry of the pastor's split-level house. She hugged Jeffrey tightly. "Jeffrey, why don't you take your stuff to the guest room. You know where it is. And I hope the both of you are hungry because dinner will be ready in just a few minutes."

After Jeffrey headed up the stairs to his room, the pastor and his daughter embraced.

"Jeffrey's gonna stay with us for a while," said the pastor.

"Of course," Megan said. "And how's Grayson doing?"

"He should be checking himself into White Marsh Psychiatric hospital right about now." He sat on the steps. "I've had some scary moments in my life," he said, "but today had to be one of the scariest moments in my entire life."

Megan sat beside her father and put her arm around his broad shoulders. "What made it so scary?"

"Satan's presence. I don't mean his actual physical presence, but the power he has is greatly underestimated. His lies are more destructive than any man-made weapon. I know that Satan only has the power that we give him, but that's the scary thing. People will willingly giving him this power because they believe his lies. Grayson almost killed himself because of Satan's lies. He believed that he was worthless, had nothing and no one, when a person gets to feeling like that, it's easy for Satan to take advantage of him. Helping Grayson today reminded me of a time when I felt exactly the same way he did today. It felt like I was the one who had the shotgun in my hand."

"But that's what made you so effective in helping people who threaten to commit suicide. You have empathy for them in a way that others cannot understand, unless they've been where you've been. Grayson was blessed to have you there today."

"I don't know how blessed he was. If he would have done it, if he would have killed himself..."

"But he didn't. God used you to help him."

Pastor Willis smiled at Megan and placed his hand against her soft cheek. "However did you get so smart?"

"Easy," Megan laughed. "I got my smarts from Mom."

"True. Your mother was a lot smarter than me. And I see her in you."

Megan glanced at the picture of a beautiful Asian woman holding five-year-old Megan asleep in her arms. "Dad, are you happy?" Megan asked.

"Why are you asking that?"

"I was just thinking about mom. And how happy you were when she was here. You'd smile so wide and your eyes lit up in a way that I haven't seen in a long, long time."

Pastor Willis stood and picked the picture up from the table in the hallway and brought it to the step where he rejoined Megan.

"Maybe you should start dating again."

Pastor Willis was quiet, lost in the picture of his beautiful wife. He missed her terribly.

"Mom would want you to find love again. You never dated anyone when I was a kid because you were busy raising me. But I'm a grown woman now. It's okay to move on. I just want to see you have that light in your eyes again."

Pastor Willis put his arm around Megan and pulled her close. "Baby girl," he said sweetly. "Your mother was the one woman that could put that light in my eyes. I'm fine sweetheart. And besides, I'm married to the church now. So, please don't worry about me."

Pastor Willis placed the picture back on the table and they both headed to the kitchen for some cookies and milk.

"How did Bruce do today with the sermon?"

"He has the gift. He could become lead evangelist when you're ready to retire."

Megan opened the cabinet to get Chunky Chips Ahoy cookies—her father's favorite. She put a few cookies on a small plate and then placed it on the kitchen table.

"I knew he had it in him. I always liked Bruce, he's a strong godly man, and he's single," the pastor said, smiling coyly.

"Dad," Megan said. "Don't go there. I like Bruce as a friend and that's it. There is *nothing* between us."

The pastor threw his arms up in surrender. "Well," the pastor said, "I'm just saying, you're worrying about me but what about you, sweet-pee? You know, Bruce will make for an awesome husband and father someday." He sat and helped himself to a cookie.

Megan poured them each a glass of milk.

"I have no doubt he will, just not as my husband. God has his own plan for me and he'll lead me to the right man when I'm ready."

"You can't blame an old man for trying," the pastor said. He dunked a cookie in the milk.

Megan smiled and kissed her dad on the top of his bald head. "You're far from old. And I do love you for trying. Good night Daddy." Megan left the pastor alone with his thoughts and headed to bed.

The following day Pastor Willis was drawn downstairs by the aroma of bacon and eggs.

In the kitchen, his plate was ready and set on the table beside the morning newspaper. He poured them each some juice while Megan was fixing herself a plate.

They sat across from each other at the kitchen table.

"I tried getting Jeffrey to come downstairs," Megan said, "but he wasn't hungry. So, I've set aside a plate for him in the microwave. It would be nice if you could let him know, later, that it's here when he wants it."

The pastor nodded.

Megan followed her father's lead as he bowed his head in prayer.

"Lord God," said the pastor, "thank you for the food this morning, and for the privilege to just be able to sit in a comfortable home and eat breakfast. But mostly for being able to come before you and know that you are hearing our prayers. Surround us with your spirit as we go about our day. In Jesus' name we pray. Amen."

After breakfast, the pastor went upstairs and knocked on Jeffrey's door.

"Come in," said Jeffrey. He was sitting on the bed. He had been reading a comic.

"Breakfast is ready," said Pastor Willis. "Are you feeling up to eating?"

"Miss Megan already offered me breakfast, but thank you anyways."

The pastor nodded.

"What comic is that?" the pastor asked.

"Captain America. I love to read comics."

"Captain America is alright, but Wolverine's my man," said the pastor.

Jeffrey put down the comic. He seemed surprised. "You know about Wolverine?"

"'Of course I know about Wolverine. He's my favorite X-man. Which one do you like best?"

"Professor X."

"Yeah, he's cool. Reaching out to those who are lost would be much easier if I could read minds like Professor X does."

"If I could've done that, I would've been able to know how sad Grayson really was."

The pastor sighed. "If only it could be that easy. But God's grace is sufficient for us all. Grayson is going to be okay."

"You really think so, Pastor?"

"Yeah, I do. It may take some time, but he'll be fine. While he's recovering, I want you to think of this place as home, alright?"

Jeffrey smiled.

Pastor Willis patted him affectionately on the shoulder and then headed towards the door. "I do have one rule in this house. You do have to eat your meals when they're ready."

Jeffrey got the hint and followed the pastor downstairs.

Megan was on her way out the front door. "Dad. I might be late for dinner," she said. "I have that bible study with Lisa tonight. She's gonna get baptized, I can feel it."

The pastor clapped his hands. "Well. Amen. So we'll just grab some takeout, or something, tonight."

"Sounds good." Megan crouched to pick up the newspaper and handed it to her father before leaving.

Jeffrey headed to the kitchen for breakfast while Pastor Willis scanned the headlines on the front page. There was an article about a murder. Its headline read: *Congregation of the Central Jersey Church of Christ Found Murdered during Sunday service.*

"Oh my God," said the pastor, and realized that he had gone weak in the legs. He staggered to the closest chair and slumped into it. "Ivy. Jessica. The whole congregation?" He didn't know how long he sat like that, in utter disbelief of what he had read. A knock at the front door startled him out of his stupor.

An African American man in his mid-thirties entered, dressed in a dark business suit. Pastor Willis blankly handed the newspaper over to the young man.

"I know," said the young man. He did not take the paper. "That's why I came over right away. It's all over the news."

"Who would do this? Who would wipe out an entire congregation? And the children... They even killed the children. Who would do this, Bruce?"

Bruce shrugged and put his arm around the pastor's shoulders. "I'm so sorry about Ivy. I know he was your best friend."

"Have you talked to any of the church leadership this morning?"

Bruce shook his head. "But I guess that by now they all know what happened. Should we call an emergency meeting?"

The pastor was burning up inside and he began to feel lightheaded. He raised his hand toward Bruce and left him standing there as he stumbled to the bathroom down the hall.

He splashed water in his face. Water and tears dripped off his face as he looked into the mirror. It was a blur. With his fist he shattered the mirror and before he even realized what he had just done, he dropped to his knees amid the shards of glass and prayed.

He must have been lost in prayer for quite some time because when he stood he noticed that his face was dry. One by one he placed the shards of glass in the wastebasket beneath the sink and took a deep breath before stepping out of the bathroom.

He found Bruce where he had left him and wondered

whether Bruce had heard him break the mirror, and if he had, then why had Bruce not knocked on the bathroom door?

The pastor cleared his throat and tried to keep his voice from wavering as instructed Bruce to gather everyone at the church. Told him to hurry.

"And what about you? I can't leave you like this."

"I'll be fine," said the pastor. "We must act now so that we can properly grieve later."

When Bruce was gone the pastor went to find Jeffrey in the kitchen.

Jeffrey held his fork in his hand as he gaped at the news on the small television Megan liked to watch while she prepared the meals. There was still food on his fork and he had not yet finished chewing the food in his mouth. Pastor Willis turned the television off.

"It's on just about every channel," said Jeffrey. "What happened to the church in New Jersey?"

"We don't know all the details yet. All we know is that the entire congregation was murdered last night, during worship service. It doesn't seem like anyone knows the hows and the whys. No details have been released."

In Jeffrey's face the pastor saw that he looked as defeated as he had sounded.

North Brunswick, New Jersey,
Central Jersey Church of Christ

The Central Jersey Church of Christ—a community center and a Christian school, K-12—stood right off of Route 130, in North Brunswick, New Jersey, a large gray marble building that had finished being built merely six months ago. Its perimeter was sealed off by dozens of North Brunswick police cars and a crowd of police officers. The area was taped off; onlookers were kept at a distance.

A black Jeep Liberty was cleared through the checkpoint. Its driver was a bald, dark skinned African American man wearing diamond earrings and a wedding band. His passenger was a Latino woman dressed in a well-tailored suit. She resembled the actress Rosalyn Sanchez, with her shoulder length brown hair and hazel eyes. The duo approached the entrance of the church, from which emerged a man with a police badge hanging from his neck. He was hardly able to hold himself upright and leaned over, placed his hand firmly against the wall of the church and vomited into the rosebush.

The man and woman waited for him to finish and then flashed FBI badges.

"I'm Special Agent Navaro," said the woman, "and this is Special Agent Phelps."

The man wiped his mouth with his sleeve and identified himself as one of North Brunswick's coroners.

"This is an FBI investigation now," said Navaro.

"We're looking for Detective Rowan," said Phelps.

The man gestured toward the double glass doors, which led into the church. "Ask Detective Rowan for vomit bags," he said meekly.

In the hallway leading to the sanctuary, body parts and corpses were scattered on the blood stained floor. Police examiners were taking pictures and labeling the evidence.

Navaro and Phelps had to navigate around the crime scene. Navaro struggled to keep from vomiting.

"I'm going to look around here," said Navaro. She pulled out a small digital camera and began to take pictures of the crime scene.

Phelps headed to the sanctuary. It was also littered with bodies, positioned as if they had been trying to flee when they were killed.

Phelps overheard a policeman say that no one had been able to find any signs of forced entry.

Medical examiners were examining the bodies before they could be removed.

Phelps approached the stage where paramedics were placing a corpse in a body bag. Phelps hopped onto the stage to look a closer look at the body. "Is this the pastor?" Phelps asked.

"Yes."

"Do you know what killed him?"

"Undetermined," said an assistant M.E. as he pointed out multiple wounds, seemingly both entry and exit wounds. "All we know is that these were caused by a high-powered projectiles. We haven't been able to locate any shell casings anywhere, and we also can't find a single bullet hole in the walls."

"It just doesn't make any sense," said another medical examiner. "No forced entry. No traces of any kid of projectiles; just these odd wounds."

Navaro came upon two more bodies as she walked down the stairway. She knelt and examined the long slash mark running down the victim's back. The second body had a slash mark across its neck.

When she reached the bottom of the stairs she tried to turn on the lights, but they did not come on. She figured the power had been cut.

In the first classroom she found the body of the Sunday school teacher and that of her assistant.

The back door to the classroom had been left open.

Navaro thought she heard a faint whimper come from within the supply closet. She reached for her gun and placed her ear to the door. "My name is Agent Navaro," she said. "I'm with the FBI. Can you tell me your name?"

"My name is James. My sister, Marie, is in here with me. Our teacher locked us in."

"Do you know where she keeps the key?"

In a small voice Marie suggested the agent try looking in the teacher's desk. "It's a little key. It should be in the top drawer."

From her cell phone Navaro texted her partner: *2 survivors locked in closet.*

Navaro found the key where Marie had said she would. She unlocked and opened the closet. She was astounded to find that it was empty. "Marie? James?" she called out.

The lower section of the back wall slid open and out crawled a couple of Latino children. The girl hugged Navaro tightly. She was much smaller than her brother. The boy must have been ten years old, so Navaro estimated Marie must have been around seven. The little girl clung to Navaro and did not seem as if she would be ready to let go anytime soon.

"Do you know where's my mom and dad?" Marie asked.

"I don't know, honey," Navaro said sadly. She crouched to the child's eye level. "Can you tell me what happened? Did either of you see what happened?"

Marie shook her head and covered her ears.

"I heard screams upstairs," said James. "The teachers opened the back door, to get all of us out, but they couldn't. The bad men were like shadows. You didn't hear them coming and you couldn't see them until it was too late. Our teacher only had time to hide us in the secret compartment of the closet and lock us in."

Phelps entered the classroom and startled the children.

"It's alright," said Navaro. She explained that Phelps was with her in the FBI; he was her partner."

The children settled down and Navaro asked what it was like upstairs.

"It seems likely that some of the children were able to get out," Navaro said to Phelps, "so I'm gonna check the rest of the classrooms to see if there are any other survivors. Can you take these two out through the back? And also, could you call child protective services?"

Phelps gestured for the kids to follow him.

Navaro searched classroom after classroom, and closet after closet, but found only the dead left behind.

The bad men were like shadows, James had said. *You didn't hear them coming, you couldn't see them until it was too late.* The boy's words kept coming back to her as she went from room to room.

Outside she found Phelps alone. James and Marie had been taken into child protective custody.

"I was able to get something out of the kids," said Phelps.

"'The assailants looked like shadows, undetected until it was too late."

"Sounds like professionals. Highly trained professionals. Any theories?"

"A few," said Navaro.

She waved over a medical examiner that was carting a body away and unzipped the body bag. A long slash mark ran down corpse's chest. From her bag Navaro pulled out a small metal detector and passed it over the wound but it couldn't detect any trace of metal.

"No metallic fragments in the wound. What kind of weapon can cut through flesh and bone and leave absolutely no trace?" she said, rather than asked.

"The type of weapon Tanaka would be able uncover," said Phelps.

San Antonio, Texas, Pastor Willis' house

The leaders of the San Antonio Church of Christ had congregated in Pastor Willis' dimly lit study. Megan brought in extra chairs for new arrivals. The meeting had been opened for some time. Pastor Willis sat behind his desk. Bruce sat beside him and had been taking down the minutes.

The room was quiet. Attention was focused on the flat screen that was mounted on the back wall of the study.

"We now have just received new information regarding the massacre of the Central Jersey Church of Christ," said the news anchor. "We take you to North Brunswick, New Jersey, where Vera Mysakovskaya is standing by."

The broadcast switched to a live coverage from the Central Jersey Church of Christ, where the coroners were still busy removing the bodies.

"Thank you, Jim," said a young blonde in a red pantsuit; she had a lingering Russian accent. "I'm standing about two-hundred yards from the Central Jersey Church of Christ where, earlier today, police discovered a grisly scene. FBI and North Brunswick police have discovered 150 deceased men, women, and children. Not all of the victims have been identified as of yet. We do have a shred of good news. It has been confirmed that anonymous FBI agents discovered two survivors. The survivors are children, whose identities will not be revealed. Again, they are the sole survivors of this tragedy. We'll have more, as things develop."

Pastor Willis turned the television off.

A tense pause followed and several of the men wiped tears from their face.

A church leader asked no one in particular, "What are we going to do?"

"I called you all here so that together we could pray for the families of the victims of this massacre," said Pastor

Willis. "And also, we need volunteers to go out there and see if they can help out in any way"

Megan raised her hand, as the pastor had expected she would.

"I'll go, too," Bruce said.

"Good," said Pastor Willis. "Let's see what we can do out there, but before, let us pray."

All heads bowed.

"Father, God, this is a terrible time for the church and we need you, Lord. We need you to help us rely on your strength and carry us through this tragedy. Help the two children who survived the tragedy, Lord. They're alone and you alone know the horrors they have witnessed. Be with them tonight, Lord, and help us, as a church, unite in spite of the tragedy. In Jesus' name we pray."

After the prayer, conversation was sparse and somber.

The phone rang and Megan picked it up. Pastor Willis accompanied the visitors to the door.

A woman's voice asked, "Is this the Willis household?"

"Yes, I'm Megan Willis. How can I help you?"

"My name is Lucretia Mott. I'm with the North Brunswick, New Jersey Child Protective Services. Do you know James and Marie Taylor?"

"Yes," said Megan. She took a deep breath and braced herself.

"I just wanted to inform you that the children are alive and doing quite well, considering the circumstances."

"Thank you. Oh, thank you so much to update us with such wonderful news."

"You're most welcome. And can you tell me if Willis Ware is around, by any chance? I would like to talk with him."

"Of course. He's here. I'll go get him."

Megan called the pastor back to his study and handed

him the cordless phone and then waited around so that she could be there when he received the good news about the children.

"Hello?" said the pastor. "Yes, this is Willis Ware."

"My name is Lucretia Mott. I'm calling about the Taylor children, James and Marie. They were the fortunate two survivors of the massacre at that church, and I wanted to contact you because you are listed as their emergency contact."

Pastor Willis dropped to his knees and looked up toward Heaven. "Praise God," he whispered. "Praise God they're alright. I'll be on the first plane out. Thank you, Miss Mott. Thank you so very much for this call."

He hung up and asked Megan to book him on the first flight to New Jersey. "They have James and Marie Taylor, and I'm going to pick them up."

"I'll go with you," said Megan and then she sat down at the computer and began looking up flight information.

The pastor removed his glasses and rubbed his eyes.

"Daddy, go get some sleep. You look exhausted. Why don't I fly out tomorrow and get James and Marie while you get some rest. Even Jesus slept, you know?"

The pastor smiled. He walked up behind Megan and kissed the top of the head.

"I don't know how I'm going to be able to rest at all during a time like this, but I guess I could give it a try. I'll go check on Jeffrey before I go to bed."

Jeffrey's bedroom door was ajar. The pastor knocked on the crown molding, and asked tentatively, "You okay, Jeffrey?" He found the young man at the desk, finishing up his bible study.

Jeffrey shut the bible and turned to the pastor.

"I just wanted to check on you, see how you're doing," said the pastor.

"I'm okay. Just scared."

Pastor Willis sat at the edge of the bed. "I'm scared too, you know? I'm scared that what happened to the Central Jersey church could happen here." He gently placed a hand on the Jeffrey's shoulder.

"We're supposed to be the light of the world," said Jeffrey. "Who would want to kill all those Christians, children and all?"

"Darkness," said the pastor. "Darkness is always around, waiting to devour the light, but it can't. Light can pierce darkness, but the darkness can never drown out the light unless it extinguishes itself. But that won't stop the darkness from trying. In times like these, we persevere, just like the early Christians had to. In their time, mass murders of Christians was a regular thing, and still they persevered."

"I guess that times like these really do test our convictions," said Jeffrey, "and our trust in God."

"Indeed, they do," said the pastor, and he glanced at the clock on the nightstand. "I have to go to New Jersey tomorrow. They've found two survivors, my niece and nephew, so I'm going to bring them back here. You know, it was encouraging for me to come in here and see you into the word, rather than allowing yourself to get so stirred up by what happened that you would neglect it."

"During times like this, I need the word of God more then ever."

Chapter Three:
A New Path Is Set

Tamuramaro village, Two years ago

Jubei had returned from killing Shinza Tanaka and went to his bedroom to rest. He closed his eyes for only a moment. There was a knock at the door. The white screen was pulled back and a servant girl stood in the doorway; her eyes were fixed on the floor.

"Your mother wishes to see you. She awaits in the garden."

Jubei had avoided the garden for years. He took a deep breath and went to find his mother.

From the bridge she was feeding the fish in the small pond below. Matsumi sensed her son's presence and turned, smiling. "You completed another mission. You went after Shinza."

"How did you know?"

"I make it a point to know my son's affairs, and his well being." Warmly she took his hand. "Something troubles your ninja focus, you can't disguise that. Something about the last mission. What is it?"

"Mother, what is our purpose? Jubei asked. "Do we serve a purpose or are we killing, spying, and sabotaging as a service for the highest bidder, regardless of cause or reason?"

"You never asked me anything like this before." Matsumi's tone was soft and tender.

"I'm asking now. What is our purpose?"

Matsumi led Jubei by the hand to a small bench at the foot of the bridge. "What did Shinza say to you before you killed him?" she asked.

Jubei took in the fragrance of the cherry blossoms. He could not look his mother in the eye, but knew that she was gazing lovingly at him. "I did not know Shinza, but his reputation for being honest was a well-known fact. And he confessed something to me, that, had it come from anyone else, I would have dismissed it. Shinza told me of the reason he betrayed us, feeling betrayed himself when he learned although we are ridding the world of evildoers that deserve to die, innocent people are often eliminated due to a high price tag that someone placed on their heads."

Jubei stood and glanced over at a small tree that was knee high. He could see himself as a boy, with a girl that he would come to love as a woman and later kill for being a traitor.

Matsumi followed her son's gaze and noticed the tree that Jubei and Maki had planted together. A small gravestone rested against the tree trunk. Matsumi ached for her son.

"A mother's tragic fate is to see the pain their child is going through, and be powerless to take it away." Matsumi joined her son by the small tree and turned him around so that he would face her. "The path to the truth is a road you must not take lightly. You must measure the cause and effects it will have. And it is a lonely road, one you must travel alone. All I can do is direct you to the road. Ask yourself this question: What kind of man would have his son kill the woman he loved just to prove his loyalty?" Although in this moment Matsumi could not read Jubei's face she knew she had struck a nerve.

"She was a traitor to the clan," Jubei said coldly. "The penalty is death."

"Do you truly think that Maki would have betrayed your love? Did you bother to investigate to see whether this was true? You simply receive the scrolls and go accomplish your missions without asking any questions." Again, Matsumi took hold her son's hands in hers. "There's so much blood on these hands, as much guilty blood as innocent blood."

Jubei pulled his hands away. "Mind your tongue," he said. "You speak of things you do not know. No one is innocent. And you have also helped turn me into this weapon, mother. And now you wish for me to seek the truth? What is it you hope to gain?"

"Our Freedom."

Matsumi began to walk away. Without stopping she said, "Already, the seed Shinza planted is beginning to sprout. You have just been put on the path."

Jubei watched his mother until she was out of view, and then dropped his head. His eyes widened. For the first time he saw his hands covered in blood. He blinked and the blood was gone, but he felt it still.

On the small gravestone was carved the Kanji symbol for "Double Happiness," Maki's name. Jubei bowed down before it. He could see her smiling face as if she were there, with him. Gently the wind blew her hair into her face. He reached out to tuck her hair behind her ear but like the blood she was gone, and like the blood he could feel her there still.

He crouched and with his finger he traced the Kanji symbol. In almost a whisper he said, "I'm sorry for the sin I committed against you. I am not deserving of your forgiveness, but I only followed the command I received. I love you Maki. I've always loved you and I will always love you. Every day you haunt me." He sat in the grass and crossed his legs. "I have killed priests who were molesting children in their church. I have killed corporate monsters that were exporting drugs, financing child slavery, pornography. The most evil and corrupt men have died from my blade. Oh, Maki, is there truth to what Shinza told me?" His eyes teared up at the thought of innocent blood. Women. Children. Maki.

Jubei balled his fist and punched the soft ground. And he wept. He wept for the women and children. He wept for Maki and her entire family. He wept for them all.

What kind of man would have his son kill the woman he loved just to prove his loyalty?

The path to the truth is a road you must not take lightly. You must measure the cause and effects it will have, and it is a lonely road where no one can travel with you. All I can do is direct you to the road.

Jubei said aloud, "I can't atone for what I've done to you, my love. All I can do is continue down this path and search for the truth. I don't know what I will find and I don't know what I will do with what I find, but I swear that I will make this journey." Jubei got back to his feet and bowed at the gravestone one last time.

A few hours later

At the local tavern, elders swapped stories of the old ways. The curtains to the stage opened. Women in Kimonos took the stage and danced a sultrily, drawing in the drunken men. One dancer slowly approach the edge of the stage, her gaze fixed on Jimbo Sanoki, a clan elder having long since retired. He was a man in his mid-fifties who, like most other retired men in their mid-fifties, loved women and was loyal to the drink. However, Jimbo Sanoki was a rather sought after commodity. He had a wealth of knowledge and, a treasure of sorts; he knew all there was to know about the clan as well as its well-kept secrets.

He drank his Sake and giggled as the dancer began to untie the belt of her kimono with every step she took towards him. She tossed it into the audience, aiming it towards him. She went to his table and, dancing around it, teased him, revealing a little shoulder, a little leg. She whispered into his ear and Jimbo happily followed her to a private room.

She pulled the curtains closed behind him and offered a massage.

He promptly slipped out of his shirt and laid, face down, on the bed.

"You like massage oil?" the woman asked, just as she drizzled cherry blossom oil over his skin. Her hands pressed into him.

Jimbo moaned. "I love your touch. Such strong hands," he said.

Shyly, she thanked him.

He groaned.

The woman playfully nibbled Jimbo's earlobe.

"I bet you've seen many things in your life," she whispered.

"I was a Dragon ninja," he boasted.

"How impressive." She asked whether he had been on any missions.

"More missions than I can count."

The oil felt warm on his skin, or perhaps it was just the friction of her skin against his.

"I have always wondered how the Dragon ninja receives a mission."

"In my day, we would receive our orders on a secret scroll that had only been seen by the clan ruler. Nowadays, the order comes in through a computer, and then it is transmitted to a scroll. The intelligence has always been locked in a vault, deep beneath the palace."

"That sounds very mysterious," the woman whispered, and right away Jimbo realized he had said too much. He turned over and grabbed the woman by waist. "You are very sly. I nearly told you my secrets."

She offered to spend the night with him, if he would only tell her more. She turned Jimbo back over and resumed stroking his back. Jimbo laid out the secrets to the underground archives as the woman listened intently. When he had nothing left to say, he turned over, anticipating the sex she had promised. The woman leaned in, as thought to kiss him, instead, striking Jimbo in a pressure point. She knocked him unconscious.

She slipped out the back entrance and uncovered a secluded path to the forest, which she followed and upon reaching a safe distance she took out a small remote kept hidden in the sleeve of her kimono, pressed a button, and her skin and silken hair melted from her body, revealing Jubei beneath.

Later that night

Upon entering his room, a dart hit Kuma Tamuramaro in the neck. He dropped, but Jubei dashed in and caught him before he hit the floor. He laid Hanzo down on the bed and with a miniature scanner he scanned Hanzo from head to toe. He flopped him over to scan the other side of his body and, once the scanning was complete, Jubei tucked Hanzo in bed and stealthily exited through the window. Like a shadow he seemed to glide across the rooftops.

Back in his own bedroom chamber, Jubei toggled on the lamp on the nightstand. A secret compartment under his bed propped open and from it he retrieved a laptop computer.

He plugged in a USB drive and uploaded Hanzo's body measurements. Jubei clicked on an icon with his own picture. The screen split in half, with Hanzo on one side and Jubei on the other; each of the men's measurements was displayed on either side of the screen. Jubei scrolled the arrow onto his image and highlighted it, and then highlighted Kuma. He pressed *enter* and the images of both men fused and the bodily measurements adjusted as Jubei transformed into Kuma. According to the image there were extra layers of skin, which was easily adjusted with a few keystrokes the extra skin was trimmed off to fit his body type. Again Jubei pressed *enter*, and the image was highlighted. Within moments Jubei waved his hand over a section of the carpet and a secret opening containing a glass encasement lifted out. The glass slid open. A bodysuit slid on a metal rack toward Jubei. He disrobed and slid into the suit, which spontaneously molded to his body and metamorphosed Jubei into Kuma. He then helped himself to tinted contacts from the automatic lens dispenser and after disinfecting his hands he gently placed the lenses into his eyes. The transformation was complete.

A separate concealed compartment held hundreds of small digital chips with differing labels. Jubei held one of the chips to his neck and upon contact, a minuscule green light on the chip switched on and microscopic prongs stuck into the latex surface and instantaneously the chip amalgamated to the synthetic skin. Jubei recited his ninja Dragon vows and incrementally his own voice attuned to Kuma's sharper pitched voice.

Jubei went down the stairs, deep down in the palace. He propped open a vent, into which he crawled and then put back the vent. Inside, he looked over a control panel and pressed the appropriate button and the elevator took Jubei further beneath the palace.

When it finally came to a stop, a guard in full uniform opened up the vent covering. Jubei slid out. The guard proceeded to confirm his identity, scrutinizing Hanzo, front and back, peering into his eyes. He patted Jubei down and then allowed Hanzo to proceed.

After passing through several similar checkpoints, Jubei gained access to the intelligence center where Usagi Yumagato, Kuma's best friend, approached him.

"I thought you were going to the matches tonight."

"Didn't you hear?" asked Usagi. "A tavern waitress killed Jimbo Sanoki. But then they found her dead in a storage closet. It looks like we have a rogue Dragon ninja. Only Dragon ninjas are trained in that level of disguise."

Everything came to a respectful standstill while a ninja a scroll was carried through the room. Work resumed once the scroll was sent up.

"I'm aware of what happened," said Jubei. "And Lord Ukyo thinks that a Dragon ninja is trying to infiltrate the underground. He sent me down here to go over the surveillance videos so I need to use your terminal. However, Lord Ukyo does want to keep this quiet and he expects us to be discreet."

Usagi gestured for his friend to follow him to his terminal. He logged in and then gave his seat up to Jubei.

"So, who do you think the rogue ninja could be?" Usagi asked.

"Could be anybody."

There had been a surveillance camera in Kuma's room an Kuma's assault had been captured on video and now played on Usagi's computer screen. All Usagi was able to do was flinch before Jubei turned and snapped his neck.

Jubei checked around for other witnesses.

An alarm rang out. Dragon ninja guards scrambled to

lock everything down. Jubei killed a couple of them as he fled.

"We've got a traitor among us! We've got a traitor! It's Kuma!"

Jubei disappeared through the vents. As he crawled through he came upon a gas mask and put it on just as poison gas had been released into the lower parts of the vents. Jubei kicked open the vent and came out in the hallway. Two Dragon ninjas hurled throwing darts at Jubei as he ran at them. Jubei did a dive roll as the darts passed over his head. He reached into his synthetic skin and pulled out two razor sharp discs. He hurled them while in mid-roll and they both killed the Dragon ninjas.

Jubei found an elevator, which he rode up to the level with the stairway where Dragon ninjas were waiting in the stairwell.

Jubei slipped a gas pellet through the vent. Upon hitting the ground it released a knockout gas. Jubei kicked off the vent cover and jumped out the window. He landed in a river. He took a deep breath and dove underneath the water just as an enormous spotlight was aimed at the water.

Ninja snipers took up positions along the palace's rooftops and emptied entire clips of ammunition as they indiscriminately sprinkled the river with gunshots, but no matter where they aimed they could not hit their target because Jubei was swimming a few feet below the range of the bullets.

Chaos erupted in the palace hallways while Ukyo was visiting his favorite concubine. He was about to send out a servant to check on the cause of the brouhaha when another servant brought him the report. "Sir, we have an infiltrator. Only one, from what we can tell. And Kuma is dead. He was killed with this dart, sir," said the servant who was holding a dart out to Lord Ukyo.

Gunfire could be heard in the distance.

Ukyo took the dart from him and with his eyebrows lowered and eyes squinting he looked over a Japanese character on its shaft and a black feather at the end of it. "This is a Yagyu ninja dart," Ukyo said in almost a whisper, and then he clenched his teeth—but the Yagyu had been crushed during the ninja wars.

Ukyo turned toward his concubine and dismissed her; the woman wrapped herself in a towel, picked up her clothes and excused herself, just as a ninja entered.

The man bowed to Ukyo, and then knelt down. "Master, the infiltrator is in the river. He appears to be wearing a Yagyu ninja uniform."

"Dispatch a recovery team and bring back the body. Where is Jubei?"

"I do not know, my lord. He was not in his room."

"See if you can find him and send him to me."

Smaller lights skimmed the top of the water as Jubei swam toward the surface. He carefully peered out.

Patrol ships were searching the river in a pattern. Ninjas leaned over the sides and scanned the water for any disturbance.

Jubei ducked beneath the surface and swam toward the closest boat.

He placed a small round disc the size of a hockey puck on the hull and swam hurriedly to a safe distance.

A ninja spotted him and opened fire. He shouted, "Yagyu ninja!"

The disc exploded, blowing an enormous hole in the hull. The boat took on water and began to sink.

A second explosion followed, before the first boat had even sunk.

At the Palace

Matsumi stood at her window. A smile crossed her face. She almost reveled in the chaos of the bodies being discovered. Explosions. "He has begun to walk the path," she said quietly to herself.

Once back on shore, Jubei double backed toward the palace, through the forest in which Dragon ninjas had been dispatched.

Dressed as a Yagyu ninja, Jubei continued to lure the Dragon ninjas. He quickly vanished up into the trees and from high above he could see a lone Dragon ninja running in his direction. Jubei braced himself, jumped down from the tree, and stood before him, Yagyu ninja facing Dragon ninja.

Alike the Yagyu ninja, Jubei's identity was concealed beneath a mask. He wore metal gauntlets inscribed with the Yagyu symbol. Jubei drew his sword and attacked the Dragon ninja, who was able to block Jubei's attack.

In a brilliant display of acrobatics and swordplay, the two ninjas battled in the moonlight.

However, the Dragon ninja was no match for Jubei's swordplay, and he disarmed the Dragon ninja and then sheathed his own sword. Now Jubei would fight his opponent in hand-to-hand combat.

Jubei blocked the Dragon ninja's attack. He grabbed his wrist, and kicked him in the stomach, and then in the back of the neck. The Dragon ninja rolled to his feet as Jubei dashed towards him and spun a crushing side kick, which shattered several ribs, despite which the Dragon ninja meant to keep fighting, but with another spin kick Jubei knocked him out.

Jubei removed the unconscious man's uniform and then slipped out of his Yagyu uniform. He quickly put on the man's uniform and took his sword. And then he redressed the Dragon ninja in the Yagyu uniform he had been wearing. Jubei stood over the unconscious man and raised his sword, readying to impale him, but Dragon ninjas stepped out from the trees before he could. One man said, "No, brother Jubei. Lord Ukyo wants him alive."

At first, Jubei was taken aback at having been identified, and immediately realized that he was not wearing his hood and mask. He sheathed his sword and picked the body up and along with his fellow Dragon ninjas they started back toward the palace.

Ukyo sat on the throne with Matsumi seated beside him. Jubei walked through the doors, carrying the unconscious ninja in Yagyu uniform. Callously, he dropped the ninja at Ukyo's feet. The fall startled him awake. He seemed disoriented as he tried to lift himself.

Ukyo commanded for his mask to be removed. "I want to look at the face of this Yagyu coward."

Ukyo slapped the ninja and then proceeded to punch him in the face, again and again, until blood poured from the man's grimacing face.

Matsumi was cringing.

"Where are you from?" Ukyo yelled. "Where is the rest of your clan?"

The ninja's silence was stunning.

Ukyo hit him again. "What were you looking for in the underground?"

"Father," Jubei pleaded. "Allow me to question him with my methods. I can get the results you need and by the time I'm done, death will be a privilege."

Ukyo granted his son's request and, as Jubei headed out

with the prisoner, Ukyo called out. "After you extract the information from of him, Jubei, bring me his head."

Jubei noticed that his mother frowned ever so slightly.

A secret room of the palace held a bevy of torturous devices. Surfaces in the room had collected dust. It had primarily been used during the last ninja war to interrogate Yagyu enemies.

Jubei unsheathed his sword. Meekly the ninja looked up at Jubei and nodded. Jubei raised his sword.

The ninja pleaded, "Promise me that my family will be taken care of."

"I promise you," said Jubei, "that your sacrifice will not be in vain." Jubei brought the sword down and its blade cut through flesh, bone and air. The sound of the severed head hitting the ground was heavy and wet.

Jubei rolled the severed head towards Ukyo's feet. Matsumi turned her head in disgust. Ukyo stood and approvingly patted Jubei's shoulder. "Well done, my son. What did that coward say?"

Jubei glanced at his mother, and then he addressed his father, "He was able to infiltrate our compound with inside help. It seems that we had a Yuga ninja amongst us for a while now, but do not worry, father, for I have already killed the other Yagyu spy. It was our own Jimbo Tamuramaro."

Ukyo raised his brow in disbelief. "Jimbo? Are you sure?"

"I know this firsthand. I was that woman in the massage parlor. His Yagyu tattoo was concealed in a place that only one of his whores would be privy to. Jimbo was passing on vital security information to his companion, about how to bypass our security system. The Yagyu made it all the way into the underground. That was where I caught up with him, but he used our own escape plans to elude me. Obviously, he did not elude me for long."

"What was he doing in underground?" Ukyo asked.

"I don't know for sure," Jubei said. "He chose to die rather than reveal this."

Ukyo began to pace the room, seemingly in deep thought. And when he stopped, he asked, "The location of the Yagyu, did he give you a location?"

"He did. The Yagyu have resurfaced in Kyoto-Nigawa. They have been gathering strength secretly for over thirty years. My guess is they sent the infiltrator to test our defenses because they are preparing an invasion."

"I want you to go Kyoto-Nigawa, find the Yagyu, and report back."

"Father, could you please send one of my comrades instead? With your permission, I would like to investigate the underground to figure out what the Yagyu had been looking for. Whatever it that is, it is key to the Yagyu invasion and we need to know what it is so that we can better counter it."

Matsumi approached Ukyo and lovingly wrapped her arms around him.

"My husband, our son is right. The underground has been compromised. For all we know, there may be more than one Yagyu infiltrator. And, by sending Jubei into the underground, you will be able to uncover the truth. Whether there are more Yagyu amongst us. What they are seeking. In the meantime, why don't you send your soldiers to the Yagyu camp? Jubei will serve you best here."

Ukyo tenderly rubbed Matsumi's hand. "Very well," he said.

Jubei sat cross-legged on his bed. His head hung low. Matsumi entered but Jubei did not look up. She gently slid the door shut.

"I did not want to kill, Hiamaryu," said Jubei. "It was not part of the plan, mother."

Matsumi went over to her son and took him in her arms as she did when he was a boy.

Six hours earlier

At a small house in the village, Hiamaryu answered the door and was horrified to find Jubei on his doorstep, but, before he could shout for help, Jubei barged in and placed his hand over Hiamaryu's mouth. "Hush. I'm not here to kill you. I'll take my hand off your mouth, but if you scream I will snap your neck."

Hiamaryu nodded, so Jubei released him.

"If you're not here to kill me, then why are you here?" Hiamaryu asked, trying to steady himself.

"You were once a Yagyu weaponsmith and Jimbo spared your life after the Yagyu were destroyed. Your past will help me and in return I shall help you."

"How can you help me?"

"Your wife and child are sick, are they not?"

Hiamaryu sighed deeply.

In the back room, Hiamaryu's wife laid in bed with a cold rag over her head. Her skin was covered in boils.

Hiamaryu mixed some herbs into a teacup and helped his wife drink it down. He stroked her forehead and looked lovingly at her, with such sadness.

Jubei appeared unmoved.

In the next room slept a four-year-old girl, who was in the same dire condition as her mother. Although she was asleep, she would occasionally flail around and groan.

"She's in constant pain," said Hiamaryu. "How is it that you can help us?"

"With the money that I shall give you, you'll be able to

help your wife and your child. I will also provide travel visas and tickets for the three of you to go to America."

"You would help a Yagyu?"

"This comes at a high price."

"Anything worth having always does. And I must admit that I was wrong about you. The mere fact you are helping me shows that you are the not a merciless killer."

Jubei interrupted him. "Make no mistake. I am that. But I don't have a reason to kill you or your family. Nevertheless, remember whom you are speaking to. "

Hiamaryu nodded sternly, and Jubei went on to clarify what it was that he expected from Hiamaryu .

In Jubei's room

In her son's face Matsumi could see his anguish and regret at having killed Hiamaryu.

"Is this the price I must pay for the path of truth that I have chosen?" Jubei asked.

"You will pay a heavier price while traveling this road, Jubei. "But I can give you a grain of truth. And that will cost you nothing at all."

Matsumi stood and went over to the window. The moon was full. The peaceful facade she wore on her face slipped away and the affliction she usually hid so well became apparent. Jubei hurried to comfort his mother but she held her hand out so that he would keep away.

Matsumi admitted that she had not wanted this sort of life for her son. "I did not want you to be molded into a killer. I wanted something better for you. I considered faking your death so that I could arrange for you to be adopted by a family in America. You could have been an American and never known what it is to be a ninja. You would have been free to live and love. I failed you, my son." Matsumi slipped her kimono off and uncovered severe scars along her back, where she had been whipped repeatedly.

Tears welled in Jubei's eyes. He balled his fist and shook in anger as his mother slipped her kimono back on.

"This was the consequence of my failure. I could only watch as they turned you into the most ruthless Dragon ninja I have ever seen. At a young age, your skills were already superior to your father's. I stood by as your soul was weighed down with every life you took. I said nothing as you swallowed your own humanity, which enabled you to obediently, and blindly, follow every order handed to you. There was a time when this ninja clan only eliminated the bad people to improve the quality of life of those who are good. And now, what you decide to do on this path for truth will shape the fate of this clan."

Matsumi kissed her son on the forehead, and then left him to contemplate his new path.

Chapter Four:
Dark Days

San Antonio

Pastor Willis was preparing a sermon for Sunday service when there was an urgent knock at the door of his study.

"Come in."

Bruce entered looking downcast. "Have you seen the news?" he asked somberly.

Pastor Willis had not.

Bruce turned on the television to a CNN news report set outside a high school in Denver, Colorado. The pastor and Bruce watched in disbelief while the reporter informed viewers about another massacre, which involved the Denver Church of Christ. Pastor Willis turned the television off and dropped to his knees in prayer. Bruce followed.

The telephone rang and when the pastor pulled himself off the floor, to answer the phone, he could not tell how much time had gone by.

"Hey Willis. This is John," said a man's voice. "Have you

heard about the Denver church, and about the one in Santa Fe?"

Pastor Willis was shaken. "I just saw the news report about the church in Denver. Dear God, what is happening?"

"I know. The reason why I'm calling is to set up a meeting with all the lead evangelists so that we can discuss what's going to happen to the remaining churches. Leaders from the churches in Europe and Asia are meeting as we speak. How soon can you fly out here, Willis?"

There was a moment of silence and static.

"Willis, are you there?"

"I'm here," said the pastor. He rubbed his smooth head. "I can take the first plane out." He hung up.

"What did John say?" asked Bruce.

"He wants lead evangelists to meet. You're gonna have to preach the sermons this week, Bruce. I got to get to New York."

"No problem," Bruce said, reassuringly. "I'll be prepared."

"I was going to start with Sermon on the Mount. For mid-week we'll continue with the beatitudes."

Bruce jotted a few notes in his notepad and the pastor handed over his own sermon notes.

Megan the children entered the house as Pastor Willis and Bruce were leaving the study. When the distraught children saw Pastor Willis, their faces lit up. They ran over to him and hugged him.

"I'm so sorry," the pastor whispered.

Both children clung to the pastor and dissolved into tears.

Megan waited for them to settle down a bit and then told the children to go get washed up. "I'll have dinner ready soon."

Bruce grabbed their bags and led the children upstairs.

Megan knew her father well. She could tell he was downtrodden. She took him by the hand and asked him softly, "What's the matter?"

"Two churches of Christ were attacked. Everyone's dead."

Megan's legs weakened. She reached for the closest chair and slumped into it. "My God," she said. "What's happening to the churches? Three churches in a week?"

"John Sharp called from the New York church. He wants the lead evangelist from every stateside church to meet in New York."

"I'll make your arrangements. Why don't you go ahead and pack?"

Pastor Willis smiled gratefully at his daughter and then headed for the staircase.

FBI Forensics Lab, San Antonio, Texas

Jeremy Tanaka was a Japanese Crime Laboratory Technician at the FBI. He adjusted his glasses. They were always sliding off the bridge of his nose and adjusting them had become a habit, a tic of sorts. He wore his short hair spiked and most of his colleagues had never seen him in anything other than his nondescript white lab coat.

Tanaka was pacing the hallway that led to his laboratory, anxiously awaiting Agents Navaro and Phelps. He hurried over to them as soon as they came off the elevator. He handed a file to Navaro, and announced, "The results of the autopsies."

Navaro seemed puzzled as she looked over the results. "Inconclusive?" she said, rather than asked.

"Ballistics can't trace the weapons that were used ," Tanaka said excitedly. "No fingerprints found on the body either. But there's something very interesting inside the wounds themselves." He grabbed the file back and flipped through till he found what he was looking for, and then returned it to Navaro. "Now, what do you think about this?" Tanaka rubbed his hands together in anticipation while Navaro read over the indicated section.

She was perplexed. "Traces of water in the wounds?" she said inquisitively.

" Yeah, water. And the results were consistent in at least twenty of the bodies." Tanaka insisted on showing the evidence to Navaro and Phelps, and led them to a refrigerated room on the third floor. He pulled open storage drawer 14 and on the metal slab laid a young victim of the massacre with two deep slash marks across the boy's chest, in the shape of an *X*.

Phelps leaned in, over the corpse. "The traces of water in the wounds could suggest that the weapons were made of ice," he said. "Special Forces will often use ice bullets, which do not leave any ballistic trace that could be used as evidence.

Tanaka agreed. "But no Special Forces that I've heard of uses swords. These slash marks were not made by any of the standard knives used by Special Forces. The strokes are too long and the incisions are too wide. These wounds were made by two different swords"

"Swords?"

Tanaka slid the drawer shut and opened another, one row up, on the left. This elderly victim had been wounded between his eyes.

"This one wasn't made by a bullet dart or a knife. Notice how the wound is shaped like a triangle, and simply widens as it goes deeper. This could've been made by a Shuriken weapon."

"You mean, one of them throwing stars?" asked Phelps.

"Could be," said Tanaka. "But without us having the actual weapon to compare it to, all this remains speculation."

Navaro and Phelps exchanged a puzzled look and shrugged.

Navaro turned to Tanaka. "So, bottom line. Whom do you think did this?"

"The people that wiped out those church folks, they're hard core. And it's going to be nearly impossible to find them."

Phelps interjected, "Maybe by finding out the *why* behind the church massacres, we can find the *who*.

Navaro and Phelps thanked Tanaka as he excused himself to return to his work.

Outside the J. Edgar Hoover building, Navaro answered her phone.

A Middle Eastern man was on the other end of the line. "Agent Navaro, there have been two more massacres. I want you in Santa Fe, and Phelps in Denver, ASAP. There's already a fallout within the churches. Please tell me you have a lead."

"Sir," said Navaro, "we may be dealing with an elite Special Force unit," she paused a took a breath before continuing, "or ninjas."

"Did you say ninjas?"

"Yes, sir," Navaro said, trying her best not to sound certain, as if she herself might not believe what she had just suggested. "The only thing the autopsy revealed was traces of water found in the wounds. There were no fingerprints, no fibers of any kind. Only the wounds themselves."

"Just get your butts out there, *now*."

He had hung up before Navaro could say anything else.

"He wants us to split up and go to Denver and Santa Fe. Which one do you prefer?"

Phelps didn't hesitate. "Santa Fe."

Navaro admitted that she also would rather go to Santa Fe. She suggested rock, paper, or scissors.

Navaro and Phelps shook their fist to the count of three and then simultaneously Phelps held his opened hand out, signifying a sheet of paper, and Navaro made the V sign with her fingers, mimicking the shape of scissors. Quietly, they acknowledged the outcome with a nod, but, as the partner parted ways, neither the victor nor the loser had anything left to say. Once their backs were turned, Phelps sighed and Navaro did smile.

New York City, New York

The next morning Pastor Willis arrived at George Washington High School in New York's Washington Heights. He carried his bible with him as he walked the hallways of the vacant high school on a cold Saturday morning. The hall that led to the auditorium was dimly lit. Pastor Willis' face was solemn. He murmured a brief prayer as he passed by the trophy cases and rows of lockers.

Inside the auditorium forty-six of the church leaders of the international churches of Christ turned to look at the newcomer.

Pastor John Sharp, a slender white man in his early sixties, hurried over to Pastor Willis and hugged him like they were old friends. "Glad you made it. How was your flight?"

"Long, considering why I'm here," said the pastor.

Pastor John Sharp approached the stage and Pastor Willis took a seat. The large auditorium quieted. The mood was sad.

John Sharp sighed as he glanced over the faces of surviving church leaders. "Let's go to God in Prayer."

Heads bowed.

"Father God," John Sharp said, and then he just stood there, overwhelmed.

Pastor Willis approached the stage, put his arm around John and bowed his head, as did John.

"Father, God, it's a dark time for the church, Lord," said Pastor Willis. "But you, Lord, are our light. It is a sad meeting as we gather here today. Our emotions take us over, but, in this time of sorrow and weakness, I ask that you, precious father, be with us and strengthen us. In this moment Satan will attempt to cripple us. Lord, please help us stand firm and fight against him. We know that our brothers and sisters are home, with you, in Heaven. Lord, help us find comfort in that. In Jesus' name we pray."

John mouthed *thank you* to Pastor Willis and then he returned to his seat.

John exhaled deeply and then preceded, "I've been in touch with the FBI and local law enforcement about the three massacres," he said. "More specifically, I've been speaking with Agents Salma Navaro and Dante Phelps. The latest update was that they were going to the forensics lab to see if there was anything they could use to get a lead on the killers. I'm still waiting to hear from either one of them. I've been watching the news since the beginning of these massacres. It's causing quite a shake up in the church community. Churches of different denominations have suspended their services all over the country. It's no secret that the killings were done by professionals, and the reasons why don't really matter. We just have to pray for the killers, and pray that God will save their souls. Amen."

"Amen," the pastors said in unison.

"The reason I called us here today was to discuss our options, as a church. I personally don't see any option but one. Until this blows over, we should not resume church services."

Murmurs flared up amongst the audience. Pastor Willis leaned in closer and rested one hand in his other palm. He took a moment to glance around the room and observed the reactions of the other lead evangelists.

"Brothers," John Sharp called, waving his hand to quiet them down. "I know how this sounds, but three of our churches have already fallen victim to these murderers. There's been no rhyme or reason to it, but to spread fear."

John's controversial suggestion was being discussed amongst the evangelists. Pastor Willis kept quiet. When the audience finally quieted down, John Sharp went on to explain the reasons for his suggestion, after which the floor was opened for discussion. Other lead evangelists spoke their minds, going as far as to suggest not meeting at all. All the while, Pastor Willis said nothing.

One the lead evangelists turned to him and said, "Brother Willis, you've been quiet this whole time. What do you suggest?"

Pastor Willis shrugged and stood.

"There's forty something men in this auditorium right now. Each one of us were baptized and eventually appointed lead evangelists of our churches. We're the leaders. We're all well versed in the bible and we're the ones who set the example for our congregations. What example are we setting as *well versed* godly men if we turn and run with our tails between our legs? What are we telling those who look to us for answers? We're telling them that their faith isn't good enough. We're telling them that it's okay to worship and share our faith, and change communities, so long as it's safe, but worst of all we're telling them that God isn't powerful enough to handle this. And if they don't already think these things, I promise, they definitely will, when they see our example.

To hold church service in secret and not invite the lost to any of our services is mind blowing. To not hold services at all is a realm that I don't even want to venture to." Pastor Willis did not wait for a reaction from the evangelists. He looked sharply at John, and then stormed out.

Hours later

Megan and Bruce greeted Pastor Willis at the door upon his return home.

"What happened?" Megan asked.

James, Marie, and Jeffrey came downstairs to greet the pastor. Megan asked Jeffrey to set the table for dinner.

Jeffrey whined. "But I want to hear what's going on with the church."

"I'll fill you in later," Pastor Willis said reassuringly. "James and Marie can help you."

"Yes, sir," Jeffrey said, and he headed off toward the kitchen with James and Marie, but they stopped after turning the corner, so that they might listen in on the pastor's conversation.

"Come out, kids" the pastor called. "If you're going to listen in on the conversation you might as well hear it from over here."

The kids stepped out from around the corner. "Megan used to sneak around like that too." He smiled but soon enough his solemn expression returned.

"There's no easy way to say this, but due to the murders at the three churches, the evangelists have decided to suspend services."

"Dad, maybe the kids shouldn't hear this," said Megan.

"They'll know sooner or later."

Bruce interrupted, "So you were saying?"

"I was saying that because of the murders, church services have been suspended."

"That's insane," said Bruce.

"I just sat there for the longest time, listening to everyone shout their opinions. Some were for it; some were against it. I couldn't believe what I was hearing but I stayed quiet until I was asked what I thought. Why even bother asking?"

"John has always valued your opinion, daddy," said Megan.

"I objected to it out right, and walked out. He called me later on and told me that was what had been decided."

"Did you want me to get the word out over email and start making phone calls?" Bruce asked.

"No," said the pastor. "I'll tell the congregation at the midweek service. What you can do, Bruce, is get the word out that's it not going to be split, but one service."

Bruce nodded and left the house to begin making the phone calls.

Megan placed her hand on her father's shoulder and he took her hand in his.

"I'm gonna skip dinner tonight, sweetheart," he said. "I've got to prepare a speech for what I'm going to say during midweek."

Pastor Willis sent James and Marie off to wash their hands and then headed towards his office. Megan went to the kitchen to get dinner ready. Jeffrey followed her. He took the dinner plates out of the cabinet and set them on the table.

"Are we not going to have church anymore?" he asked, reaching into the silverware drawer and grabbing four of each utensil. Megan pulled the meatloaf out of the oven, put it on the counter and with a knife she cut it into slices.

"No," Megan said. "It won't be for good. It's just until the murderers get caught."

"Why is this happening to our church?" Jeffrey asked. "Who would want to hurt us?"

"People who are very lost," Megan said. "We just have to pray to God for strength and that He is with the FBI as they investigate. We have to pray for the murderers as well."

"Why?" Jeffrey asked. "They killed people. They killed James and Marie's mom and dad."

"Yes, what they did was horrific. But Paul killed Christians as well. And Christ called him to serve in spite of that. He still wanted Paul to be with him."

Jeffrey shook his head and finished setting the table.

"So, you're saying we should pray for the murderers to be saved?"

Megan finished cutting the meatloaf and placed it on the dining room table. James and Marie hurried in and presented their clean hands to Megan and she allowed him to sit at the table.

"Jeffrey, you want to pray?" Megan asked.

Jeffrey squirmed in his chair and bowed his head. He mumbled his words but got through saying grace. Silence filled the dining room throughout the meal. When dinner was over, the kids cleared the table and went upstairs. Megan put the food away and stood over the sink to place the dishes in the dishwasher. A tear rolled down her cheek and soon enough she was bitterly weeping over the sink. She dropped to her knees, folded her hands in front of her and cried out, "Father God, my heart is broken. How can this be happening to us? Lord, I know nothing is out of your control, but why this? How can we not hold service? Guide us all in this dark time. Lord, watch over my father, for he's exhausted. I've never seen that look of defeat on his face like he had tonight. *Ye though we walk through the valley of the shadow of death we will fear no evil.* We're going through the valley right now,

Lord, and with you we walk to make it out of the valley. In Jesus' name I pray. Amen."

Two days later

The congregation gathered at the San Antonio Church of Christ and waited for the song group to take their place on the stage. And since the children's classes were not in session, everyone was present. The song group took the stage and began with a lively upbeat song. Pastor Willis waited in the wings of the stage with his daughter. He looked over his notes, concentrating on what he was about to say.

Megan watched him. Normally, he would be bopping to the music and singing along, but today he was a different man. Pastor Willis looked tired. Older. Megan rubbed his back. It must have been her touch, but it jump-started him. Pastor Willis put aside his notes and began to clap to the song. After the song was over, the pastor took a deep breath and approached the podium. The seats were filled with disciples. His eyes fell upon Jeffrey, James, and Marie, and looking at the faces of James and Marie made what he was about to say real. Their pain was real and the safety of the church's children began to sink in. It wasn't until he looked into the faces of the children who had survived the horror of the first massacre that he realized the need to suspend church services.

Megan gently nudged him. When he looked up, all eyes were on him. He apologized. "My train of thought was seriously derailed," he said, "but I'm back. Let's go to God in prayer."

Everyone bowed their heads and Pastor Willis prayed. When he was done, everyone looked up at him again. A baby's cry broke the silence.

"Tonight, I wanted the split midweek services to be joint.

I originally was going to continue with the beatitudes, but there's been a change of plans. I'm not going to preach a sermon tonight. It's been a week since the massacres of the three churches. If you've been watching the news or reading the papers, in this area alone hundreds of churches have shut their doors. Even a few mosques and synagogues have closed. Fear and panic has spread among religious communities, and the International Churches of Christ is not an exception. Take a look around you. There are lots of empty seats and our seats are only going to get emptier."

Pastor Willis paused for effect. The congregation appeared perplexed. Megan gave him a supportive smile.

"I was called to New York by John Sharp, shortly after the... I was called to New York and met with all the leaders of the United States churches. To make a long story short, this is going to be our last service."

A voice shouted from the back row, "What do you mean, our last service?"

"Everyone decided that it would be best to suspend church services until this dark time is over."

An older male disciple stood up. "This can't be," he said. "We can't just hide out, afraid of what might happen.

"I agree," said another.

One by one, members of the congregation began to voice their objections. Pastor Willis waved his hand and gradually the room quieted. "I understand how you feel. I also felt the same way when this suggestion was brought up. I felt so indignant that I walked out before the consensus, and I had to be called back in. Then there was a vote, and the result was to suspend the services until the FBI solves the case."

The pastor had nothing left to say and the congregation dissipated until he was left alone in this very auditorium in which his grandfather had baptized him. It was also where Megan was baptized as a teenager. Now the large auditorium seemed like a ghost town, however, Pastor Willis did not see the empty seats before him but rather an auditorium filled with people and their songs of worship echoed.

Days turned to weeks and weeks turned to months. The International Church of Christ had all but disbanded. Across countries, churches of every denomination had shut their doors. Catholic and Christian schools had also closed down. Fear of worship spread like a pandemic and communities suffered. Before long, finger pointing and blaming would follow. Soon enough, religion was blaming religion; blame turned into violence. Christian extremists went on Muslim witch-hunts and bombed mosques. In retaliation, Muslims extremists burned down a Christian church. Months slipped by and horrifying news played out on the news. Pastor Willis shut the TV off in disgust. A church had been burned to the ground, and the consequence of the church burning resulted in the death of fourteen random people from different denominational sects.

A rock crashed through the window and tires screeched as a car tore down the street and the pastor dropped flat on the floor. Amid the shards of glass he could see the rock that had shattered the window. Something appeared to be attached to it, perhaps a note of sorts. At first, the pastor found that he was unable to move, and, with some effort, he willed himself to crawl over to the sharp debris and retrieved the attached note: *To hell with your church.* The pastor crumpled it and tossed it as far as he could.

Across town, Megan was leaving a Whataburger restaurant, carrying bags full of fast food. People on the sidewalk recognized her.

"Hey!" someone shouted. "You're one of them *disciples* from the Church of Christ aren't you?"

Megan kept on walking toward her car. The man stepped forth, followed by his crowd. They surrounded her.

"Yeah, you're one of them. I've been to your church before."

"Can you please get away from my car? I'm just trying to get home."

"Aren't you gonna preach to me? Aren't you going to try to invite me out to church?"

Megan tried to push her way through, but was pushed back. She dropped the bags and food spilled onto the pavement.

A woman accused her church of being a cult. "I saw it on the internet. You've been brainwashing people."

The crowd got louder and the woman got in Megan's face. "It's your church's fault that all this is happening. If I smacked you, would you hit me back or would you turn the other cheek, like Jesus tells you to?" The woman lifted her arm to slap Megan. Megan shut her eyes but did not feel the blow. When Megan opened her eyes she saw a strikingly handsome dark skinned Asian man holding back the woman's arm. He fractured it. Bone pierced through the skin. The woman let out a bloodcurdling cry. The man kicked her in the chest, sending her crashing into others. The man who had first confronted Megan, tried to punch the stranger, but he swayed to the right. The stranger kicked the man in the thigh and broke his leg. He threw a chop to the man's throat and then pushed him out of the way. Two more people rushed towards the stranger. Two others went down. A teenager pulled out a knife and went after the stranger. The stranger kicked another person in the face. The teenager stabbed at the stranger but he swiftly disarmed the teenager and kicked his face so hard that the kid spun around. The stranger grabbed the teenager and threw him through the windshield of a car. The crowd fled as the sounds of sirens became louder. The stranger gave Megan a slight nod before vanishing into the shadows.

The police pulled into the parking lot. They survey the scene and called in an ambulance. Witnesses were eager to tell their version of the event. Megan also related what she could remember to the police. They scoured the area and asked witnesses whether they had seen where the mysterious stranger had gone.

No one noticed an old woman walk out of Whataburger with a sack of burgers, get into a car, and drive off slowly. A few blocks down, the old woman pulled into an isolated park and peeled off her face. It was Jubei.

Three weeks earlier, Tamuramaro Mountains

Jubei went to the central intelligence room beneath the palace. Dragon ninja guards stepped out of his way as he passed through. Jubei held a scroll, which decreed that whomever held it ought to be granted special access to the central room.

Upon entering the central room, Jubei allowed the ninjas to frisk him, and then he commanded everyone to leave the room.

A technician asked, "On whose authority?"

Jubei unrolled the scroll and handed it to the technician. "By my father's authority. You can authenticate it, if you wish to. Meanwhile, you will be disobeying a direct decree to vacate the premises immediately. I am here to investigate the leak in our structure." Jubei shoved the scroll into the technician's chest. "I will not repeat myself."

The intelligence agents took their leave without asking any more questions. Left alone, Jubei approached the computers and searched for the location of the vault. Jubei plugged in a small USB port, uploaded a looped video recording of an empty vault and recorded himself sitting at the computer. There was a brief glitch in the security cameras and then they came back online. All the while, Jubei was aware that a secret security surveillance team was monitoring him.

"What was the malfunction?" said a voice over the loudspeaker.

"I uploaded a continuous loop to mask what I am doing in case there is more than one Yagyu infiltrator. My father is fully aware of what I am doing. For all I know, you could be the infiltrator."

"Precede, brother Jubei."

Jubei activated the loop so that his true activities might remain concealed. Jubei began his search on the computer and Shinzin Tanaka's words rang in his head.

He came across the file of the Church of Christ leaders, and the order to terminate three of them. He scrolled through the files until he came upon Pastor Ivy's profile —the first pastor to be murdered. A detailed dossier of Ivy appeared on the screen, complete with his entire biography, and his time as a leader of the Central Jersey Church of Christ. Jubei read the dossier twice and saw nothing that would warrant killing this man.

Jubei memorized the address on the dossier. He spent a few hours going through the dossier of the three pastors that had been slain; he had to find out more. However, he realized there wasn't anything here worth killing entire congregations over.

As he approached the secret entrance to the vault he scanned the door for trip wires. Jubei waved a small remote device over the vault door and scrambled the alarms. He had twenty seconds to get the door open. He pulled out a pick and worked fast with the timer on countdown. Five seconds left. Jubei had to pick the lock. Four seconds. Three. Two . One. The vault opened.

As directed by Hiamaryu, an army of a hundred Dragon ninjas descended upon the location of the Yagyu camp, which appeared to have been abandoned for years. The Dragon ninjas spread out in a fan pattern and searched the village thoroughly. They found nothing, regrouped and were vacating the desolate village when explosive arrow tips flew from the treetops and rained upon the Tamuramaro Dragon ninjas. Dozens succumbed. The arrows forced the Dragon ninjas to escape through a narrow passage. As they retreated, several Dragon ninjas fell through pitfalls and were impaled on bamboo spikes. Arrows kept coming. Few ninjas made it into a clearing. Smoke landmines exploded, releasing a thick dark cloud. The ninjas drew their weapons and kept retreating. Explosions. Arrows. Chaos. Dragon ninjas killed their comrades in confusion. Forty ninjas made it out of the minefield and ran through the forest. A trip wire activated grenades.

Only five Dragon ninjas made it back to Tamuramaro village reported back to Ukyo, who was basking in a hot tub filled with lavender rose petals. Pretty maidens gently rubbed silk sponges on his bare back. One fed him grapes. Another wiped the corner of his mouth with a silk cloth.

"Lord Ukyo, we were ambushed."

Ukyo stepped out of the tub and slipped into the robe that was being held open for him. "What do you mean, ambushed?" he asked, indignantly. He took down a sword from the rack of weapons beside the doorway.

"When we arrived at the Yagyu camp, it appeared abandoned. But without warning we were attacked."

In anger, Ukyo thrust the sword through the closest maiden and coolly watched her draw her last breath.

"How many of the Yagyu were there?" Ukyo asked.

"We couldn't tell. We only saw shower after shower of arrows coming down on us. We had to retreat into a minefield. There was all this smoke, and then the Yagyu were moving in on us."

Ukyo lifted the ninja to his feet and back fisted him. "You fool!" Ukyo roared. There were no Yagyu. You were killing each other in the confusion. The Yagyu must have received word of our attack. There is still a mole among us."

A ninja stepped forwards and said, "Master, have you considered that the traitor might be your own son? Was it not Jubei who interrogated the Yagyu traitor and received the location of the Yagyu camp? Perhaps, it was Jubei who informed the Yagyu of our arrival. We lost 95 ninjas today."

Ukyo decapitated the ninja with a single motion. His head rolled into the tub, turning the water crimson.

"Does anyone else share his opinion?" Ukyo asked.

"Master, forgive me," The ninja leader pleaded. "But Jubei has been given access to the underground, by you, while we were ambushed by the Yagyu. If anyone could become a spy for the Yagyu Jubei could do it well."

"Remove your mask and open your mouth," Ukyo commanded.

The ninja hesitated, but did as he was told, and Ukyo stabbed him through the mouth. The sword exited the back of the man's neck.

"Anyone else care to accuse my son of treason?"

"My lord," a brave ninja said, "I am far from accusing Jubei, but if you want to verify whether or not he is the one behind this betrayal, then review the surveillance video of his interrogation of the Yagyu spy. Unbeknownst to Jubei, a secret video surveillance monitors interrogations. It has been installed recently. We haven't had a chance to brief you on the new system."

"Show me," Ukyo said.

Moments later

With a balled fist and fire in his eyes, Ukyo watched the interrogation of Hiamaryu while the Dragon ninjas stood by, awaiting his orders. Ukyo punched the monitor in a fury. "Bring Jubei to me alive. And make sure he suffers along the way."

As the ninjas turned to head out, Ukyo's stopped them. "This is Jubei you are going after. You'll need more men."

The ninjas bowed and left Ukyo rubbing his fist as he stared at the broken surveillance monitor.

Jubei had finished installing the spyware on all the computers and entered the mysterious vault, which to his surprise was empty. Jubei returned to the main room. The download was complete, so he disconnected the small USB and hid it a secret compartment in his tabi boots. He exited the security room and headed down the hall toward the elevator. The elevator door opened. Throwing knives flew out of the elevator toward Jubei. He dropped back and then rolled to his feet. Another elevator opened at the end of the hall and several other throwing knives soared toward him. Jubei dodged most of them, but two knives lodged into his shoulders. He yanked them out and quickly retreated to the main central intelligence room. Ninjas broke down the door. They unsheathed their swords and slowly fanned out to search for Jubei. One man kept his back along the wall to prevent Jubei from sneaking up on him. Jubei was hiding in the utility closet the ninja had just passed by. Jubei exited the closet and stalked the ninja. The ninja moved away from the wall and doubled back to the utility closet. He fired multiple shots into the closet and then opened it. From behind, Jubei snapped the ninja's neck and gently laid the dead man to the floor. He hurriedly stripped the ninja of his armor, sword, and smoke bombs.

A ninja snuck up on Jubei and swung. Jubei dodged the attack but was cut across the stomach. The sword was out of his reach. The ninja swung again. Jubei stepped to the side and back fisted the ninja. Two others came at Jubei with their swords raised. Jubei grabbed the closest ninja as the two ninjas thrust their swords and impaled their comrade. Jubei vaulted over the men, killed them, and yanked his swords out them in time to deflect another attack.

Jubei found himself smothered in a crowd of ninjas. He valiantly threw down two smoke bombs. Killed. By the time the smoke had cleared, six ninjas were dead. Two others threw knives at Jubei, which he deflected. He hurled a sword and impaled a man through the chest.

Jubei vaulted over another ninja but was hit in the thigh with a throwing star. He landed on his side. Ninjas warmed in on him. Jubei got up and staggered. His vision was getting blurry. Jubei pulled the sword out of the impaled ninja and held it out in front of him. A couple of ninjas moved in. They died. Two more ninjas moved in. Jubei shook his head to clear his vision. His legs felt wobbly. A ninja attempted to rush Jubei from behind. Jubei stabbed him in the stomach. As another ninja moved in, Jubei pulled out the sword with which he had just killed a man, and decapitated the one who had snuck up on him.

Another ninja did a flying side kick with spikes and struck Jubei in the face. Jubei fell forward and he was kicked in the ribs.

Jubei slammed another smoke bomb on the floor. And when the smoke began to clear, he was standing; blood dripped from his face. In a whirlwind he annihilated every ninja in the security room and then staggered into the hallway in which an elevator opened, packed with ninjas. Jubei could barely hold his sword. He pulled the pin on a grenade and tossed it, just as reinforcements were stepping out of the elevator. The explosion was deafening. Jubei pressed his hands against his ears. Another elevator opened and ninjas spilled out, charging at Jubei who was standing ready, but already knew he would be overtaken.

Ukyo observed the construction of the water tank. Servants in uniform carried in bucket after bucket of salt water, which they poured into the tank that maintained thousands of Box Jellyfish—the most poisonous known to man.

Jubei was carried into the chamber. His naked, battered, and bruised body was dropped onto the table in the center of the room.

Matsumi entered and rushed towards her son. A ninja held her back. She threw her leg straight up and kicked the startled ninja in the face. Other ninjas stood side by side, blocking her way to Jubei. Matsumi's eyes burned with anger and hatred. "What are you doing to my son?"

"There is undeniable proof that Jubei has betrayed our clan," said Ukyo. His voice was unwavering.

"But, this is your son."

"And he is not above the law. I have been betrayed by my own son and so he shall be interrogated and executed as the traitor that he is."

"Spare him, my husband. He has done so much for the clan. Please, do not kill our only son. Banish him. Let him live with the shame of knowing that he had betrayed his own people, but let him live.

"It is only because he is my son that he will die a quick death, once I retrieve the information I need from him."

"He would rather die than reveal anything to you."

"Either way, he will die."

Matsumi retrieved a hidden knife from her sleeve, raised it and charged Ukyo. Ninjas stepped in and were easily able to restrain her .

"Ukyo, I despise you. You have turned this clan into a travesty."

Ukyo waved his hand and the ninjas carried Matsumi off.

"Spare my son," she pleaded. "Allow him to live, or, so help me, I will topple your reign over this clan with a single confession. And so, should something happen to me, or my son, Ukyo, you will lose it all. Your empire will crash down on you and your sin will be uncovered."

Matsumi glared at her husband as she was dragged away.

Ukyo signaled the ninjas for them to stop. He approached his beautiful wife and punched her, knocking her out.

"Take her to her suite and keep her there in until I decide what to do with her."

The guards dragged the unconscious woman away.

A few hours later

At first Jubei's vision was blurry, then his eyes began to adjust to the light. He tried to move. A sharp pain stiffened his entire body. He grimaced, teared up.

He came to the realization that he was immersed, up to his waist, in a tank full of jellyfish, and, whenever he would move, droplets of acid trickled onto his skin.

Ukyo was there. A doctor stood by, holding the antidote to the jellyfish poison.

Jubei looked up. His mother was in the window, locked in her private suite. Jubei could barely keep his head up but raised his eyes, filled with hatred, back toward his father.

Ukyo nodded to the doctor and the man injected a shot of the antidote into Jubei's shoulder .

"You almost had me fooled, my son," Ukyo said. "But did you really think you could betray me and get away with it?"

Jubei said nothing. He wanted his father to look into his eyes and see the loathing and deep seeded hatred he felt for him.

Ukyo signaled the master torturer to pour more acid on Jubei's shoulder. It burned through the skin. Jubei shut his eyes into a reddened darkness and tried to absorb the pain tearing through him. Meanwhile the jellyfish kept stinging him.

Ukyo signaled the man to cease dropping acid on Jubei's shoulder.

"I saw the surveillance video of your interrogation of Hiamaryu. You were in league with him, weren't you? What did you promise him? Who aided you in this plot? Were you trying to take my power for your own?" Ukyo questioned Jubei relentlessly, without even waiting for an answer. And when he was finally done talking, he anxiously awaited for Jubei to say something that might clarify all of Ukyo's doubts at once.

Jubei slurred, "I was alone."

"You lie!" Ukyo shouted. "Very well. I know that the pain ripping through you is more than any man can bear. However, this slow agony can be replaced by a quick death, if you would only confess your crime."

Jubei mastered enough strength to raise his eyes. Members of the council were seated around him. Behind them stood the villagers.

The acid had nearly stripped Jubei's shoulder to the bone. While a regular man would have succumbed long ago, Jubei chose to say nothing and endured the torture and questioning. Time after time, he was brought to the brink of death, only to be snapped back by a carefully measured dose of the antidote. Ukyo continued to interrogate Jubei until Jubei lost consciousness.

From Matsumi's private suite she could do nothing but watch her only son be tortured by his own father.

The Dragon ninjas standing watch outside Matsumi's suite stepped aside to allow in a couple of maidens who were carrying trays of food in to their mistress. One maiden walked in front of the other, to provide cover to the one who was pulling out a blowgun concealed in her kimono. The maiden in the lead moved aside and the young woman behind her shot a tranquilizing dart into the guard's neck before he could call out for help. The man dropped. The second maiden grabbed his keys and unlocked their mistress' door.

"Everything's in place, my lady. We must get out of here, now."

"Not without Jubei," Matsumi said.

Jubei was forced to regain consciousness so that the torture could resume. By now, most of the clan had gathered in the gardens to witness the torture. The crowd was divided on how they reacted to Jubei's torture. Shock. Delighted. One person murmured, "The mighty Jubei has finally fallen."

Jubei was in and out.

"This could all end, should you only confess your betrayal," Ukyo said. "Just confess, my son, and your death shall be swift."

"Father, I confess," said Jubei.

Ukyo smiled. He paced victoriously around the tank, and announced to the crowd, "My son has something to confess."

Jubei struggled to speak, but managed to hiss, "I confess that I will kill you."

Jubei's words stung Ukyo, but he kept a placid face, knowing that none other had heard what Jubei had said.

"Jubei has confessed his crime, and so, his death will be swift."

Matsumi shouted, "No. Show mercy! Please!" She humbly crawled to Ukyo. "Please," she pleaded. She wrapped her arms around her husband's legs. Tears streamed down her face. "Let us go, Ukyo," she whispered. "Remember that I have the power to bring your rule to an end."

Ukyo tried to pry Matsumi from his legs.

"No one will ever find us," Matsumi said. "You will have what you want, and we will have a chance to live a life free of you. But remember, should anything happen to me..."

Ukyo continued to address the crowd. "Jubei has betrayed us. He had been working with the Yagyu ninja, sending them secrets. But there was a time when I did call him my son, and his mother, my wife. Such a bond cannot easily be broken, not even through betrayal. I have decided to spare Jubei's life, but he is to be banished from our clan. Should he ever step foot in Japan again, he will forfeit his life."

None dared oppose Ukyo's decision, but most were disgusted with it and to publicly admit disgust would mean certain death. Therefore, the council and the ninjas bowed respectfully. Ukyo gave the signal and Jubei was removed from the tank. Immediately the physicians began treatment and proper protocol to remove the jellyfish from Jubei's body and administered the antidote. His flesh, raw around the shoulders, were treated with disinfectant and bandaged. Once Jubei was treated he was taken away. Matsumi tried to follow her son. Ukyo grabbed her by the arm. She tore away from him, ripping the sleeve of her kimono. A guard standing by, escorted Matsumi from the palace while Jubei was taken to the docks, where a boat was awaiting. Matsumi was close behind. Jubei regained consciousness and looked around.

"Mother," he called out. "Mother."

Matsumi approached Jubei and took his hand. "I'm here."

A slight smile crossed Jubei's face. "What's happening?" he asked. "Where am I going?"

"You're free," Matsumi said, clasping Jubei's hand in hers. "That is all that matters. I've made arrangements and you're going to America, like I always wanted you to."

"You're not coming?"

Matsumi choked up. "I can't go with you. I have to stay here and secure your legacy, and keep this clan from total corruption. One day you will return, and forever shape the clan's destiny. But until you return, I must stay."

"No," said Jubei. "This is your chance to be free."

Matsumi knelt and kissed her son's forehead. "I am free because you are." She released his hand and he was carried onto the boat. She held back her tears, comforted by her servants who had just arrived and placed three sacks on the deck of the ship. Matsumi only allowed herself to break down when the boat's engine sputtered as it pulled away.

Chapter Five:

Journey of Truth

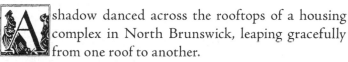

A shadow danced across the rooftops of a housing complex in North Brunswick, leaping gracefully from one roof to another.

Upon reaching his destination, Jubei noticed two police cars parked out front the townhouse.

Navaro and Phelps got into the SUV and drove off. A few neighbors were standing outside, watching the activity around the house. Jubei laid down flat against the black-shingled roof, blending in with it. He crawled over to the skylight. Through it he saw the police pull off. Jubei opened the skylight and dropped into the office. He activated his night vision goggles. Pictures of Pastor Ivy and his family covered the wall and a small picture frame of his wife, Jessica, was on the desk on which you could make out the dusty outline of a desktop computer. The police and FBI had already been though there.

After examining the room thoroughly, Jubei headed to the bedroom, across from the office. It was Pastor Ivy and Jessica's room. There were some highlighted notes, as well as an open bible, in which a particular passage was highlighted.

Jubei flipped through the bible, looking for anything that might be hidden between its pages. Then, he went through the drawers and closets, making sure to put everything back in its place. He continued his search upstairs, room-to-room, but, finding nothing of interest, he went down the stairs to the living room where more pictures of the family were on display. Pastor Malcolm had his arm wrapped around Megan who was smiling from the mantle above the fireplace. Jubei found himself drawn to her.

Jubei proceeded down into the basement, which had been finished and turned into a playroom for the children, but the state of the playroom was unsettling. It had been ravaged. Indeed, the police and FBI had combed through this room. If there had been anything to be found, they would have found it.

Jubei knew who was responsible for the murder. He also knew how the murders had been committed. What he still had to figure out was the reason. Jubei used to not concern himself with the whys, but now he walked a different path and sought the truth, the truth about his clan, a truth about himself he had not journeyed to, yet.

Jubei slipped out of the house without leaving a trace. He headed to the church. The area was still taped off. The parking lot was empty. Jubei entered the building from an underground passage. Silently he moved through the dimly lit corridor to a staircase that led him through the main sanctuary, backstage.

Flashlights approached Jubei and he had to think fast. A couple of North Brunswick police officers were doing a routine check of the premises. Once they had passed by, Jubei landed behind them, on the stage, without making a sound. The officers exited the stage through the side door and then Jubei hurried across the sanctuary to the main doors. They were locked.

Two more lights were headed his way and Jubei hid between rows of seats. The police officers had begun searching between the rows, when one of them had to pause so that he could answer the radio. Jubei crawled beneath a seat and crept out the unlocked doors, across the main sanctuary to Pastor Ivy's office. He tried turning the doorknob, but the office was locked. He picked the lock and entered the office, which he could tell had already been searched.

More pictures of Pastor Willis and Megan sat on the desk. Jubei noticed a slightest unevenness in the floorboard. He knelt and ran his finger along the seam of the floor and found a concealed glitch, which he triggered, uncovering a shoebox beneath. In it there were letters and newspaper clippings. One letter condemned the church and denounced it as a cult. It depicted, in great detail, the church's rigid rules and regulations for its disciples, and hostilely addressed an old claim that the church was the one true church that had been closely modeled after the first century church. The letter was signed by Henry Krite.

Another letter was an editorial, by Henry Krite, to the general public, warning all to stay away from the church. One newspaper article related the major upheaval caused by the Krite letters. Violence had even erupted during a church service, according to an article in the Asbury Park Press another in the Star Ledger.

Jubei noticed a journal tucked in the corner, under other floorboards. So he set down the shoebox and reached down, just barely touching the journal with the tips of his fingers, easing the journal closer, bit by bit, until he could pick it up.

Stuck between the first pages was a letter addressed to Pastor Willis.

My dearest brother,
   It is indeed a dark time for the church. Numbers

have dwindled since the outbreak of the Krite letters. Kip Monroe and so many of our leaders have stepped down and now speak out against a church they had helped establish. It may have been true that the church had become so legalistic that it was only a matter of time before a purge would occur, however, we must keep our focus on God and his will. Communities need to be served, and souls need to be saved. We can't get caught up in the protocol anymore. The reason I'm writing this letter to you is that I have discovered something disturbing about Henry Krite. All I can reveal to you is that he is a spy that was sent to infiltrate our church and sabotage it from within. I can't explain in this letter the manner in which I have uncovered this information, which is the reason why you must find all your answers within this very journal. If you have discovered this journal hidden beneath the floorboards, then I am already dead and it will be up to you to keep the church going. I'm afraid the dark times are about to begin. Should they come after you, seek the Narrow Gate. They will help you.

I love you, Willis. You have been my very best friend and for that I am grateful. See you when you come home, brother.

Matthew 5:10-12 Blessed are those who are persecuted because of righteousness, for theirs is the kingdom of heaven. Blessed are you when people insult you, persecute you and falsely say all kinds of evil against you because of me. 12 Rejoice and be glad for great is your reward in heaven, for in the same way they persecuted the prophets before you.

Jubei folded the letter and then stuffed the journal into the shoebox along with the other letters and news clippings.

He had finished replacing the floorboards when he noticed a shadow beneath the door. By the time the policeman opened the door, Jubei had fled out the window and vanished into the dark night.

Upon reaching his rental car, Jubei typed *Henry Krite* into his Blackberry, and an address and photo appeared. Jubei inputted the address into the GPS and turned on the ignition.

Patterson, New Jersey, forty-five minutes later

Henry Krite, a tall, slender man, in his late forties, watched the news report of the murders in his living room while sipping a martini and petting his 130-pound Rottweiler. The dog pricked its ears and ran out.

"Saul," Henry called out. "Come here, boy." But Saul did not return. Henry stood. "You better not be in that trash."

In the doorway of kitchen, Saul was lying on his side, unmoving. The butt of a dart stuck out his neck. Henry saw red as he was thrust backward, slamming into the wall, head first, landing flat on his back, and before he could even make sense of what had just happened, he was grabbed by the collar, dragged down the hallway and into the living room where he was shoved onto a couch. Jubei was standing before him.

"I knew, it was a matter of time, before *they* would send someone, to kill me," Henry said. "I did my job, and now it's time to die."

A woman's worried voice called out, "Henry? What's all the trouble?"

"Nothing," Henry said, trying to sound calm and collected. "A friend stopped by. Go back to bed, sweetie. I'll be up in a bit."

The woman did not heed the veiled warning and

came down the stairs. Jubei knocked her unconscious and redirected his attention to Henry Krite.

"I don't want you dead," Jubei said. "But you owe me some answers. And if I don't get the answers I want, I'll kill her. Do you have any children Henry?"

"Yes," Henry said, reluctantly. "I'll tell you what you want to know so please don't hurt my children. Don't hurt my wife."

Jubei smiled. "I wouldn't dream of hurting them. I'd just kill them and be done with it. But you caught me on a good night. All that would happen is that they would be orphaned. For starters, who do you think sent me here?"

"I can't say. All I can tell you is that their order is as old as Christianity itself. They want nothing more than to destroy the church. I don't know who they are. I was recruited and sent to infiltrate the church, to cause havoc from within and bring the system down. I was beginning to see the fruits of my effort, but then something strange happened. The church began to rebuild. Multiplied."

"Why did they have the entire congregation of the Central Jersey Church of Christ?" asked Jubei.

"I don't know. Once I saw the damage done, I repented for my sins and fled. I don't know why those three congregations were selected to be slaughtered."

Jubei knew he was lying. He pulled out a knife and walked towards Mrs. Krite. "Henry, Henry, Henry," Jubei teased. "The last thing you want to do is lie to me. I'm going to split your wife open, from ear to ear. *That* is the truth."

"All right. Enough already. The Pastor of the Central Jersey Church began to sniff around during the purge and uncovered something that could potentially reveal the identity of my employers. Not only that, but the Central Jersey Church supported missions in Africa and Asia, and their support was compelled multitudes to get baptized and convert to Christianity. That's all I know. I swear it. My employers figured that if they wiped out at least three churches, the churches would just shut down and no one else would need to die. That's all I know. I swear."

Mrs. Krite regained her sense and crawled to her husband and desperately clung to him, as if he could protect her from the intruder. "Who are you?" she asked. "What do you want with us?"

"Your husband is partly responsible for the massacre of the congregations of the Church of Christ."

"You can't stop them," Henry said. "You're just one man."

Jubei shrugged dismissively and turned to walk away. In a burst of indignation, Henry Krite reached into the nightstand and took out a gun, which he aimed at Jubei, but before he could pull the trigger, Jubei swung around and thrust a throwing knife that sunk into the barrel of the gun. Henry Krite pulled the trigger and the gun blew up, taking off Henry's hand. The man stumbled in his own blood. His piercing cry echoed through the house.

"That was stupid. I was leaving," Jubei said to the stunned wife, without turning to look at the squirming man. "You can be stupid too, and join him in hell, or you can think of your children and live to be their mother. Some men were headed here, to murder your husband. He was a dead man before I even came into your home. Leave this place and start over, or you can try shooting me."

FBI headquarters, later that night

Navaro and Phelps were going over the evidence gathered from the first crime scene when an agent peeked into their office. "There's a man out there who says he has information about those murders."

Navaro hopped out of her seat and followed the agent to the reception area where a Latino man, with short black hair and unusually piercing blue eyes, awaited. The man extended his hand and Navaro shook it. Agent Navaro introduced herself. "Agent Nicks informed us that you have information on the church massacres. May I have your name, please?"

"Paulie Diaz," said Jubei. "The traces of water that were found in the wounds of the victims were from weapons that were made of ice. Practical for non-detection."

Navaro pulled her gun out, but Diaz snatched it from her and took it apart. Agent Nicks reached for his gun but Jubei pinned him against the wall with the sole of his foot.

"No need for any of this," said Jubei. "I was not involved in the murders. But I do know who was."

Agents stormed in with their guns drawn and aimed at Jubei. He pressed his foot on agent Nick's throat. "Tell them to lower their guns and I will gladly tell you what you need to know."

Navaro ordered the agents to put their guns away and they complied, reluctantly. Jubei released agent Nick and allowed himself to be handcuffed and taken into an interrogation room. Jubei was handcuffed to the chair, arms behind his back.

Navaro and Phelps entered. Phelps threw the case file onto the table. A grisly photograph faced Jubei.

"What do you know about these murders?"

"I told your partner," said Jubei, "that I did not have anything to do with the church murders. You need my help to solve this case, otherwise you will not get anywhere with what you have right now."

"What do you know?" asked Navaro. "You mentioned weapons made of ice. How do you have this information?"

"It's a signature of the Tamuramaro ninja clan."

"Ninja clan?" Phelps asked.

"You heard me correctly. I have a doctorate degree in Asian studies, and a black belt in ninjitsu. I have studied the ninjas for more than ten years and, I am telling you, these murders were committed by the Tamuramaro clan."

"Do you believe any of this?" Phelps asked Navaro.

"You know what?" said Navaro. "That's exactly what Tanaka said."

"It does not matter if you believe me or not. It is what it is."

Navaro leaned in with interest. "Go on."

"To kill multiple targets would normally have to be done in a more discrete manner. Their communion wafers and grape juicer poisoned or CO_2 through the air vents. These murders were committed in a manner designed to instill fear. The crime scene was overtly gory, was it not?"

Navaro and Phelps concurred without a word.

"That was done at the request of the employer. The Tamuramaro have a history of lending their services to the highest bidder. Whomever hired the Tamuramaro would have wanted the very best, and is wealthy enough to afford the best of the best." Jubei pulled out a small USB. "On here, you will find all the information available on the Tamuramaro."

"So, who was it that hired the Tamuramaro?" Phelps asked.

"I do not know. "Or at least, I didn't know until tonight. We receive orders and then they are placed on an ancient scroll and assigned. No one but the head of the clan has knowledge of the identity of the employers. As soon as the orders are assigned they are destroyed."

"All the clan does is assassinate?" Navaro asked.

"But why Christians? Why kill men, women and children who worship God?"

"They do whatever they are hired to do and will not stop until their mission is accomplished. Rest assured, these three massacres were not the end of it. For whatever reason, they want to exterminate this church and its legacy."

"That is all you have?" Phelps asked.

"Forgive me, agent, but ten minutes ago you had nothing. In my pocket you will find a journal. The first murder was probably committed because the pastor discovered the truth about this secret society and was about to expose it. The answers you're looking for will probably be in those pages."

"Can I see you outside for a moment, Agent Navaro?" asked Phelps.

"Stay put," Navaro said sarcastically to Diaz.

Navaro and Phelps shut the door behind them.

"You're not buying any of this are you?" Phelps asked. "A ninja clan? Come on."

"You should have seen how fast he took apart my gun and disabled agent Nicks. He held him against the wall with his foot."

"So, he might be good at martial arts, but a ninja clan? That's like something out of a movie. I say he's one of the killers playing some sick game with us. This guy's some psycho getting his kicks off. How else would he know about the murders unless he was there?"

"I hear what you're saying, but there's something about him that suggests he may be telling the truth. I don't know what that is but I can't shake this feeling that he's for real."

"I don't buy all this stuff about a ninja clan."

Agents Phelps glanced through the window on the door and could not see Diaz. They flung open the door and indeed the room was empty. All that was left of Diaz's presence were the handcuffs dangling off the back of chair.

Navaro shook her head. "Believe him now?" Navaro asked.

Phelps noticed a note on the table. He read it and Navaro asked what it said.

"*The next potential target is Willis Ware, from the San Antonio Church of Christ. Find him, if you want to save him.*"

Navaro got on the phone and issued a code red. The building went into shutdown mode. Phelps placed a few calls after Navaro gave him Diaz's name and, in a matter of moments, Phelps had located an address for Diaz.

Off highway 130, in the Renaissance apartment complex, the North Brunswick police broke into apartment 25 D and found Paulie Diaz watching television with his feet up on the coffee table. Diaz appeared baffled by the unexpected invasion and hardly protested when they cuffed him.

Navaro entered. "This isn't "Diaz" she said. "Uncuff this man."

The handcuffs were taken off of Diaz's wrists.

Diaz was indignant. "What's this all about?" he asked.

"Mistaken identity," Navaro said. "Sorry for the inconvenience. The FBI will pay for the damages done to your front door. Send us a bill."

Phelps was going through the files on his laptop. "Wow!" Phelps said to himself as Navaro shut the car door. "This ninja stuff is real after all. The Tamuramaro were some bad dudes. They're excellent masters of disguise, capable of disguising themselves as just about anyone, masters of escape, which would explain how our guy got out of the cuffs and escaped the interrogation room." Phelps scrolled down the screen and Navaro chuckled. "I didn't realize you were such a research geek, Phelps."

"I'm not, but this is some fascinating stuff. The Tamuramaro were off da chain. There's footage on here that shows them doing things I would never have believed was possible."

"Anything showing their faces? Navaro asked.

Phelps said nothing and Navaro sighed, started the car and put it in gear.

"If they can be disguised as anybody, then who's to say that the guy who came to see us was even Latino?" Phelps asked.

"Whomever he was, he's long gone by now."

Jubei parked his car in the darkness of the night. The area was so secluded that the last car he had driven by was over an hour ago. From where he sat he could see the Delaware memorial bridge. He got out of the car and stretched, hopped on the hood, sat and crossed his legs. He was alone. Weeks had passed since he last saw his mother's beautiful face. Her last words to him echoed in his mind. He balled his hands into fists, unbridled power surged through him and he trembled. If only his mother could be beside him. He stared at the stars above, wondering whether they were those he had gazed at with his mother, with Maki. They seemed eternal in their clarity. He felt the corruption that had poisoned him for so long. He could now make out the faces of those he had murdered and had once believe meant nothing to him. They would be with him always, like the stars piercing through the murkiness of night. And Henry Krite, his last victim, was engraved in Jubei's history, memory. Jubei felt immobilized beneath the weight of the souls he had amassed like a thief. He could hardly breathe. He did not deserve to breathe. He was alone and more than ever did he wish he had someone to love, someone who would love him. His purpose had been to take and take and take until there was nothing left to take. Never had he given. Truly. And he knew this now and wished he could change it, but despite his awareness he feared he could not. He had turned on the one he had once loved, without even questioning the reason behind his orders, words dispensed by another for him to execute, and he did do that, execute, execute her, Maki. What would this newfound freedom mean without her? This freedom that had cost him a father, mother, brotherhood, just about everything he had ever cared for, believed in, loved. From his pocket he pulled out a picture of Pastor Willis and his family, which he had taken from Pastor Ivy's office. The young woman beside the pastor, Megan, what was it that drew Jubei to her? He believed he had the answer, but could not retrieve it, like a faded memory. Frustrated, he shoved the picture back into his pocket and looked out at the lights of the cars crossing the bridge in the distance. He had decided to let the FBI take over from this moment onwards so that he could return home and slay all those who stood in his way to liberate his mother and claim his birthright. His course of action was evident and yet he felt his work was not done here. That highlighted verse he had read just hours ago in the bible resonated within him. He had never known faith like this, an eagerness to serve God at any cost. And that blind faith was what drove the Ware family and he couldn't turn away from them, from this purpose that promised to fill the emptiness he felt. The Ware family might have been strangers, but they validated his need to fight for justice, truth, and honor. In their faith he had perhaps found a cause worth killing for, and, more importantly, worth dying for. It was clear to Jubei in this moment; his birthright would have to wait.

San Antonio, several nights later

Shortly after the Whataburger incident, Megan unlocked the front door of the Ware home .

Megan called out, "Dad, you home?"

Pastor Willis peaked into the foyer. "I'm here," he said. "What's the matter?"

"I was coming out the restaurant and people standing

outside recognized me. They harassed me. One of them was about to hit me, but some man stepped in, almost out of nowhere, like an angel, and he save me, dad." Megan carried the grocery bag to the kitchen and her father followed. The children must have heard Megan's voice because you could hear them run down the stairs.

Pastor Willis' brow was knotted up with worry. He pressed Megan for details.

"I was surrounded. They said all sorts of awful things about the church, and then one of them tried to hit me, but, like I said, this guy came out of nowhere and like some Jackie Chan-like hero, he karate chopped his way through those punks and saved me. I know it sounds ridiculous but it's true. He moved so fast, dad. It was incredible. I don't think I even had time to blink and they were all knocked out cold. I didn't even get a chance to look at him. I couldn't even tell you if he was young or old, handsome or not. He was so fast that if those people hadn't been lying flat on their faces, I would have to tell myself I dreamt it all. He was gone before I even realized what had happened. And to tell you the truth, I'm not sure I understand what happened back there but I'm glad to be home."

The pastor tried to check Megan for bruises. She gently moved away. "I'm okay, dad," She said. "No one was able to lay a hand on me."

Pastor Willis seemed relieved, and more than anything, Megan's nonchalance reassured him enough that he was able to compose his face so as not to worry the children. He even smiled at them as he distributed the food Megan had brought home. They were gathering around the table when Bruce entered the kitchen through the side door. He was carrying a bag with some ice cream and all the fixings to make banana splits. Megan set a plate for him beside her and once they were all seated they joined hands and bowed their heads.

"Father god, bless this time in fellowship and the meal you have prepared before us, in Jesus name. Amen."

The food was passed around. Only after they had all served themselves did they begin to eat. You could only hear the sound of cutlery clinking against the dishes.

Pastor Willis cleared his throat and said, "I saw Grayson today."

"How's he doing?" Jeffrey asked.

"Better. He's off suicide watch so he can start receiving visitors soon, if you want to go see him."

"Yeah," Jeffrey said. "I can show him the new comics I've been working on."

"Have you seen Jeffrey's comics?" James asked no one in particular. "They're really good, you know?"

Bruce helped himself to some chicken nuggets. "I know," he said. "I really like the one about the baby that has super powers. Do you know what's that one's called?"

"Samurai Baby."

They cut. They chewed. They swallowed.

Bruce asked, "Did you hear what happened to the Mosque, over on Sam Houston Boulevard? It was completely trashed."

"What about our building?" Megan asked.

Bruce sighed. "So, far it's been untouched. Maybe now is the time for us to start again."

Megan put her fork down. "Start again?" she asked.

Bruce stood from the table and began pacing around the table. "We could have a great revival," Bruce suggested with enthusiasm. "Think about it."

"It's not going to happen," Pastor Willis said. "It's far too dangerous, with those murderers running around."

Bruce tried to interject but the pastor would not hear him. "I said it's not going to happen," the pastor repeated; his tone was final. There would be no arguing on the matter. He stood abruptly and left the room.

Bruce was dumbfounded. He looked inquisitively at Megan in search for an answer to a question he had yet to ask but that his face had already expressed.

"It's okay," said Megan in a pacifying tone. "You know, losing the church really hurt him. I think that deep down, there's nothing he'd rather do."

"Maybe I should go talk to him," Bruce said.

"He'll be alright. You should join us and eat."

After dinner, the children cleared the table and Bruce and Megan prepared banana splits. Pastor Willis could hear the laughter from his study where he had been pacing while the others finished dinner. He slumped into his chair and looked over at an old picture of Pastor Ivy and himself, when they were both in their mid-twenties, seemingly a lifetime ago.

After desert, the children were sent upstairs to do their homework, and Bruce and Megan went for an evening walk. Megan was about to mention how much cooler the air was at this time of day when a black Jeep Liberty passed them by and pulled up to the house.

Phelps doubled checked the address and gave his partner a nod so that she would know it was the right house and that she could ring the doorbell.

Pastor Willis answered the door.

"Willis Ware?" asked Navaro.

"Yes?"

The agents presented their badges and introduced themselves. The pastor invited them in.

"Can I get you anything?" the pastor asked. "We just had dinner and there should be plenty left over."

Phelps began to turn down the gracious offer when Navaro interjected, "Actually, I am kind of hungry."

Pastor Willis led the agents to the kitchen and plated a burger and some onion rings, which were now soggy and room temperature. He poured some ice tea for Navaro while she marveled at the size of the burger.

"This is huge," she said. "You guys like things big in Texas, after all."

She said a quick prayer before biting into the burger and delighted in its juiciness. She wiped her mouth and declared, straight-faced, that this burger alone was reason to request a transfer to the Texas office.

Pastor Willis smiled and sat down across from Navaro. Phelps sat in the other chair and crossed his arms.

Phelps blurted, "Mister Willis we're…"

Navaro cut him off. "I'm sorry we didn't get a chance to meet earlier. We're the agents that have been assigned to the International Church of Christ murders. Can you tell is whether you've been approached by anyone unfamiliar in the last few days?"

"No" said the pastor. "Not me. But my daughter, Megan, had an incident earlier tonight, at the Whataburger."

""What happened?" Phelps asked.

"I'm sure you noticed how things have been since so many of our churches have closed down," said the pastor.

Navaro nodded.

"Christians are attacking Muslims and other people of faith. And Christians are attacking each other. We've been subjected to a lot of persecution, recently. Megan was minding her own business as she came out the Whataburger when she was approached by a mob. She would have been assaulted had it not been for a stranger whose intervention was a blessing. According to Megan, the stranger was more like a guardian angel with ninja skills who vanished into thin air after saving her."

Phelps took out a notepad and a pen. "At which Whataburger did this altercation take place?" he asked.

"The one on Route 3, West bound. Does this man have something to do with those murders? Should I be worried that he saw my daughter?"

"We're not sure," Navaro said and, in the way she spoke, the pastor could tell she was being honest. "He showed up at our office, claiming to have information on the murders. We did witness him use advanced martial arts moves against our agents. We were able to take him back to the interrogation room, only because he allowed us to capture him. He had a message for us. He revealed information that only the murderers would know, or someone closely involved with the perpetrators. I suspect that although he has intimate knowledge of the case, he does not have anything to gain by these gruesome crimes."

"He knew how the murders were committed?"

"He accurately described a murder victim and the manner in which he was murdered. We have not released such detailed information to the press, yet."

"Well, if he wasn't directly involved in the murders, then why is he here?" the pastor asked.

Navaro and Phelps exchanged a glance and sighed.

Phelps began, "What I'm about to tell you is gonna sound far fetched. We didn't believe it at first either, but our mysterious stranger has confirmed that," Phelps paused and Navaro finished his sentence, "ninja assassins have been hired to slaughter members of your church."

"I think I know why he's here," the pastor said. "I figured, he's not here to kill me but rather to protect me, and my family."

Navaro handed the pastor a piece of paper that Jubei had written on in the interrogation room. "He wrote this right before he escaped."

The pastor read the note and then rubbed his forehead in deep thought. "Why has he targeted me? My family?" he asked.

"We don't know for sure," said Navaro, as though she were excusing herself.

A cell phone rang and Phelps excused himself to answer the call.

Navaro glancing in Phelps' direction, to make sure he wasn't coming back, and then she asked, "Can I be frank with you Pastor Willis? I was baptized in the Church of Christ in my teens. My partner isn't a Christian and can't understand this. We went through the church's records. From the central Jersey Christ alone, more people were being baptized than in the east coat combined. The Central Church of Christ also supported missions overseas that were baptizing new Christians. To Phelps, they were just new members to the church. But to me they were lost souls given grace and changing their lives. It meant something to me that so many souls were being reached out to. I admit to have slacked in sharing my faith. And in my line of work there is more reason for me to do so. I also know how compelling and meaningful it has meant to me, to look at the numbers that the Jersey church was pulling in, and that there are others out there who are compelled by hate and whose aim is to destroy it. I can't prove it, but Pastor Ivy, and the members of his congregation have been taken out for that reason. The other murders were random."

"Okay, but why me. Why my family? Why do you think we'll be next?"

Navaro sipped her drink and then placed her hand on the pastor's shoulder. "I've looked into your career, Pastor Willis. You've also been blessed and have a special anointment on you. During the whole Henry Krite thing, you were the one who stepped up and took steps to bring the church back together.

Someone with your charisma is able to radically transform the world. To the godless and the wicked, transforming the world for God makes you a wanted man."

"Have you considered Krite in all this?" asked the pastor.

"I thought so at first, but turned out to be a dead lead. Listen, if you are the next target you need to go into protection.

Phelps walked in just as the pastor noticed a small tattoo of a golden gate with open angel wings on Navaro's hand.

"You're not gonna believe this. Krite is dead," said Phelps. "We got to roll." He turned and walked out.

Navaro handed the pastor her card. "Should you need anything, or anything comes to mind, gimme a call. Let me know if you want to consider protection."

Pastor Willis escorted Navaro to the door. She turned around to face Pastor Willis and recited, "*You believe at last. But a time is coming, and has come, when you will be scattered, each to his own home. You will leave me all alone. Yet I am not alone for my father is with me. I have told you these things, so that in me you may have peace. In this world you will have trouble, but take heart I have over come the world.* John 16:3-4." She patted Pastor Willis on the back and said, "Should you need me for anything, or if our mystery man gets in contact with you, call me."

Pastor Willis stood in the doorway until the agents drove off. Jesus' words, quoted by Navaro, lingered.

Meanwhile, a few blocks from the pastor's home, Megan and Bruce enjoyed the warm Texas night. A slight breeze blew through Megan's long dark hair. Bruce watched as she tucked her hair behind her ear, again and again.

"And then," Megan said, "he broke the ladies arm, and kicked her in the chest. He kicked her so hard that she went flying into the crowd. Some other guy tried attacking him and he was thrown through the windshield of a car. This guy was amazing. He was so fast. He moved like he was on fast forward."

"Did you get a good look at him?" Bruce asked.

"It all happened so fast. I think he had dark hair."

"You're gonna be telling this story for a long time, aren't you?"

Megan laughed. "It was pretty exciting. God was definitely watching over me."

"Yes, He was."

Once again she brushed the hair out of her face and caught Bruce glancing at her.

"Megan, I have to confess something," said Bruce.

Megan nodded.

"I'm crazy about you. I've always have been, ever since we were on campus together."

Megan blushed. "I never knew that," she murmured.

Bruce smiled bashfully and looked at his shoes.

"How come you never said anything to me?"

"I was worried you wouldn't like me back."

Megan took Bruce's hand in hers. "Does this help?"

They exchanged glances and Bruce felt like a teenager again. He looked down at his hand, intertwined with Megan's. It made him smile. They said nothing for a while. It felt like there was so much to look forwards to. Bruce asked Megan if she would like to go out with him sometime.

"I would love to," she said.

They turned the corner and headed toward the house.

"I'm sorry about earlier. I don't know what got into my father. He shouldn't have snapped at you like that."

"It's fine. I probably shouldn't have brought it up. It's just that I've never known your dad to give up."

"I know, but given the circumstances, he closed the church for safety reasons."

"I realize that. And I know this is very hard on him."

"I hear him praying everyday. He prays for everybody. There's nothing more he would rather do than be in church."

"Then why not just do it?" Bruce asked. "Then why not have a revival? If your father wanted to reopen the church, others would surely follow."

They walked in silence for a couple of blocks. As they passed by the church, the sounds of sirens could be heard in the distance. You could make out the flickering lights and smoke in the horizon. A police riot van screeched through red lights, speeding towards the fire. Fire trucks followed.

"That's why we need the churches," Bruce said sharply, pointing toward the pandemonium. "It's why we need God. We've become islands that are cut off from the mainland, and we're struggling."

"We just have to keep praying that this tribulation will end soon. We must continue to trust God through it all, whether it ends shortly or drags on and on."

Bruce agreed. He knew it was time to lighten the conversation and squeezed her hand tenderly.

Unbeknown to the couple, a gray car trailed them closely. Jubei was behind the steering wheel. He followed them until they went back indoors, and then he drove off, with the Journal and the letter in his lap.

Chapter Six:
The Ninja and the Pastor

Far from San Antonio, within the walls of one of New York City's hot spots, a meeting was taking place. Hidden by the shadows of the dimly lit back office, a couple of men sat before a large screen looking at digitized photographs of men and women in a variety of settings.

"These are the men and women that have already been silenced," said the lanky man. "However, there is someone else that is causing quite a mess in San Antonio. A photograph of Pastor Willis Ware came up on the screen. The heavyset man pointed his chubby finger at the screen. "Out of all our targets, this one has been making the most impact. It's Willis Ware. His wife, Deborah, was killed in a car accident, years ago. He was instrumental in the church's revival, after Henry Krite."

"Why hasn't he been killed yet?" asked the heavyset man.

"There's no need to kill him right now. The Church of Christ is finished. Over. The congregation hasn't met in weeks. The concern now is with the journal. The journal was one of the reasons that the assassinations were set up in the first place. That, and the perversion the Church of Christ was spreading. Got any news on the journal?"

"None," said the heavyset man.

The men were interrupted by a knock on the door.

The man that entered knelt down before the others. "Henry Krite is dead," the third man announced.

"Good. One more loose end tied up." said the heavyset man. "Anything else?"

"The journal has been found."

"How do you know?"

"Agents assigned to the case interrogated a witness who was able to describe the murders in detail. I've managed to get the tapes from the room. He left the address to Pastor Willis with the agents. This stranger could be bringing the journal to the pastor."

"The stranger's a ninja, isn't he?" The heavyset man asked.

"I believe so. He escaped from the interrogation room. It's all on the video."

The third man handed the DVD to the lanky man who slid it into a DVD player and pressed the play button.

The camera only caught Jubei from the back. The interview was brief and then the screen went dark.

"Should the ninja deliver the journal, our existence may be compromised," said the third man. "Looks like we got to eliminate the good pastor and his entire family after all."

"Excellent job with the intel, Agent Nicks," said the heavyset man. "Keep us informed."

Agent Nicks was about to excuse himself when Pastor Willis appeared on the screen.

"Let our friends know that they have multiple targets, including one of their own."

Agent Nicks acknowledged his order and excused himself.

Tamuramaro village

Ukyo was practicing his swordsmanship in his dojo, surrounded by students that were armed with *Bokens* (wooden swords, used for training). Two of the students moved in and were easily defeated. Ukyo countered against another pair. Ukyo rolled underneath one young man and quickly sprang back to his feet and backflipped over the student. Ukyo charged with a downward slash and cracked the student's Boken. Ukyo landed and then front kicked the student in the chest. The student flew back. The other moved in. Ukyo placed his Boken right up to the student's neck and swung away and then back in, forcefully, cracking his Boken on the student's head.

The student managed to get back up, holding his head, and bowed low. He took his place in the circle.

Ukyo lectured the students on swordsmanship and the fundamentals necessary to simultaneously take on multiple enemies. A messenger approached and held out a scroll. Ukyo unrolled the scroll and read the message. Without another word he left the dojo and headed underground to a private chamber that had a large viewing screen. After sealing himself in the room, Ukyo turned on the screen and agent Nicks appeared on it.

"Why this breach of our arrangement?" Ukyo asked.

"My employers have a new mission for your Dragon ninjas. This one promises to pay handsomely."

Ukyo remained in the shadows so as to remain anonymous. "That still does not answer my question. Why contact me directly?"

"I'm afraid your protocols have been compromised by

one of your own, but I will go into that after I give you the details. Before the first murders, a journal, which could reveal the identity of my employers, was hidden away and it was impossible to retrieve it until now."

"The journal is your employer's problem. We did our job."

"Money is of no object. You must kill all that have come in contact with the journal. We can't risk exposure. Pastor Willis, his entire family, and all his associates must die. How soon can it be done?"

"As soon as arrangements are made," Ukyo said. "And one last thing, don't ever contact me this way again." Ukyo cut off communication. He summoned the best of his Dragon ninjas and entrusted them with a scroll on which was the kill order.

The next morning

Pastor Willis went into the kitchen in his robe. He put a pot of coffee on the stove before taking a bible, with a small notepad on it, out of a drawer. He sat at the table and began to read highlighted scriptures.

Megan walked in, yawning. She kissed her father and then took the eggs out of the fridge.

"Daddy?" Megan said. "I know what's on your heart, and I understand why you snapped at Bruce yesterday."

"I feel bad about that," Pastor Willis said, in an apologetic tone. "I have to apologize to him. His spirit is in the right place."

Megan cracked the eggs on the edge of a glass bowl and mixed them with a fork. "You know I agree with him," she said. "Now, would be a great time for revival."

Her father shook his head. "Not you too."

Megan put the bowl aside and took a seat beside her

father. "Daddy, I know what it's in your heart. You want to bring the church back. If anyone can do it, I know you can."

The pastor was beginning to get agitated, so Megan took his hands and looked at him in an affectionate manner. "I know that you're trying to protect us. The murders have made everyone so paranoid and everyone's accusing everyone else. And everybody's just too afraid to worship. Although all this is true, you can't protect us. It's not up to you. I put my life and God's hands. The children are in God's hands. We know the dangers and trust him to protect us."

The pastor teared up. "I saw the pictures of what the murderers did," he said. "I've had nightmares for days now and can't bare the thought of something like that happening to anyone in our congregation, especially you and the kids." The pastor pulled hands away and got up with his cup, as if he meant to refill it with coffee.

"Daddy, to see you give up like this breaks my heart. What would mom say?"

The pastor blew into his cup and watched Megan as she looked back at him with her eyes wide and her mouth agape. In her face he saw the little girl she had once been, holding on to his leg with such despair in her eyes after she had found the bird she rescued, dead in the shoebox she had left it in overnight.

"You mother can't say anything, Megan. She's dead." He put his cup down and left his daughter alone with her thoughts.

A knock on the door startled her and she answered the door to find nothing but a box on the doorstep, addressed to the pastor. She took it in and opened it. She pulled the journal out of the box. She was tempted to open it but it was not meant for her so she put it back in the box and took it to her father's study. The door was cracked open and she could see the pastor kneeling in prayer. Megan tiptoed in to the desk, gingerly put the box on the desk and snuck back out.

The rumbling sound of children coming down the stairs surprised her as she pulled the door shut as quietly as she could.

"Good morning," Megan said. "Breakfast is out. You guys can fix it. Just don't make a mess, okay?"

The boys raced each other to the kitchen and Marie stayed back. "Is Uncle Willis alright?" she asked.

Megan wrapped her arm around the girl. "I think he's a little sad today."

"Is he still praying?" Marie asked.

Megan nodded.

Mary hugged her. "God has it all under control. He'll be okay, you know?"

Megan smiled and they went to join the boys.

"Bruce Lee is definitely better than Jackie Chan," James argued.

Jeffrey said, "Can't compare the two. Two completely different styles."

Megan interjected, "Actually, Jackie Chan was offered the opportunity to become the next Bruce Lee, but he chose to do action-comedy, because even he had to admit that there could be no other Bruce Lee."

Jeffrey pointed the spatula at James. "This doesn't mean you're right."

James laughed and turned the bacon. Jeffrey poured the eggs in the pan and Marie set the table as meticulously as she would have had they been expecting guests for dinner. Marie had also set a place for Pastor Willis but Megan removed his place setting.

"He's won't be eating with us, this morning," Megan said.

They gather at the table and joined hands.

"Jeffrey, do you want to give thanks?"

Jeffrey seemed delighted that Megan had chosen him. "Dear lord, thank you for the meal you have provided for us. Please bless those that don't have a meal to eat this morning. In Jesus' name, amen."

"What's wrong with Uncle Willis?" James asked.

"Don't' speak with your mouth full," Marie scolded.

"I think he wants to rebuild the church, but he's afraid to," said Megan.

"I don't blame him," Jeffrey said. "I'd be afraid too. There's no telling what might happen if the church started up again. There haven't been any murders lately so maybe it's for the best if the church doesn't open up at all. Ever."

James stormed out. Megan shot Jeffrey a stern glance and hurried after James. Marie shrugged and put another forkful of eggs in her mouth.

Pastor Willis prayed on. "Father. Help me do what is right, and glorifying to you, Lord. I'm feeling so lost. In Jesus' name I pray. Amen."

After his prayer the pastor sat up. His eyes fixed on a picture of his wife he kept in a silver frame Megan polished religiously. His wife smiled at him and for a brief instant it felt as though she had never left him. The pastor kissed the picture.

He noticed the box and took off the lid. He was surprised to find a journal and opened it at once and a letter slipped out from the journal and landed on his desk. The pastor's name was on the letter. He recognized pastor Ivy's writing. Pastor Willis went to lock the door and hurried back to his desk. He took a deep breath and opened it.

His eyes teared up at the very first sentence and it was difficult to keep reading but he couldn't put the letter down. Tears trickled down his face and soon enough he was crying without restraint and it felt good. He bowed his head and despite himself he made an effort to regain his composure and then reached for the journal. He choked up with the thought of Ivy's murder and sighed deeply, drawing in from his innermost strength and courage and opened the journal. In it he found his best friend's life narrated from the very beginning of the upheaval caused by Henry Krite, up to the evening before his murder. Pastor Ivy had mentioned the Narrow Gate in his letter and in the journal he went into further detail. Still, the Narrow Gate maintained its secrets. Pastor Willis had never known that Pastor Ivy had been a member of the Narrow Gate.

He read on and encountered events in Ivy's life that he had kept private. At the time, he thought nothing of it, but now it all came together and began to make sense.

The journal brought up Henry Krite and an age-old organization dating back to the Roman persecution of Christians. The journal chronicled names and dates and other information, however, as the pastor read on, he came upon something that made him pause and his heart sank. A passage mentioned his late wife and the car accident and Pastor Willis could not read any further. He could hardly breathe. Pastor Willis had been at home when he got the call from Bruce. The next thing he remembered was arriving at the scene of the accident. Fire trucks and ambulances were parked on either side of the road. Charred remains were all that was left of the Pontiac Grand Prix. A loaded body bag was being carted away on a stretcher. Pastor Willis knows that he ran out of his car in hysterics and had to be held back, but he could not remember it, although several bruises on his arms and torso, which took a long time to fade, vividly reflected how he must have struggled with several police officers and emergency personnel that it had taken to restrain him—Pastor Willis was indeed a large man. The police ruled out foul play and informed him that it had been nothing more than an accident. In his gut he knew it was no accident. All these years he had been haunted about the reason he had switched cars with his wife and had been unable to remember until he read it in the journal that Deborah had taken his car on that day because he needed the minivan to pick up people for church.

The pastor whispered, "She died because of me."

He thought back to the controversial things he had said and done. He thought about the ministry in the Middle East. He had certainly made enemies along the way, but he had never done anything that would have warranted someone to want him dead. This he believed was true.

Pastor Willis scrambled for the door and dashed up the stairs to his room. In the hamper and he found the pants he had worn the day before and in its pocket was the card Navaro had given to him, should he have any information to share with her. The pastor dialed Navaro's phone number feverishly, and had to dial it several times because he kept misdialing it in his haste.

"Agent Navaro, this is Willis Ware. Someone dropped off a journal that belonged to Pastor Ivy. I now know why he was killed. Everything you need to know is in this journal. I need to bring it to you. It is imperative that you meet me in front of the Alamo in twenty minutes. All right. See you then."

Pastor Willis brushed past Megan without saying a word. He didn't notice that he had dropped Pastor Ivy's letter. She picked it up and before she could reach him, he was in his car and backing out the driveway and he did not hear her call out for him as he sped down the road. Megan went back in and dialed * 69 on her father's telephone.

A woman's voice answered, "Agent Navaro."

Megan hung up. She was befuddled. She sat on the edge

of the bed and it took her a moment to realize that by now her father was long gone and following him was not an option, therefore there wasn't anything she could do, so she went to get the children ready for school.

Pastor Willis approached some

A new construction was delaying the traffic heading downtown, so the pastor turned into the nearest side street, to bypass the traffic. A few blocks down, a crowd as picketing outside a mosque, harassing Muslims who were trying to get in the mosque, in time for prayer. The crowd shouted slurs and curses. An old Muslim man was pelted with a rock. He fell and tried crawling up the steps. Pastor Willis knew he was short on time but he could not drive on and allow these crazed people to terrorize these men whose only goal was to worship God. He got out of the car and hurried across the street, shoving and pushing his way through the hostile crowd. He covered the cowering old man with his body and shouted, "Anyone who wants to lay a hand on this man will have to go through me."

"And me," said a voice and the pastor glanced over his shoulder and saw Jubei, standing beside him.

The crowd continued to yell voraciously, but no one step forward.

"Hey!" someone amid the crowd shouted. "You're that pastor from the Church of Christ that's involved in that massacre of God-fearing Christians. All this madness is the fault of your church. Well, maybe we should go after you."

"Come and get some, then," the pastor challenged the unruly crowd. "Come on then. You want to go after me? Well, here I am. You can come after me, but what then? What are you going to do after that? I'm fed up with all this. It's been going on for long enough. A few months ago, three entire congregations were killed. And now, because of fear, paranoia, and sin, we've turned on each other, denomination against denomination, faith against faith, and for what?"

The pastor recognized some people who lived in his neighborhood, and even a few individuals that had belonged to the church.

Jubei glared at the crowd. He was ready to kill. Always ready to kill.

"I know some of you," the pastor said. "Most of you I have no idea whom you are, but you take one step forward and what will you accomplish. What has all this infighting, and interfaith fighting solved? Now you seek to persecute this man because he's Muslim? Do you think that Muslims have invented terrorism? Do you want to go after them with pitchforks and fire?" Is this what being Christian means to you? Well, according to my bible, it is not. The murders involving the Church of Christ were not random. Certain men were specifically targeted, and I hold the proof. I know *why* these atrocities took place." The pastor pointed at the man he was sheltering from the mob. "And this man is not the cause. His religion is not the cause."

Someone yelled, "Where is this proof you speak of?"

"Yeah," we want to see this proof."

A news van pulled up and its crew began to set up. Pastor Willis left Jubei with the old man and made his way through the crowd to his car. He retrieved the journal and all the while Jubei kept his eyes on the pastor.

"He's either brave, or insane," Jubei muttered.

The pastor returned with the journal and photographs in hand. "The first man murdered, was my best friend," he announced. "You've all seen pictures of him and his wife on the news. The Pastor passed out photographs of himself with Pastor Ivy to the crowd. Passersby join the crowd. The reporter related the events to the camera, live, discretely from the sideline.

The pastor did not notice the news crew was filming him as he held the journal high, for all to see. "This was Pastor Ivy's journal. I can't tell you exactly what is in it, but the proof that the murderers targeted my church is in here. Pastor Ivy stumbled on some evidence that would have blown the lid off of an age-old cover up that concerns the church. And Pastor Ivy was silenced. So was the entire church. This journal holds the reason for all this death. It was sent to me anonymously last night."

Jubei concluded: Pastor Willis was both, brave and insane.

"My friend wrote me a letter, as if speaking from the grave. He asked me to keep the church going. Somehow he knew he was in trouble, but he never shared this with me. I was on my way to turn this in to the FBI. It will help them solve the case and bring this nightmare to an end. And then I passed all of you, here. Shame on you."

Meanwhile, at the Alamo

Navaro and Phelps awaited Pastor Willis at the Alamo. Pastor Willis was running late.

"He's not showing up," Phelps said.

"Something must have happened."

"We've been sitting here for about half an hour. He's not going to show."

Navaro shook her head. "Gotta give him more time. Maybe he got caught in that construction traffic."

"Well, I need something to eat. I'm going to get a sub at Subway. You want something?"

"Nah."

Phelps looked both ways and then crossed the street. He was walking by an appliance store when he noticed Pastor Willis on one of the television screens in the window display.

Phelps stopped a passerby and asked the man whether he knew the building in the background of the scene.

"Yup. That's the 5ᵗʰ Street Mosque. Six blocks east."

Phelps ran across the road, dodging a cab and a cyclist.

"Your boy's on TV," Phelps said to Navaro, almost out of breath. "He's on TV. In front of the 5ᵗʰ Street Mosque."

The partners wasted no time and sprinted toward the parking garage.

Fifth Street Mosque

"I was driving to meet the FBI agents in charge, when I saw all of you harassing these people." This madness has got to stop, *now*." Pastor held the journal up. "There's no more reason to be afraid. Paranoid. Return to your neighborhoods. Reopen your churches. Repent and trust in God, knowing that there's nothing to be afraid of."

The crowd slowly began to disperse like drunks at closing time. Jubei loosened his grip on the knives concealed beneath his sleeve. His face was placid, however, in his core he was astonished at what the Pastor had just pulled off. Jubei stepped aside as a news reporter, Jana Dicosmo, approached Pastor Willis.

"Pastor Willis, what was going on through your mind, as you revealed what you claim is crucial evidence for the FBI to crack the case?"

Pastor Willis glanced over several Muslim men anxiously standing at the top of Mosque's steps. "The needs of others," the pastor said candidly and then he began to walk towards his car, with Jana and her cameraman following close by. She was barraging the pastor with questions, which he ignored. Jana recognized that she would not get more information from the pastor and signaled to her cameraman that they were done here.

The old man hurried to the car and held his hand out to the pastor. "Thank you," he said. His accent was thick and his voice had a trustworthy quality like that of a storyteller. "You are a good man. Most people are quick to condemn and harass us. Thank you for standing up even though you were alone to do so."

"You're welcome," Pastor said humbly. "May God be with you."

"And Allah, with you."

The old man turned and the pastor was about to open his car door when Jubei startled him. The pastor was befuddled at how Jubei could have reached him so quickly, when just a moment ago Jubei was all the way back at the steps of the mosque. The pastor coughed and then said, "Don't sneak up on people like that. You could give someone a heart attack."

Jubei cracked a smile. "You showed a lot of courage," Jubei said, without a trace of an Asian accent. "You do not see that type of character in men anymore."

"Weren't you ready to take on the same mob as I was?"

Jubei nodded, humbly.

"Well, at least two of us have that type of character. Thanks for being my backup."

The Pastor held out his hand and Jubei's first instinct was to bow respectfully but then he took Pastor's hand.

"I'm Willis. Willis Ware."

"Jubei." He glanced at the journal and said, "Aren't you afraid of the consequences of putting yourself in harm's way because of that journal?"

"Of course," the pastor said. "But it wouldn't be the first time I've been in danger."

"So, you were a police officer," said Jubei.

"How did you know?"

Jubei pointed to the faded sticker pasted to the back windshield of the pastor's car and the pastor chuckled. "True, but I am actually in more danger as a pastor than when I was a cop."

Jubei did not appear amused by the pastor's pleasantries. His face remained expressionless.

"But you don't even know me. What made you stop and back a stranger up? Those Muslims were strangers to you as well, and yet there you were, ready to lay down your life for them as well." The pastor cocked his head and, looking quizzically at Jubei, he asked, "Why would you do that?"

"I admit that I'm not a champion of the people, like you. Protecting people is not what I normally do, but even I cannot ignore a defenseless person faced with adversity."

Jubei's words appeared to have had a profound effect on the pastor, as though he had heard them before, or at least heard of someone who applied this same philosophy. "Spoken like a champion of the people," Pastor Willis said. "Thank goodness there are still a few good men out there. Like the other night, my daughter was attacked by a mob as she was coming out the Whataburger restaurant just minding her own business, and a lone champion came to her defense. And because of him, my daughter returned home to me, unharmed, the same way I will be retuning home to her unharmed thanks to you. And she will be forever grateful to you, as I am so very grateful to that stranger."

Jubei tried not to smile and the pastor continued, "If I ever get a chance to meet that mystery hero, I would express how deeply grateful I am that he stepped in when there was nothing for him to gain."

In the pastor's words, Jubei recognized the world of difference between a good man like the Pastor and his own father. It was nauseating to think that he was the son of such a dishonorable man. "So what happens now?" Jubei asked the pastor. "Are you still planning on going to the FBI?"

"Yes. I am on my way there now."

"And then what?"

"And then I go home and do exactly what I told those angry and confused people to do. Can't expect to be a leader that people would want to follow if I'm not willing to do what I ask my congregation to do." The pastor pulled a small card from his pocket and handed it to his new friend.

"Listen, you helped me when I was alone. The least I can do is buy you dinner. Here's the address of where I'll be with my family tonight, if you're interested in joining us."

"That's not necessary."

"It is for me. It's the least I can do, for helping us out. I mean, helping *me* out."

Navaro and Phelps' car screeched to a stop and they both got out, indignant.

"What were you thinking?" Navaro asked the pastor in a patronizing tone. "You have just put yourself at risk."

Pastor Willis noticed that Jubei was gone and he had no idea even what direction he had gone in. He felt relieved that Jubei had at least taken the business card.

Navaro rambled on. "And you may have just blown any chance we had at cracking this case."

Pastor Willis nodded along, fully appreciating Navaro's frustration.

Gradually Navaro ran out of steam; her tone softened and her breathing steadied. "But I guess that if I were in your position, I would've done what I needed to do to protect those Muslims too."

Phelps interjected "Still, Pastor, that was a stupid move. Please tell me you still have the journal in your possession."

Pastor Willis handed the journal to agent Phelps. "I hope you get the people that did this," said the pastor, as he was about to get into his car.

"Wait," Navaro said. "You might have put yourself in

danger because of what you did today. You may need to go into protective custody."

"If I go into protective custody, you might lose your chance to get them, because now they'll be coming after me, for sure."

Navaro and Phelps exchanged looks.

"What are you saying?" Phelps asked.

"I was a cop for fifteen years, before I became a pastor. I was a member of the SWAT. So, I know the dangers and the risks involved. This is the only way."

"Are you saying that you planned this?" asked Phelps.

"No. I just improvised. We set up a trap and sooner or later they'll be coming for me."

"This is crazy," Phelps said. "It could blow up in your face."

"Sure, it could, but it won't. They will come for me, for sure. I'll get my daughter and the children out of town, tonight. This has got to end. People need their churches; they need a safe place to worship."

Navaro and Phelps consulted each other and ultimately agreed with the pastor's suggestion.

"We'll have to run this by our supervisor but we should be able to come up with something."

Phelps waved the journal. "Are you sure you want to do this?" he asked.

"No," the pastor admitted. "But if I can help bring all this to an end, then it will all be worth it."

Navaro and Phelps left Pastor Willis to his own thoughts and the pastor felt the weigh of responsibility. He sighed deeply and murmured, "Lord, please guide me. I hope I made the right decision."

Fifth Street was quiet again. The call to prayer was announced and, for the first time in weeks, cars pulled into the mosque's parking lot. Pastor Willis smiled as he watched people file into their beloved sanctuary.

Chapter Seven:
Return of Faith

Megan and Bruce were anxiously waiting on the front porch for the pastor and, as soon as he stepped out of the car, Megan asked him question after question, without waiting for an answer. She had been crying and was beside herself with concern for her father. She could not believe that her father had knowingly put himself in harm's way. He could have been killed. He could be dead. No matter how much Megan unloaded her frustration and fear upon the pastor she could not manage to calm her nerves, so she stormed up the stairs and slammed her bedroom door. She went upstairs to talk to the children and make arrangements for them to travel to their Grandparents' house, in Pennsylvania.

Pastor Willis took Megan's place on the empty swing.

"Would you rather be alone, right now?" Bruce asked; his voice was compassionate and the pastor was grateful.

"It's alright," Pastor Willis said. "Come join me, won't you?"

Bruce took a seat in the lounge chair. "She already packed for the children so they'll be ready to leave to Pennsylvania first thing in the morning. Their grandparents must be thrilled to have them visit."

Pastor Willis nodded. "They're good people."

Bruce said nothing more and for a while they sat there, taking in the aroma of the gardenias Megan had planted last spring.

"Go head and say it," the pastor said in a defeated tone.

"Say what?"

"That it was crazy, what I did. I know it was crazy I sat here for hours and tried to convince Megan that it was the right thing to do. But it didn't go well. She gave me quite an earful."

Bruce chuckled. "Well, she is your daughter."

The pastor smiled. "Spitting image."

The two men shared a brief laugh and then the chirping of birds took over and the men said nothing, as though in awe of their delightful melody.

The pastor was the first to interrupt the whimsical moment and blurted, "You were right, Bruce. You were right about the time being right for a revival. I was being prideful, and I shouldn't have snapped like that." The pastor patted Bruce's knee. "You've been with me for a long time and I couldn't love you any more, were you my own son, but it's not for me to lead the revival, brother. This is your time now."

Bruce mouth was agape and he looked as if he could not find the words he meant to say. The pastor was amused and for the first time that day he felt good, like everything would be all right after all.

"You want *me* to lead the revival?" Bruce asked.

"I've been leading the church for twenty-five years and I will never stop serving God as long as I'm alive, but I am tired. My time is over and yours has just begun."

Bruce remained quiet for a while. He was so still that it

seemed like he had forgotten to breathe. Finally he snapped back, "Do you really believe I can do this?"

The pastor looked into his friend's eyes so that he might understand he meant what he was about to say, and he took his time saying it. "Brother, there's no one else I would want to take my place."

Bruce sat upright and stiffened with respect. "It would be an honor to follow your footsteps."

"Do not follow in my footsteps, Bruce. You must set your own path."

The men shook hands, thus sealing the deal. Megan came back out carrying small travel bags. Her face was no longer reddened and she almost seemed relieved as she loaded the bags into the car.

Pastor Willis waited for her to slam the trunk shut and then he announced, "We got some great news. We're going to reestablish the church; I'm thinking a big tent revival."

Megan ran into her father's open arms. "Oh, dad, that's wonderful."

"And there's more," the pastor said, and he grabbed Bruce by the arm and pulled him into their embrace. "Bruce is going to be new leader of the San Antonio church."

"Daddy, are you serious?"

"I'm serious, baby. It's Bruce's time now."

Megan smiled a wide smile at Bruce. She could hardly take her eyes off of him. She held out her arms, hugged Bruce and whispered into his ears, "I'm so proud of you." After a brief hug, they broke the embrace.

"I want to help," Megan said.

"You can help by leaving town for awhile."

Megan crossed her arms defiantly. "I know what's going on here. I know the dangers we face, and I do want to help."

The children joined the adults on the porch.

Megan informed them that they would be bringing the

church back. They gleefully squealed and took turns hugging one another.

"Daddy, we know the dangers and what's at stake. But it will all be all right, since we'll do this together. We'll do it as a family."

Pastor Willis shook his head. "I don't know about this. Do you truly understand what's going on here?"

"I know. I know that part of the reason for this revival is to bring Ivy's killers to justice. I know the cop in you hasn't died, dad. It's like I said, it will all be all right because we'll be doing this together It's like it says in the good book: *No weapon formed against us shall prosper,*" *Isaiah 54:17,* right?"

Pastor Willis saw himself in his daughter and it filled him with pride

"We want to help Uncle Willis," James said. "After what we've been through, we can handle it."

Pastor Willis looked at the eager faces surrounding him and he raised his arms. "Okay. This calls for a celebration. I'm thinking Hibachi, tonight. Besides, I've invited someone I met today, for dinner."

"Who was it, daddy?" Megan asked.

"A young man named Jubei. Although he had nothing to gain from it, he stood with me against the mob, at the mosque. There's something special about him and invited him to dinner tonight. I hope he'll join us."

Later in the evening

Blindfolded, Jubei practiced his Kata sword in his motel room. Slow ballet-like motions of grace and poise, Jubei moved his sword in every strike position and then struck without notice, swiftly cutting through the air with determined precision. Jubei sheathed his sword, unbuckled and tossed the belt aside. He put his hands together and then bowed, and untied his blindfold.

From his wallet and he retrieved the card Pastor Willis had given him. A beeping sound called his attention to his laptop. He read an email in Japanese as he finished getting dressed, grabbed the pastor's card and headed out the door.

Entering Tagawas Hibachi Restaurant was like stepping into an enchanted Japanese garden. Jubei arrived shortly after Pastor Willis and his family had been seated. A beautiful hostess escorted Jubei to the dining area where Pastor Willis enthusiastically waved him over and stood to greet him as the others turned their attention towards the pastor's new friend. Megan was smiling and seemed delighted by the sight of him. Jubei leaned into a respectful bow and was taken aback when Pastor Willis hugged him instead, uncertain as whether he ought to disarm the pastor or hug him back. Unaccustomed to this display of affection, Jubei stiffened and the pastor recognized his own gaffe and apologized profusely.

Megan laughed it off, "We're a huggy type of people," she teased.

"No apologies necessary."

"This is my family. My daughter Megan,"

Jubei and Megan shook hands. Megan smiled coyly. "Welcome, Jubei. I'm so glad you have come. It's lovely to meet you after my father told us all about how you backed him up at the mosque earlier."

Bruce held out his hand. "I'm Bruce, nice to meet you."

Jubei shook Bruce's hand and said, "Likewise," and it was hard to believe this man would say anything he did not mean.

When he was done introducing the children, the pastor invited his guest to sit across from him.

"Hope you're hungry," Pastor Willis said. "Ya ever had Hibachi?"

"I am Japanese," Jubei said as though this fact were an answer in itself. They all laughed out loud, the way people laugh a bit too hard at something that they wish had been funnier than it was.

Jubei caught Megan looking at him and smiled. She blushed, and turned away, as if to say something to Marie.

"You're from Japan?" Jeffrey asked.

"I was born in Japan, but America has been my home for quite some time now."

The Hibachi chef set his cart alongside the table. He repeated each order and then went through the motions of preparing to cook as though he had done this far too many times before.

"So Jubei, what brings you to San Antonio?" Megan asked, over the clanging of the cook's blades.

"I'm on vacation."

"What do you do?" Bruce asked.

Jubei took a sip of his water and then said, "I am the Chief of Security for the Japanese consulate."

"Whoa!" James said. "That must be a cool job. I bet you know martial arts and stuff."

Jubei smiled politely. "Only when I play Street Fighter."

The mention of the video game further peaked Jeffrey's interest. "That's my favorite game. Who's your best character?"

"I like Ken and Ryu," Jubei replied.

"Me too. They're the best."

An elderly woman tripped as she walked by and Jubei spun out of his seat, catching her before she fell to the floor. All eyes were on Jubei as he helped the older woman regain composure and escorted her to her seat. Once the patrons realized that all was well, they clapped.

The old woman was grateful. She kissed Jubei on the cheek.

"Nice reflexes, Street Fighter," the pastor teased, when Jubei returned to the table.

James shouted, "That was awesome. I never saw anyone move that fast, except in cartoons"

Megan caught herself gazing at Jubei and looked away.

The cook slid sizzling shrimp onto each plate and smoothly delivered carefully rehearsed cooking trick after cooking trick as he meticulously prepared each order.

Marie had been struggling with her chopsticks and was about to give up and use her fork when Jubei leaned in and said, "Here you go, little one. Let me show you how to use them. It very easy, you'll see."

Jubei properly positioned the chopsticks in Marie's hand. "Now you try."

Mary successfully picked up slippery noodles with her chopsticks.

Jubei patted her hand affectionately as she licked her sticky lips. "All you need is a little practice."

"I'm just so fired up about this revival," Bruce said.

"Me too," said the pastor. "I've been thinking of some great ideas. Like, something that will really get the people out there and praise Him."

"What is revival?" Jubei asked bashfully.

"It's a special church service that kinda breathes new life into the church," said Bruce.

Pastor Willis interjected, "We're going to reestablish the church, Jubei."

"Is it safe to do that, considering what has been happening to your congregations?" Jubei asked.

Pastor Willis put his hand affectionately on Jubei's shoulder. "Now's the perfect time. Look what's been happening to our communities since the churches have closed. Once more, God needs to be celebrated as the nucleus of our lives. We need to remember who we are and what is most important."

"You all have such a deep commitment to the church," Jubei said, at the same time perplexed and in awe.

Bruce corrected Jubei, "Not merely to the church. That is only a part of it. Truly we're committed to God himself, our Lord and savior."

Jubei set his chopsticks down. "I, too, understand what it is to have deep convictions and devotion toward a purpose. I've lived my life deeply committed to a cause, only to discover how very wrong I have been."

"I think we've all been there," Pastor Willis said. "How the light of revelation shines when it illuminates our ignorance."

Jubei acquiesced, smiling genuinely as he eased into a comfortable zone with the pastor, all the while ready to strike down any enemy, if need be. He fiddled with the butter knife, twirling it between his fingers. He intently followed the conversation about the revival, admiring Pastor Willis' convictions. Never before had he come across anyone as passionate about serving others and the pastor was remarkable in his unassuming humility.

Jubei was on unfamiliar grounds, with the pastor and his family, and yet he had not ever felt as serene among strangers. He had killed wicked men as well as men that could not be labeled as wicked, but in the Pastor and his family, Jubei could not distinguish any trace of depravity or sin.

A Japanese party comprised of a woman and four men were being seated at a nearby table. Jubei could make out the mark of the Yakuza tattooed on the woman's neck. He recognized the man with spiky hair died red and a teardrop tattooed beneath his left eye. He knew him by reputation, Kenzin Tanaka, a ronin without familial affiliation besides his ties to the Yakuza as their most notorious assassin. The tattooed woman beside him was Mishi Tanaka, also a well-known assassin. Jubei did not recognize the others accompanying them. As the only other Japanese in the restaurant, Kenzin nodded at Jubei, and Jubei politely acknowledged him in return before taking another bite.

Kyoto, Japan, two years ago

The Jade Dragon nightclub was filled to capacity with elite clientele, among the country's most powerful of present, Hiamaryu Fujimoto, a largely built man whose black spiked hair was graying on the sides. A black Dragon was tattooed on his face, with the Dragon's tail coiled around his right eye. Fujimoto's reputation stretched over the country and reached into parts of China, Korea, and the United States. With Kenzin Tanaka standing beside him, Boss Fujimoto conducted business with government officials while strippers gyrated on nearby tables. One stripper attempted to climb on Fujimoto's table, but Kenzin snatched her arm and tossed her into the wall. The stupefied woman landed in the corner and Kenzin picked her up by her hair and shoved her away before returning to his post, alert and vigilant.

Fujimoto passed a briefcase to the official beneath the table, and then the official excused himself, followed by his bodyguards.

Another stripper boldly tried to approach Boss Fujimoto. Kenzin shoved her aside. A muscular bouncer was displeased by Kenzin's treatment of the girls and pinned him against the wall, but before the brute could hit him, Kenzin headbutted him and broke his nose. Kenzin kept headbutting the bouncer. Blood splattered. Kenzin snapped a front kick hard on the man's chest, sending the big man flying into a rival

Yakuza boss' table. The boss's went after Kenzin. One by one, Kenzin struck the men down with graceful strength.

Across the bar, a couple of mysterious figures standing in the shadows began shooting with assault rifles. Frenzied patrons were screaming, ducking, fleeing, and trampling over each other. A spray of bullets stuck down groups of people at a time.

A gun in each hand, Fujimoto returned fire at the other Yakuza bosses, but a poison dart hit his neck.

Kenzin held a bodyguard in front of him, like a body shield, and made his way over to Fujimoto, unharmed, and then fired a volley of bullets to cover their escape out the back, through the stripper stage.

A stripper hurled a couple of incendiary Shurikens and both exploded upon striking Yakuza members. Blood had splattered over the walls.

Kenzin and Fujimoto ran down a flight of steps, to the parking garage where Fujimoto finally collapsed. Kenzin examined him, found the wound and pulled the dart from Fujimoto' thick neck. He forced him to his feet and Fujimoto staggered to a car.

Seemingly out of nowhere, a black shadow breezed past them and vanished as promptly as he had appeared. Fujimoto dropped to his knees. A thin line of blood ran across his neck like a crimson necklace. Fujimoto's head dropped onto the concrete, his eyes still wide open. Kenzin backed up against a car and quickly reloaded. A ninja hopped on the roof of the car. The masked man aimed a taser at Kenzin who he did an X block and pulled the trigger. Hot lead sprinkled the ninja.

Kenzin tossed the guns and began undressing the ninja. As he tried to swap clothes he was kicked in the face. Kenzin fell back, into the arms of second ninja. Another approached with a taser in hand. The one holding Kenzin disarmed Kenzin And Kenzin could just movement his wrist enough to press a button concealed in his suit jacket and spikes impaled the ninja who was restraining him. The spikes retracted and Kenzin pulled a sixteen-inch knife from his sleeve and stabbed the other ninja in the stomach.

Kenzin picked up his guns and hurried toward Boss Fujimoto's limousine. Its tires had been slashed, so Kenzin shattered the windshield of the nearest car— a Hummer with a sunroof. He hot-wired it and accelerated through the gate.

Jubei watched from the rooftop across the parking garage. A ninja knelt before him and reported, "He killed three Dragon ninjas."

Jubei grabbed the ninja by the throat and lifted him up.

"Dead ninjas don't concern me. Was the tracking device planted?"

"Yes, Jubei-san," said the man in a small voice.

Moments before

Kenzin had just been grabbed by a ninja from behind and the ninja planted a tracking device on Kenzin's suit jacket before Kenzin detracted the spikes and killed him.

Moments later

Jubei released the ninja from his grip. The ninja knelt again and awaited further orders.

"Gather the others and return to the compound. I will go after the target myself."

Kenzin Tanaka typed in the entry code on the keypad of a beachside mansion outside Kyoto. The door unlocked and Kenzin stepped into a dark house. He switched on the light switch. Corpses littered the living room and before Kenzin could process what he has seeing, he was punched in the face and landed hard on the cool marble floor. He swiftly rolled back to his feet and pulled out his guns. No one was there besides the dead. Seemingly out-of-nowhere, a leg swung towards his head But Kenzin blocked the kick, countering it with a palm punch to the aggressor's chest. It was Jubei. Jubei staggered a bit but brushed off the attack. Kenzin fired. Jubei dodged the shots and disarmed Kenzin with a kick. Jubei kicked Kenzin again and sent him crashing through the study doors. Kenzin sprang back to his feet and Jubei moved in, but Kenzin blocked his attack and punched Jubei in the face. Kenzin pulled a knife from his back pocket and charged Jubei. Jubei dodged him and threw a ridge hand chop to Kenzin's neck. Kenzin fell, but rolled back to his feet only to be kicked in the chest. Jubei lifted Kenzin. Kenzin clawed at Jubei's face and ripped off his mask. Jubei stuck Kenzin and knocked him out cold. He hoisted the notorious Yakuza assassin over his shoulder and carried him out of the mansion.

Tamuramaro Palace, a few hours later

Kenzin Tanaka awakened with a splash of cold water to his face.

Sawa's Hibachi restaurant and grille, present

Kenzin stood from the table and asked the waiter to point out where the bathroom was located. Jubei politely excused himself and followed. Another patron was walking out of the bathroom when Jubei entered. Kenzin was at the sink washing his hands. Jubei glanced over the stalls. They were vacant.

"A long way from home," said Kenzin, as he dried his hands with a paper towel. "Far from your ninja stronghold and the support of your fellow ninjas."

"Last I checked I did not need any help in capturing you. And you killed three Dragon ninjas. Not an easy feat. You earned my respect for being able to hold your own against me, even if it was brief."

Kenzin kept his eyes on Jubei via the mirror. "Your respect means nothing. Word has it that you've been banished from your clan. You're a fallen Dragon ninja. A disgrace." Kenzin spat on the floor. "That's what your respect means to me."

Jubei punched Kenzin in his mouth twice and blood sprayed the mirror. Kenzin hit the ground. Jubei locked the bathroom door. He took a paper towel and knelt down besides Kenzin who spat up a few teeth into the palm of his hand. Jubei gently wiped the blood from Kenzin's mouth.

"If you kill me, my men have orders to take out the pastor and everyone else in the restaurant, if need be."

Jubei just smiled and continued to clean the blood from Kenzin's face. When Kenzin was finally clean, Jubei unlocked the bathroom and excused himself, leaving Kenzin on the floor.

On his way back to the pastor's table, Jubei passed by Kenzin's party and said in Japanese, "Your boss has lost a couple of teeth and is bleeding on the bathroom floor because he disrespected me by spitting on the floor. You all know who I am, so you know what I will do to each one of you, including Kenzin, should you raise a hand on the pastor or his family. There aren't enough mops to wipe up your blood from the floor." Jubei bowed and proceeded to his seat.

"Were you speaking in Japanese, Jubei?" Jeffrey asked. "What did you say to those people?"

"I was giving advice about areas they ought to stay away from during their vacation," said Jubei.

Kenzin returned to his table, slumped into his seat from which he openly glared at Jubei, without daring to make a move.

The evening unraveled pleasantly. Desert was served and the family continued to talk and laugh. Pastor Willis shared stories of his childhood in Georgia. You could tell that Megan had heard the same stories many times before, and still she laughed candidly along with everyone else. Jubei had not experienced this sort of familial bonding and warmth. He felt at ease with this family and knew the feeling was mutual.

"You know, the circus is coming into town," Bruce said.

Pastor Willis exclaimed, "The circus? That's it, Bruce. That's our way back in."

"You want to go to the circus, daddy?"

Pastor Willis was ebullient. "The circus. The circus has got a big top. So, I'm thinking, what about a big tent revival for the church?"

Bruce liked the pastor's idea. "We can even have a church-circus combo service."

The pastor's smile was infectious. Megan choked up with emotion. "Okay. All right," she managed to say. "The first thing we need to do is get in touch with the people who are running the circus, and find out if we can work something out."

Bruce pulled a small notebook from his rear pocket and jotted some notes down. "I can get started on this tonight."

"A big top church revival," the pastor said to himself. "What a fantastic idea."

Megan took the pastor's hand. "It's wonderful to see your eyes light up again."

"I gotta get back to the office. I have a lot of planning to do. I'm so excited, I lost my appetite."

Bruce agreed. "If we can pull this off, it's going to be off the hook."

In the parking lot, Jubei shook Bruce's hand.

"Nice meeting you man," said Bruce and then he helped the children into the car.

Jubei extended his hand towards Megan, but she hugged him instead. She could tell that he was surprised by her forwardness, and she was amused. "Hope to see you again, Jubei. Sooner than later," she said in a singsong voice.

Jeffrey lowered the rear window and invited Jubei to can come over and play Street Fighter sometime.

"I'd like that."

"I hope you can bring it.' Cause' I'm gonna bring the pain!" said James, mimicking a martial arts move with his hands and Jubei did a move in return.

The car pulled out of the parking lot and left the pastor alone with Jubei.

"Thanks for coming out tonight," Pastor Willis said.

"Thank you for inviting me, Pastor Willis. Your family is wonderful."

Pastor Willis crossed his arms and leaned against his car. "Yeah, I guess they're all right," he joked.

"I've never known such closeness in a family as yours has."

The pastor agreed, "I'm a blessed man, my friend."

"Your daughter is very fortunate to have you as a father."

"I'm the one that's blessed to have her as a daughter. I raised her on my own. You see, my wife was killed some years ago and it hasn't been easy, man. I'm telling you, there have been times when I had no idea what I was doing."

"Well, she turned out to be a lovely young lady," said Jubei.

"That was God's doing. I spent many a time on my knees, praying for guidance and strength. God had to be the center of raising her. So, in some ways, she did have two parents."

"This church revival you spoke of tonight…"

"I'm excited about it."

Jubei warned the pastor that it could be dangerous. "People could get killed."

Pastor Willis' smile faded, and right away Jubei regretted making that statement. "I'm sorry. I don't want to deny the joy you have for reviving the church, but we must be vigilant because these are dangerous times. Just yesterday, we defended a group of Muslims who were only minding their own business from a vindictive mob, and it was your church that was targeted by murderers. Maybe this revival will bring back the massacres."

"Maybe," Pastor Willis whispered. "Maybe the murder spree will begin again, but the Lord's work must be done despite fear of persecution and death. And I'm not afraid of a being that can only take my body. I fear the one that can take both my body and soul. Can I let you in on a secret, Jubei?" Pastor Willis approached Jubei and leaned in close to say, "I know I'm next on the hit list. I've known that for sometime now. The fact that I'm still alive now is due to the churches having remained silent. Someone out there wants me killed. They did the same to Jesus, so, of course they would do it to me."

"And yet you are willing to die?"

"People have died for a lot less."

Pastor Willis placed his hand on Jubei's shoulder. "Living in fear is not living with God in your heart. You can't serve two masters at once. All I can do is to put my life into the hands of the One who gave it to me in the first place"

Jubei in turn put his hand on the pastor's shoulder. "And I will do everything I can to help you make this revival possible. Besides, you may need someone to protect you, in case things go badly."

"I appreciate that, Jubei. We can use all the help we can get." The pastor took out his car keys and Jubei stopped him.

"Just one question, Pastor. You just met me today so why did you confide in me?"

"I'm not sure. Maybe it was something about your eyes, I think," said the pastor and he chuckled lightly. "Just listen to me. I sound like a teenage girl."

The men parted ways, got into their own cars and drove off in opposite directions.

Tamuramaro Palace

The latest Dragon ninjas stood to attention, shoulder-to-shoulder, as still as statues, their dark gaze was sharp behind their snug masks. Ukyo inspected them one by one, as he passed them by. Without cause or warning, he roundhouse kicked a ninja's face. You could hear the man's jaw crack and yet the man did not flinch or reveal any sign of weakness, although there was no doubt that behind that mask the skin was bruised and his flesh was throbbing. Ukyo nodded his approval and resumed inspecting the line of masked men.

A stunning young woman in a pale yellow kimono approached and, with her head lowered, she knelt before Ukyo. "My lord," she said in a melodious voice, "Kenzin Tanaka wishes to make contact with you. It's extremely urgent."

Ukyo followed the servant girl to a private room where Kenzin Tanaka was sitting lazily and got to his feet as Ukyo entered. Kenzin bowed slightly but Ukyo did not return the gesture. Instead he dropped into in his chair and picked up a pear from a bowl of fruit on the side table.

"We have a problem," Kenzin said. "The pastor has protection. He must be aware that he is being targeted."

"Whomever is protecting the pastor does not concern me. I expect him to be dead before the end of the week.

"It's Jubei," Kenzin said. "He is the one protecting the pastor."

Ukyo clenched his fist and leaned forward. His eyes narrowed and you could only make out black irises like the eyes of a shark, soulless and devoid of compassion. "Are you certain that it is Jubei?"

"I was seated no more than three feet from him in the restaurant."

"This means that Jubei has seen you too. How could you let this happen?

"There was no way of knowing that Jubei was acquainted with the pastor. We had just gotten into town and ran into the pastor and his family at a restaurant by mere coincidence."

"Then you must kill Jubei," Ukyo said coolly.

"Jubei is not the problem, Ukyo. The problem is however did Jubei get connected with the intended target in the first place? Somehow, Jubei is privy to information on your clan's activities. If you do not want Jubei to interfere with your plans, you ought to identify the source of the leak and neutralize it."

Ukyo stood abruptly, knocking his chair back. He was indignant. "You, just handle what you are paid to do. I would have no qualms eliminating you as well if you give me any excuse to."

Kenzin chuckled. "Your threats are meaningless to me, Ukyo. Kill Jubei yourself, if you can."

Ukyo balled his fist, stood, and walked through Kenzin's hologram, which simultaneously vanished. With a knifehand strike, Ukyo reduced the side table to splinters. Pears rolled across the floor.

A ninja entered the room, kneeled before Ukyo and awaited instructions.

"There's been a change of plans," said Ukyo distractedly. "Kenzin Tanaka has compromised himself. Somehow, Jubei has been able to retrieve pertinent information from us. Thoroughly search the palace and the underground for signs of tampering."

Matsumi was confined to her chambers with her maidservants. She had a foreboding presentiment and stood as her chamber door busted open and Ukyo stormed in, like a tornado through a farmhouse. His eyes were crazed; his face distorted with ire. The maidservants fled. Ukyo grabbed Matsumi's hair and dragged her across the room. She tried to make him release his grip but he wouldn't so she palm punched her husband's chest and he staggered. She kicked high but he blocked it, grabbing her leg. She backflipped and kicked Ukyo in the chin. She tried to run but he grabbed her ankle. She stumbled, rolled on her back and kicked Ukyo in the face. She quickly stood up and he in turn sprang to his feet, beat her to the doorway, blocking her way out. Matsumi threw several kicks at Ukyo but he managed to block each one of them. He punched her face and she fell on the bed. Ukyo leaped across the room and crouched over her on the mattress where so many times they made love. She tried to sit up but Ukyo smashed his fist in her face, again and again.

"You have meddled in a mission for the very last time." Ukyo roared. "Die!" He wrapped his hands around his wife's delicate neck and stared into her frightened eyes as she lost consciousness and when she no longer struggled he released her. She looked so peaceful it enraged him. He balled his fist and once more struck his wife across the face.

Later on that morning

The gates to the main courtyard opened, allowing the villagers to join the uniformed ninjas gathered in the courtyard. Logs of wood were stacked high in the center of the courtyard; a tall post was planted upright in the middle of the stack of wood.

Seated on a balcony overlooking the courtyard, Ukyo brushed silk, torn from his wife's kimono, against his skin. He breathed in the scent of her, cherry blossoms, spring, oh, how he had loved her. He watched the crowd part to allow a Dragon ninja through. The man carried Matsumi, still unconscious, over his shoulder like a sack of rice, up the logs where he dropped her, stretched his back and then picked her up and propped her up against the post and held her there until another masked man could secure her to it with tick rope. The second ninja held smelling salts up to Matsumi's face and she regained consciousness only to find herself nude, tied to a pole, and ogled by a crowd. She struggled in vain. Screamed. Cried. A ninja stuffed a gag in her mouth and another lit a torch and stood beside the logs, his face turned towards the palace balcony.

Matsumi despair was muffled but Ukyo could see the dread in her eyes. It was difficult for him not to avert his eyes but he took a deep breath and stiffened up, put aside his love and compassion and signaled the ninjas to proceed.

The masked man lowered the torch and dropped it on the oil-doused wood, which went up in flames, crackling, popping consuming itself.

A ninja stepped out on Ukyo's balcony and reported, "Lord Ukyo, I have news." The ninja presented the computer and bugging devices that Jubei had planted underground. "These are just a few of the devices that we found. All the computers are being meticulously searched and a thorough sweep is being done on the entire property as we speak, my lord.

As my wife burns, thought Ukyo.

The ninja continued, "Jubei planted these while he had unlimited access to the grounds. The most recent information that was downloaded was of the next target. Matsumi was not the traitor."

Ukyo rushed to the railing of the balcony and hollered but you could no longer tell that a human being had been standing amid the heated whirlwind of flames and smoke. In response to the urgent cries of their lord, ninjas sprung into action and with consorted effort they managed to extinguish the blaze. Alas, a charred form was all that was left of Matsumi.

Ukyo wiped his tears and once more his face became placid, unreadable, as though human only in its form. Ukyo returned indoors and the ninja followed, shutting the doors behind them.

"We have additional information, my lord," the ninja said. "We can pinpoint Jubei's exact location."

"How is that possible? Didn't he remove the tracking device we had implanted in him?"

"Since Shinza Tanaka's escape, we have developed our tracking devices for the Dragon ninjas. Someone as dangerous as Jubei should not be able to wander around freely. It is true that Jubei removed his tracking device, but the one he excised was a fake device. The genuine tracking device is a product of nanotechnology and it was injected into Jubei's bloodstream in a saline solution. This device is utterly undetectable and will remain in his system so long as he is alive. The life of the nanobytes, lord Ukyo, is linked to the life of the person it resides in."

"So find Jubei, and then report to me. I will personally handle my son."

Chapter Eight:
Road to Revival

Downtown San Antonio, Texas

Agent Navaro was asleep in her River Walk View Hotel room. Her cell phone vibrated, sliding across the nightstand. Blindly she fumbled for the phone and answered in a daze, "Navaro speaking."

Whatever she heard caused her to instantly sit up in her bed. Now she was wide-awake. "Are you sure? Well, thank you. Yes. Your arrangements have been taken care of. I'll see you soon."

Navaro disconnected the call and immediately called someone else. "This is Navaro. We've got a leak. It's Nicks. Bring him in and I'll handle him. Just bring him to San Antonio. He's at 125 Hillsdale Road in Elberon, New Jersey. How soon can you get him here? Good."

Elberon, New Jersey

A black Viper was not an unusual sight in the rich town of Elberon and Agent Nicks turned into the driveway of a large mansion. He got out of the car and went around the Viper and opened the passenger door for a striking Asian woman. She hardly got out of the car as Nicks pressed up against her and kissed her passionately. She welcomed the kiss but broke away from it so that she could better marvel at the mammoth size of the mansion.

"Wow! Is this your house? I didn't realize the FBI pays so well."

Agent Nicks laughed. "I made some investments. They paid off well."

"Extremely well," she said and approached the front door. Nicks typed in a combination of numbers on the keypad of the sophisticated alarm system and the lock unlatched. The girl put her lips against Nicks' neck and gently sucked on it. Nicks pick her up and carry her into the house, promising her a memorable evening.

A man disguised in a nondescript dark uniform crept up behind Nicks, and with the speed of a hawk snatching a fish from the lake he placed a handkerchief over Nicks' mouth. Chloroform. Nicks dropped to the ground; the girl fell. She began to crawl away and just as she readied to scream, a second attacker chloroformed her. A black Van pulled in behind Nicks' car and the side door opened. The men placed Nicks in the van and left the Asian girl sprawled in the doorway.

Four hours later, San Antonio, Texas

"Who are you? Where am I?" asked Nicks. He had awoken to find himself handcuffed in an old wine cellar, seated across from a very large, bald, black man wearing a black tank top and sporting tribal tattoos. The man crossed his muscular arms

"Da one ting me can't stand is a traita, mon. you de traita me talking about."

The man poured water into a glass. "You must be thirsty. Da chloroform done left a bad taste in your mout." The man pushed the glass toward Nicks.

"I can't get a drink," Nicks said desperately.

"So, I guess you don't get to drink, mon."

"Zula, is that any way to treat a guest?" Navaro asked, stepping out into the light.

"You!" Nicks shouted. "What's going on here?"

Zula brought the glass to Nicks' lips and allowed him to sip.

"You can let him go, Zula. If he tries anything I'll just shoot him."

"Shooting him would be too good for dis traita. I say we filet him like a fish."

Zula dangled a Bowie Knife with a ten-inch serrated blade in front of Nicks. "Oops, tis isn't me filet knife, but it will do. A little messier but it'll do."

Nicks tried to conceal his fear, but Navaro could see it the way his eyes shifted around the room. "Zula, do I have to make you leave the room?"

Zula put the knife away and backed up, all the while staring at Nicks.

"You've been dimmed out, Nicks," said Navaro. "Don't deny it. The truth is contained in this USB. We know whom you've been secretly working with. We also know your role in the murders. So, the more you deny it, the harder it will be for you."

"I know my rights."

"Wrong. You have no rights here. You only have one choice to make. If you want to see sunlight again, then you better tell me where your employers are."

"You're bluffing. You're not going to harm me."

Zula placed his knife against Nicks' throat. "She might not do anyting, but I gonna."

Nicks asked Navaro, "Are you CIA?"

"CIA's got nuttin on us, mon," said Zula.

"It's true. My associate here can make you disappear off the face of the planet, and no would even notice that you're gone. If we have to, we'll bring your Asian girlfriend in here too. She's probably still unconscious in front of your big fat house. Could swing by and grab her, and make her vanish as well, but it doesn't have to come to that."

"You have no idea of the power these people have," said Nicks.

"Their power means nothing to me."

The scar on Nicks' neck reminded Navaro of the bond they had once shared, when he had even taken a bullet for her. He had been her first partner. Throughout their time at the academy they were as close as friends could be, but this man before her had been corrupted, he crossed the line and was partially responsible for the murders of hundreds of Christians.

"So what now?" Nicks asked. "You offer me some kind of deal in exchange for what I know? There's nothing you can offer me that I would want."

"No deals," Navaro said flatly. "That's not the way it works, and you know it. You're gonna rot in prison, the rest of your life. And with your pretty looks, you are sure to be someone's girlfriend. And since you'll be locked away in prison, your employers won't be able to retaliate against you. I got a feeling that your baby sister won't be so lucky. You know these people, Nicks. They won't just come after you; they'll come after your family. And the last impression you'll leave your family with is that you've disgraced your country. So speak up. You're gonna tell us what we need to know."

"Doesn't matter what happens to me, but my family…"

"You should have thought about them before you switched sides."

Navaro stood. "Since you don't want to speak, Zula here has some convincing ways to loosen your lips. I'm not one for torture. Don't want to get any blood on my new shirt, so, after you've been screaming for a while, I'll come back down and see if you're ready to talk. Hey, Zula. When you're cutting him open, make sure not to hit an artery."

Navaro started up the stairs and Zula approached Nicks slowly, his knife in hand.

"All right. All right, I'll talk."

Navaro came back down. "That's something. Keep talking."

Zula backed up and again Navaro sat across from Nicks.

"But you have to promise you'll protect my family. Please, Navaro."

"I told you, no deals."

"I'm begging you!" Nicks shouted.

Navaro said nothing for a while, and then she nodded. "Fine, you tell us what we need to know, and your family will be safe. I guarantee it."

Navaro took out a tape recorder. Zula turned on a video camera that had been concealed in a darkened corner of the cellar.

Navaro listened intensely as Nicks revealed what he knew about the secret organization and its affiliation with the Tamuramaro ninja clan. Nicks had so much information to share that Navaro had to put in a new tape, twice.

Hours had gone by and Navaro had some food brought down. She paused the recorder.

"So what happens now?" Nicks asked.

"We arrange to get you and your family into a program."

"Witness protection?"

Zula laughed and when the other two looked at him, Zula regained his composure. "Sorry," he said. "Witness protection. I just thought that was funny." Zula excused himself and left the old partners alone.

"To answer your question, its sort of like witness protection, only that this program is privately funded. Our success rate is one hundred percent. We never lost a witness on our watch. We'll get you processed, and then we'll go get your sister."

"But what about prison? What kind of time am I looking at?"

Navaro reached across the table for Nicks' hand. "As a person, I would like to shoot you, but I can't. Prison is all I can offer. When I look at you, I can still see the man I once loved, like my own brother. You couldn't have been closer to me if we had actually been related. God still sees the good man you were, and can be. Couldn't call myself a Christian if I didn't try and do the same." She sighed. "Well, lets get you upstairs and processed."

She called Zula back and he escorted Nicks upstairs.

Navaro called Phelps on her cell phone.

"Yo, what you find out?" Phelps asked.

"We gotta assemble a team. We've hit the mother load. Nicks gave enough information to bring this whole thing down."

Navaro ran up the stairs, excited that this nightmare was coming to a close.

A special FBI task force broke into a room at a motel outside San Antonio. They found five Tamuramaro men and forced the Japanese occupants to their knees. The FBI sifted through their personal belongings. They found ninja uniforms and a vast supply of weapons and intelligence on Pastor

Willis and his family. Across town, at another hotel, other Tamuramaro ninjas were being arrested. A total of twelve Tamuramaro ninjas were arrested and taken into custody. Navaro and Phelps took part in the Texas raids. Later, they congratulated one another and planned to celebrate their having cracked the case that led to these arrests.

San Antonio, Texas:

At his hotel room, Jubei sat before images of the exterior of Pastor Willis' house on the screen of his laptop. He typed and brought up audio from inside the house. Megan sang 'His eye is on the sparrow' in the shower, her voice clear and melodious, ethereal. He listened to her for a while and then switched to the children who were animatedly reminiscing about the fun they had had at Hibachi's. Then he shifted to the pastor's study where Pastor Willis was praying. All was well.

Jubei took out a sword wrapped in beautiful silk from the closet. He unwrapped the sword, grabbed a sharpening stone in his other hand and settled on the bed. He used the remote control and turned on the television just as All My Children was interrupted by a special news report. San Antonio's channel six news reporter Javier Ramos appeared on the screen. The raid at the first motel unraveled in the background.

"We're here, in front of the Siesta Inn, outside the loop of San Antonio, Texas. We have a break in the case of the International Church of Christ murders. The FBI have just raided this motel and arrested twelve Japanese assassins and taken an arsenal of ninja weapons into custody.

Jubei leaned forward and turned the up volume and looked at the computer screen, on which the pastor was done praying and had turned on the news. Javier Ramos was simultaneously broadcast on both Jubei and the pastor's television.

"It has been confirmed that an additional twelve Japanese assassins have been arrested at a nearby hotel, two miles from this one. So far the FBI have made thirty-two arrests in San Antonio in connection with the International Church of Christ murders that began six months ago, starting with Central Jersey Church of Christ. The FBI also found evidence of the intended target, however, the name of the target shall not be released."

Pastor Willis changed the channel. The same news was being reported on the other channel. Another reporter. Same story. Only the order of the words differed.

The pastor's phone rang at the same time as his cell phone. Pastor Willis let both phones go to voice mail and continued to watch the news.

Ukyo watched CNN in his chambers. News reports of the arrests had spread across the world.

A ninja crouched before him. "My lord, we're being invaded. The Japanese government has…"

The sound of helicopters interrupted the ninja. Gunfire followed. Japanese defense soldiers swarmed upon the ninja village and palace. The Dragon ninjas were surrounded but would not go down without a fight. Ukyo quickly pulled two swords from a secret compartment and strapped them to his back.

Explosions and gunfire drowned out the screams of innocent Tamuramaro villagers. The defense team showed them no mercy. Many casualties were to be expected.

Ukyo was being hurriedly escorted to his secret escape hatch when a defense soldier crashed through the French doors. He open fired. The ninja was shot down. Ukyo dodged the bullets and swiftly ran towards the defense soldier and cut him down. Another soldier roped down from above. Ukyo grabbed his ankle, yanked him from the rope, and stabbed him.

Ukyo deflected shots and tossed a sword towards the soldier aiming for him and impaled the man as yet another soldier charged at Ukyo. Ukyo spun around and kicked the gun from the man's hand. The soldier unsheathed his sword. Ukyo pulled his own sword from the corpse, still warm, and wielded two swords. The soldier was no match for Ukyo and they both knew it. Ukyo leaped twenty feet and landed on a balcony from which he jumped off, swords raised, and slashed the soldier below, landing into a forward roll and onto his feet. Four more soldiers were cut down without effort.

Helicopters were closing in; missiles fired at the palace. The Tamuramaro counsel was trapped in the palace with other town officials and their families. A missile struck the room in which they were trapped and annihilated all upon impact. The helicopters continued to fire at the palace and the ground battle continued. Additional Japanese defense soldiers were sent in and they brought heavy firepower, which began to overwhelm the Dragon ninjas, however the latter would not surrender and would battle to the death, if need be.

Hours later

The siege had gone relentlessly. Ukyo decimated many soldiers. The Dragon ninjas were finally beginning to over take the Japanese defense force, but cost was astronomical. The Tamuramaro village had been reduced to ash the palace was under siege. Ukyo and a couple of ninjas slipped out unnoticed and ran through the darkened woods in search for the source of the rockets and missiles that were pummeling the building. The stealth posse snuck up on the soldiers and decimated them, and then they sabotaged the missile launchers, however, on the battlefield it was becoming apparent that the Dragon ninjas were losing their initial advantages and the soldiers' overwhelming firepower would eventually lead the soldiers to victory.

Ukyo retraced his steps only to discover that a massacre had taken place at the palace while he was on his disarming mission.

A soldier took aim and fired a rocket at Ukyo, but he perceived the rocket and he focused all his energy to slow it down in midair and blow it up before it even reached a hazardous vicinity of its target. Ukyo hurled a knife at the soldier who had shot that rocket and hit the man between the eyes.

Ukyo turned and was startled by a man behind him who dropped dead as Ukyo readied to defend himself. A few feet way stood a man who wore an eyepatch over his left eye and had with his thick hair pulled back in a low ponytail. He recognized Tamayo Tamuramaro, his chief advisor and friend had killed the soldier. The men expanded nods.

Tamayo shouted, "We have to get out of here. If we're going to preserve the Tamuramaro, we must retreat now."

"What about the counsel and chief advisors?"

"They were in the east wing. They're all dead."

As the battle persisted, an unmarked helicopter landed amid the raid and its door slid open. Ukyo and Tamayo fought their through the crowd of enemies and over the inert bodies of their men to reach the helicopter.

"We have to get out of here. The clan's preservation depends on it. A few helicopters have already carried some of our people to safety."

Ukyo and Tamayo hardly had any strength left as they were helped into the helicopter.

The black aircraft rose up and seemed to have vanished as it flew through the thick smoke stretching through the evening sky.

A single explosion momentarily lit up the sky, as the surface of the earth seemed to go up in flames, decimating structures and obliterating any form of life; a fuming crater left in their stead.

San Antonio, Texas

"Megan! Megan, come quick!" Pastor Willis called out from the bottom of the stairway and then he hurried back to his office.

Megan found her father standing flabbergasted before the television.

"What's the matter? Is everything okay?"

Pastor Willis turned the volume up. The reporter was repeating himself, unprepared for the news he was delivering live to the audience. Megan's mouth dropped. "I cannot believe this."

"Yes. They really arrested the assassins. This footage is live, Megan. So far, the FBI has made thirty-two arrests."

Megan pointed out that the motel in the background was but five minutes away from where they lived. Her face was flushed as was his. She could hardly breathe. She could not put into words her fears, relief, excitement, all bundled in her stomach, chest, and throat. She turned to God and her words returned to her, the familiar words of prayer and praise for Him and the gratitude she felt, all flowing through her at once, an awareness that made her shudder and yet she welcomed. Her father took her into his arms and held her tight

"It's okay," Pastor Willis whispered. "This isn't a time to get all sad and think about what could have been."

"I know." Megan wiped the tears from her eyes. "But I can't help it. Those assassins were here to kill you. What if they hadn't gotten arrested?"

"*When evil men advance against me to devour my flesh, when my enemies and my foes attack, they will stumble and fall.*"

"*Though an army besieges me,*" Megan continued, "*my heart will not fear, though war break out against me, even then will I be confident.*" (Psalm 27:2-3)

"That's become one my favorite psalms. It speaks volumes to me, because we're always in some sort of situation. Someone is always out to get us, whether it is spiritually or physically. No matter what could've happened, those people cannot steal my peace. Besides, in a weird way it's kind of flattering."

Megan looked at her father dubiously. "How could this be flattering?" she asked.

"If someone wants me dead that badly, then I must be doing my job right," the pastor said in a joking manner.

Megan pushed his shoulder playfully.

"Does this mean it's over?" she asked.

"Perhaps. Regardless, if it's over or not, the revival will go on, as planned."

Megan seemed relieved. She hugged her father one last time and then returned to bed. It was late.

Pastor Willis went out to fetch the morning paper while the kids ate breakfast and Megan was putting her make up on in her bedroom. He found agents Navaro and Phelps about to knock on the front door, still dressed in raid outfits from the previous night.

"Do you have a moment?" Navaro asked and Pastor Willis invited them in.

"Mr. Ware, have you seen the news?" asked Phelps.

"It was on every single channel, last night."

"We've made other significant arrests since then. We might not have gotten our hands on the ninjas that had carried out the assassinations but we got the people who hired them, the responsible parties. Our Japanese counterparts have informed us that they have staged a raid on the Tamuramaro ninja clan and have destroyed the palace and captured many members of the clan."

"For all intents and purposes," added Phelps, "it's over."

"Over?" asked the pastor. "Just a few days ago, you guys didn't have any information on the murders. And now you're making arrests? This is miraculous."

"We were tipped off by someone on the inside," said Phelps.

"Would you give me a moment with the pastor?" Navaro asked her partner and he excused himself. Once alone with the pastor, Navaro said, " Phelps wouldn't understand what I'm about to say." She took a seat. "I guess I don't need to tell you who the assassins were after?"

"I know they wanted me."

"But they didn't get you. The Lord has placed his hands on you, protected you. It was His grace that led to the arrests. Someone tipped us off, with enough information on this mysterious clan that they were uncovered and were able to be taken down. I just wanted to tell you that I will keep you in my prayers."

"Thank you," said Pastor Willis. "Thank you for everything you've done."

Agent Navaro handed Pastor Willis a business card, but on this one small golden gate with angel wings was embossed besides her name .

"The Narrow Gate could sure use a strong man of God like you, Pastor Willis."

"What's The Narrow Gate?"

"You know the scripture and therefore you already know what we do."

"Ivy. He was a member."

"He was an awesome man. I could see why the Central Jersey Church was so successful."

"Did you know him?"

Navaro nodded. "He was going to perform my wedding ceremony, but that was a lifetime ago. It's how we first recruited him. Now, I should probably get going. Just wanted to swing by and personally tell you that it's over."

Megan peeked through the door opening. "Dad, breakfast's ready."

Megan and Navaro exchanged smiles.

Pastor Willis introduced them to each other and the women shook hands.

"I better get going, Pastor Willis. "It was nice to meet you, Megan. Your father is a good man."

Megan smiled. "I know. And it was nice to meet you too, agent Navaro." Megan returned to the kitchen.

"We're having a huge revival to reestablish the church. Already got a lot of people coming."

"That's awesome," said Navaro. "Let me know when it's going to be and I'll be there."

Jubei turned down the top of his laptop, grabbed his keys and went out.

Navaro and Phelps returned to their motel to pack their things. They both stood outside their rooms, keys in hand.

"Navaro, I was kind of thinking. When we get back to D.C., maybe I'll go to one of those bible studies with you."

Navaro hugged Phelps. "What changed your mind?"

"Maybe it was just a matter of conviction."

Navaro looked puzzled.

Phelps continued. "We put ourselves on the line every single day and we bring in the bad guys but am I truly convicted in my job? Well, I can't say for sure that I am. I might not really believe in God, and Jesus, but I've seen the things that churches and people do when they are convicted in their beliefs in Him. They get things done. They change the world in ways that we could never do, so I've started telling myself that there's gotta be something to this whole Christian thing."

"Indeed, there is. His name is Jesus Christ."

Navaro was smiling and Phelps was grinning as they went into their respective rooms. Navaro shut the door behind her and looked towards the ceiling and mouthed, *thank you, God.* She walked by the bathroom and reached for her bags in the closet. Jubei grabbed her from behind.

"Don't scream," he said. "I'm not here to hurt you." Jubei removed Navaro's gun, removed the clip and the bullets and tossed them out of her reach. "I'm glad to see that you've acted on what I revealed to you in the interrogation room. Listen, I'm gonna let you go, but don't turn around and don't make any sudden moves. Do you understand me?"

Navaro nodded and Jubei released her. Navaro stared straight ahead and remained still. "How did you know where to find me?" she asked.

"That's not important. It's not over."

"What do you mean?"

"The Tamuramaro will return. They won't stop until the pastor is dead."

"You're wrong. The Tamaruamaro have been defeated. The Japanese defense was tipped off by an anonymous source and they raided the clan. Now there's nothing left. If you don't trust me, then I'll just show you. Don't worry. I won't try anything stupid."

She reached for the remote control on the dresser

drawer and turned the on the television, flipping through the channels until she found CNN, and just as Navaro had said, the reporter was going over the details of the raid that had gone on for a few hours.

"See?" Navaro asked. "It's already over."

Jubei was taken aback, but did not show it. He thought of his mother as he stared at the screen.

"I'm sorry," said Navaro's and her apology broke Jubei out of his spell.

"The only thing that matters now is protecting the pastor and finding the actual assassins. Those you arrested were decoys. Even if my home was destroyed and Tamuramaro crushed, those who remain alive will not stop coming after their target."

"How can you be so sure that this isn't over?"

"I would sacrifice as many Tamuramaro as I need to, to accomplish my mission and trust me, so will they. Do what you have to do, but I will stay here and protect the pastor."

"What can we do?" Navaro asked.

"Stay out of my way."

Navaro turned but Jubei was no longer there. She ran into the hallway. He had vanished. She banged on Phelps' door and he opened.

"What happened?" he asked, his eyes wide open with worry.

"Our ninja friend from the interrogation room was here, in my room. He's convinced that it isn't over. The ninjas that have been arrested were just decoys and the clan is still out there."

"And you believe him?" Phelps asked.

"I do."

Phelps cell phone rang. He put it on speaker.

"Hello, Agents Phelps and Navaro. Good work out there

in San Antonio, but you got to get your butts out of there and back here by tonight."

"Sir, we have reason to believe there's another team out there planning an assassination."

"What are you basing this assertion on?"

Navaro glanced at Phelps and he gave her a nod so that she knew that it was all right to divulge their source.

"Our ninja witness, sir," said Navaro.

"Oh, yeah. The one you let get away."

"Sir, he approached me and divulged that there's another team that has been instructed to kill the pastor and possibly wipe out the congregation."

"Do you have anything else to back this up, other than speculation from a ninja?"

"No, sir," said Phelps, regretfully. "But he would be able to anticipate his clan's tactics better than we ever could. I believe he could be right and I suggest that we move forward with the assumption that he is correct.'

Navaro blurted, "Wait. If he's right, then the team out there is probably a sleeper. They might be waiting for an opportunity to kill him, like in a public place. Pastor Willis told me today that he's been planning a huge tent revival."

"Unless we get something concrete there's nothing we can do right now," said the man on the phone.

The circus was coming to town and had agreed in advance to have a combined church service along with the circus' show. The news of church's reopening was covered by all over the news agencies, as well as the reports about the Tamuramaro. Pastor Willis' leadership incited other at The Churches of Christ across the country to start planning their own revivals.

Early during the day, Pastor Willis, Bruce and Megan made calls to jump-start the revival, reaching out to former congregation members to get the word out that the Church of Christ was reopening. A wave of overwhelming phone calls and letters came through to Pastor Willis from people wanting to express their admiration of him and their enthusiasm for the revival. In the afternoons, the pastor and Jubei bonded as they hit the streets and passed out the flyers.

On the last night before the revival, Pastor Willis took everyone out to celebrate. After dinner, Jubei and Pastor Willis went to get some fresh air out on the porch while Megan and Bruce did the dishes in the kitchen.

Pastor Willis said, rubbing his full belly and said, "Whew! That girl can throw down in the kitchen."

Jubei agreed wholeheartedly. "It was very good. I've never had, Collard Greens, before. Tastes like seaweed."

"Sea weed?" the pastor asked.

"When cooked right, it is very tasty."

"I'll take your word for it."

The men laughed.

"Thanks for helping us pass out the flyers. The revival is going to be great. You're going to come, right?"

Jubei took a deep breath and said, "I can't."

"Why not?"

"I'm sorry, but there's something I have to do tomorrow."

"I was hoping you'd be able to attend. You're a part of making this happen. You should be there too."

A moment of silence came between them, and then the pastor cleared his throat and asked Jubei, "Let me ask you something, my friend. Do you believe that God loved us so much that he allowed his only son, Jesus Christ, to die on the cross for our sins?"

"I don't believe that, but I do understand having a father that would easily sacrifice his son for any purpose that might suit him."

Pastor Willis nodded. "Is that how you see God?"

"I do not see God. I've seen so many terrible things, and come across terrible people, and never before have I seen God in any of it."

"I get it. You just don't believe. And yet you helped us all week, passing out flyers and everything else. Where a man puts his treasures is also where he puts his heart, you know?"

Megan joined them outside and Jubei smiled at her.

"Daddy, Bruce needs you inside, for a moment."

Pastor Willis stood and placed his hand on Jubei's shoulder.

"If you change your mind, it starts at seven. I hope to see you there."

Megan waited for her father to go in and then took a seat besides Jubei.

"You're not going to come tomorrow?" she asked.

"I can't. There's something I have to do and I cannot change that."

Megan dropped her head and briefly touched Jubei's knee. "Daddy really likes you. You two share some kind of connection."

"I'm also fond of your father. He is a good man; a man worth protecting and there aren't too many men like that in the world."

"Well, I know of at least two men worth protecting."

Jubei and Megan were facing each other. Jubei hoped Megan was referring to him, but there was also Bruce.

"You're a mysterious man, Jubei. You appear into our lives out of nowhere and make an impact on my father in such a short amount of time. God's anointed you. You might not believe this right now, but there are some things that you must go through before your anointing can take hold. But it's there all right."

In this moment he felt as though she could see his inner self. Never before she had been so beautiful and he felt his heart accelerate and before he knew it, it was as though he was in the garden with Maki, besides their tree. He leaned in and kissed her but as he opened his eyes to gaze into hers he realized that he was kissing Megan. Abruptly he stood up and is had been years since he had felt like a boy, vulnerable, pained, and he wanted her to reach for him. "I'm sorry," he said. "I shouldn't have. I must leave."

"Jubei, no." She grabbed his hand and stood as well.

"I'm sorry," Jubei said again.

Megan tried to reassure him but he pulled away and hurried to his car and had already driven off when the pastor returned to the front porch. "Where's he going?" he asked his daughter.

"I don't know," she said in a whisper.

Chapter Nine:
Twist of Fate

Japan

The crew went to work securing the boat to the dock. The small reception party comprised several handmaidens clad in black kimonos, their hair pulled up into intricate updos adorned with flowers and ornaments. They greeted Ukyo and Tamayo with respectful bows and then knelt down before Ukyo.

The maidens escorted the men during the two-mile walk through the woods until they came upon a palace similar to the one recently decimated. Men in gray Yagyu ninja uniforms stood guard at the gates and seemed to have been expecting their arrival, allowing them into the grand courtyard decorated with colorful Yagyu flags, emblems and banners. Tamayo mouth dropped and he stopped.

"You were my most trusted friend," Ukyo said," and I wanted to give you a chance to rebuild with me."

"In this place?" Tamayo said without concealing his revulsion.

"Yes." Ukyo said dryly.

"You've joined forces with Yagyu?"

Ukyo reached for a Shuriken knife concealed in his sleeve and said, "Joined forces with the Yagyu? But I am Yagyu." Ukyo hurled the knife, which struck Tamayo in the heart. "I'm sorry old friend, but you've outlived your usefulness."

Ukyo left Tamayo sprawled on the ground, face up, his dead eyes wide open, and sat in a nearby chair.

The surviving Tamuramaro members were brought to Ukyo and made to kneel down before him.

"The Tamuramaro have seen the last of their days. I have fulfilled my mission and now the Yagyu have returned to power, marking the beginning of a new era, the Yagyu era. Now each one of you must chose whether you want to embrace the Yagyu and live, or hold on to old Tamuramaro loyalties and die."

Tamayo's body was nailed to a post, as an example of what would happen to those that dare challenge him. The surviving Tamuramaro remained in a kneeling position and swore their eternal loyalty to lord Ukyo. Their eyes kept shifting back to the bloody corpse that had once been one of them.

"You've made a wise choice."

Inside the place, Morimoto Niga-Yagyu greeted Ukyo. Morimoto was a tall man with short hair; his goatee was streaked with streaked with white hairs.

"My lord, it could take years to rebuild the Yagyu to its former glory," Said Morimoto.

"Time no longer matters, my friend. We are no longer slaves to the Tamuramaro, which was the first step to our freedom. Now there is only one thing that could stand in our way, but that will be dealt with soon enough. Very soon, to be exact."

"My lord, we don't have the man power to send anybody after him."

Ukyo smiled and placed his hand on Hanzo's shoulder. "Have you heard of the saying, no matter how good someone is at something there is always someone better?"

Morimoto understood what Ukyo said. "Tonight he will finally die."

Jubei got off the elevator on his floor, at the hotel. Down the hall, a maid's cart was parked outside a vacant room, a few doors down from his room. Jubei went into his room where he sat on the floor and crossed his legs. He was consumed with thoughts of Megan and Maki. He needed to clear his mind. Focus. He closed his eyes and began to breathe deeply, in and out, in, out. Silence. The world around him came back into perspective but as though in a dream. Sounds were accentuated and slower, like in a dream. The maid was cleaning the room next door. She exited the room. There was movement outside Jubei's door; a clicking sound; not a door latch unlocking but something else.

Jubei dove between the beds just as the door was kicked open by a stunning tattooed female assassin who stormed in, armed with an AK-47 assault rifle. She open fired and missed him by a hair. The sound alerted hotel security and guests ran out of their room and down the hallway in a panic. Jubei tossed the chair at the assailant. The assassin dodged the chair and it landed in the hallway, smashing against the wall. Jubei speared toward the woman and knocked her to the ground. She monkey-flipped Jubei but he managed to land on his feet and spun around and kicked the AK-47 out of her hands. The assassin pulled out a two nine-millimeters and Jubei dropped to the ground just as she fired. The bullets passed over his head and stuck a hotel guest.

Jubei sprang to his feet and swerved to the side, disarming

the assassin by kicking her gun away. The assassin cracked Jubei's jaw with her other gun and his blood sprayed onto the wall. She pointed the gun at Jubei and he front snap kicked her in the chest. The woman staggered.

The elevator doors opened and the assassin shot down the security team inside. Jubei kicked the second gun out of her reach as well. She detracted long silver blades that were hidden in her sleeves and went after Jubei. He dodged to the left, and right. The assassin matched him, move for move. She slashed Jubei's chest from the left, and then from the right. She also cut his arm. She thrust forward to stab him but he moved aside in time and her blade stuck into the wall. Jubei threw a ridge hand chop to the woman's neck and she fell hard, but sprang back up faster than he had expected. Jubei threw a kick but the assassin disappeared in a puff of smoke and reappeared behind him. Jubei swerved but she managed to slash his back. He threw a back kick, which she blocked. Jubei immediately threw another kick but again the assassin disappeared in puff of smoke only to reappear in front of him and she came across with a vertical downward slash as Jubei jumped back. She disappeared once more and when she reappeared, Jubei had anticipated her move and grabbed her neck, lifted her and slammed her to the ground. He balled his fist and as he was about to deliver a final blow, a chain wrapped around his neck and another assailant, a six feet tall male assassin yanked Jubei hard off his feet.

The man wore a white tank top and his bulging muscled body was covered with tattoos. A mechanism that powered the chain was strapped to the man's arm. All the while laughing and taunting Jubei, the man swung the chain and sent Jubei crashing into a loveseat. Then he pulled Jubei toward him and shot him forward like a slingshot.

The chain around Jubei's neck made it nearly impossible for Jubei to draw in any air and he struggled to remove the chain from around his neck as he was being hurled from one side of the room to another.

The assassin increased the power of the chain and sent Jubei crashing through the wall and into the vacant room next door. Jubei hit the floor. The man was still laughing as Jubei was turning blue and he felt his life slipping away. In a last attempt to break the chain, Jubei channeled his chi and when he broke the chain, Jubei was as surprised as the assassin was. Jubei gasped for air as he unwrapped the chain from his neck. He was still gasping for air when the female assassin entered through the other door and kicked Jubei in the ribs. He slid across the carpet and into the sliding glass doors. She jumped into the air and came down hard onto the back of Jubei's neck, miraculously missing the kill spot. Jubei fell face down. The woman lifted Jubei up and readied to shove her blade through him, but Jubei mustered a burst of strength and elbowed her stomach. She staggered. Jubei threw a back fist and struck the woman in the temple. She was dazed. Jubei turned and kicked her in the face. He was shocked that she recovered and charged at him, but he stepped aside and kicked her face again. The chain-assassin entered through the hole in the wall and shot another chain toward Jubei who managed to dodge it.

Jubei reached down and plucked out the woman's pretty eyes and she hollered and once again he kicked her face. In a rage the female assassin blindly swung her swords and Jubei easily ducked underneath her, grabbed her by the neck, ripped out her throat and tossed it at the chain-assassin. The man shot another chain and the end of the chain took on the shape of a ball and hit Jubei in the chest and into the wall. The chain-assassin pulled back the chain and fired another shot at Jubei who managed to block the ball. The man shot another chain at Jubei's feet and then pulled Jubei toward him, lifted Jubei over his head and slammed him into the ceiling. Jubei wrapped his legs around the man and squeezed hard. The man peeled Jubei off of him and tossed him onto the balcony. He powered up his chain and fired the chain-ball again. Jubei swerved, grabbed the chain and leaped over the side of balcony, thus dragging the assassin along and as they plummeted, Jubei climbed the chain until he reached the assassin and delivered bone-crushing blows to his face. The man spat blood. Jubei double-broke the man's neck and flipped in the air a few feet from the ground and landed on his feet while the dead man crashed onto a car just a few inches from Jubei. The car was smashed in. Jubei slowly lowered himself onto his hands and knees.

A stranger hurriedly dodged through the traffic over to Jubei and examined him carefully. He noticed the bloody wounds. "Buddy, are you okay? What can I do to help?" The stranger helped Jubei up.

Police pulled up to the front of The River Walk Hotel. The stranger assisted Jubei to cross the road. Missiles fired from a white repair van killed the police officers. The back of the van opened and another assassin stepped out with a 52-caliber armor-piercing rifle.

Jubei tried to push the Good Samaritan out of the way, but the man was struck nevertheless. The assassin fired continuously. Jubei weaved through oncoming traffic and limped across the street. The third assassin didn't care whom he might hit. He kept firing at Jubei, as if caroling him to go towards a certain direction.

Across the street was the Alamo. The third assassin followed Jubei across the street and fired another shot at Jubei, but missed, ran out of shells and dropped the weapon in the street. The shell went through the door of the Alamo. Jubei was forced to go into the Alamo and the assassin followed him. The door leading to the courtyard was locked.

The assassin was close by. Jubei kicked the door open and ran into the courtyard.

Standing there, waiting for him, was Kenzin Tanaka. The assassin came over the fence and flipped in the air, landed on his feet as he pulled out a sword. Jubei was unarmed. He took a fighting stance and was ready to die but would go down fighting.

Kenzin laughed out loud and pointed his sword at Jubei. "Look at the great Jubei now," Kenzin said. "Looks like you took a quite a beating. Not unstoppable after all. I've been waiting a long time to kill you."

The assassin moved in first and so did Kenzin. Jubei leaped and grabbed onto a branch to evade the attack. In anticipation of Jubei's evasive tactic, Kenzin was already in the air slicing through the branch. Jubei hit the ground, landing on his back. Kenzin stabbed down at Jubei and Jubei rolled out of the way. The assassin also stabbed down at Jubei but Jubei held onto the branch as the assassin stabbed at it. Jubei back rolled onto his feet. He searched for something to help defend him against both assassins. Jubei was in trouble. Never before had he come face to face with foes of this caliber. The assassin moved in on Jubei. Jubei evaded his sword attack but Kenzin predicted his step and kicked Jubei in the face. The assassin kicked Jubei toward Kenzin. Jubei quickly blocked Kenzin's attack, disarmed him and kicked him in the chest. Kenzin hit the ground and rolled onto his feet. Jubei reached for his sword but the assassin kicked it at Kenzin. Kenzin brushed the dirt off and then charged at Jubei. Jubei rolled underneath his feet and ran. Kenzin and the assassin split up to flank Jubei.

Jubei scrambled and came across several dead armed security officers. He patted down their stiffened bodies for weapons but found nothing. A Shuriken flew through the darkness toward Jubei who spun around and kicked it out of its trajectory. Another Shuriken was on its way and Jubei did a split and it passed over him.

Jubei broke into one of the museums and came upon an old sword encased in glass. He shattered the glass, activating the silent alarm. Jubei took the sword and hurried toward the other exit on the other end of the long room. Kenzin blocked that way out and the assassin blocked the other exit. Holding his sword up in a defensive stance, Jubei stood in the middle of the room while Kenzin and the assassin closed in. Jubei deflected the assassin's attack and right away he spun around and parried Kenzin's attack. Kenzin and the assassin attacked again. Jubei jumped up on a glass casing and backflipped from it onto the other side. Kenzin and the assassin destroyed the section of the display case and went after Jubei. An all out display of swords skills was displayed in this duel of swords. Jubei had met his match.

The assassin came up with a downward slash. Jubei angled the sword and deflected the blade. Kenzin moved in with a horizontal slash but Jubei blocked the attack. Jubei leaped as Kenzin jumped into the air, and Kenzin kicked Jubei's chest, sending him into a vertical standing glass display.

The third assassin attacked with a stabbing motion but Jubei was swift and thrust the sword into the assassin's belly. The man staggered backwards. Jubei pulled the bloodied sword out. The assassin roared and readied to retaliate as blood poured steadily from his wound. He clumsily swung his sword. Jubei spun around so that he ended up behind the man and drove the sword through the back of the assassin's head; it came out his mouth and jabbed the wall. Jubei grabbed the assassins' sword.

Glaring at Jubei, Kenzin trembled with hatred. "I've waited a lifetime to kill you, Jubei. For years I've trained in secret to become your killer. Tonight my goal will be fulfilled. Do you have any idea who I am?"

"You're my next victim," Jubei replied coolly.

Jubei and Kenzin ran towards each other. The swords clanged together. Kenzin matched Jubei for every stroke. He moved just as fast. The men swung simultaneously and slashed each other in the same area, diagonally across the chest. Both staggered and felt the same sharp pain. Kenzin shook the blood off his sword and Jubei wiped the blood off with his fingers. Then they charged at each other once more.

As they battled to kill each other the men demolished the priceless treasures that had till then been safely guarded at the museum. Jubei swung at Kenzin. Kenzin sidestepped the attack. With the blunt end of the sword Kenzin struck Jubei's face and Jubei then side kicked Jubei in the chest and sent him flying into one of the last remaining glass displays. Jubei backflipped in the air and landed on his feet. Kenzin moved with supernatural speed upon Jubei who somehow managed to block the exceptional attack and swept Kenzin off his feet. Kenzin did a back handspring and landed on his feet to break his fall while Jubei had sprung to his feet and again the swords clashed. Jubei and Kenzin battled their way into the yard. Brutal swings. Powerful blows. Both men were covered with blood, theirs and that of their opponent.

Kenzin swung at Jubei and Jubei swung and they locked blades. Kenzin matched Jubei in strength and yet Jubei sent Kenzin's sword flying. Jubei swung down on Kenzin but Kenzin caught the blade between his palms and twisted, disarming Jubei who immediately countered and kicked the sword from Kenzin's hand. Kenzin punched Jubei's face and Jubei punched Kenzin's face. Kenzin punched Jubei in the face again and, in response, Jubei punched Kenzin in the face. Kenzin attacked Jubei but his attack was blocked. Jubei flipped and kicked Kenzin in the chest. Jubei lifted Kenzin up and with his other hand he threw a palm punch at him, which Kenzin blocked. Jubei countered with a throat strike and Kenzin held his throat. Jubei spin kicked Kenzin's bruised face and he went down and then rolled onto his feet. Jubei moved in for another attack. Kenzin pulled out a knife and cut Jubei across his leg, severing the femoral artery and blood sprayed from the wound. As blood spurted Jubei fell to his knees. Kenzin picked up the sword and swung at Jubei's head. Jubei countered the sword strike and disarmed Kenzin and turned Kenzin's attack against him and cut off Kenzin's left hand. Kenzin howled and maddened by the pain and the horror of seeing a part of his body inanimate on the ground, Kenzin hurled himself at Jubei who swerved aside and cut off his adversary's other hand.

Jubei could not stand up. With the amount of blood he was losing he would be dead in a matter of minutes.

The sounds of sirens could be heard. Police and paramedics hurried into the courtyard of the Alamo and encountered a grisly scene, Jubei lying in a pool of his own blood, his life slipping from him. Kenzin's hands were besides Jubei, but Kenzin himself was no longer there.

Four hours later

Jubei woke up connected to an IV. His wounds had been stitched and he assumed he had received blood transfusions otherwise he would not have regained consciousness. He recognized the sterile white room to be a generic hospital room. Through the windowed upper half of the door he could make out the back of a policeman guarding his door. Jubei realized he was cuffed to the bed. From the treetops outside his window he assumed he was on the sixth floor of Wilford Hall medical center of Lackland Air Force Base. His was in an isolated unit of the hospital.

Jubei told the police officer that he needed to go to the bathroom and when the man unlocked the cuffs Jubei struck the cop in the neck. The man dropped. Jubei helped himself to the keys of the handcuffs, undressed the police officer and then laid him in his bed. Jubei hurriedly put on his uniform. He took a couple of steps but felt so weak. He summoned the strength and pushed forward, escaping without being confronted through the front entrance of the hospital.

Meanwhile

Ukyo dismissed the Yagyu counsel from the counsel chambers. He was about to head out when the phone rang. Ukyo answered by pressing a button and a holographic projection of Kenzin materialized.

Kenzin announced that Jubei has been removed. "But it cost me my hands."

"A small price to pay. Is he dead?"

"Yes. After I cut an artery in his leg, I left as he was exsanguinating ."

Ukyo got up from his seat. "Therefore, he still lives."

"It doesn't matter. He is out of the way. I did what no other was able to do. The pastor and his family no longer have their protector, and besides there's poison in his system that will kill him in twenty-four hours at most. He will suffer before falling into a coma, followed by death. So I have indeed killed Jubei Tamuramaro."

Ukyo smiled at Kenzin. "You've done well, my son."

Kenzin bowed respectfully.

"Thank you, father. But what about my hands?"

"What about them?" Ukyo said before disconnecting the link.

He summoned Tamayo.

"Jubei has been eliminated. By this time tomorrow, the poison would have taken effect and killed him."

"The reserve team is in place, my lord."

"Good. At tomorrow night's revival, kill everyone."

Chapter Ten:
The Narrow Gate

Outside San Antonio, Texas, present day

avaro began to administer CPR and chest compressions on Jubei. Megan cried as she watched Navaro try to bring Jubei back to life. She dropped to her knees and prayed. Pastor Willis joined Navaro and took over the chest compressions while Navaro did mouth-to-mouth. Jubei spat up blood but remained unconscious. Navaro grabbed her cell phone again and called for emergency assistance.

Soon enough a black van sped down the road. An emergency crew for the Narrow Gate loaded Jubei in it. They did everything they could to keep Jubei stable. Pastor Willis and Megan rode with Jubei in the first van. A second van, with Navaro, followed the one transporting Jubei.

It was a four-hour drive from San Antonio to the small town of Ozona, Texas.

"We need to get him to a hospital, fast," Megan said to Zula, the driver.

Zula checked the rearview mirror. "We go to da hospital

and risk exposing him. He'll get betta care wit us. Almost at ta house."

Zula made a left turn off Main Street onto another dirt road. They passed a few trailer parks and a couple of farmhouses and reached at a Victorian farmhouse.

Jubei was rushed inside. An elevator led to a secret underground command post. Jubei was wheeled through the command center and taken to the hospital ward. Pastor Willis and Megan followed, but were not allowed further when Jubei was taken into a room where doctors immediately tended to him.

Pastor Willis and Megan waited nervously outside the hospital ward. The doctors scrambled stabilize Jubei. They ran a series of tests on him. He kept slipping in and out of consciousness and convulsed, due to the pain. He was sedated to provide some relief.

After Navaro consulted with the doctors she approached Pastor Willis and Megan. "The doctors ran several toxicology tests on him," she said. "Jubei's been poisoned. He's been stabilized, but if he were to fall into a coma, it's all over."

Megan took hold of Navaro's hand. "There's got to be a way to save him. We can't let him die, after what he's done for us."

Navaro squeezed Megan's hand in an attempt to comfort her. "We're gonna do everything we can for him."

Pastor looked around and asked, "What is this place? What exactly is the Narrow Gate?"

"I guess I owe you an explanation. Come with me."

Pastor Willis and Megan followed Navaro upstairs, to a private room. She gestured for them to take a seat and began to pace. "So how can I explain what we are?" Navaro asked, as if she were asking herself for an easy answer. "You've heard of the Witness Protection Program? We're something like that except for we're privately funded. We've been around since the first century. What we do is provide a safe living environment and protect people of all faiths from religious persecution. We're part of the reason the Christian faith has been able to be spread all over the world. In a time when Christians were being slaughtered, we hid them by any means necessary. In our two thousand years, we have never lost a single person that was under our protection. The federal witness protection cannot boast a claim like that."

"I'm beginning to understand what you meant earlier," said the pastor. "But what makes the Narrow Gate more effective than witness protection?"

"Let's just say that the world is a safer place now that some of our members have become Christians. And who better can protect the innocent than those who used to prey on them."

Zula entered without knocking.

Navaro slid her arm around his waist. "Zula, here, used to recruit children to fight in the rebel army in Sudan. He's also one Sudan's former drug lords, but now he's a child of God and a valued member of the organization."

Zula smiled and whispered something into Navaro's ear. She nodded and Zula left.

"To sum this up, our organization is made up of ex special forces, former terrorists, murderers, drug dealers, embezzlers, rapists, and also just ordinary people. Despite our colorful background we've all got one thing in common. Everyone has been sanctified by the blood of the lamb and are devout Christians. People you would never expect to be open to the word of God and accept it as the truth have been baptized into grace."

"How does this affect us?" asked Megan.

"You're under our protection now, and you must decide for yourselves if you want to go through our program. Like with the federal witness protection, you'd be given new identities, a new place to live, and your old life will be totally wiped away. You'd have to severe ties with everyone you know."

Someone knocked on the door.

Navaro opened and found a Middle Eastern woman standing in the doorway.

"There are some people that want to see the pastor," said the woman, and she moved aside to allow the children into the room. They ran toward Pastor Willis and Megan and threw their arms around them. Navaro smiled and left the room for the family to some privacy for their tearful reunion. She went to check on Jubei in the hospital ward on the lower level.

She stood by his bed and gingerly lifted his shirt to get a peak at his abs and pectoral muscles. She nodded her approval. Suddenly Jubei grabbed her wrist, opened his eyes and realizing it was just Navaro he released her.

Navaro rubbed her wrist but said nothing of it.

"Pastor Willis, Megan?" Jubei asked, trying to sit up.

Navaro gently helped Jubei lay back down. "Don't try and sit up. Pastor Willis and Megan are fine. The children are fine too. You'll see them soon enough."

"You must protect them now. My father, he won't stop until they're all dead. It is the Tamuramaro way."

"They're in good hands, I assure you."

"Forgive me for not sounding convinced. I want to see Pastor Willis."

Navaro called for the pastor and within moments he was beside Jubei. Jubei smiled at the sight of him and Navaro excused herself.

"I'm glad you're okay," said Jubei. "It means I did my job." Pastor Willis smiled and took Jubei's hand.

"I'm sorry I deceived you," said Jubei. "It was the only way to protect you."

"I don't understand," said the pastor. "You went against your clan to protect me? Why would you do that?"

"You are worth protecting, I've never known a man to be truly good until I met you. My father is an evil man, and you're everything that he isn't. I would have protected you for the rest of my life, if I needed too. The world needs you and it does not need me. I'm glad to die doing something honorable, for once."

Pastor Willis snapped "Stop right there. Enough with the all this talk about dying. You're not gonna die in some hospital bed. The Lord has a plan for you."

"It's all right," said Jubei. "I'm not afraid." His eyes rolled and then shut. His hand went limp. He had slipped into a coma.

Doctors gathered in the room and tried to bring Jubei back, but he had slipped too far into the darkness, teetering between life and death.

"He's in a coma. There's nothing more we do."

The doctors left. Pastor Willis took Jubei's hand, bowed his head and prayed over his unconscious friend.

After more than an hour had slipped by, Pastor Willis returned upstairs and the look revealed what had occurred. Megan broke down and cried. Her father put his arm around her and they all prayed together. When they were done, the pastor asked everyone to take a seat.

"We have something we need to talk about," Pastor Willis said, looking at the children.

"We already know," said Jeffrey. "The agent lady filled us in, while you were with Jubei."

"Is it true?" asked James. "Is it true that Jubei's a ninja?"

"It's true," said Megan.

"Is he a member of the same ninja clan that killed our mom and dad?" James asked sadly.

"Yes," Pastor Willis said. "But he wasn't one of the ninjas

involved in that murder. He was protecting us against his own people."

"Why do they want to kill us, Uncle Willis?" Marie asked.

"I don't know. But these people we're with, they're called the Narrow Gate. They're going to keep us safe until we can decide what to do. These are good people here. They help people who are in trouble start a new life. They can help us start a new life, but there's a huge sacrifice that we'll each have to make."

"We'll have to go into hiding and change our lives right?" Jeffrey asked.

"Yes," Pastor Willis said dryly. "We'll get new names, a new place to live, and we'll have to forget about everyone we have ever known."

"What about Grayson? He's the only family I have."

"I'm not sure how it all works exactly, Jeffrey. I'll talk to Navaro and then we'll decide what to do."

It had been a while since Navaro had had a moment to herself as she reclining in a chair, in a private room; shook her head and sighed deeply. She lost a good friend tonight. Her final thoughts were of. She dropped to her knees and prayed for agent Phelps. She tried to ignore the knocking on the door but Zula came in anyway. He knelt beside her and placed his arm around her. She welcomed the warmth of his embrace as he patiently waited for her to finish her prayer.

Slowly, she opened her eyes, as though waking from a deep slumber. "I don't know how much longer I can keep doing this," she said. "I lost a good friend tonight. And this country lost an amazing agent. Can you believe that after years of getting on him, he finally agreed to study the bible? He told me that never in his life had he had any convictions, and then he witnessed the pastor's convictions and was moved by how much they meant to him, and how they shaped the pastor's life and those around him. So much faith. So much love. He was taken by it all and had decided to study the good book." She paused and dropped her head. " I keep losing my partners," she continued. "The things I see compromise my faith, daily."

"Maybe it's time to say goodbye to da FBI, Salma."

"Perhaps you're right."

Zula stroked her hair and smiled as they looked at each other. Navaro made an effort to smile back. And as if he had remembered something important, Zula's smile faded and his forehead creased giving him a more severe air.

"I just came to tell you da ninja Mon took a turn for ta worse. He slipped into a coma. The doctors don't know anything about his condition, but dey tinkin he won't come out of it."

Navaro stood up and said, "I wouldn't count him out just yet. God's still got a plan for him."

"What can be done for him at dis point?"

" A few hours ago I put in a call to our Japanese home. We have a new member who's an expert in poisons. God, willing she'll be able to help Jubei."

A couple of days later in Ozona, a black sedan pulled up to the farmhouse. The driver went around the car, opened the passenger door and a tall Japanese woman stepped out gracefully. Navaro greet her at the door. The woman bowed respectfully and the followed Navaro in, as the driver retrieved her bag from the trunk.

"As soon as we get settled, we'll take you to him," Navaro said, but the woman asked politely whether she could see him immediately.

Navaro consented and led the woman to Jubei's room in the hospital ward.

When the woman entered the room, Megan was asleep in the chair besides Jubei's bed and her hand was resting on his limp hand. She had held vigil throughout the night, praying until she fell asleep in that same chair with the bible draped over her lap.

Navaro noticed the woman was hesitating to approach the bed in which Jubei was on life support.

Navaro asked whether everything was all right.

"Everything's fine," she said in a small voice. "I just never saw a victim of poisoning in this bad a shape."

"These machines are what's keeping him alive?"

"I'm afraid so."

"How long has he been like this?"

"Two days."

The women's voices woke Megan up and she rubbed her sleepy eyes.

"This is Megan," said Navaro. "She's been sitting with him."

Megan stood up and shook with the woman's hand.

"Megan," said Navaro, "she's here to help Jubei. Hopefully she'll be able to do what the doctors couldn't to help him."

The woman approached Jubei and examined him carefully.

Megan excused herself from the room and although she left, she remained outside the door and looked in through its small window.

"He was administered a concoction of poisons that is just about untreatable. And even if I could cure him, he may never recover to be the way he was before he was poisoned. Death just may be better than what he might have to live with." The woman seemed saddened by Jubei's condition.

"Well, if the poison is incurable, how can you help him?"

"I said that this poisonous concoction was created to

be just about incurable. I did not say that it was absolutely incurable."

Navaro handed the woman a manila folder containing a meticulous toxicology report.

The woman waved her hand dismissively. "This is not necessary. I'll take care of it from here so you ought to leave, now. I cannot allow for you to see what must be done, and you have to stay away until I let you know it is safe to return."

Navaro took a few steps toward the door and paused, taking a long look at Jubei before closing the door behind her. Right away the woman locked the door, shut the blinds, and disabled the cameras through the room. Once she was satisfied that the area was secure, she took out acupuncture needles and various herbs, powders and liquids out of her bag. The powders were kept in bags made of seaweed; the liquids in small glass vials. Everything was in order. Finally she took out a miniature portable burner and incense, which she lit up on the nightstand. She slapped her hands and shut her eyes, and without opening them she reached into some of the bags of the powder and sprinkled the powders onto Jubei's arms and legs and rubbed them into his skin until it was absorbed. And only after she slid a needle into his brainstem she opened her eyes. Then she lit the burner and in it she mixed a clear liquid with purple and red powders, and added in crushed dry herbs. In no time the mixture blackened and she removed it from the heat and put it aside. She put another beaker on the burner and poured liquids and other powders, dropped in live worms and leeches and mixed it all until turning the concoction turned grayish and dull. She kept pouring ingredients and mixing different concoctions until six beakers were filled with differing colored liquids. The woman smelled each one and their rancid smell made her grimace. They were ready. Six syringes were laid out and she filled each one with one of the concoctions.

She stuck the first needle into Jubei's neck and injected the black concoction into his vein. Jubei's eyes opened wide and rolled back. His body shook violently. She watched quietly until his shakes appeased and once more he was laying still. She had to paralyze Jubei's nerves to keep him from injuring himself. Black liquid spewed from his mouth and from the corners of his eyes. Again she stood by nonchalantly until he finally stopped shaking.

His eyes were open and he appeared lifeless. She wiped the black liquid from around his mouth and down the side of his neck. She proceeded to inject Jubei with the second syringe. Jubei convulsed again, but this time the spell lasted much longer, nearly an hour until he calmed down. She injected the contents third syringe and the cycle of shakes recurred. The woman applied more powder on Jubei and rubbed it into his skin. Six long hours had passed before the woman was done with the first round of treatment. She neatly put everything away and waited and waited and waited some more while upstairs Pastor Willis and Megan prayed, and Navaro read the bible in her room.

Twelve hours after the treatment Jubei started to move on his own. Jubei opened his eyes. At first his vision was blurry and he reached out and touched the woman's blurry face. "Mother?" he asked, before he fell unconscious once more.

Japan, 1990:

At eight years of age, Jubei's head was shaved head and he wore nothing but a loincloth. It was raining steadily and he knew his mother and father both watched as he stood unarmed in the center of a mud arena, across from which another boy, twelve or thirteen years old, brandished a sword that seemed quite large for his size. Lightning streaked across the sky and thunder rumbled in the distance. The older boy charged at Jubei with his sword raised and swung it furiously. Jubei dodged the attacks with a finesse that surpassed other boys his age. He easily flipped over the boy, kicked him in the back and sent him face first into the mud. Jubei moved in but the boy turned over and kicked Jubei in the face. The boy regained his footing, picked up his sword and once more he charged towards Jubei. Jubei disarmed him and with the boy's own sword he cut him behind the knees and the boy dropped. Jubei held the sword over the screaming boy and then looked at his own father whose face was unmoved.

"Finish him," Ukyo snapped.

In the boy's eyes Jubei saw the maddening pain and desperate desire to live, grow old and learn to love and be loved in return. Ukyo trembled.

"Kill him!" Ukyo yelled in a menacing tone Jubei knew well.

He glanced at the boy's distraught parents and Ukyo leaped from his chair, grabbed the sword from Jubei with one hand and slapped him hard with the other before killed the horrified boy himself. The wailing parents ran out into the muddy arena to retrieve their son's bloodied body. Ukyo picked Jubei up and raised him to eye level. "You hesitate, Jubei, and that moment of weakness may kill you some day. Learn to kill, my son. It is your destiny." Ukyo threw Jubei into the mud and tossed the sword beside him. "You will learn to kill, even if it kills you." He summoned several older boys into the arena with a wave of his hand and pointed at Jubei, who was on his hands and knees.

Ukyo commanded the boys to kill his son. "He is not worthy," he said.

The boys surrounded Jubei and waited for him to stand up. Jubei picked up the sword and stood, holding the sword out in front of him. The boys attacked all at once and Jubei dodged but was cut. Merciless, the boys kept swinging at him, trying to carry out the mission their lord had charged them with.

Matsumi ran out into the arena with a knife in hand, ready to defend her only child, but her husband grabbed her by the arm and restrained her.

"Let me go," Matsumi pleaded. "They're going to kill him!"

"They will have to, if he doesn't kill them first."

Matsumi twisted around and the rain on her skin made it easier to slip from Ukyo's grip and she put the knife to his throat. "Stop this now, or I will slit your throat."

Ukyo laughed. Ninjas suddenly surrounded Matsumi, as if they had dropped from the sky with their blades pointing at her. Ukyo disarmed his wife and kissed her forehead as though she were a child. "You have such fire in you. Jubei is your son. He is our son and you should trust that he will succeed."

Jubei was covered in his own blood and turned his fear into anger and his anger into a source of power and he sliced and stabbed and slashed and cut one boy after another until he was the only one was left standing amid his dismembered friends. Jubei moved in lightning streaked across the darkening sky and the boy's intestines spilled onto the mud. Jubei dropped the sword and kicked the inert boy as he stared maniacally at Ukyo. Matsumi turned but she would never forget the moment her son had become a murderer. Jubei was in such a rage that he didn't even feel the multiple wounds he had suffered. He just kept kicking the dead boy, kicking him and kicking him as Ukyo walked away.

The crowd dispersed and Matsumi lifted her catatonic son from the mud and carried him to his room. Behind closed doors she sung a Japanese folk song that her son loved so very much. She stroked his soaked hair and caressed his filthy face, and then she proceeded to treat his physical wounds, but those inflicted on his spirit, they would never heal.

Present day

For six days the woman treated Jubei until all her ingredients had been used up by the end of the sixth day.

She met with Navaro in her office.

"I have done all I can," the woman said. "I will stay here with him, until I see what the outcome is."

"What can we expect? Did the treatment work?"

"The poison is out of his system, so all we can do now is wait. Are you a praying woman?"

Navaro nodded and the woman seemed pleased. "Good. Praying will help."

Upon returning to Jubei's room, she found Megan looking at Jubei through the window.

"I'm sorry," Megan said. "I know you gave strict orders for him not to be disturbed, but I couldn't stay away from Jubei. He saved our lives."

The woman nodded and said nothing. There was nothing to be said.

"Do you think he knows that I've been sitting with him?" asked Megan.

"He has heard every prayer," the woman said softly. She opened the door to Jubei's room.

Megan waited until the woman was checking Jubei before walking away.

The woman wiped the sweat from Jubei's forehead and then checked his vitals. His eyes flickered as if struggling to open, and when they opened at last, he took a while to adjust to his surroundings and the first thing he that seemed real to him was the woman smiling brightly at him and yet he looked at her as if she were the one thing that he truly believed could not be in that room with him. He opened his mouth to say speak, but though he knew what he meant to say, he could not speak. He struggled to sit up, but couldn't. The woman leaned and kissed Jubei tenderly on the forehead and began to sing softly to him.

Jubei managed to say, "Mother." His throat was dry and his voice cracked.

Matsumi looked into his eyes and teared up as she finished her song.

Japan, weeks earlier

Gazing out into the garden her son loved so much, Matsumi thought of him. Jubei had been exiled from the clan and she knew well that Ukyo would not keep his word. Matsumi's bodyguard knocked and she called her in. Yumiko, similar in size, shape and height as Matsumi, knelt down before her mistress.

"Yumiko," said Matsumi warmly, "how often do I have to tell you that you do not need to kneel for me?" The women had been friends since they were children. Matsumi turned back to the window.

As she stood up, Yumiko noticed a letter on the table. Matsumi was writing to Jubei. Yumiko blurted, "You must leave this place. It is steadily stealing your life."

"I cannot go." Matsumi placed her hand against the window. It felt cool to the touch.

"The other night I bedded Tamayo-san and in his drunken state he revealed something about a purging of the clan. And your name was mentioned. I don't know the details but your husband is planning something terrible and without a doubt he will betray you. You must leave."

"But how?" Matsumi asked. "I am a prisoner in my own home. I cannot get past the gate so let him do his worst."

"Why not kill him? After all, you are a master of poisons," said Yumiko.

"I have thought about that for a long time now, but in killing him in Jubei's absence would only trigger a civil war for control of the clan. Too much blood will be shed. Jubei ought to be the one that defeats him. And besides, it is only fitting for the monster, Ukyo has groomed his son into being, be the one to kill him."

"If you will not kill your husband, you must leave. Why don't you join your son in the United States and start over? You could have the freedom you have wanted."

Matsumi did not see how she could even begin to put such an ambitious plan into motion and so Yumiko excused herself, but she did not allow her mistress to fret unnecessarily for too long and soon enough Yumiko had returned to Matsumi's chambers. But she returned as her mistress. Matsumi was staring at herself but it was Yumiko's voice she heard say to her, "You can escape without even leaving."

Matsumi was stunned by the perfection of her likeness that mimicked her facial expression for facial expression.

Yumiko pressed a button hidden in her sleeve and the disguise melted off and she was exalted. "Ukyo will never know the difference," she said triumphantly, as if Matsumi had already put her plan into motion.

"I have been married to him for many years. He would know that you are not me, no matter how well you might impersonate me."

"But not if you teach me to be you." Yumiko dropped to her knees, lowered her head, and said pleadingly, "You saved my life when we were children, and I swore to serve you and protect you at all costs. Please, allow me do this for you, for me."

Matsumi turned away.

"If I can fool Ukyo, I know we can get away with this. By the time he discovers the truth you will be gone. You can disappear. Join your son. Be whom you were meant to be."

"But, your life is precious to me, Yumiko."

"But it is my life, and I will gladly sacrifice it for you. Never have I disobeyed you, but I shall do this without your consent if need be. Thanks to you I have had the opportunity of living a full life. Now, it is your turn to live your life, freely."

"I will teach you to be me," Matsumi said reluctantly and looked gratefully at her friend.

Matsumi kept her word. Daily she drilled and instructed Yumiko on her mannerisms, and confided in her intimately, about herself, about Ukyo. A month had gone by and Yumiko had not only learned, but also come to understand, even the minutest things about Ukyo that had allowed Matsumi to once love Ukyo. Indeed, Yumiko had come to see him not merely as an unscrupulously ambitious individual who had spent a lifetime obsessing about his own power, grandeur, greatness, but she had also come to see him as a man, flawed in his humanity and his ability to love and be loved truly; a life wasted. Yumiko was sickened at feeling compassion for this one person she had loathed always, and yet she could not help being saddened for the tragedy he had carefully set in motion. Yumiko knew then that she was ready.

Matsumi had been summoned by Ukyo and, as soon as they were alone, he pulled her in and kissed her neck, took in the sweet smell of her. He ran his hand over her skin, gazing into her eyes as he felt her smoothness and her inviting warmth. He undressed and disrobed, picked her up and carried her to bed. Gingerly laid her down. Kissed her passionately and she kissed him back, welcomed him.

She awoke to the melodious chirping outside and the sun had already begun to rise. The air still felt wet from the evening rain. Ukyo's arm was draped heavily across her chest. She carefully moved it aside, slid out of bed, and returned to her own chambers. Matsumi came out of hiding and right away Yumiko removed the disguise. Matsumi could tell that Yumiko couldn't take it off fast enough and yet she could not help feeling happy. The plan was underway.

Chapter Eleven:
Ninja Reborn

Mother," Jubei said. "Is it really you?" He had not sounded as excited as he felt and he desperately wanted to hug her, but the pain was nauseating, and, despite his discipline and training to control pain, it was like a thousand needles were pressed into his nerves and he twisted, cringing, and held in a cry. Unwillingly he gave in to his body's weakness and rested back on his pillow.

"It's alright," Matsumi said. "I'm here. Don't try to move, my son. Poison has injured your nerves and I don't know yet whether the damage is permanent."

Jubei opened his mouth. He wanted to ask about Pastor Willis and Megan. His mother anticipated his question and told him they were both alive and well.

He smiled, but he was exhausted and shut his eyes, fell asleep again.

Matsumi could not contain her glee and skipped out of the room to look for Navaro and was informed by a nurse that Navaro had left town but would be returning shortly.

Matsumi found Megan reading the newspaper on the porch with a fresh cup of coffee on the table. It was a pleasant morning, bright and not too warm. Megan pulled out a chair for Matsumi who was trying her best to remain composed but this only made her appear uncomfortable.

"Please, have a seat," said Megan. "You look exhausted."

Matsumi did not sit. "He's awake," she said. "Jubei has come out of his coma."

Megan jumped out of her chair with joy and in her excitement she knocked the mug off the table and broke down in tears. She shouted thanks and praises to the Lord.

"Can I see him?" she asked.

"He was awake only for a moment, and we exchanged a few words. He fell back asleep, but he's going to be all right."

"So, what happens now?"

"He'll need a significant amount of rest. He may never be able to walk again because the damage to his nerves is so great. Only time will tell."

"Oh, thank you. Thank you so much. I have to go and tell my father the incredible news. He's going to be thrilled. I had a feeling this was going to be a wonderful day!" She hurried off to find the pastor and Matsumi followed.

Pastor Willis and Zula were playing the Wii with the kids. Megan rushed into the den like an excited kid. "Dad" she shouted. "He's awake! Jubei's awake!"

Pastor Willis did not consider putting the game on pause and dropped the remote control. For an instant he seemed disoriented by what he had just been told and then he found his words. "Jubei? He's awake?"

"Yeah, daddy. He's gonna live."

"Dat's good news," said Zula.

Al-Kazim burst into a den with a gun in hand and was surprised to find everyone beside themselves with happiness.

"What's with all the shouting? I thought we were under attack again."

They all laughed. Al-Kazim put the gun back in the holster and walked out as Matsumi entered.

"Dad, this is Matsumi. Jubei's alive thanks to her."

Matsumi bowed respectfully to Pastor Willis and because her eyes were lowered she did not notice that her beauty struck the pastor.

"You are Willis," Matsumi said. "And I am Matsumi Tamuramaro."

Willis repeated her name thoughtfully and said, "You're a ninja?"

"Hai," said Matsumi.

"And how do you know our Jubei?" Pastor Willis asked.

Matsumi smiled coyly and said, "He is my son." Silence filled the room. All eyes were on her. "I did not introduce myself earlier because my sole focus was Jubei. I do apologize for my rudeness."

"I would've done the same thing," said Pastor Willis.

"Well, my son woke up, briefly and the first thing he asked about was you, Pastor Willis." Matsumi turned toward Megan. "And he asked about you too."

Megan smiled.

"When can we see him?" Willis asked.

"He's asleep right now. I will send for you when he is stronger."

Pastor Willis suggested that he could sit with Jubei. "You've been down there for six weeks and had very little rest. You can sleep in my bed." The pastor cleared his throat and blushed. "What I meant was, you can borrow my bed, if you'd like."

"Thank you. I certainly could use some rest. Are you sure this will not inconvenience you?"

Pastor Willis escorted Matsumi to his room where she thanked him again before closing the door. As soon as she laid down and shut her heavy eyes, she was fast asleep.

Four hours later

Pastor Willis had fallen asleep in the chair next to Jubei and he awoke Jubei looking back at him. Pastor Willis smiled a wide smile. Jubei was glad to see him too and whispered, "It's good to see you."

"Not as good as it is to see you, my friend."

"Friend," Jubei repeated after the pastor. "I thought that once you learned the truth about me you would not call me friend."

"Well," said Pastor Willis, "I do have lots of questions on my mind."

"Ask, and I will answer."

Pastor Willis looked up, thoughtfully. "That day we met on the steps of the mosque, that was not a random meeting, or was it?"

Jubei sighed. "No. I knew all about you and your family from the intelligence my clan had gathered. I had been watching you for weeks."

Pastor Willis nodded. It was easier to ask these difficult questions than he had expected it would be.

"Were you originally sent here to kill me, and then had a change of heart?"

"No. I was exiled from my clan. I recovered here but still kept tabs on what was going on. I could not allow my clan to kill you and your family. I apologize for not protecting the other pastors. I was blinded by my loyalty to the clan, and my duty."

"And then why me?" Pastor Willis asked. "Why did you protect me?"

"There was a time when I would not have cared to protect you, but when I followed you around I witnessed your life and realized that you were a man worth protecting, worth dying for, if necessary."

"I don't know what to say."

Jubei smiled. "You move people. You touch their hearts and change their lives. It is refreshing to see a man that can lead people with such love and compassion. You have a way to get people to do things for you, because they feel compelled, by their love for you, to do them. You're a bright light at the end of a dark corridor"

"Do you know whom you're describing?"

"I am describing you," Jubei replied.

Pastor Willis chuckled. "You're describing Jesus Christ, my friend. What you see in me, Jubei, is Christ's love and grace that fills me."

Pastor Willis rolled up his sleeves and showed Jubei his scars. "There was a time when I was the darkness. These scars are from a time when I was lost and didn't know God. God had a plan for me, like he does for all of us. I knew there wasn't anything that God wouldn't bring me to, that he wouldn't bring me through. To not serve a loving God like that, and surrender myself to his will, was not even an option, once I heard his word."

"God," said Jubei. "The only thing God has ever been good for, in my life, was to judge the souls I sent his way."

Pastor Willis said nothing as he absorbed Jubei's cold and blunt words. Corpses left behind by Jubei; by this man he called his friend. Blood. Violence. Jubei was an angel of death in human form. Mercilessly. Cold. Void of emotion. Robotic in his tasks. Unfazed by the countless lives he took.

Jubei watched the pastor as if he were waiting for him to say something that might comfort him.

"Well," Pastor Willis finally said. "I was wondering what

the delay was with God answering my prayers. Now I know. You've been keeping him busy." The pastor attempted to smile but Jubei's face was blank.

"That was my attempt to lighten the mood a bit, but I digress," said the pastor.

The men just sat in silence for a while until the pastor asked in a small voice, "Did you kill many people?"

Jubei nodded. "There was a time when I would not have hesitated to kill you, and your entire family, if ordered to do so, regardless of how good of a man you are."

"But instead you were willing to die to protect us. Why, Jubei?"

Jubei shrugged.

"I bet that in short time you went from being a ruthless killer to a man whose only mission has become to protect worthy souls, and you can't even explain why you have changed but you have." Pastor Willis leaned in closer to Jubei and pressed his hand over Jubei's heart. "That's the lord, already at work in your heart."

Pastor Willis sat with Jubei for a while longer and waited for him to close his eyes and fall back asleep. Once Jubei's breathing had slowed and deepened, Pastor Willis placed his hand on Jubei's forehead and prayed for him.

Tokyo, Japan

Mishi Tanaka entered a large office with a large picturesque window from which you could admire the gorgeous skyline of lights of Tokyo at nighttime. In front of the window was an 18th century French desk with a large dark leather chair turned towards the window. Mishi approached the desk and bowed just as Kenzin turned his chair around to face her. "He is alive, isn't he?" Kenzin asked.

"Hai," said Mishi. "Ukyo is tied up with the Tamuramaro demise. It falls onto us to finish the job."

Kenzin stood up, balled his new cybernetic titanium hands and smashed the table to pieces with a single blow. "But, I killed him!"

"My sources have informed me that Jubei is still alive. He killed several Tamuramaro before succumbing to the poison, but was rushed in a van. We tried to follow, to confirm his death but…"

Kenzin shouted, "He is dead! No, doctor could help him. The only person that could have saved him was put to death in front of the entire village."

"We need to confirm his death, Kenzin."

Kenzin leaped across the room and came to stand face to face with Mishi. "I know what needs to be done. We will find Jubei and kill him. Ukyo gave us a mission, and I shall not rest until Jubei is dead." He pushed Mishi to the floor. Mishi got back up and pulled out a Razor sharp fighting fans and went after Kenzin, but he blocked her attacks and disarmed Mishi. He attempted to put her in an arm bar but Mishi brought her leg up and kicked his face. Kenzin staggered. Mishi dashed at Kenzin with a spin kick and Kenzin caught Mishi's leg in time and threw her towards the wall. She backflipped and her feet landed against the wall, from which she pushed off, and flipped forward, landing on her feet. She hurled her fans at Kenzin and deflected them with his hands. Mishi attacked with a side kick to his chest but Kenzin caught her fist and palm punched her in the chest. She flew into the wall and then slumped to the ground. Kenzin moved in with a flying knee. Mishi rolled underneath him. Kenzin's knee hit the floor where Mishi's head had been and cracked the floor. Mishi grabbed Kenzin and placed him in a chokehold. Kenzin tried to catch his breath, all the while fighting, pummeling Mishi in the ribs until she was forced to release him. She crossed her arms around her ribcage and grimaced in pain.

The siblings glared at each other. Mishi attacked first and Kenzin blocked her punches and kicks. Her hands were pretty damaged by his prosthetic hands; they were not easy to defend against; they were covered in her blood.

She threw a kick at Kenzin's head. Kenzin stepped to the side and blocked the kick with an open handed block. Snap! Her leg was broken and still she managed to stand. Mishi jumped up with her good leg and kicked him in face. She landed on her good leg and did her best to stand, ready to fight again, but collapsed.

They laid on the floor besides each other, glaring at one another until Mishi cracked a smile and they both broke out in laughter.

"The two of us combined, my dear sister, we shall destroy Jubei," said Kenzin.

A medical officer burst into the office and rushed to Mishi's side to help her with her broken leg. He did not expect her to kick him in the face and sent him flying to the other side of the room.

She got up with some difficulty and hobbled over to the medical examiner. She pummeled the stupefied man until his face was a bloody mess. Then she dropped into her brother's chair and with a nothing more that a hiss and low grunt she snapped her leg back into place.

Although Kenzin already knew that the medical officer was dead, he crawled over to the man and checked his vitals.

His sister shrugged. "I killed that fool because I pictured him as Jubei. Just imagine what I will do to anyone else that gets in my way."

Kenzin wiped the blood from his mouth, got up and

went over to Mishi. Affectionately, he slid his arm around her. "You are without a doubt your father's daughter."

Kenzin pulled up a chair and sat down besides Mishi. "Now, how are we going to find him?" he asked.

"The real question is not how, but when. Finding Jubei is inevitable, and so is our death if we fail."

There was knock at the door. The Japanese woman who entered wore her hair short and had a red Dragon tattooed on the left side of her face. She did not seem surprised at the chaotic state of the office, or at the disheveled and bloodied appearance of the siblings, and not even at the dead man on the floor. She bowed to Mishi and then handed her a USB port. "This is the latest information on Jubei."

"Excellent. Arrigato, Asti."

Asti bowed and excused herself.

Kenzin and Mishi reviewed the information on the USB.

Meanwhile, a teenage boy leaned against a fence and watched the horses. Jeffrey was deep in thought. He did not notice that Pastor Willis was heading towards him. He was holding a small brown bag in his hand.

"Thought I'd find you out here," the pastor said.

"I just needed to get out of the house for a minute, to think, you know?"

"I know. Tomorrow's a big day for us. Everything is going to change."

"I don't know if I can do it, Willis. I don't think I can leave my brother behind."

A dark mare and her colt galloped by. Both the man and the boy took a moment to admire them.

"I figured you might be hungry after skipping lunch," said Pastor Willis, and he handed the bag to Jeffrey.

Jeffrey checked what was in it. A sandwich. He put the

bag on a fence post and told the pastor that he would eat it later.

Pastor Willis frowned, and caught himself. His face softened and he said in a reassuring tone, "I spoke with agent Navaro, over the phone. She thinks that you might not be in danger. The ninjas were after me. But this is your decision, Jeffrey. No one can force you to do anything you're not comfortable doing."

"And what are you going to do?" Jeffrey asked.

"I've spent the past few days in constant prayer over this. I think it's best to go through the Narrow Gate program."

Jeffrey looked sadly at Pastor Willis. "If I decide to go home, would I ever see you again?"

"Not likely. But as the saying goes, never say never." He tried to smile and put his arm around Jeffrey. "I'm proud of you. Through all of this, you've remained faithful and did not once turn from God."

"I had a good teacher."

A white horse trotted up to Jeffrey, whinnied, and dropped its head. Jeffrey patted its elongated face. The horse turned and sauntered off.

"I have to be with my brother," said Jeffrey. "He's the only family that I've got left. I want to go home."

The pastor nodded his understanding but was sad to hear Jeffrey's decision.

Jeffrey grabbed his bag and as he turned to head back to the house, Pastor Willis took hold of his shoulder.

"You're wrong about one thing, Jeffrey," said the pastor. "Grayson's not the only family you have left, son."

Jeffrey hugged the pastor with the warmth he would have hugged his own father with.

Lavender filled the air and Jubei felt a soft hand gingerly touch his hand. He opened he sleepy eyes. Megan was standing beside his bed. He smiled back at her and asked her to help him sit up, which she was glad to do.

A tray of food was untouched on his side table.

"As soon as I heard that you were awake I just had to come see you. I owe you my life, Jubei."

"You owe me nothing, but I am glad you've come. I really needed to see your smile again."

But Megan was no longer smiling, still she looked at him tenderly. "It's because of you that I'm alive. I don't know if I could ever pay you back. How is that even possible?"

With much effort and pain, Jubei slowly took the lid off the breakfast tray. Megan grabbed the fork as though she meant to help Jubei eat. He shook his head. She put the fork back onto the tray. Jubei struggled but managed to pick up the fork, hold it, and scoop a forkful of tepid mashed potatoes into his mouth. He chewed with some discomfort and swallowed. He paused, as if allowing his body a moment to process what it had ingested, and then said, "There isn't anything you can do to pay me back, because I do not need to be paid back."

"At least let me help you eat. At this rate you'll be able to collect on social security by the time you're done." Megan began to mimic Jubei's eating. His face was placid and she did not know what to make of it so she stopped. Suddenly, Jubei burst into laughter and, relieved, Megan laughed along with him. The laugher took a while to die down but it did and Jubei nodded towards the tray. Megan picked up the fork and patiently helped him eat as much of his lunch as he could.

"Tomorrow, your family has a big decision to make," said Jubei.

"I think we pretty much decided. We're going to go through the Narrow Gate program. However, poor Jeffrey's torn. He has a brother and that's the only real family member he has left. But what about you, Jubei?"

"As soon as I am back on my feet, I'm going to end this for good."

Megan raised her brow. "What do you mean, *end this?*"

"I'm going to kill my father and destroy whatever is left of the Tamuramaro clan."

"Why do you have to kill anybody?"

"It's the only way to make sure that you will be safe."

In Megan's face, Jubei saw that for the first time she was seeing him for what he was. The lives he had stolen. Death. She backed away from him. She was indignant. "Is this all you know? Murdering people to solve your problems?"

"It is what I am, Megan. I am a killer."

"No," Megan yelled. "You're more than that. You are better than that. You do not have to kill anyone. Ever again."

"Understand this, my clan will not stop. They will not rest until they hunt you down, and kill you, kill everyone you have ever loved, anyone you have ever cared for, and they will kill any man, woman, child that gets in their way. I know this because it was what I was trained to do. We have all been trained to do this, to kill. The Tamuramaros are killers. I am a killer. These hands, that can barely hold a fork, have taken countless lives. You have seen what I am capable of, with your own eyes."

"But that was different. It was self-defense. Going after your clan, now that's murder."

"If I don't end this and something happens to your family, I..."

Megan interrupted him. "*My life* is *not* in your hands, Jubei. My life is the hands of our Lord. If your clan finds us, then it is by his will that they will be able to do so. Know that I am *not* afraid of your clan."

Jubei bellowed," You should be." His sharpness in his

tone, eyes, they conveyed a truth she could not afford to underestimate.

"And if your clan kills you, what will stop them then?"

Matsumi walked in and interjected, "She is right, Jubei. You can not go after the clan."

Megan knew that this moment was between this mother and her son. Megan stood and walked out as quietly as she could.

"Let them think you're dead, my son. I want you to have this life I have always longed for you to have."

"And I am lying in a hospital bed. My body is broken, mother."

"It will heal."

"If I do what you ask of me, I will spend the rest of my life looking in the shadows, and besides, you know that as long as father is alive, the clan will not rest until Pastor Willis and his entire family are dead."

"Going after the Tamuramaro isn't something you need to do, Jubei. Ukyo is no longer concerned with the pastor or his family. He is preoccupied with the Yagyu."

Jubei was surprised at the mention of the Yagyu and for a mere instant he forgot about the pain and sat up on his own. He cringed, and between clenched teeth he asked, "The Yagyu have resurfaced? When did this happen?"

"It happened since Ukyo is Yagyu."

Jubei looked confused. He tried to make sense of Matsumi's words but could not.

"There are things about your father that I have never told you. Things I've kept secret for so long, but all that is over. We can leave the secrets and that life behind us, now." Matsumi took Jubei's hand and held it tight. "Jubei, the past cannot be changed. The future cannot be determined. And the present, the present, my son, cannot be halted."

Jubei pulled his hand away and said sternly, "I want to know everything, mother. Everything."

Matsumi sighed deeply. A tear trickled down her cheek and she began to tell the tale she had for so long kept to herself:

It all began in the Yagyu Mountain, circa 1964 in Japan. The Yagyu ninja were the only ninja clan that rivaled the Tamuramaro clan. Our two clans alone had survived the ninja wars.

In the main Yagyu palace, the Yagyu warlord, Hiroshi Tanokawa-Yagyu, was meeting with his top assassins. He was intimidating with a long scar running down his face and neck. . His snow-white hair was streaked with a black streak on either side of his head.

The great door opened and a five-year-old child ran in with a Boken in his arms. Hiroshi and threw his arms around the boy. This young child was Ukyo.

"Ukyo, show me your stance," Hiroshi said.

Ukyo obediently broke into a fighting stance. Even at this young age, his form and balance were near flawless.

"Kata Sword!"

At Hiroshi's command Ukyo demonstrated his control of the short wooden sword. Ukyo performed his Kata swordsmanship beautifully, until he tried to throw a spin kick and come around with an, in air, downward slash upon which Ukyo slipped onto the floor. Hiroshi encouraged Ukyo to get back up and continue, so he did. And when Ukyo was done, Hiroshi nodded, smiling, pleased with his performance. "Very good, Ukyo-san," he said, "but you need to practice your landings. I will show you how, later. Now run along. Your mother is waiting for you. I will be home shortly."

"All right, Papa."

The doors closed behind Ukyo and the meeting resumed.

Little Ukyo went down into the market place, where his mother, Yeh-Shen, was waiting for him, flanked by her bodyguards. She took her boy's hand as they walked through the market place and those around them stopped and bowed as they passed by.

A hissing sound could be made out and within seconds the clear summer morning was eclipsed as arrows rained upon the village, hitting everything and anyone. In the first wave of arrows alone, dozens of people were killed.

A brave Yagyu man climbed the tower to sound the alarm when a ninja in Tamuramaro uniform appeared in a cloud of smoke and cut off the supporting legs of the tower, which fell, along with the brave man who was instantly crushed.

A second wave of arrows dropped from the sky and those on the streets ran for shelter, as they would have from hail. Yeh-Shen pushed Ukyo to the ground and laid over him, sheltering him as best she could with her own body. She was wounded.

Suddenly, hundreds of Tamuramaro ninjas descended upon the Yagyu village. The genocide had begun.

Hiroshi and the counsel heard screams, which could be made out from the highest level of the palace. He grabbed his sword and ran to the window from which he saw Yeh-Shen laying face down with three arrows in her back.

Hiroshi did not even take the time to shout and leaped out the window, and flipped three times before landing on a flagpole, from which he leaped off and landed steadily on his feet. He drew his sword and charged the nearest Tamuramaro. The man was no match for Hiroshi.

Explosions shook the ground and the sound of gunfire was deafening.

Hiroshi had to fight a path to reach Yeh-Shen.

A Tamuramaro pulled her to her feet and readied to kill her but she was unexpectedly swift and stabbed the ninja before he could strike her. With some effort she lifted her son and tried to usher him to safety. Ukyo pulled a dagger out of a dead Yagyu guard and slid it into his sleeve. A Tamuramaro snuck up from behind Yeh-Shen and cut her behind the knees. She fell over. Ukyo rolled to the ground. Ukyo saw the Tamuramaro raise his sword and slash Yeh-Shen across her chest. She went limp and then the man rushed towards Ukyo, grabbed the boy by the throat and began to choke him. Ukyo could not breathe and he knew he was not strong enough to fight off the man. Instinctively he pulled out the knife and cut the ninja's throat. Ukyo coughed as he was sprayed with warm blood and he tried to catch his breath, then scurried behind a couple of wooden barrels. From his hiding place he watched the Tamuramaro brutally slaughter people he knew. He was panicked and did not think of remaining safely hidden and ran into the open, towards his mother's bloodied body.

Hiroshi killed one Tamuramaro after another, any who stood in his way. Dozens surrounded him and he struck them all down.

Hiroshi's bitter rival, lord Usagi Tamuramaro wore his raven dark hair in a ponytail, his staple black kimono, and a leather patch over his left eye. He had lost his eye to Hiroshi in a duel during the wars, but Hiroshi spared his life in exchange for peace between the clans. Viciously, he was cutting down any Yagyu still standing.

The ninja lords stared at each other from across the dirt road, which was littered with their fallen men. They ran at each other and stuck down anyone in their way. Usagi pulled out a gun and shot Hiroshi several times. Hiroshi fell to his knees. Usagi took Hiroshi's own sword and with it he decapitated the Yagyu lord. The head dropped heavily and rolled towards Ukyo who was lying on the ground beneath his mother's body, inert, as if dead. In his terror he had wet himself. For several hours, the little boy remained there while the Tamuramaro annihilated the Yagyu clan. After the majority of Yagyu men, women, and children were no longer standing, Lord Usagi walked around the village, inspecting his victorious massacre while his men checked every body to ascertain that no one would be left behind alive. A Tamuramaro kicked over Yeh-Shen's body and discovered Ukyo trembling beneath. Ukyo stabbed desperately at the ninja but was easily disarmed. The ninja raised his sword and as he brought it down to finish the boy off Usagi deflected the ninja's sword with the one he had taken from the Yagyu lord.

"No," he said sternly. "Chain this one up." Something in Ukyo's eyes struck him.

The few Yagyu who hadn't been killed had been chained to one another and Ukyo was chained to other Yagyu children. Most of them were bloody. Some of them were covered in their own blood, others, like Ukyo, in that of loved ones.

Usagi ordered his ninjas to set fire to every last building in the silenced village. As they were led away from everything that they had known and loved, the Yagyu turned to take a last look at the little that was left be consumed by a roaring fire that reached up into the darkening sky.

It was an extensive march to the Tamuramaro village and the captors only made the trek more arduous and unbearable through deliberate starvation, molestation, rape, vicious beatings and torture. Six hundred Yagyu captives began the journey but merely seventy-five of them reached their forced destination where they were eventually sold as slaves to the hierarchy of the Tamuramaro.

Ukyo only made it through because Usagi paid special attention to him, making sure that the boy was cared for and protected from the cruelty of his men.

Narrow Gate headquarters, present day

Matsumi allow Jubei a moment to take it all in.

"My father, a Yagyu? But how did he become lord of the Tamuramaro? The Yagyu were crushed and treated as inferior."

Matsumi agreed. "But Ukyo was different. Your grandfather saw something special in him. Not only did Usagi spare him but he also defied the counsel and, against their advice, he trained Ukyo. Ukyo's ambition, skill in ninjitsu, and his uncompromising will, helped him to later rise to become leader of the Tamuramaro. However, what primarily catapulted him into leadership was treachery. Lord Usagi had a young son to whom Ukyo was assigned to protect. That son was the true heir to the Tamuramaro. Indeed, your father could never have become Tamuramaro unless he took what he desired by force. So he killed Usagi's only son...your real father."

Matsumi noticed Jubei's hands were balled into tight fists.

"All these years, you knew Ukyo killed my real father, and you did nothing?"

"Ukyo defeated him in lethal combat for leadership. It was a fair match, and as a result, he won me, as was the custom back then. Jubei, you need to know that I never loved Ukyo the way I loved your father. Ukyo was a cruel leader, but to understand him it is important to understand that his childhood was warred in nothing but misery. Do consider that he could have killed you, but he chose to raise you as his own. I waited for a time that I could get my own revenge but I never went through with it. If I had, you would not have become the most powerful and skillful ninja to have ever lived, and more than likely, the pastor and his family would be dead. Ukyo took the Tamuramaro to the heights of power that Usagi had not dreamt of. But, deep down in his soul, Ukyo truly hated the Tamuramaro. He privately lusted for vengeance. He wanted nothing more than to destroy the Tamuramaro one day. And finally, he has. All that has transpired recently was to cover his true motives. The Tamuramaro have been crushed. Now he is rebuilding the Yagyu clan, which was always his goal. I didn't know this at first, but as time passed by I figured out his true intentions."

Jubei shook his head. He felt nauseous. "Why did he keep me alive? Why spare me?"

"In his own way he did love you; he could not have loved you any more had you been his natural son. Whereas Ukyo, even though was treated fairly by Usagi, he did not allow himself to feel anything but hate and anger. Imagine a lifetime of feeling diluted emotions because you are consumed with so much rage that you cannot feel anything else."

"I wouldn't know that feeling, because I was lucky to have you as my mother," Jubei said.

"You are the farthest thing from Ukyo's mind. Now that his vengeance is complete, he will redirect his efforts into rebuilding the Yagyu clan."

"Then what happens after that, mother? Will he resume his hunt for me?"

"I don't know that for sure. But if you do go after him, you will leave the pastor unprotected. Let the past remain in the past. Do not chase ghosts."

Matsumi kissed her son on the forehead and left him to his own thoughts.

Jubei couldn't lie in the bed any longer. His anger pushed

him. He gripped the bed rails and turned his body so that his legs hung over the side of the bed. Slowly he edged his way off the mattress so that his feet touched the cold floor. Jubei breathed in deeply. Exhaled. This much movement had tired him out, but he had to continue; he needed to get his strength up. Again Jubei carefully edged off the bed, and pushed off the bed to stand up. He momentarily managed to steady himself on his feet. It was the first time in six weeks. His legs were shaky. He leaned up against the wall for support. He eyed the door, only ten-feet away and yet it seemed miles away. Jubei began to take tiny steps all the while keeping his hand on the wall and thus he moved forward, inch by inch. Minutes went by and he made it into the hallway where he continued to make his way alongside the wall.

A Narrow Gate medical tech walked toward him.

"You shouldn't be out of bed this soon," said the man. He gripped Jubei's shoulder.

Jubei stiffened and growled, "Take your hand off me or I'll break your arm."

The medical technician backed away.

"I'm sorry," Jubei said and he continued down the hall at a snail's pace.

The man cried out. "Wait! I have something that can help you." He hurried off to the supply closet and brought Jubei a walker. "This will be helpful." He unfolded the walker and proceeded to show Jubei how to use it.

"I don't need instructions," Jubei snapped. "You may go."

The medical technician shrugged.

Jubei grabbed hold of the walker and continued up the hallway, venturing from the hospital ward to the living room where he found Zula and some of the other members of the Narrow Gate. The others were in the dining room eating.

When Zula noticed Jubei, and stood up and clapped. Other stood up as well and clapped. They were cheering.

In the processing room, Pastor Willis and a Narrow Gate agent were discussing the processing procedures of the pastor's new life. He heard the clapping and followed the cheerful sound to see what it was all about.

James and Marie had been packing the new clothes the Narrow Gate had purchased for their new life, which was set to begin the following day. They could also hear the merriment from upstairs. They hurried down and joined the others who had gathered around Jubei. The clapping continued. Jubei looked around at the strangers who were celebrating him and inadvertently caught his own reflection in the mirror. He opened the top of his hospital gown and saw the multiple scars he received from the battle with Kenzin, and the night of the revival. They had since healed and yet he still looked like he had been used as a cutting board.

As the onlookers dispersed to resume their activities and conversations, Jubei was left with Pastor Willis, Megan, and the children who stepped forth to hug Jubei but Megan held them back. Jubei set the walker aside and then opened his arms and welcomed James and Marie into them. Jubei cringed because he was still quite sore, but hugging the kids felt good.

Marie whispered to him, "Thank you for saving our lives."

Jubei whispered back, "I'd do it again in a heartbeat."

"You two need to finish your packing," said the pastor. "Tomorrow we start anew."

James and Marie headed sulkily toward the stairs. James turned and rushed back to Jubei. "Glad to see you," he said, and then hurried to catch up with his sister.

Jubei grabbed the walker and asked the pastor if he could speak with him.

"Sure. Let's go outside, on the terrace."

At a slow pace Jubei followed Pastor Willis through the double French doors and onto the deck. Jubei eased his way to a yard chair and the pastor helped him into it.

"It's good to see you out of bed," Pastor Willis said.

"Those people, inside, why were they clapping?"

"You're a hero," said the pastor, but what the pastor told him did not move Jubei who did not care for that sort of acclaim.

"If they knew I was a killer, would they still cheer?"

"They know who you are and what you've done," Pastor replied. "But they were cheering because of the lives you have changed. Do you know where you are?"

"Megan told me something about this place."

Pastor Willis nodded. "Then you fit right in. These people were at one time or another among the most dangerous individuals on the planet, but through the grace of the Lord they've been redeemed, and born again. Now, they help others like me, who need to start over. So, Jubei, what did you want to talk to me about?"

"I don't know."

"It's great to see you walking. Soon you'll be at full strength. Been praying for you."

Jubei looked away and said, "Tomorrow, you start a new life and our journey together will be over."

"My journey would have already ended, had I not met you on the road. There's no reason why it has to end, my friend."

"My life takes me in a different direction."

"Back to Japan?" Pastor Willis asked.

Jubei knew why the pastor asked that question.

The pastor continued. "Megan told me what you wanted to do. Why would you want to go back to that life?"

"Why do you say, *go back to that life*, as if I had ever left it?"

"Because you already have, Jubei. Your heart left that life long before you met me."

"Once a ninja, always a ninja."

Pastor Willis chuckled. "That's like saying, once a sinner, always a sinner. And that there's no hope. Imagine if the Lord thought that way about us."

Jubei took in pastor's words and then he said, "I don't want to do this, but I have too. I must end this."

"What makes you think you're supposed to end it?" Pastor Willis asked.

Jubei seemed puzzled.

"Megan said almost the same thing."

"I know she did. She's just like me."

"I don't expect you to understand."

Pastor Willis held up his hand as if he would not listen to any more of that sort of talk. "I understand perfectly. You're in unknown territory. You're in a world you know nothing about, because you have spent your whole life cut off from it. You only come into this world long enough to do your job and then go back to your world. Tell me honestly, do you want to return to your world? Do you honestly want to shed more blood?"

Jubei glanced down at his hands; countless lives he had taken, and they would forever be stained with their blood. The pastor might not see it. Megan might not see it. But Jubei, he knew well his hands were soaked in blood and there would not be any redemption for that level of cruelty. "For some of us there is no other option."

"That's crap! There's always an option. And besides,

that doesn't answer my question. Do you want to shed more blood?"

Jubei stood up and shouted, "No!" as if he were in perfect health. "No, I don't want to shed any more blood!"

Jubei smashed the wooden table with his fist and he was taken aback by what he had done, as was Pastor Willis. Members of the narrow gate ran out to see what the fracas was all about.

"Then don't," snapped Pastor Willis and he walked away leaving Jubei standing there with his fist clenched like an angry child, unable to channel his emotions. He stared blankly at the mess that had been a picnic table. For the last few weeks he barely had the strength to move his arm, and now he had just broken a table without any effort.

Pastor Willis turned around upon reaching the doors. Jubei looked like a deer in headlights. The pastor knew he had moved Jubei like only a parent can.

People were asking what had happened. Pastor Willis left them waiting for an answer and returned to Jubei and put his hand on Jubei's shoulders. "Why don't you start over with us? You're my best friend and I'd like to keep you around."

"Start over? I'm not sure I can do that."

"Never know until you try. Your mother can come with us, Jubei. You saved our lives. The least we can do is offer you a home. At least until you are fully recovered."

Jubei in turn placed his hand on Pastor Willis' shoulder. "If the world had more men like you, there wouldn't be a need for men like me. Thank you for your invitation."

Jubei reached for his walker and slowly made his way back in.

The next morning

Navaro brought the travel visas and new documents for the pastor and his family. After six weeks in the Narrow Gate house, it was time to move on. Behind Navaro's car was another black SUV that would be taking Jeffrey home.

Inside

The family had just finished packing.

James ran into Pastor Willis' room and asked, "Where are we moving to again?"

"Clovis, New Mexico."

"Sounds boring."

"After what we been through, boring will be a nice change of pace."

Megan was in her room packing her hygiene products into her single suitcase. She glanced out the window, which faced the field with the horses. She sighed. She had become attached to this place.

Megan left her room and went down the hall to Jubei's room, where he had been moved to the day before. She knocked lightly. It was still early in the morning and Jubei could still be asleep. There was no answer. She wanted to say goodbye before leaving, so she opened the door and peeked in. Jubei's bed had not been slept in.

Navaro shouted from the bottom of the stairs, "Time to go!"

Members of the Narrow Gate were downstairs and waiting to say good-bye to them all.

James and Marie were the first to come down with their suitcases. Pastor Willis, Megan, and Jeffrey followed. Everyone exchanged goodbyes. Jeffrey teared up as he hugged

Megan, and the kids. He then hugged the pastor tightly, as if it would be the last time they would ever meet.

Pastor Willis whispered, "Whatever you do, hold on to your faith. And don't worry. We'll see each other again."

Jeffrey struggled to let go of the pastor.

Pastor Willis looked around and could not find Jubei. He headed to the door and took a last look up the stairs, but Jubei did not appear at the top of the stairs. Pastor Willis and Megan exchanged worried looks. They both wanted dearly to see him and say goodbye. Where could he have been?

"Let's move out," Navaro said in a commanding tone. "We got a plane to catch."

She ushered everyone outside.

Jeffrey cried as he hugged the family and got into the SUV that would take him back to San Antonio, to his brother. Jeffrey waved out of the window as the SUV drove away.

A Narrow Gate agent loaded the family's bags into the back of the tinted minivan. Navaro opened the van door, and invited everyone in. Pastor Willis stepped in and saw Jubei and Matsumi seated in the back.

"Maybe I can become a man like you," Jubei said with a big smile. "Only way to do that is to be around you."

Pastor Willis was elated and his face blushed with delight. Megan got in and squealed with excitement when she saw Jubei and Matsumi. The kids joined in the laughter and it took a while for them all to settle so that Navaro could shut the door.

"You know, we wouldn't have to go into hiding if I could just end this," Jubei said. Navaro had scooted into the driver's seat and turned around. All the passengers were glaring at Jubei. Navaro laughed. Jubei shrugged and said, "I'm just saying..."

Chapter Twelve:

Before Leaving Earth

Clovis, New Mexico

The family had been assigned new identities. Pastor Willis' name was changed to Malcolm Ross; Megan's, to Paty Ross; James and Marie's, to Marcus and Mara Ross. Accordingly, they were to henceforth address each other by their assigned names. Together they lived in a big house on a four-acre lot. After weeks of physical therapy, Jubei was beginning to make excellent progress. Jubei and Paty were getting closer. Malcolm found work as a principal at an elementary school. Paty was progressing well in her new job in the next town over, as a counselor at the university.

Matsumi and Jubei built their own house on the Ross' property, as well as a dojo, and opened up a martial arts school that had a successful after-school program. Life in New Mexico was sweet.

Jubei was roused from a deep sleep by a loud horn, on Sunday morning. He sprung up into a fighting stance and glared at Malcolm. He already knew what the pastor wanted.

"You don't scare me, ninja. We've been here for six months now and today you're going to church. It will be good for you. And besides, your mother's coming along."

Jubei shook his head and sighed as Malcolm left his room. First thing in the morning, for months, Malcolm had been after Jubei to go to church. This morning Jubei did not want to go either, but today felt different. Today Jubei felt guilty when he looked into Malcolm's pleading eyes. He could not continue to refuse him. He reluctantly slipped into his pants, a shirt and tie, and then headed over to the main house where Paty and the kids were eating cereal in the kitchen. She was dressed casually and laughed when she saw Jubei. Jubei looked over his outfit and didn't see what was wrong with him. Perhaps he had something on his face. He wiped at his face and smiled boyishly. Paty approached him and began to undo his tie.

"You've got the tie all wrong," Paty said.

"I don't wear this type of clothes. I can go change."

Paty took a step back and admired the perfect knot she had tied. She had fixed her father's tie so many time before that she could do it with her eyes closed. "You look great. I really like the way you look in a suit."

"Why aren't you dressed?" he asked.

"I am dressed."

Jubei looked confused and said, "I thought that you had to be well dressed for church." Usually the family had already left for church in the mornings and this was the first time he saw Paty in her church attire.

"The Lord doesn't care about your outward appearance," Paty said and she placed her hand over Jubei's heart. "He cares about your heart. Your whole heart."

The two locked eyes and as they gazed at each other, could feel his nervous heart pounding and worried that she might feel it and know just how deeply she made him feel.

Paty herself was in no hurry to take her hand or her eyes off of him. Slowly she leaned in and Jubei was following her lead when Malcolm entered and said, "Everyone's in the car, waiting on you two." They both lowered their heads and hurried after the pastor.

A large cross was prominently located in the front of the building, over the main entrance. Malcolm pulled into the parking lot where church staff was directing the cars to where they could park. His car was next in line to be assisted.

"Wow," Paty exclaimed. "This church is massive. Look at all these people going in."

Jubei was also impressed. He had never seen anything like this.

Matsumi just shrugged her shoulder and, like her son, she watched individuals of differing race, ethnicity, and age, file into the church, some in a pair of jeans and a t-shirt others in a suit or a pretty dress.

After parking, the Ross party went inside and Marcus and Mara went to the children's services while the usher led the rest of them to their seats, in the second row from the stage.

The sanctuary took a while to fill up, but it did.

The choir entered the stage. The choir director cued the choir to take their positions and led them into an upbeat song. Its lyrics appeared on an elaborate screen above the stage and the congregation clapped and danced along. Jubei admired their love for the Lord in their united fervor. Malcolm and Paty were also engrossed in the joy that filled the sanctuary. Matsumi tapped her foot and nodded her head a bit.

On cue, the congregation quieted and sat down when the song came to an end.

A hefty Hispanic lady took the stage and slow music began to play; the choir hummed softly. The singer delivered a powerful rendition of Amazing Grace; her voice was angelic and filled their hearts. Jubei leaned forward in his chair. Never before had he heard anything so beautiful. The words she sang sunk into him and it was as if they carved into Jubei's heart and extracted the darkness that had festered there for a long time. He teared up, overwhelmed by the Holy Spirit, more powerful than the ninja in him. He wiped tears from his chin, cheeks, and eyes. Megan glanced over and was moved by his tenderness.

A short bald Hispanic man came on the stage after the song was over. "Amen! Good morning church," he said, with a thick accent. "I am so glad to be here. Here are announcements of up and coming events…"

The announcement appeared on the jumbo screen as the man read them out.

Once the announcements were over, the choir sang His Eye Is On the Sparrow, while crackers were passed out.

When the plate reached Jubei, Malcolm directed him to take a piece of the cracker and then pass the plate on. Jubei helped himself to a piece of cracker and held onto it, looking around to make sure that no one ate his or her cracker.

Grape juice was passed around while the communion message was being preached. Jubei drank the juice and then ate the cracker.

Once the communion services were over, the pastor took the stage. For nearly an hour he spoke of letting go of the past and welcoming God into one's heart. Jubei carefully listened as his past crept up on him; his first lesson when he had turned eight years old; the torturous hours spent honing his skills to be a killer, being molded into a living weapon. Jubei was the most skilled ninja among the Tamuramaro. His kill average was well over a thousand, not including the lives he took during training. Jubei had killed his victims without remorse, emotion, or thought. He obeyed order without questioning them. Men, women, children, babies all fell to Jubei's sword. In this moment the pastor was preaching about grace and Jubei wondered whether the sermon would have differed if the pastor had been privy to every horrible act Jubei had committed. And then the pastor said something that startled Jubei. "I'm sorry, but I have to stop this sermon for a moment." The pastor glanced over the area Jubei and his family was seated. "One of you here today has committed heinous crimes. And God wants you to know that, even though you took those lives, he loves you unconditionally and wants to give you grace." After these words, the pastor resumed his sermon.

Jubei was dumbfounded. He needed to get out of there and motioned to stand up, but Paty wrapped her arm around his and Jubei sat back. Matsumi noticed the exchange. She knew her son well and could tell in his face that emotions stirred within him. He was feeling deeply, substance, essence, God, and love. Jubei was struggling to find harmony.

Despite the lively conversation on the car ride home, Jubei remained quiet, engrossed in the past, and yet the sermon echoed within.

Once home, Jubei got out of the car without saying a word to anyone and retreated to his house as Paty watched on.

"Uncle Malcolm, what's wrong with Jubei?" Marcus asked.

"*For the word of God is living and active, sharper than a double-edged sword, piercing until it divides soul and spirit, joints and marrow, as it judges the thoughts and purposes of the heart. -Hebrews 4:12.* Jubei was touched by the sermon and he's dealing with some things in his heart."

Matsumi bowed. "I enjoyed the church service very much. Arigato. I look forward to going again next week." She excused herself and went to the back house.

"Okay, kids." Malcolm said. "You got homework to do. Get to it."

Marcus chased Mara up the stairs.

Paty went to prepare lunch and Malcolm followed her to the kitchen.

"Got a minute?" Malcolm asked. Paty knew that tone. She sat at the kitchen table.

Her father continued. "What did I almost walk in on, before church, with you and Jubei?"

"I know what you're going to say," said Paty.

"I'm not saying anything. Just want to know what's going on. So, you two have feelings for each othe?."

Paty denied it.

Malcolm raised his eyebrows, as fathers have done since biblical times.

Paty knew she couldn't lie to him and she dropped her head in defeat. "Is it that obvious?" she asked.

"Yeah. And that's what has me worried." Malcolm reached across the table and took her small hand in his. "You know, I love Jubei like a son. He's like my right hand. But he's not evenly yoked with you, spiritually. As much as you love him, you can't be with him. You know that, right?"

"I know, Dad. I almost lost my head. Despite our differences in faith, I love him. But I do know that I have to keep my distance from him."

"I raised a smart woman."

Paty corrected him. "You raised a godly woman. Still, I can't help how I feel about him."

"I know that beneath all that pain he's a good man. And I know that if something was to happen, you would be protected."

Paty smiled. Her father stood to leave and she looked out the kitchen window. She saw Jubei sitting on the front porch and turned away.

A few hours later

Malcolm was enjoying popcorn in the den when someone knocked on the back door.

"Come in!" Malcolm yelled and Jubei entered.

"Hey. I fixed myself a big bowl of popcorn and am about to watch all six of the Star Wars films."

"What is Star Wars?" Jubei asked.

Malcolm looked dumbfounded. "Are you serious? Even headhunters of Borneo have heard of Star Wars. Oh, son. You got to sit here and get schooled on Star Wars."

"I'm just kidding you. I know Star Wars. I especially like Captain Kirk." Jubei laughed. "I'm kidding you again."

Malcolm laughed as well. "Didn't realize you had so many jokes, ninja. Then again, nothing surprises me about you anymore."

Jubei stood by the recliner while Malcolm finished programming the DVD player. He popped in the DVD and pressed a few buttons, but nothing happened. "I could never figure these things out," he said. He checked the back of the television. The RF cable jack was not connected. Once connected, they were ready to watch.

Marcus came down with his math homework. "I'm all done with my math, Uncle Malcolm."

"What kind of math are you doing, Marcus?" Jubei asked.

Marcus presented his math book to Jubei.

"Ah, yes. Beginning Algebra." Jubei took a moment to look over Marcus' homework. "Everything is correct. Good job."

Marcus closed his textbook and set it aside. "Can I play the Wii for a little bit?"

"Well, we were about to watch Star Wars."

"Cool!" Marcus plopped on the couch and helped himself to a handful of popcorn.

Malcolm looked at Jubei and nodded for Jubei to take a seat.

Jubei just stood there. "I need to speak to you," he said. "It's important."

"But Star Wars is about to begin," Malcolm whined, jokingly, but Jubei did not even crack a grin.

Malcolm put the movie on pause and gestured for Jubei to follow him into the living room.

"What's up?"

Jubei looked distractingly around the room. He was unsure as to how to start this conversation. He couldn't find his words. "I am not one to use many words," Jubei started. "But something about the sermon in church has affected me."

Malcolm took out two sodas from a small refrigerator and handed one to Jubei.

"How did it affect you?" he asked.

"In my life, growing up, I did not experience the type of feelings that I felt in church today, or in being a part of your family during these last few months. I believed in the clan, and I owed my loyalty and obedience to my father. There was no target I failed to kill, all in the name of my clan. I've been killing since I was eight years old and have kept killing since then. I still have an urge to kill. It's all I have known. But it is not all I want to know."

"What do you want to know, Jubei?"

"How I can have the peace in my soul that you do. I'm raging inside. And I want the rage to stop."

Malcolm nodded. He took a wooden box from the bookshelf and handed it to Jubei. He told him to open it. Inside was an old bible.

"All you need to find peace with yourself, and peace

with God, is in this book. In your training, do you have instructions?"

"Yes," said Jubei. "We have our basic principles, on eight-hundred year old scrolls. They are the foundation of ninjitsu, written by several ninja masters over the years, each contributing a different technique."

"Sort of like this bible here. It's an instruction manual as well. B.I.B.L.E. Basic Instructions Before Leaving Earth. This, Jubei, was my great grandfather's bible. He was a conductor on the underground rail road, and when he reached the north he became a preacher."

"So your lineage is of pastors?" Jubei asked.

"Heck no. My daddy was a plumber. I was a cop. This bible was passed down from father to son over a hundred and forty years. Now I want you to have it, my friend."

Jubei was stunned. "I cannot accept this."

"Yes, you can. I want you to have it."

Jubei gently took the bible from the case and opened the inside cover. *Property of Moses Wilkin-Wares, conductor of the under ground railroad 1863-1864.* On the bottom of the inscription were the names of slaves he helped bring to freedom. Jubei closed the book and placed it back in the box.

"This is a part of your family's history. It should stay within your family."

Malcolm pushed the box toward Jubei. "Jubei, you're family. You're my son. I want you to take it. Read Psalms and John. After you're done, we'll talk some more. I was convicted when I read them, and maybe you will be too."

Jubei accepted the box and bowed low. Malcolm returned the bow.

"I'm glad we had this talk," Jubei said. "Thank you."

"Hey. Since you're here, watch Star Wars with us."

"I cannot. I want to start reading this."

Dressed head-to-toe in black, Kenzin and Mishi got out of an SUV with tinted windows, armed with swords and assault rifles, and headed toward the quiet house down the street. When they were close enough, they split up, with Mishi going toward the main house and Kenzin toward the back house, where Jubei and Matsumi were.

In the main house, Paty was in the living room preparing lesson plans, Marcus watched television with Malcolm in the den while Mara was coloring at the coffee table. Suddenly, the house went dark. Mara asked what happened in a hushed voice.

Malcolm took the flashlight from the drawer and went to find the circuit breaker.

Mishi glided through the house like a ghost and crept up to the pastor. Quietly, she pulled out her sword and the pastor turned around. Mishi slashed him down the chest. Blood splattered across the wall. She brought the sword up and slashed him once more. Malcolm fell to his knees and Mishi ran the sword through his neck. Mishi heard the sound of footsteps and hid around the corner, in the hallway leading to the kitchen.

Marcus happened upon the bloody scene. Before he could scream, Mishi's sword went through the boy's head, impaling him to the wall. She pulled the sword out with some effort, his body hit the floor with a thump and she stood there looking at the boy for a moment before putting the dripping sword away. Then she snuck up on Paty in the living room and placed the assault rifle to her head. She pulled the trigger.

Mara's eyes were wild with horror. She scrambled to her feet and ran toward the window. Climbed out. As soon as her feet hit the ground, Mishi's bullets shot through another window, in the girl's direction, miraculously missing Mara as she sprinted towards the back house.

Jubei had heard the distant sound of glass shattering. His instinct kicked in and he dropped the bible, and in a matter of seconds he was at his closet, retrieved his sword and loaded up on throwing knives.

Matsumi had also heard the commotion and grabbed the spear she had hidden beneath the couch.

The front door burst open and she dove behind the couch just as Kenzin stormed in and began shooting. Matsumi was trapped. Kenzin was standing in the middle of the living room.

Matsumi grabbed onto the bottom of the couch and flipped it over, immediately kicking it across the floor. The couch clipped Kenzin and he fell.

With her spear in hand, Matsumi side kicked the gun from Kenzin's hand and with her other foot she kicked him in the chest. He staggered, regained his footing, and then pulled out his sword and went after Matsumi.

Jubei had heard the pandemonium on the ground level and was rushing down the stairs to help his mother when Mara's shrieking outside the window caught his attention and he leapt through the glass, rolled to his feet and headed toward Mara.

Mishi had climbed out the same window after Mara and now pursued the girl across the lot. Jubei was running toward Mara. Mishi stopped to better aim. Opened fire. Jubei simultaneously pushed Mara out of harm's way and deflected the bullets with his sword. Mishi kept on shooting. A bullet struck Jubei's hand and he dropped his sword. Another bullet ripped through his left shoulder. And then both his arms and his stomach were hit. He struggled to shout, "Mara, run!"

Kenzin swung his sword, brilliant controlled strikes that disarmed Matsumi. Then he side kicked her and sent her flying into the wall.

Kenzin's blade came at her she stumbled back to her feet and she swiftly stepped aside. Kenzin stabbed the wall. She leg swept him, quickly disarmed him and tossed his sword toward the back of the room.

Kenzin punched Matsumi's jaw. She returned the punch. Both back rolled to their feet, but Kenzin was faster and grabbed Matsumi by the neck, punched her repeatedly in the face, and then tossed her into the yard.

Mishi shot Mara in the leg and she dropped, screaming in agony. Mishi grabbed the girl by the hair, dragged her over to Jubei and said to him, "You're going to watch me blow her head off."

Jubei was holding his stomach and warm blood flowed between his fingers.

Matsumi shouted, "Jubei!"

Kenzin delivered a jaw-shattering blow to Matsumi's face and knocked her out. Mishi's gun was pointed at Mara's head. She pulled the trigger. Mara dropped heavily to the ground.

"Now, your mother," said Mishi.

In a burst of ninja super speed, Jubei sprang up and delivered a blow to Mishi's face, shattering her nose. He grabbed the assassin's head and snapped her neck, left and right.

Kenzin howled and kicked Jubei behind the knee. He picked up his sister's gun, and said between his teeth, "I've waited a lifetime for this, Jubei. And this is even better than I had dreamed. Before you die, you're going to watch me kill your mother." Kenzin pointed the gun at Matsumi and pulled the trigger.

"Jubei!" Matsumi shouted out. She felt a sharp pain in her left hip and shoulder. Her heart was pounding; she was disoriented and drenched in cold sweat. She propped herself up with some difficulty and looked around. Everything was in order. She had fallen from the couch in her sleep.

Jubei had heard his mother yell and rushed to her side. "What happened?" he asked her as he helped Matsumi up.

From the window, she could see the main house. The lights were on and Paty was outback, putting trash in the cans. It all appeared as expected. Paty returned inside.

"We have to leave here," Matsumi said firmly, and her son could not understand what his mother was talking about and tried to lead her to the couch so that she might be more comfortable, regain her composure.

"You know how ninja's operate. They will not stop and sooner or later they will descend on us. And Malcolm and his family, they will be caught in the middle. We cannot remain here any longer."

"No," Jubei said. "I will not leave them. They are family. These people are warm and compassionate and I love them. They love us and I will protect them with my life."

"I am fond of them as well. Our Malcolm is a better man than Ukyo will ever be, but you must understand that by leaving, we are protecting them."

"I won't run anymore."

Matsumi did not want to sit on the couch. She walked over to the coffee table. "Then, this must end, so that you no longer have to run." She picked up a paperweight and hurled it at her son's chest. He moved but the paperweight struck his shoulder and he grimaced with pain, glaring at his mother.

"In your poor condition, running is all you can do. The Jubei I knew, could dodge bullets, and even deflect them with his sword. This Jubei before me now, could barely dodge a paperweight."

He rubbed his shoulder and reminded her that barely six months ago he couldn't walk. "I'm getting stronger and faster by the day."

"Not fast enough. You've allowed yourself to become too soft. You cannot protect anyone in the state you're in right now."

Matsumi went to get an Icy/Hot therapeutic pack from the kitchen and applied it to Jubei's shoulder. "They're coming for us, my son. I've seen it in a dream. They are coming, and I think that deep down you know it."

"I'm not going to live looking over my shoulder every single day, as if it may be my last day on Earth. If the ninja do come, I will be ready."

"Will you?" Matsumi asked. She pressed Jubei's shoulder, just enough for him to feel it. He grunted. She smiled lovingly and kissed his cheek before starting up the stairs.

Jubei reapplied the Icy/Hot and thought about Matsumi's words. She had a point, as usual. He was not ready to take on anyone.

Matsumi stopped half way up and turned. "And what if you went to them?" she suggested.

Jubei was surprised by her words.

"The last thing Ukyo would expect would be for you to attack them. Besides, he is preoccupied with rebuilding the Yagyu right now. They are still in a weakened state. This would be the perfect time to strike them. If anyone can destroy the ninja once and for all, it is you, Jubei. And you could do it by challenging Ukyo to what is rightfully yours. I know you can defeat him, Jubei. Perhaps not in your present condition, but you will be able to defeat him. You know that it's the only way to keep this family safe."

Jubei put down the Icy/Hot pack. "What if it's not the only way?" he asked.

Matsumi came back down the stairs and put her hand against her son's face as she had done countless times before. "My son. My beloved boy, there's something in your heart that is changing. You're becoming the man I have always wanted you to be. But you won't be free to go through that transformation until Ukyo is defeated once and for all. And if you do nothing, I fear that the consequences will be dire. Everyone you love could be killed."

A long silence passed between mother and son. She patiently waited for him to say something.

He looked out toward the main house and saw a figure pass by the window. He sighed with relief. Paty was sitting on the back porch and he felt like he could watch her always. He suspected that she was taking a moment to herself so that she could pray.

Matsumi watched her son, and he watched Paty for a while. When she returned indoors, turned back to Matsumi. "You're right," he said. "No, one will be safe until Ukyo has been crushed."

"I hate what you have to do, but I promise this, it will be the last time you will ever have to kill anyone. Soon enough there will be no need for you to have blood on your hands."

"The thing about blood is that although it rinses off the skin, it drowns the heart."

Matsumi saw the agony in Jubei's eyes clearer than she had never seen it before and it pained her. She pulled him to her, like she used to when he was just a boy, and hugged him tightly. "Tomorrow we start your retraining," she whispered.

The following day

Jubei and Matsumi had driven an hour, outside of Clovis, to the rural village of Taiban, New Mexico. Which used to be a thriving town at the beginning of the twentieth century until a train derailed and nearly wiped out the town. It had not built up again since then. All that remained was a post office, a church, and a few scattered houses.

On the grounds of the old church, they got out of the car carrying silk wrapped objects. When they reached the trail that led from the church to a small grove of trees, Matsumi turned to Jubei and said sternly, "When you face Ukyo, your sword skills will need to be more honed than they have ever been."

Both kneeled and each unwrapped their Boken. Matsumi slowly pulled her wooden practice swords from its sheath, as did Jubei and they were ready for combat.

Jubei moved in on Matsumi and swung at her, but she was no longer standing there and had appeared behind him. She struck him on the back.

"You move like a crippled hippo," said Matsumi. "Clumsy."

Jubei sighed and retook his stance. Matsumi ran at him and flipped in the air. Jubei backflipped. Matsumi landed on the ground and swung her Boken behind her to deflect Jubei's attack. Then she spun around, dug her foot into the ground and kicked up dirt at his face. Jubei managed to block the dirt but, while he was distracted, Matsumi moved in.

"Distraction," Matsumi said as she struck Jubei in the chest, "can lead to death."

Jubei staggered.

Matsumi sprang forward with another attack. Jubei side stepped the attack. Matsumi had anticipated his move caught him with her heel. Jubei dropped to the ground and back rolled to his feet. He held the Boken in front of him.

Matsumi moved in. Jubei parried the attack. The clanking of the Bokens echoed through the grove, like the sound of clapping, whenever they clashed against each other.

Relentless, Matsumi did not let up on attacking. She came at Jubei from all sides, drawing from her uncanny ninja speed.

Jubei was able to defend against most of her attacks,

except for when she struck his face. Blood sprayed from his mouth. Matsumi jabbed him in the stomach and he doubled over. Matsumi struck him on the back and he hit the ground, face first.

Matsumi shook her head disapprovingly. "If I can defeat you, Ukyo will surely kill you."

Jubei got back to his feet and held out his Boken and said, "One more time."

"Do you need another beating?"

"You won't get another chance."

Mother and son ran at each other. The Bokens abruptly connected.

Jubei's swings were becoming more controlled and he was starting to overtake Matsumi. With a powerful swing Jubei shattered Matsumi's Boken. But she did not concede. Swiftly, she tossed tiny silver balls at him and they released a jolt of electricity, disarming Jubei. Matsumi picked up Jubei's Boken, pointed it at him and swung. However, he had pivoted to the side just as the Boken went past him.

He threw a leg sweep, but Matsumi flipped out of the fall and landed on her feet. Jubei caught the Boken in the air. Matsumi did a back handspring and knocked the Boken from his hand. Both leaped to catch it, Matsumi with a flying side kick. She grabbed the Boken and came back down with a slash, as he rolled away. Barely missing him, she struck the ground where he had been. He sprang to his feet with hyper speed.

Matsumi came at him. He dodged to the left, then to the right, evading her attack.

"That's it," Matsumi said, to encourage him.

Jubei swung around a tree with a pole-like trunk and kicked the Boken out of Matsumi's hand. Matsumi did a dive roll and took hold of the Boken again.

He picked up a hard stick from the ground and used

it as his Boken. Mother and son continued to fight it out. Matsumi ducked a head swing and then Jubei brought the stick down on her head, stopping just about an inch over her head. He appeared pleased with himself. Matsumi directed Jubei to look down. Her Boken was between his legs. Jubei dropped the stick.

They bowed to one another.

"Jubei, you have a lot of work ahead of you. Your mind is clouded and you know well that you will need absolute clarity to destroy Ukyo."

Jubei dropped his head.

Matsumi wrapped her Boken in silk again. When she looked up, she saw uncertainty in her son's eyes. "What's wrong?" she asked.

"I don't know if I am the killer I used to be."

Matsumi gently placed her hand on Jubei's shoulder. "What is it, that Americans say? Oh, yes. It is just like robbing a bike."

"Riding a bike," he corrected. "Not robbing a bike."

They laughed.

Matsumi composed herself quickly. This was no time for amusement. "I cannot press you to go through with this. It might not even be necessary to kill him…"

Jubei interjected, "No. You're right. Ukyo will not stop until everyone is dead. I must end this. The killer is within me and he will return. And when he does, blood will flow."

Matsumi smiled lovingly at him, as they put their silk-wrapped wooden swords back in the car.

An hour later

Jubei and Matsumi pulled into the driveway.

The children were out playing while Paty was working in the garden.

Matsumi went inside to take a nap.

Paty waved at Jubei, put down her gardening tools, and started heading towards him. She was stunned that Jubei turned from her without even acknowledging her. He got back in the car, turned the ignition and drove away.

Jubei trained for hours in Ned Houk Park, outside of Clovis, where he could be by himself. He practiced running up trees and balancing across thin wire among several other acrobatic feats. Time slipped by and he kept practicing with the same intensity. His mother was right. It was like riding a bike. Advanced ninja skills were coming back to him, improving with every move.

The sky was pitch black when Jubei entered the house, rubbing soreness from his shoulder.

Matsumi and Paty enjoyed a chat and tea in the living room. The women noticed Jubei. Paty smiled but Jubei only nodded and went up the stairs. Paty was baffled. Wide eyed, she looked at Matsumi who merely shrugged.

The next day

Jubei was balancing on the rafters, in the barn, leaping from one beam to another. His backflips were unerring, much like those of a seasoned gymnast. He leaped from the beam to the ground, he ran up a wall, from which he sprang and landed on his feet.

He broke off the prongs of an old pitchfork so that he could use it as a staff. He twirled it with methodical control and accuracy. He was profoundly concentrating on the staff training and did not notice Paty enter the barn.

With his hands leaning on the staff for support, Jubei went into a handstand and then pushed off the ground and twisted around for a faultless cyclone kick. He landed back on his hands and repeated the cyclone kick. He flipped over and landed on his feet; twirled the staff around him once more and then brought it in front of him. He exhaled deeply as he put the staff down and when he turned around, Paty was standing there.

"I thought I'd find you here," she said. "Can we talk?"

"I'm training right now." Jubei was about to return to his training but Paty took hold of his arm.

"You walked in last night and didn't even say hello," she said. "Are you avoiding me?"

"I've been busy training."

"It's more than that. I haven't seen much of you at all since we came home from church. I think you're been avoiding all of us lately."

"No. Just you," Jubei said as he walked away. He did not see the pain and anguish his words had inflicted upon Paty. For a moment she was stunned, unable to form a coherent thought, aware only of the profoundness of her heartache. When she snapped back to her sense, she hurried to catch up with Jubei and grabbed him by the shoulder; turned him so that he had to face her.

"Why?" she asked in a whisper.

Jubei stepped back. "Because of the way I feel about you. We come from different worlds. I understand that, and I cannot afford to have such feelings for you, feelings that cannot be nurtured, feelings without an outlet."

"Yes, we do come from different worlds, but that doesn't mean that you have to avoid me."

"What then?"

She shrugged. She did not know.

"How do you feel about me?" he asked.

Paty just stood there, unprepared for this moment. A tear ran down her cheek.

Jubei's voice softened. "Paty, I will always be here for you."

"I know that. If only things were different…"

"But they are not. And I don't know that they ever will be."

Paty wiped her eyes and peered intently into his, as though it was the last time they would meet. This look of his she had not seen since the revival. And he was training. Avoiding everyone for the last five days. "Jubei, what are you planning?" she asked. "All week you've trained all day and late into the evening. Why?"

"It's best that you don't know." He tried to walk around her but she sidestepped.

"No." she said. "Something's definitiely going on. You better tell me. And don't you dare lie to me."

"I would never lie to you."

Paty pleaded with him. "No lies. No secrets. I know that look in your eyes. You're going to go after someone, aren't you?"

Again, Jubei moved away and again she blocked his path. She grabbed his arm. She would not allow him leave this barn without giving her an answer. Her face was twisted with worry and her voice, broken. In her eyes he saw the depth of her distress, of her love. Her love for him, his love for her, together they dispelled his stifling apprehension. Jubei took a deep breath and asked, "Do you trust me?"

"With my life."

Jubei reached towards her as if he meant to touch her face. Instead he placed it on her shoulder. "Let me explain my world. In my world, there is no rest or peace. In my world, the enemy does not renounce. It will keep coming, and coming, until its mission is fulfilled. I can say this with conviction, for I have been the enemy."

"You're going after your old clan? You're going to kill them?"

Silently, Jubei acquiesced.

"Is there no other way?" Paty asked.

"It must be done or they will be coming for us. I must bringing the fight to them before they come to us."

"But we're safe here, Jubei." Her words were confident but her tone gave her away. She felt afraid.

Jubei continued as though she had not said anything. "There was once a Tamuramaro ninja that had deserted the clan and had started a new life. No other deserter has lasted as long as he had. For ten years, ten years evaded the clan, and then I killed him."

Paty felt as though she couldn't breathe, horrified by what Jubei had told her, by what he had done. To hear it from his own mouth was almost unbearable. "After ten years?"

"Like I said, it doesn't matter how much time goes by. They will not stop. Paty, I do not want to leave you. This is my home. You are my home." Jubei caressed the side of her smooth face. "I will not allow anything to happen to you." He gingerly placed his hand over her heart like a parting kiss and then he left her alone with her thoughts, with his words.

Jubei returned to his room and read his bible by the window. He did not see her cry as she walked back to the house.

For the next two weeks, Jubei continued to read the bible beyond the books Malcolm had recommended, all the while continuing to train and hone his skills as a killer. He became faster, more powerful. Daily matches with Matsumi improved his swordsmanship. And still he went to church

Jubei did his best to avoid the pastor and his family. He trained in isolation, somewhere outside of Clovis. Only in the evenings did he go home to dine with them.

Two weeks later

As Jubei put his bag in the trunk of the car, Matsumi said, "Arrangements have been made. You will have what you need when you get there."

She hugged him tightly and whispered into his ear, "You are ready. Defeat Ukyo. All that is wrong shall end with him."

She noticed Malcolm approach, said her goodbyes and then returned the house.

"I knew you would come sooner or later," Jubei said. "You can't talk me out of this."

The pastor shook his head. "By now, I know that once you get something into your head, trying to change your mind is pointless. But it doesn't mean I can't try. Don't do this, my friend."

"I have to," Jubei said. He shut the trunk.

Malcolm grabbed Jubei's shoulders. "No! You don't have to. By going off on your own, you're taking control away from God. Believe me, the last thing he wants is for you to kill."

Jubei pulled away. "Let God tell me so himself." Jubei looked upwards. The sky was clear. "Speak!" he yelled. He paused and made as if he were waiting for a response, and then he looked triumphantly at the pastor.

"The Lord has steadily been changing your heart, and still you put him in a box. Don't do this. If they come for us, they come for us. Let it alone and know that it's in God's hands."

Jubei smirked. "How do you know God isn't working through me to end this nightmare?" he asked, without expecting an answer.

Malcolm sighed deeply. He leaned against the car with his hands folded in front of him.

Jubei's brow softened, as did his tone. "It has to end, and I must do all that I can to ensure that it does."

Malcolm dropped his head. He appeared disheartened.

"No matter how often I explain this to you, you just don't get it," Jubei said sadly. "There will not be a threat. When the time comes, and it will, death will fall upon this family before you even know what is happening. But they will come. *That* is certain. So what I have to do now is take out my father and this looming death sentence will end." Jubei got in the car.

"Jubei. Jubei, listen, please. Do not lose yourself. Do not lose the person you have become. The killer is no longer who you are."

Jubei shut his door. The engine turned and Malcolm began to pray.

Paty stood at her bedroom window and teared up as Jubei drove off, leaving the pastor in the dust. The car turned the corner and was gone.

Chapter Thirteen:

Mercy

Two days later

When Jubei came out of the baggage claim area at Tokyo Narita International Airport, a man with dark sunglasses greeted him and handed him a sheet of paper before turning and walking away. Jubei put the paper in his bag and then went to the Hertz counter where he rented a car to drive out to the country, about four hours outside of Tokyo.

The small lodge was located in the forest and had a breathtaking view of Mount Fuji. Jubei did not take the time to make himself comfortable as soon as he entered the lodge, and opened his bag from which he pulled out a map and a few photographs of the Yagyu compound, which he set aside. He sat at an old wooden desk and studied the blueprints to the palace. Once comfortable that he had memorized the crucial details, he set them aside and opened the map. It represented the area surrounding the lodge. Jubei folded it back up and took it along on a four miles hike into the wilderness, referring to it until he located another isolated log cabin.

This one was empty of ornamental objects and furnished with basic furniture and useful tools. On the stove he found a kettle with steaming hot tea. He poured himself a cup and settled at the table, upon which there was a plate of food that looked as though it has been recently plated. He had begun eating when he footsteps outside, approaching the cabin. The door swung open and a woman walked in, carrying firewood in her arms. She did not notice anyone else was there, for Jubei moved like a shadow over the old wooden floor that did not creak beneath his light footsteps.

Jubei snuck on the woman from behind, as she was putting down the logs by the fireplace. He grabbed her around the chest with one arm, simultaneously muffling her scream with the other. He held her like this until she realized her struggling was in vain. The person holding her had the upper hand and she knew it. Her breathing was still heavy but she stopped trying to get away.

Jubei released the woman and she turned to face him. He was surprised and did not conceal his astonishment. "I know you," he said in a faraway voice.

The woman stepped back. "A few years ago, you kept a promise to my husband to help me and my daughter. Your mother had told you arrangements have been made."

The woman leaned over to the fireplace and opened a secret compartment from which she dragged out a case and left it at Jubei's feet.

"Our arrangement has concluded," she said. She left the cabin.

Jubei picked up the heavy case, placed it on the table and opened it. In it he found an assortment of ninja weapons: a collapsible high powered bow and a quiver of arrows; several

Shuriken knives; smoke bombs; grenades; spring-loaded wrist blades, a Katana sword; a ninja uniform.

Jubei picked up the sword and removed it from its sheath. The blade glistened in the candlelight. Jubei held the sword out and tested it for balance. In one powerful swing he cut a wooden chair in half. Grinning with satisfaction, he sheathed the sword and began to prepare for his mission.

Later that night

A shadow gracefully slid through the wilderness with grace and utter silence. Soon enough he could make out lights, piercing the darkness: the Yagyu compound. Jubei stopped short. It looked like an easy shot to reach it. He pulled out a sensor and activated that the thermal imaging, which revealed camouflaged ninja guards.

Jubei hurled several heat-seeking silver orbs that zigzagged through the trees and found their marks with ease, exploding upon contact, releasing a potent sleeping gas that knocked out the ninjas before they could reach for their weapons.

Jubei performed another scan before continuing. Satisfied that the way was clear, he followed the trail till he came upon a long suspension bridge that crossed a deep gorge, which appeared abysmal in the night. Ninjas on guard duty flanked both ends of the bridge.

Jubei crawled on the cool ground, creeping up on them like a snake in the grass. He sprang up and split kicked the ninjas, knocking them out cold. He stripped them of their weapons and uniform; tied them naked to the pole.

Jubei crawled beneath the bridge and startled the ninjas on the other end, handling them as he did the others.

Jubei cut the ropes to the suspension bridge and then kept proceeded through the night, toward the well-lit palace, evading and or taking out the perimeter guards with uncanny ease.

All of a sudden, a net fell upon him. He had tripped a net trap. Ninjas sprang from the darkness and began stabbing at the net before they realized that it was empty. They fanned out in search of the intruder.

Jubei appeared in the exact location that they had cut the net.

The ninjas drew their swords and charged him all at once but Jubei timed his maneuver perfectly and sprang into the air as they merged and impaled one another.

Jubei moved on, getting closer to the palace, the lights of Yagyu village becoming brighter as he advanced. When he was close enough, he climbed a tree and with night vision goggles to overlook the village that was bustling with people and activity. A celebration was taking place. Kabuki actors performed in the village square.

He would have to go through the village to reach the palace. It was the only way to get there.

A no man's land surrounded the village, stretching all the way up to the palace. Not a single guard was posted in this area, which in itself revealed to Jubei that it was peppered with landmines.

Jubei located the guard towers, climbed higher and shot a zip-line to the guard tower. He slid across and disarmed the guard on duty. He knocked the man out.

Then Jubei zipped to the other tower and positioned himself.

The palace gates allowed a black limousine through. It proceeded slowly up the lantern-lit driveway, and into the courtyard where handmaidens in kimonos greeted its passengers; men in business suits. Yakuza bosses.

The imposing men and their bodyguards were escorted to a holding area. All of them were searched thoroughly before being granted entry to the dining room were masked clowns and pretty dancers performed for the Yagyu counsel seated at the table. The yakuza were shown their seats, near the head of the table.

The music stopped. Two solid gold doors opened for Kenzin and Mishi. Ukyo followed. When the latter entered, every person in the room bowed and kept their heads bowed until he was seated.

The servers made their way around the long table with tray after tray of delightful hors d'œuvres.

"It's an honor to have been invited to your compound," said boss Usagi. "However, I must admit, we are curious as to the reason you have extended this invitation."

Ukyo helped himself to a brochette of grilled shrimp. He plucked a shrimp off the stick and put it in his mouth. Chewed slowly, all the while staring at boss Usagi.

"So, you wish to skip the pleasantries and go straight to business? Good. Let's cut to the chase, as Americans would say."

A collective chuckle erupted around the table. As soon as it died down, boss Yokoma leaned toward Ukyo and asked, "What is it that you want, Ukyo-san?"

"It is not so much about what I want, but what you will want."

The guest exchanged puzzled looks.

Ukyo nodded at Kenzin and Kenzin reached into his single-breasted jacket and from it he pulled out a large brown envelope and placed it on the table, in front of boss Usagi who promptly opened it. The photographs he lay out on the table were of dismembered bodies. Disfigured faces. Blood splattered walls. The guests were uneasy.

"Men? Women? Children? It's hard to tell, I know," said Ukyo. "As you can all see, we do not have qualms about eliminating anybody," Ukyo said. "And we do it better than anyone else in the world. What you see on these pictures is a modest example of the services we provide."

Hefty boss Sato asked Ukyo for the reason he was showing them these gory pictures.

Like a salesman, Kenzin continued Ukyo's macabre pitch. "For a nominal fee we can eliminate your enemies. Every single one of them. But we do ask for the exclusive rights to contract assassinations."

"We don't need to hire out. We have our own."

Kenzin was about to speak but Ukyo stopped him.

Mishi stared coldly at the bosses. Beneath the table she was playing with her knife. She was itching to put it to use.

Ukyo gestured a servant across the room. Remotely the man lowered a screen from the ceiling and started a video that displayed, one yakuza boss' family after another, at school, in their homes. Anger and outrage erupted at the table and the bodyguards, which had thus stood at a respectful distance, stepped toward their bosses, but before they could reach them, ninja guards closed in, seemingly out of nowhere, and held knives to the bodyguards' thick throats.

"It is nearly effortless for us to get to your families," Ukyo said. "Your security is ineffective against us. These photographs are of the remains of your assassins."

"How dare you threaten us?" one boss shouted. Other chimed in.

Ukyo remained calm. Grinned. "I never issue threats. And this should not be taken as one. This is merely a demonstration of our abilities."

Boss Usagi asked, "What happens if we refuse?"

"Well, we finish our dinner and then send you on your way, with no hard feelings."

Boss Sato snapped, "You are not as effective as you think, Ukyo-san. We are well aware of the betrayal amongst your clan. One of your own has gone rogue and you have failed in your many efforts to eliminate him. And this traitor, it's your own son, isn't it?"

Ukyo gestured to another servant who spoke into a walkie-talkie.

A live video started on the screen and on it several Yagyu ninja brutally murdered members of boss Sato's entire family, one by one.

At the table, jaws dropped, eyes widened in shock and horror.

Ukyo interrupted the dumfounded silence and said, "You are responsible for having your entire family killed." He signaled Mishi and she hurled her knife, hitting boss Sato between the eyes. He slumped forward and his blood spilled into his plate.

A couple of servants hurriedly removed the corpse from the dining room, leaving a trail of Sato's blood.

"Do any other critics want to share their opinion?"

The other bosses remained quiet.

Ukyo smiled. "If you graciously decline my offer, then our business is concluded. But I guarantee, you will not regret our services." He clapped his hands and said jovially, "Very well then, let us eat."

The yakuza bosses momentarily conferred amongst themselves, and then boss Usagi nodded at Ukyo. Ukyo was pleased. Discretely he dismissed the hidden ninjas that had been standing by.

All lifted a glass of sake and drank to the new partnership between the yakuza and the ninja.

Jubei zipped to the last guard tower overlooking the courtyard from where he used his binoculars to search for Ukyo. Jubei located the dining room window. Ukyo, Kenzin, and Mishi were in his sight. He meticulously assembled a high-powered bow and screwed specialized arrow tips into the shafts. He positioned an arrow on the bow and pulled the string back. Jubei looked through a special targeting system installed on the side of the bow and aimed for Ukyo's heart. Instead of shooting, he then aimed for the wall above the dining room window and released the arrow, which split into three separate arrows in mid-air and each one struck the wall in three separate points that lined up horizontally. Jubei was satisfied with his shot. He positioned another arrow and drew the bow, with Ukyo, Kenzin and Mishi in sight.

As he held the bowstring back, he could feel the tightness of the string. He had just killed dozens on his way here and now he had but a few more to kill. He was sweating and his heart was pounding. It was unlike him and he tried to concentrate. And simply in trying, he realized that he did not use to hesitate to kill, but that was before the sermon, the friends he had made, the woman he had fallen for, and knew that she loved him as well. He put the bow down and rubbed his face, took a deep breath, and picked up the bow, held the string back again. All he had to do now was release the arrow and it would all be over. Ukyo, Kenzin, and Mishi would be dead.

"End this," Jubei murmured to himself. Had this taken place a few months ago, the job would have been done.

"Jubei?" a soft voice called.

Jubei turned and saw Maki, the last person he had killed with a bow. His beloved. He had killed her. She was dead. She could not be there with him. Jubei turned back toward the palace and aimed at Ukyo. Maki walked in front of Jubei's line of sight and knelt down; gingerly touched his face.

"You killed us with this bow, Jubei," Maki said. "Hanzo and I, you killed us, my love. And you killed us both without even hesitating. But now you hesitate to kill the man who is ultimately responsible for my death, for my little brother's death, and for the hell that has been your life. You are hesitating now because you have been touched by something more powerful than the venom that Ukyo has been instilling in you since you were a boy."

Jubei put the bow down and looked into the dark eyes of the one he had loved and killed long ago, Maki. Still as young and beautiful as he remembered she had been. He had killed her and yet here she was, speaking to him with the same affection in her voice.

"Today you are filled with unselfish love, Jubei. True love. I recognize it because it is the way I loved you. I see that you are no longer the same man who killed me and all those I loved. In your heart you know what you want. Let go of this bitter life you have led and know that you can let go of me as well. I forgive the man you are today."

Jubei felt that Maki was no longer with him although the idea of her was clear, and her words, they rang true. He no longer was the ninja Ukyo had filled with rancor. He took the bow apart and readied to make his escape. He climbed to the outside of the guard tower and to the guard tower roof, from which he leaped off and pressed a button that propelled a glider from his back. Jubei glided over the palace, descending into the woods. Jubei released himself as he approached the treetops, leaped, and flipped from branch to branch. He landed gracefully on solid ground and proceeded to escape undetected.

A ninja patrol reported a breach to Ukyo and, in his rage, Ukyo flipped over the dinner table. The alarm was raised and the entire Yagyu clan went on high alert, but by the time this news had reached Ukyo, Jubei was long gone.

Patrols searched the area. Half naked ninja guards tied to the posts of the suspension bridge were the only trace left of Jubei's presence.

Ukyo summoned Kenzin and Mishi to his chambers at

which time a ninja presented Ukyo with the arrow discovered above the dining room window. Ukyo grabbed it from the ninja's hand and shouted, "Jubei was here!"

Mishi pointed out that it could have been shot by any ninja and before she knew it, Ukyo back fisted her and she fell over the desk.

"Only Jubei would miss on purpose," Ukyo said between clenched teeth. "This is a warning." He turned his attention to Kenzin. "Well, now that we know he is alive, let's finish it."

"Why would he spare you?" Kenzin asked.

"The reason does not matter. What matters is that he won't live to regret it."

Mishi picked herself up and knelt before Ukyo, begging for forgiveness as blood trickled down the side of her mouth. She did not dare wipe it away.

Kenzin suggested that they use the arrow to identify his contact. Ukyo agreed and dismissed Mishi and Kenzin so that they could begin their search for Jubei. It would not be easy.

Before the sibling shut the doors behind them, they heard Ukyo's final warning:

"If you fail..." Ukyo left it at that.

Jubei was back at the second lodge. He removed the ninja uniform and placed the weapons and supplies back in the case, doused it with oil and lit it up. He stood there until it had all burned beyond recognition. "My old self is dead. Gone." He felt lighthearted. Smiled.

Two days later

It was a warm on Sunday afternoon on the front porch, after church, when Malcolm, wearing a bright yellow apron, was laying out several sausages and patties of ground beef on the grill. Marcus and Mara were playing freeze tag with some of their friends from church.

Indoors, Matsumi was making a cucumber sesame salad while Paty prepared potato salad, from an old family recipe. From the kitchen window Paty saw Jubei pull into the driveway and she rushed out the back door to meet him.

Malcolm handed the cooking tools to a man standing nearby and ran around back.

Jubei got out of the car. Paty was about to reach for him but hesitated. Malcolm stopped beside her. They starred at Jubei with anticipation; all remained in quiet for a little while. You could hear the children squeal with delight.

Finally, Jubei said, "It's over. I'm done." He took his bag and went inside. Paty wanted to follow, but her father held her back. In his face Paty saw that he needed to talk to Jubei first. She watched her father follow Jubei inside.

"So, it's finished?" Malcolm asked.

Jubei nodded.

Malcolm looked disappointed. Sad. Jubei's nonchalance disturbed the pastor. The changes Jubei had undergone, his progress, all in vain. A killer void of emotion was all that Malcolm could see now—a damned man. Malcolm could not stand to look at the one he had once called *friend*, and began to walk away from Jubei. He reached for the door.

"I didn't kill him," Jubei said.

Malcolm turned, stunned. "What?"

"I did not kill him, though easily I could have. I had an arrow pointed at his heart, but I couldn't go through with it. I no longer am *that man*. I do not want to be *that man*."

Upon seeing Malcolm smile from ear to ear, Jubei smiled as well.

"Well, my friend. What kind of man do you want to be?"

"I want to be a godly man, like you. I tried living my way for long enough, covered in the blood of my victims. Now I want to live God's way."

Malcolm shouted, "Amen!" He grabbed Jubei and hugged him tight. From the window he could see Paty, eagerly waiting for her turn to see Jubei.

When Malcolm left, he put his hand on Paty's shoulder as he passed her by, but he said nothing. Just smiled.

Paty went in. Her first impulse was to run into Jubei's arm. Instead, she kept her distance, longing to feel him hold her, embrace her, but she controlled herself. She smiled awkwardly. "I'm glad you made it home," she said. "Are we finally safe?"

Jubei nodded and Paty shook her head. She could hardly look into his eyes.

"I didn't kill anyone," Jubei said.

"But you said it was over. I thought it meant you killed him."

"I almost did, but chose not to."

Paty threw her arms around Jubei, rested her head on his broad shoulders.

"The last time I saw you, you had a scary look in your eyes. I thought you would surely kill your father. So what changed?"

"I changed."

Jubei noticed his mother standing in the doorway. From the look on their faces, Paty knew Matsumi and Jubei needed a moment to themselves. She politely excused herself and closed the door behind her.

"Did you succeed in your mission?"

"Mother, I chose to fail."

Matsumi sighed deeply warned him of the probable repercussions resulting from his irresponsible choice.

"I know. And when the time comes, I will deal with them."

"Do not make light of this. You know well what Ukyo is capable of. You should have killed him."

Unwaveringly, Jubei said, "I did the right thing."

Matsumi put her hand around Jubei's waist. "I had a feeling you would not kill him. Your heart, it was not in the training."

"So, what should I do now?" Jubei asked.

"Live your life, Jubei. Live, laugh…" Matsumi pointed out the window, "love." She put her hand over Jubei's mouth before he could deny it. "Your eyes expose your deepest feelings. You are in love with Paty."

Jubei nodded reluctantly, and yet he seemed relieved to no longer have to withhold this truth from h is mother. "I do, love her, but it's complicated."

"It's only complicated if you want it to be. My dear son, this lovely girl is obviously in love with you as well."

Jubei looked out toward the big house.

"How much does she know about your life?" Matsumi asked.

"I haven't said much about it."

There was a knock at the door. Malcolm peeked in. "Y'all come and eat," he said. "We got fried chicken, ribs, macaroni and cheese, and loads of other deliciousness."

"Ah," Matsumi exclaimed. "Soul food."

Malcolm laughed. "We got lots of that."

"And watermelon?" Matsumi asked.

"This is a black and Puerto Rican household. We also got Goya…"

The three of them shared a good laugh. Malcolm threw his arm around Jubei and in turn Jubei put his arm around Malcolm.

"You don't smile often, Jubei," Malcolm said. "But when you do, you smile big, and I like that."

Matsumi followed them out the door and together they walked to the front yard of the main house.

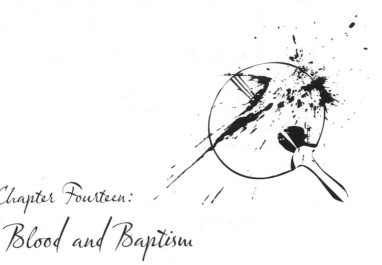

Chapter Fourteen:
Blood and Baptism

Kenzin inspected the computer for clues that might lead him to Jubei. The door to his office swung open and in walked his sister, Mishi, dragging in an old balding man who had a scar where his left eye used to be. Mishi released the man and he slumped to the ground. She kicked him in the side.

"This is the piece of trash who supplied Jubei with custom-made weapons for his mission outside the clan."

Kenzin lifted the man up and strapped him to a chair. Mishi set a knife aside, where the man could see it.

"How did you get in touch with Jubei?" Kenzin asked. The man did not answer. Kenzin grabbed a syringe filled with a truth serum that his sister had concocted from a mixture of herbs and secret ingredients, she would not disclose to him. Kenzin stuck the needle into the man's deeply wrinkled neck and pressed the plunger. The brown liquid burned as it coursed through the man's veins. He tensed up, the tendons in his neck stuck out and he suddenly began to convulse. Fainted.

Mishi placed smelling salt beneath the man's nose and

slowly he regained consciousness but he could barely hold his head up. Mishi checked his eyes, which were glazed over. She nodded to her brother and still twirling the knife in his hand, he pulled up a chair and sat face to face with the old man. "How did you get in touch with Jubei?" asked Kenzin.

The old man couldn't raise his head. "I did not speak to Jubei," he said in a faraway voice. "I made arrangements, through a woman, for her to make the necessary weapons available to Jubei, once he arrived to a designated location."

"Who is this woman?" Kenzin asked, as he raked the knife across the man's withered face.

"I don't know." The old man said slowly.

Kenzin and Mishi exchanged looks.

The man continued. "He uses different sources to contact me."

"Does anyone besides Jubei have this sort of arrangement with you?" asked Mishi.

The old man nodded lazily. "Matsumi. She contacted me."

Kenzin scoffed. "Matsumi? She is dead. Burned alive for treachery. I saw her burn, like the witch that she was."

The old man coughed. "No. It was not Matsumi who made contact with me. It was a young girl. An attractive girl." He cleared his throat. "It's like I said. Jubei uses different proxies to contact me. Then he performs saimain jutsu to erase their memory or he kills them to eliminate any potential witnesses. In all the years that I've been making weapons for Jubei, I have only met him once."

"How did you make contact with this woman?" Mishi asked.

"From a computer. But after we established contact, I destroyed the laptop so that it could not be traced."

"And when did she contact you?"

"Six weeks ago. On May 9th. She was specific about the

required weapons and supplies, as well as to the location where I had to deliver the goods. This is truly all I know."

Kenzin took the knife to the old man's throat. "Too bad for you."

Mishi stopped him. "He told us everything he could. We have no more use for him so just let him go."

Kenzin reluctantly agreed and Mishi removed the old man's restraints.

"You're free to go," Kenzin said.

Mishi helped the man out and led him to the street and told him to run before her brother changes his mind. She watched as the old man stumbled away as fast as his uncoordinated feet could take him. Kenzin came up behind her and said, "Should have killed him."

"There is a chance Jubei may contact him again."

"There's no guarantee that this will work. We're taking an awfully big risk, Mishi."

She took her brother's hand in hers. "Relax. This is going to work."

Later that night

Panicked, the old man returned to his apartment and rummaged desperately through his belongings until he located a tiny one touch I-phone. He accessed his email, and as soon as he sent out a warning, a bullet struck his forehead.

Kenzin holstered the gun and pulled the small computer from the dead man's grip. He took out a pocket-sized computer, connected both computers, via a USB, uploaded the information on the man computer and then began to track the IP address. In conjunction with a beeping sound, a green screen confirmed that he had successfully tracked the IP address to a computer in Tokyo. Kenzin transmitted these coordinates to Mishi.

Mishi followed the coordinates to an Internet café and found a teenager chatting online on the computer that was the source she had been tracking. Mishi yanked the girl from the computer and she fell to the floor, got back to her feet and ran off to find help. Mishi had to type fast, before the police would respond. She disconnected the computer and an attendant approached, yelling for her to stop. Mishi stood and walked away, ignoring the attendant, exited the café and headed to her car.

The policemen arrived and questioned the attendant. She pointed at Mishi, who was crossing the street. The policemen hurried to catch up with her. One officer grabbed Mishi's arm. She twisted around and broke the man's wrist. Kicked him in chest. The other officer pulled out his nightstick. Mishi spun around and kicked it out his hand and then roundhouse kicked his face. Nearby officers witnessed the altercation and came running, moving in on Mishi all at once. She ducked a nightstick. Another swung towards her ribcage but she sidestepped the attack. A nightstick cracked over her back and she yelped, pivoted left and kicked out one man's kneecap. Mishi disarmed the fallen man and with his nightstick she smashed his partner's head. She kneeled and took out another officer's legs, then she backflipped over a charging officer and onto the roof of her car. Police cars swarmed in with their sirens blaring. Mishi smiled, jumped off the car and with a flying side kick she struck policeman's chin and he stumbled into a wall. A couple officers with taser wands moved in from either side of Mishi. She easily dodged them and acrobatically evaded their attacks, as if taunting them. She disarmed them both and took them down with their own weapons.

Backup police officers were armed with guns.

Mishi released a grappling hook, which whisked her into the air and she landed on the roof. She pulled out her cell phone, pressed speed dial, and as she ran across the roof she said into the receiver, "Come get me." She jumped from one roof to the other and located a dumpster in the alley onto which she leaped and from which she flipped off, landing steadily on her feet.

A police car turned down the alley and accelerated towards Mishi as she began running toward it. She leaped over it and continued to run towards the street.

A second police car turned down the alley. Mishi jumped up and grabbed onto a fire escape. She lifted herself up and climbed a few levels and then kicked in a window, crawled in. A stunned family starred at her wide-eyed, quiet at their dinner table with forks and knives in hand, unchewed food in their mouth half-open. Mishi hopped onto the table and as she ran across it she knocked off rice dishes and ceramic soup bowls. She headed for the front door and kicked through it and through the neighboring door.

She climbed out the window, grabbed onto fire escape railing and headed back down to the street. Kenzin pulled up beneath the railing. Mishi hopped onto the roof of his car, then the street, and leaped into the passenger seat through the lowered window.

Kenzin sped off, turned a corner, then another, and pulled into a dark, vacant parking lot.

Mishi tried to catch her breath. Panting, she said, "In know we saw Matsumi die, burned at the stake, but listen to me. What if it *that* Matsumi was not *the* Matsumi?"

"I know she is a ninja master. Virtually incomparable in poisons and disguises, but trust me, Mishi, she is dead. Dead."

"What if I'm right, and she's still out there."

"Then, we have a big problem."

Mishi giggled. "Oh, I do love big problems. I get tremendous satisfaction when they get solved."

"Let's go back to that café and see. But this time, I'll take care of it," Kenzin said.

2 a.m.

Kenzin watched from an adjacent rooftop as the last patron exited the café. The attendant pulled down the metal screen in front of the door. Even at this late hour, people were coming out of the nearby clubs.

Kenzin sprang onto the rooftop, rolled onto his feet, all the while keeping his eye on the attendant.

The attendant was putting his keys in his pocket when suddenly he was whisked upwards, pulled onto the roof and placed in a sleeper hold until he passed out.

Kenzin grabbed the attendant's set of keys and jumped down into the alley, sneaking around to the front. He unlocked the door. Once inside, Kenzin began to sift through the sign-in logs and surveillance tapes. He located the one for May 9th and played it, section that focused on the computer Mishi had tracked the IP address to.

Throughout that day, men and women of all ages used that particular computer. Kenzin weeded out most of the women on the surveillance tape, but, around closing time, when only three people were left in the café, a final customer walked in, a beautiful woman with straight black hair, young enough to be a college student. She wore copper rimmed glasses and on her neck you could make out the tattoo that symbolized the Tamuramaro clan.

Kenzin zoomed in on the computer screen and checked the time and date stamp, which he checked against the payment records and established the girl's name and address by tracing the debit card she had used. Once the information had been gathered, he left the café.

Across town, Asti Sato opened her sleepy eyes. It was dark, sometime in the middle of the night. Her husband was asleep beside her. All was quiet in their high-rise apartment. She wanted to go back to sleep but had to use the bathroom. She gingerly opened the bedroom door and lightly stepped into the hallway, so as not to wake up her in-laws, who slept in the room across the hall. Halfway down the hall, Asti tripped and landed heavily, head first on the hardwood floor. Dazed, she couldn't catch her breath and remained unmoving. She fell hard; must have made a loud sound. In her mind she hoped her husband would be coming to help her, but at the same time she hoped he did not wake up, because she didn't want him to tell her how clumsy she was. Her body ached. She would just remain there for a little while longer. She felt someone grab her by the ankles and was about to turn to see whether it was her husband when the person began to drag her down the hall. She was so shocked that she did not think to scream and before she could even think about it, a man covered her mouth with his hand. She could not see him well but from what she could make out, she did not recognize Kenzin. This man was a stranger to her. Asti's heart was pounding. She wished her husband would come up behind this man and knock him out. They would call the police. She would kick the unconscious man before the police arrived. She knew she would kick him hard, if only she would have the opportunity to.

A woman came from around the corner. She did not know Mishi, but both strangers knew one another, exchanged looks, nodded, and Mishi pulled out two guns with what seemed like silencers on the end of each firearm's barrel. She crept down the hallway with her guns raised.

Kenzin whispered into Asti's ear, "You scream and my little sister will kill every single person in this place."

Asti nodded her understanding and Kenzin removed his hand from over her puckered mouth.

He pointed at the tattoo on her neck. "You're a Tamuramaro."

Asti did not deny it.

"You recently made contact to arrange for weapons…" he began and paused so that Asti might expand on what he was saying. But she said nothing and just stared at him with both terror and disdain.

Kenzin signaled Mishi and she opened Asti's in-laws' door.

"Please," Asti begged.

Mishi fired two consecutive shots into the dark, quiet room, and then shut the door.

Asti whimpered.

Mishi went across the hall and opened the door where her husband was sleeping and stood there, waiting for her brother's signal.

Kenzin said between clenched teeth, "Tell us what we want to know while you still have any family left."

"Alright," Asti cried. "I was the one who made arrangements to have weapons sent for Jubei so that he could to murder Ukyo."

"Was it Matsumi who instructed you to make these arrangements?"

Asti hesitated. Mishi aimed the gun, fired a single shot towards the bed.

Asti's wide eyes teared up.

Another door opened and out came a sleepy eight-year-old girl. Mishi grabbed her and put a gun to her head.

"Yes. Yes, it was Matsumi." Asti said. She was choking up and having trouble speaking clearly. "Matsumi contacted me through different people. I did not speak to her directly and I also did not speak to anyone twice. Each person passed along a code word that only Matsumi and her maidservants would know. This is how I knew that she's still alive."

"And who are these people?"

"Former members of the Tamuramaro. Matsumi had a secret network. Each member of this clandestine network did not know about the others. She kept them on rotation."

"Well, since you don't know the identity of the person who contacted you, I guess that we'll have to kill this kid," said Kenzin.

Asti screamed, "Wait! Wait! There is one more thing that I can tell you. I was contacted from an American phone number. I remember it. 1-202-292-9100."

Kenzin smiled dryly and signaled his sister. Mishi pulled the trigger and the child dropped to the floor. Asti made a low howling sound. It was as if her soul was dying. Mishi approached the heartbroken woman and kneeled, took Asti's hand and placed the gun in her hand. Asti shot herself in the head and the sibling left the apartment through the front door, closing it behind them.

Two days later, in Washington, D.C.

Kenzin and Mishi got out of their rental car in front of the Challenge Public Charter School in Washington, D.C., to which they had traced the phone number given to them by Asti. Children were lined up, waiting to board their buses. They went into the old building and checked in at the front desk.

"Hi, there," Kenzin said, in a flawless American accent. "I have an appointment with Terry about a teaching position."

"Well, you're in luck. It just happens that we have open

enrollment right now. If you don't mind waiting a bit, Terry will be right with you."

Indeed, it wasn't long before a tall man with brown hair and blue eyes came out to the reception area and approached the Kenzin and Mishi. He extended his hand and said, "Hittori Yurijama? I'm Terry Bronson." He turned to Mishi and smiled, "And you must be, Yumiko?"

They exchanged polite greetings.

"Let's go back to my office," said Terry. "I can interview you both."

Half an hour went by before the three of them came out of the office. All seemed happy.

"Welcome to Challenge," said Terry. "You guys are going to fit in great here. Come on. I'll show you to your classroom."

Kenzin and Mishi followed Terry on a tour of the school. They stopped by a few classrooms and the siblings were introduced as the new art and martial arts teachers.

New Mexico

Jubei closed his bible and rubbed his tired eyes. He put his lighter in his pocket. Malcolm was sitting across the kitchen table. He also closed his bible; set it aside.

"Do you truly understand the life you seek?" Malcolm asked.

"I do. And I'm ready."

"I saw changes in you, during this last week, while we were studying the bible. The Lord is amazing, isn't He? When you accept Him, He changes everything. I just want you to know that I love you, Jubei. I couldn't love you more or be more proud of you if you were my own son."

Jubei smiled. He didn't know what to say. "I'm not good with expressing how I feel, but if I could have picked anyone to be my father, it would have been you. You're the best man I know, Malcolm-san. And I love you too."

The men shared a warm embrace and in this moment, Paty came into the kitchen for a glass of water. She was both surprised and glad to catch her favorite men with their arms wrapped around each other. She cleared her throat. "You two still awake?" she said. "It's already after midnight."

"Jubei wanted to study because tomorrow's an important day for him."

Paty hugged Jubei. "I know. And I'm so excited for you."

"It is very late," said Jubei, as he stood up and stretched.

Paty poured herself a glass of water and went back up the stairs. "Go to bed!" She yelled down.

The next day

The last song of the mid-week service was over, which usually signaled dismissal, however the congregation was asked to sit once more. Malcolm approached the podium, adjusted the microphone to his height. Everyone was quiet. The collective attention was focused on the pastor.

"We can't leave just yet. There's one more thing we have to do." The curtain behind him, which had thus been closed, opened up, revealing a massive water tank in the center of the stage.

The congregation erupted in applause. Enthusiastic cheering.

"We have to baptize tonight!" He waited for the cheering to die down, and it did, but the excitement remained in the air. Malcolm took in the moment before speaking again. He wanted to remember it in all its glory. "Every baptism is a blessed event," he started, "but this one here is especially near and dear to my heart. Fourteen years ago, I got to baptize my own daughter. And now I get to baptize my son. Jubei Tamuramaro, come on out!"

Jubei walked out onto the stage, his eyes downcast and faced flushed due to the overwhelming attention. He stood beside Malcolm and only after Malcolm put his arm around Jubei's shoulders did Jubei smile.

"I met Jubei under some pretty challenging circumstances. Man, this guy has a testimony you wouldn't believe. His commitment to everything he does is encouraging, and I'm just so psyched." Malcolm turned to Jubei. "Brother, you know how I feel about you. I'm proud to say you're my best friend, my brother, and my son. Watching the changes you've made is just confirmation that God is truly awesome. Get in the tank man!"

Everyone laughed. Jubei climbed into the tank of warm water and sat down.

"Alright Jubei, I got two questions. Do you believe that Jesus Christ is your lord and savior, and that he died on the cross for your sins and was resurrected on the third day?"

"Yes, I do," said Jubei.

"And what is your true confession?"

"Jesus is lord!"

With that said, Malcolm tilted Jubei back and dunked him under the water. Jubei sprang back with his hair wet and grinning. He glanced at the water, which had become cold, and saw that it had metamorphosed into an oil-like black liquid as though it had absorbed the demons that had plagued him. He felt hands grab him and slip off. They could not get keep hold of him. Jubei climbed out of the tank, and took a last look at the water in which he had left his old self and his sins. The water was clear again and then he heard the audience clap. People were embracing one another as Jubei and Malcolm left the stage with their arms around each other .

Across two time zones, it was late in Washington D.C. where Kenzin and Mishi were undercover at the Challenge Public Charter School. Most of the staff had gone home but Kenzin and Mishi had stayed late to set up their classrooms and they did just that, until the night cleaning crew left and locked up.

Mishi hacked into the surveillance camera to loop the cameras, so that they could carry out their activities stealthily.

Kenzin went to Terry's office and had to pick the locked door.

You could hear footsteps echoed down the hall. Mishi went to investigate and found that a night worker was still in the building. Mishi moved lightly across hardwood floor, silently. She used her phantom steps to creep up on the woman and struck the back of her neck, just below the brainstem. She collapsed into Mishi's arms. Mishi dragged the unconscious woman to a chair, where she sat her down, placed her hand on her head, almost tenderly, and whispered into her ear. Mishi repeated a string of words several times before returning to Terry's office where Kenzin was sifting through the teachers' personnel files.

"So, did you kill her?" Kenzin asked.

"No," Mishi said dryly. "What do you think those personnel profiles are going to tell you?"

"What we need are the addresses and emergency contacts. We're going to set up surveillance at each residence and trace down every emergency contact. We're going to narrow the search down."

"How can we be sure that our target even works here?"

"That's what we're going to find out. Jubei would do what ever it takes for as long as it takes, and so shall we."

Mishi confessed that she hated Jubei.

"I do too. I'm going to enjoy killing him."

"So will I."

Mishi helped herself to a pile of records and began to copy the addresses. "Kenzin," she said, "I want to make Jubei suffer before we kill him. Because of him, we had to live as outcasts, separated from our father, denied our rightful place. We were raised as yakuza scum while Jubei was as good as if he were made of gold."

"You have it all wrong, Mishi. Father handpicked us because we are the only ones capable of killing Jubei. We were raised in secret so that one day, if it was necessary, we would kill him. And my dear sister, we will not fail."

"The sooner we get out of here, the better. I hate children. And if a single one of these foulmouthed ghetto bunnies disrespects me, I will kill them, and then I will go to their homes and kill their parents."

Kenzin shook his head, but he knew Mishi was serious. They stayed in the office for a couple of hours, copying down all the addresses and contact information for all the school's employees.

Chapter Fifteen:
Love and Violence

Clovis, New Mexico

Parents had arrived to pick up their children. Paty walked into Jubei's dojo just as he was bringing the children's class to an end. She waited while Jubei dismissed his class and watched one of the mother's flirt with Jubei, but he appeared clueless to the pretty Mexican lady's advances. She slipped him her phone number and then gathered her children and walked out with them. Jubei looked puzzled as to what he was supposed to do with this lady's phone number. When he looked up he saw Paty and his face brightened. Paty waved. He waved back. She stood by while the room emptied and Jubei put away all the gear.

"This is a surprise," Jubei finally said.

"Matsumi sent me to pick you up." Paty was smirking and teased, "So, Lillian Ortega's got the hots for you, huh?"

"What is *hots for me?*"

Paty winked at him and laughed. "I saw her flirting with you. She gave you her phone number, right?"

"Oh. You mean, she likes me, or something like that?"

Paty chuckled. "Maybe it's because you're gorgeous. And you're the talk of the church, and my school, and here as well. What girl wouldn't want a handsome Christian ninja? Aren't you interested in anyone? You know, I can always set you up with Marta Gomez, from church. I see you guys talking sometimes. I know that she would jump at the chance."

Jubei smiled awkwardly and appeared embarrassed. He grabbed his jacket and then escorted Paty out; locked the door.

Paty changed the subject. "I see that your classes are filling up. That's great, Jubei."

"Yes. It is building quite a reputation for itself."

"Plus it's a different and more exotic martial arts than most of the ones available around here."

Paty unlocked the car and they got in. She was about to start the ignition when he blurted, "I have no interest in Marta."

Paty said nothing for a moment and then asked, "Are you hungry? I could go for some tacos. My treat."

He looked at her gratefully. "I can go for tacos too."

They drove to El Rancho's, a fancy Mexican restaurant on the outskirts of Clovis. The hostess that seated kept made pretty eyes at Jubei all the way to the table. And when she left, she turned a few times on her way back to the front of the restaurant, but he did not seem to notice. Paty laughed. He was clueless and it was charming.

Paty leaned over the table and pointed out, "For a super ninja, you're not very alert."

"I am alert when I need to be. Right now there is nothing to be alert for. And besides, I have exactly what I need." He reached across the table and took her hand in his. She did not expect it.

"I have no interest in Marta Gomez, or in Lillian Ortega. I am in love with Paty Ross."

Paty was speechless, but her grip on Jubei's hand tightened.

The waitress came with Salsa and Chips and they released hands as though they were teenagers that had been caught kissing by their parents. The waitress took their drink orders and left them alone.

Paty lowered her voice. "Did you just say you were in love with me?"

"All these months. Couldn't you tell?"

Paty put the straw in her mouth but did not take a sip. It was as though she was looking for the right words. Then she spoke, tentatively. "I thought so. But I wasn't sure. You were so distant, at times."

Jubei gazed loving at her. "It had to be that way. You were a Christian and I wasn't. But now we both acknowledge Jesus Christ as our lord and savior and put him first in our lives. I think it's time that we acknowledge how we feel about each other."

Paty took Jubei's hand. "I love you, Jubei. I've never felt this way about anyone before."

Jubei was elated. They sat like that for a while, starring at each other, smiling broadly, until a strange thought seemed to have crossed Paty's mind and she became pensive. Finally she said, "We have spent every day together, for the last eight months or so, and are able to talk about so much. And yet I don't even know if you have been in love before."

Jubei tensed up. He took his hand back, became solemn. He had dreaded this moment, lost sleep over having to ever explain Maki to Paty.

Sadly Jubei said, "Yes, I have loved before I met you. But this is not the place to talk about it."

Paty agreed.

Dinner was served and they carried on as if this matter had not been brought up. Three hours passed and they laughed and shared, their hearts delighted and their guards down. Together they felt like they would were home.

By the time they returned to the house, the lights were out besides that on the front porch, which the pastor that left on for Jubei and Paty.

They cozied up on the swing on the porch. Paty's face was a bit sore from smiling all night, and yet she couldn't stop. She fidgeted.

Jubei took a deep breath and said, "I once promised you that I would always tell you the truth. Now you've asked if I was ever in love before and like told you earlier, I was. Her name was Maki. She was a member of my clan. We grew up together, trained together. Besides my mother, Maki was the only other factor that kept me from completely losing my humanity during those dark days of death and revenge. I loved her completely. I had not known that you could feel that deeply for another person. Maki and I had to keep our love hidden from my father. You must understand that love, kindness, any form of attachment to another person was viewed as a weakness. Considered a flaw. And a Dragon ninja cannot afford any sort of weakness. If you are weak, you aren't worthy. If you are weak, you cannot best serve your clan. A Dragon ninja must be able to kill anyone, at any time, and the reason itself should not concern us. But somehow my father discovered the love we shared, and sent me on a mission, to keep me away from Maki."

"What happened?" Paty asked nervously.

Jubei paused. He noticed that he was trembling. He opened his mouth but said nothing. He swallowed hard. Tried again. "Our missions, Paty, our missions were given to us on scrolls, that my father issued personally. I received my orders. I carried out my mission, no questions asked." Jubei stood abruptly and leaned against the railing of the porch with his back to Paty so that she would not see the tears in his eyes.

She considered going to him, but she hesitated.

He continued. "My mission, it was to go after a traitor. It was specific in that I had ed the traitor and completely eradicate the traitor's entire family, anyone associated with this family that might take revenge." Jubei balled his hand into a fist. He could hardly breathe.

"So what happened with you and Maki?"

Jubei wanted to lie, but knew he had to answer with the truth. He looked upwards. The dark sky was speckled with stars. "Lord, give me the strength," Jubei murmured.

Paty was waiting quietly for a response. Slowly Jubei turned to her. His face was wet with tears. He wanted to find comfort in her arms Paty but clung to the railing. "Maki. Maki was that traitor."

Paty's face dropped. Nothing could have prepared her for what he had revealed to her. And he could not take it back.

"The love I felt for her could not matter. I had been trained my entire life to worship the mission above all and my mission instructed me to kill the one I loved. And I did it. I killed her without hesitating. I killed Maki. I killed her little brother. I killed her mother, father, every single person I found in that house. All this I was able to do to one woman who loved me. The one person I had loved truly and completely. Maki"

Paty was eerily still. So silent that it seemed like she had stopped breathing.

Jubei was desperate for her to say something. Anything. "I understand if this is too much for you, Paty. I have to live with what I have done, every single moment of every day, for the rest of my life. Her face, it haunts my dreams. All my victims do."

Paty got up and went inside the house. The porch light turned off.

Jubei went around the corner towards the back house and collapsed under the crushing weight of his sorrow, consumed with boundless guilt. He put his face to the ground and prayed.

Paty made it to the stairs before she could no longer hold back her tears. She wept bitterly and did not notice the hall light upstairs had come on.

"Paty?" Malcolm called down. "You okay?" He hurried to her side and gently wiped her tears, but they kept flowing.

Paty blurted, "He loves me, dad. He told me so, tonight."

"I'm confused. It's a good thing, isn't it?"

"My heart bleeds for him, but I can't. I just can't..." Paty could hardly stand. Her father helped her walk and guided her to the kitchen.

"Come on. I'll fix ya some hot chocolate the way you like it. Marshmallows and all."

Paty dropped into a chair at the kitchen table where they had all shared such happy times. "I love him so much, dad. I have always loved him. I prayed for Jubei, but now I no longer can. I don't think I can get past what he was, and all the monstrous things he's done."

Malcolm dropped a packet of powdered Swiss Miss mixture with marshmallows in a mug of water and placed it in the microwave. "What happened?"

"I asked him if he was ever in love before. He said, yes. But he killed her, dad. He killed the woman he loved and her entire family. Massacred them all. He received his orders and just carried them out. He admitted that he didn't even question the orders. He just carried them out. What kind of man does that? What kind of man kills the woman he loves? It wasn't that long ago that he went to Japan so that he could to kill his own father. He told me that a ninja has got to be willing to kill anyone, anytime, and not care about the reason why."

The microwave beeped. Malcolm took out the steaming mug and carefully brought it to Paty.

"Why did he have to tell me that?"

"He wanted to tell you the truth, Paty. Jubei has never held back the truth from any one of us. And he has given everything up for us. I can excuse his past, because Jesus already delivered him from all that he has done in his previous life. That was then. This is now."

"But you're not the one who's in love with him. You're not the one who wants to spend the rest of your life with him. To have children with him."

"Whoa! You want to marry Jubei? This is the first time I'm hearing this."

Paty looked down and nodded despondently.

"Then what's stopping you?" Malcolm asked. "His past?"

"Yes. I'm afraid that his past is going to come back to haunt us."

"Pray, baby girl," Malcolm said. "Pray and whatever you decide, I will stand beside it. But I do want to ask you something. Are you so righteous that you can cast the first stone? I love you Paty, but I want you to think about it. Think with your heart." He sat across from her.

Paty took a while to stop crying and her father waited patiently. He did not press her further. When she calmed down, her drink had had time to cool down and she took a sip.

Malcolm reached out for her hand. Together they bowed their heads and prayed for a long while.

That night, Paty cried herself to sleep.

Right away Matsumi knew something was wrong. "You were crying?" she asked her son. She went to him but he pulled back.

"What happened?"

"I told her about Maki." Jubei sat heavily in the couch.

Matsumi sat on the other end and waited for him to continue.

"I told her I would never lie to her, or hide anything from her. What she decides now is up to her."

"But you love her. And she loves you. It will all work itself out. Love is more powerful than anything else. After all, wasn't it love that compelled Jesus to die on the cross? If he can do that, then Paty can love you despite your past. Give her time, my son." She kissed Jubei's cheek. "The fact that you are in love again is a big step for you, Jubei. Consider this a blessing in disguise."

For the next few weeks, Jubei and Paty passed each other like ships in the night. Those around them could feel the tension. None said anything of it.

Besides working in his dojo, Jubei was engrossed in reading his bible and praying to the Lord.

Day felt like weeks; weeks like months; both longed to say something to the other, however, neither gathered the courage to.

Jubei, Marcus and Mara played kickball in the yard. Laughed. The children squealed gleefully.

Paty called out from the back porch, "Dinner time, you guys. Come on and wash up."

Marcus and Mara frowned. They turned their pouty faces towards Jubei.

"We'll play some more, after dinner," Jubei said.

Marcus and Mara ran towards the house.

Paty offered Jubei to fix him a plate of food, but he declined and walked away.

She called his name. He stopped, turned to face her. Suddenly, she could not find her words and just stood there for a moment with her mouth agape, and then she pulled herself together and went inside, closing the door behind her as Jubei started walking toward the back house.

At the table, the children ate with gusto and did not notice that Paty and Malcolm were quiet. Malcolm had noticed that Paty seemed despondent. She looked out the window; held her fork up with no food on it.

"It's about Jubei, right?" the pastor asked Paty.

She nodded and put her fork down.

"Baby girl, you need to go after him. I know what you've been praying for, but what good is praying for something and then not working towards it. Don't allow pride or fear get in the way."

From the window, Paty could see that Jubei had reached his porch. She looked at her father with questioning eyes. He waved her on and she excused herself from the table and ran outside.

She shouted Jubei's name and he turned around, surprised at the sight of her running toward him, her face flushed, determined. He began to run toward her and when they came together they embraced lovingly.

She tried to catch her breath and said, "I've been such an idiot. I was scared, though I really have no reason to be. God knows I love you. I want to be with you, Jubei."

She gazed at him with ingenuous devotion and he could no longer suppress his longing and kissed her. She kissed him back, passionately. He held her lovely face. She wrapped her arms around his strong back and held him tight, pressed body against his. Their lips parted so that they could look at each other. The happiness they saw in the other only enhanced their own bliss. They kissed again. He ran his fingers through her dark mane. He loved it when she wore her hair down. The feeling of her breath on his skin was maddening. He loved her completely; could not imagine a life without her in it. He held her tight, as though afraid she would slip from his grasp.

She leaned her head on his shoulder. He brushed a strand of hair from her face and tenderly kissed her forehead.

Jubei murmured, "What do we do now?"

"Love the lord. Love each other. Take it day by day, and live our lives fully."

From inside the main house, Malcolm smiled. He closed the blinds.

Washington, D.C.

It took Kenzin and Mishi over three weeks to complete setting up surveillance in the homes of Challenge Public School employees and they were now able to monitor everyone and everything from the comfort and privacy of their hotel room.

On the television screen, the news reported on the bodies of a yet unidentified Asian couple found washed up on the shore of the Potomac River. An artist's rendition of their likeness was presented to the public, along with requests for any tips on the identity of the deceased. Mishi turned off the television. She went to check the laptop, scrolling through several scenes, in real-time, of the private lives of those they were surveilling.

Mishi called her brother over. "Look at this," she said urgently.

Terry was at his desk, in his den at home, making a phone call. Mishi raised the volume while Kenzin checked for Terry's name on a list on which most of the names had been crossed off. Terry's was one of the few that hadn't been eliminated.

"We're getting close," Kenzin said. "There are only four more left to go."

The call went through and a woman's voice greeted Terry.

"I wanted to see how the replacement for Willis was doing," said Terry.

"He's doing fine," the woman said. "Although, between us, it's just not the same without him."

"I know what you mean."

"So what's new with you and Sarah?"

At that same moment, a tall and svelte mulatto lady walked into Terry's desk. "Who's on the phone?" she asked, seemingly in a Canadian accent.

"It's Salma," he said, "from the San Antonio church." He switched the call to speakerphone mode.

The women exchanged greetings.

"I'm actually coming out there next week for the leadership conference."

"That's wonderful!"

Mishi muted the computer and turned to her brother. "This is our mark: Willis Ware."

"He was speaking as if Willis is dead, but we know well that Willis Ware isn't dead. He and his family have gone into hiding."

"We've been following the wrong lead," said Mishi. "It would take too long to track Matsumi. If we track the pastor, we'll find Jubei."

"What was the name of the agent that exposed the Tamuramaro?" asked Kenzin.

"Navaro."

Kenzin picked up the telephone and dialed the number

to the D.C. branch of the FBI headquarters. The call center patched Kenzin's cal through to Navaro's cellular phone.

When Navaro picked up, Kenzin said, "I have information on Willis Ware."

"Whom am I talking to?" asked Navaro.

"My name isn't important. You need to know that the Tamuramaro have located Willis Ware."

"How do I know your information is credible?" Navaro asked.

"I used to be a member of the Tamuramaro clan. I can't tell you what I know over the phone. Perhaps we can we meet up? But I don't know this area, so it would be best if you suggest a place for us to meet."

"Where are you now?" asked Navaro.

There was a pause. And then Kenzin said, "The Presidential Hotel."

"Meet me at the White House Park in ten minutes. It's only a few blocks from your hotel. I'll be driving a black Hummer."

Kenzin loaded his weapons and headed out to meet with Navaro.

Meanwhile

Navaro paced anxiously, waiting for someone to pick up her phone call. When the call eventually went through, Navaro didn't take the time to identify herself. " I'm going to need back up," she said. "Someone just called me and said that Jubei has been compromised. We may have a leak in the Narrow Gate."

She reported where she would be meeting the caller, and then tossed the cell phone out of the moving vehicle.

White House Park

With the exception of Navaro's car, the parking lot was empty. She flashed her lights before turning the engine off, and before getting out of the car she verified that both her guns were fully loaded, and double checked the functionality of her earpiece and the push-to-talk button concealed in her wrist.

She headed toward the benches. Navaro pretended to fix her hair and whispered into her wrist, "Are you in place?"

Zula's voice answered through her earpiece, "Yeah Mon."

Navaro came upon a homeless man who was digging through a garbage can. He seemed pleased to find something, which he quickly slipped into his cart. Navaro observed the man move on to the next garbage can.

Kenzin crept up behind Navaro and her. "Agent Navaro?" he asked.

Startled, she pulled her gun and said, "That's close enough!"

"You may call me Mijo. Thank you for meeting me."

"You indicated that Willis Ware has been compromised. What exactly did you mean?"

"The Tamuramaro have placed a liquid-tracking device in him, as they customary do with their own Dragon ninjas. It was simply a matter of activating the device. A ninja hit team has been dispatched to find him. Agent Navaro, you ought to warn him before they get to him."

"The news reported that the Japanese defense force destroyed the Tamuramaro compound after it had been exposed. The Tamuramaro have been annihilated."

"Not the entire clan. The handful of survivors was assimilated into another clan. But their mission remains the same. They will find the pastor and his family, and they will kill him. You must relocate them, now."

Navaro seemed pensive. "So you say that a liquid tracking device was injected into Willis Ware?"

Kenzin nodded.

Navaro aimed her guns at Kenzin. "Down on the ground!" she yelled.

Kenzin was taken aback.

"Get down on the ground now, or else I'll put you down."

Slowly Kenzin kneeled and then laid down on his stomach.

"Did you really think you could use me to locate the pastor? Whomever you are, if you move, I *will* shoot you."

Kenzin laughed arrogantly. The back of his coat split open and a grappling hook shot up. He was whisked up into the trees.

Navaro took cover behind an oak tree and aimed into the foliage above. She yelled at the homeless man who was running in their direction, "He's a ninja, Zula!"

Narrow Gate agents came out of hiding, though some remained out of sight. All pointed their guns towards the area Navaro was aiming hers.

Kenzin appeared behind an agent and stabbed him in the back. Kenzin jumped back into a lush tree before a nearby agent even noticed his fallen comrade. He ran to his side, but it was too late. The dead man's gun was missing. Kenzin had taken it and with it he shot an agent. The man did not die. The guns were loaded with rock salt. Unbeknown to Kenzin, Narrow Gate agents did not carry live ammunition. However, Kenzin realized at once that there was something off with the gun and it would not serve him well. He chucked it.

"Where is he?" one agent called out. " I can't see him."

Kenzin snuck up on the man and broke his neck. A female agent fired at Kenzin. He dodged the bullets, spun around in the air, simultaneously hurling a Shuriken knife into the agent's head. Kenzin dove behind the fountain and from there he crawled towards an unsuspecting agent and killed him.

"Where'd he go?" asked Zula. No one had an answer.

Navaro noticed a shadow move from one tree to another. She fired, but missed.

Zula flanked Kenzin from the right. Navaro moved in from the left like a pincer. Kenzin jumped down and performed a split kick, hitting both Zula and Navaro. Another agent came up behind Kenzin. Kenzin ran up the closest tree trunk and from it he leaped onto the agent's shoulders and dug his fingers into his eye sockets. The man howled and began stumbling aimlessly, his eyes dark and blood trickling down his horrified face. Kenzin hopped off and slammed the injured man, head first, into a tree. As the man dropped unconscious, Kenzin vaulted over him and kicked Zula in the face. Zula staggered back. He had not seen it coming. And now there was no one there. He was left only with a throbbing pain in his head and disoriented.

Kenzin turned his attention to Navaro. Navaro blocked the ninja's kick. He kicked again and again she blocked it. He dropped to his knee and spun leg swept her. Navaro dropped to the ground.

An agent hurried over to help her. Kenzin threw a roundhouse kick and a blade emerged from the tip of his shoe and raked across the agent's throat. Another agent approached from behind Kenzin with a gun. Two more approached from the other side. Navaro and Zula also moved in. Kenzin was surrounded.

Kenzin skillfully took out multiple agents. One moment he was there, the next he was gone, and there was no way to tell what direction he would be coming from. Some agents were killed. Others had been severely wounded. He kept taking them down but more of them came out of hiding. They kept coming and coming. He leaped and spun and kicked and stabbed and they just kept coming.

In a final attempt he released, from his sleeve, two chains with long curved blades at the end. He spun the blades around and took down several agents, but there were too many of them. He retracted his blades and dropped his arms. He was no longer smiling and stood there with his hands at his sides. They were moving in on him like a legion and all he could do was wait, and he did not have to wait long. Navaro pulled out a taser wand and right before she tased Kenzin, he punched Zula in his chest, so powerfully that it sent Zula a few feet away, and when he heavily hit the ground he didn't get back up. Navaro stuck Kenzin in the back of his neck to bring him down and tased him. Zula started moving again just as Kenzin stopped jerking. Zula was helped to his feet by and agent. He wobbled slightly and held his chest. He was breathing hard. Staggered. Navaro helped steady him.

Zula was wheezing. "I'm okay," he said. "Just got to catch my breath."

They looked around. Dozens of agents had been wounded. Several were dead.

"Dis is gonna sound crazy but I coulda sworn dere was anoter," said Zula. "Someone kicked me and I'm sure it wasn't him. Too many of our agents went down for it just to be one mon."

Navaro did not know what to say.

"Let's get dis guy outta here."

Navaro and Zula restrained Kenzin and placed him in the back seat of Navaro's vehicle as a Narrow Gate cleaning crew arrived on the scene. They began to remove the injured and the dead. They would have this area cleaned up in record time. No one would ever suspect anything had taken place here.

"To be on the safe side, get back to the Ozona headquarters and pull Willis Ware's file. We may have to relocate them."

"What about Jubei and Matsumi?" asked Zula.

"What they do is up to them. We have to get this done quickly. But no radio or cell phone contact. They can use that to trace where you are."

Zula patted Navaro's shoulder. "Well so much for peace and quiet, huh?"

Navaro scoffed and got into the hummer and waved goodbye

During the drive she was consumed with images of the fallen men. Good men. Courageous men. She looked in the rearview mirror. Kenzin was gone.

Navaro slammed on her breaks, slapped the steering wheel, and shouted, "I *hate* ninjas!" She got out of the car and slammed the door. A dart hit her neck. She dropped before she realized what had happened to her.

Mishi stepped out of the shadows, grabbed Navaro, threw her over her shoulder and vanished into shadows.

At Zula's hotel, he slid his card key into the slot. The green light flashed and, as he readied to enter his room, green smoke blew into his face. He fell to the floor, unconscious. The elevator rang. A shadow lifted Zula up and before the elevator door had time to open, both the shadow and Zula were gone.

Yagyu compound, Japan

Ukyo met with Kenzin and Mishi in the privacy of his chambers. The siblings were present via a 3-D hologram projection. Kenzin and Mishi knelt down before him.

In a composed tone Ukyo addressed the siblings. "I hope you have something worthy of reporting, otherwise, I will have lost two more children."

Kenzin and Mishi knew he was the sort of man that carries through with his threats. They were visibly shaken.

Kenzin gathered the courage to speak and announced that they were closing in on Jubei. "It won't be long now. We know he is somewhere in Texas, and has gone through a private witness program called the Narrow Gate. Tomorrow, we will be infiltrating their headquarters and pinpoint Jubei's exact location."

Mishi interjected, "There is something else, my lord. Matsumi is with Jubei."

Ukyo stood at once and roared, "I saw her burn."

"You have been deceived, my lord," Mishi said. Her voice trembled. "What you saw was one of her maidservants burn in her stead."

Ukyo felt flustered and his face was flushed. Many times he had thought back to Matsumi's final days. He had thought of that last time they had made love. It couldn't have been a maidservant. He would have known the difference. Or would he?

Ukyo picked up his chair and shattered it against the wall. Although the siblings were merely present via hologram, they both took a step back. And for a short while, Ukyo just stood there, breathing heavily, his hands in the shape of claws, stiffened and ready to pounce. Slowly he regained his composure, but there was no doubt that the rage was within him, seething, brewing. He cleared his throat and in the most collected tone that he could muster he asked, "Are you certain that your information is accurate? Make sure you think over your answer, because, I will hold you both responsible if you are wrong."

Kenzin looked at his sister from the corner of his eye.

She was pale. He could tell that she would not be the one to give their father this answer. "Yes, master," he said. "I guarantee that Matsumi is alive and well and hiding out with Jubei in the United States."

"When you find them do nothing," said Ukyo.

"Sir?"

"I said do nothing!" Ukyo snapped, and dismissed the siblings who vanished, leaving him only with the thought of her. Alive.

Ozona, Texas, Narrow Gate headquarters

At the farmhouse, Narrow Gate members greeted Navaro and Zula .

"What brings you back so soon?" asked Al-Kazim.

"Security has been breached. Pastor Malcolm and his family could be in danger and we are not going to take any chances. We are relocating them ASAP."

Al-Kazim was surprised and wanted more details. He needed to make sense of what he had just heard, which seemed impossible. A breach in the Narrow Gate was unheard of. Inconceivable.

"The other night, in D.C., we walked right into a trap and were attacked by a couple of ninjas. Luckily we had back up. Anyhow, they ended up escaping. But if they know who I am, chances are, they know about the Narrow Gate. So I need to access to the pastor and his family so that we can relocate them."

Inside, Navaro and Zula were given access passes to the records department. Al-Kazim sealed the room up before entering the passcode to access the Narrow Gate's records.

Al-Kazim said, "You guys could have just called for this information. You didn't have to come all the way from D.C."

"They bugged my communications," Navaro said. "They could have traced our call here.

"That was a good move, I guess," Al-Kazim said. "They must not have had a chance to plant a tracking device on you. If they had, it would've been detected when you entered."

A login screen appeared. Al-Kazim stepped aside and gestured for Navaro to go ahead and take a seat at the computer.

She appeared taken aback, but smiled coyly and gestured at the seat. "Why don't you go ahead and do it, " Navaro said to Al-Kazim.

Al-Kazim insisted. "It's the new passcode system I told you about, just the other day. You don't remember? So, I put my password in, and now *you* have to put *your* password in. We can't access the records unless we *both* put in *our own* passwords. Come on. We better get this done because if the pastor and his family are in danger, we better get them to a safe house."

"Right. Right." Navaro pulled out a piece of paper from her pocket. On it was her password.

Al-Kazim laughed. "You were always bad with passwords."

Navaro chuckled as she sat down. She typed in her password. Access was denied in bold red letters.

Al-Kazim asked Navaro if he could see that piece of paper. He checked it and rolled his eyes. "You wrote it down backwards. Again."

She tried again, this time reversing the numbers. Access was granted. Navaro retrieved the necessary information she had come for.

"Let's go! We have to move the family *now*. How fast can you get us in the air, Al-Kazim?"

"30 minutes."

Meanwhile, in D.C.

A team of police officers had gathered outside of Kenzin and Mishi's hotel room. The manager opened the door with the master key and the police moved in, fast, yelling, aiming left, right, but Navaro and Zula were the only occupants, both tied to chairs and alive, although covered in dried blood and still hooked up to an IV.

"I've got to get to a phone." Navaro yelled. "I need a phone, now!"

The officers first checked the closets, bathroom, beneath the beds, and all was clear. An officer began untying Navaro and Zula. An EMT was called in. He unhooked the IV from Navaro just as she was released from her restraints. She grabbed the closest agent's cell phone and started dialing.

The EMT checked the IV bag and announced to the officers, "This is more potent than Sodium Pathanol." And then he tried to talk to Navaro. "Listen, you should sit down and we'll bring in a stretcher and take you both to the hospital. The doctors are going to want to run a series of test to make sure you're all right. I mean, who knows what side effects you might have from this psychoactive drug?"

She pushed the young man aside. "Kazim, listen to me carefully," she said into the phone. "Two ninjas, disguised as Zula and I, will be coming your way any minute to gain access to the Narrow Gate's records. They look exactly like us, and even their voices..."

Al-Kazim interrupted her. "It's already gone! The Helicopter, it left about three hours ago."

Navaro had to think fast. "Call Malcolm Ross immediately. Don't bother going into details. Just tell him that he has to get his family out of there right away. Send them to the safe house in Portales. Hurry!"

Navaro hung up and sat back down, exhaled loudly, and waved the EMT over, so that he could resume her exam.

Clovis, New Mexico, three hours later

"Thank you so much for your help today," Jubei said to Malcolm as they got out of the car. Jubei seemed both nervous and happy. He was clutching a small shopping bag.

"Trust me, she's going to *love* it."

The front door was wide open. Malcolm and Jubei exchanged worried glances and picked up their pace. "Hello?" Malcolm called out. The house greeted them with a deafening silence.

Malcolm went up the stairs. Jubei headed down the hallway towards the den. Before he entered, he saw blood splattered on the door. Inside the den, Marcus and Mara were awkwardly slumped in a puddle of their own blood. You couldn't tell where his blood ended and hers began. Their throats had been slit. The walls had been sprayed red.

"Malcolm!" Jubei shouted. Not the children. Not like this. He choked. He was overwhelmed with sorrow. Guilt.

"No!" Malcolm yelled. His eyes were open wide with horror and disbelief.

Jubei ran off to look for Paty and he found her, in the living room, impaled to the wall by her wrists with knives. Her throat had been slit. A message in Japanese was written in Paty's blood. The arrow that Jubei had intended to use to kill Ukyo was stuck into the wall. Jubei collapsed. In losing her he felt that he had lost it all.

Malcolm called out Paty's name. He was approaching. Jubei stepped out of the living room and tried to obstruct his way in. But Malcolm was a strong man; his strength in this moment was amplified by his desperation. Both men dropped to their knees, broken men.

Malcolm wept bitterly. Jubei yanked the knives out of Paty and took her down as gently as he could. He cradled her body in his arms. His tears watered down the blood on her skin. They cleared miniature paths, revealing her soft skin beneath.

Jubei did not notice that Malcolm had left the room. Malcolm had gone to the kitchen to call the police.

Jubei stroked Paty's hair. It was limp and wet. He leaned over and kissed her cold cheek. She felt stiff. He knew he had her blood on his lips and he let her go. Stood. Walked out.

In the kitchen, Malcolm was lying on the floor. Jubei rushed to his side and checked his vitals. He was alive, but bleeding profusely. Jubei turned him over. Malcolm moaned. His stomach was cut open. Jubei put Malcolm hands over the wound and instructed him to put pressure on it.

Mishi stepped out of the shadows. She kicked Jubei in the chest before he could notice her presence. Jubei fell into the hallway. He got up in time to block her kick and took hold of her leg. She shot multiple darts from her shoe. Jubei dodged them. Backflipping, she struck his chin and he stumbled backwards. Mishi took advantage of her momentum and leg swept him to the floor.

She sprang back to her feet and pulled out a knife. Jubei rolled back, onto his feet. Mishi slashed Jubei horizontally across the chest, and then vertically down his face. Jubei moved stealthily, like a shadow, and appeared behind Mishi; kicked her back. She fell forward. Her hands broke her fall and she kicked her legs backwards and up, like a mule, sending Jubei crashing into the hallway table. As he was getting up, she stabbed down at him, but he shielded himself with a picture frame and she stabbed through the frame, wrapped his legs around her neck, and then twisted the frame, so that in turn Mishi would be forced to release the knife. She did. He tossed her over.

Now standing on opposite ends of the hallway, Jubei and Mishi began to run toward each other. Kenzin appeared in between them and side kicked Jubei through the window and onto the deck. Kenzin dove through the window and speared Jubei. Jubei landed on the ground. Hard. Kenzin kicked Jubei just as Mishi joined him, and together the siblings kicked Jubei mercilessly. They kicked and kicked. Stomped him. The onslaught seemed interminable. He was struggling less and less and he knew that soon enough he would be dead. And in this moment he did not mind dying. Paty was dead. He no longer had a reason to live. However could he live any life worth living without her, without her love and her kindness? The goodness in her had helped draw out the goodness in him and now it was all gone. And they had done that to Paty; taken her life. They had taken his love.

He felt warmth within, but not of the sort that soothes a man. This feeling burgeoned. It set him ablaze. He felt like he was about to erupt and he opened his mouth and from deep within him a roar escaped, amplifying as it emerged, virile, guttural, honest; the entire house and its foundation vibrated; from beyond, Paty would have heard echoes of Jubei's heartbreak.

Stupefied, Kenzin and Mishi stared at Jubei in disbelief. He rose to his feet and just stood there drenched in his own blood, which dripped. Kenzin and Mishi were mesmerized. Jubei should be dead but instead he looked rejuvenated. His eyes caught the light and they seemed to beam. He appeared unearthly. Divine. He opened his arms and once more he roared. Kenzin and Mishi took a step back. They were exhausted from the prolonged beating they had just subjected Jubei to. And his arousal frightened them. For an instant they seemed to have forgotten that they outnumbered him; neglected to consider that this intimidation might be nothing more than Jubei's last breath.

Jubei moved in and put hands against the side of their heads and forcefully knocked them together. This move snapped the siblings back; their instincts kicked in. They charged at Jubei just as he leaped into the air, spun thrice and kicked Kenzin in the face, expelling him from the window, all the while punching Mishi's neck. Mishi spun around and landed with a thud as her brother was coming back in through the back window.

Just as Mishi was trying to stand, Jubei vaulted off of her to perform a flying side kick, and once more he struck Kenzin in the chest. Kenzin fell backwards.

Mishi vanished into the shadows.

Jubei walked up to Kenzin and lifted him, but Kenzin struggled out of Jubei's hold and palm punched his enemy through a wall, into the dining room. Jubei landed on the dining room table where so many times he had shared a meal with the pastor and his family. Jubei shut his eyes tightly, swallowed his pain, and when he opened them he saw Mishi coming down on him with an axe kick. He rolled out of the way; kicked the china closet open as Mishi broke through the table.

Jubei began hurling dinner plates at her. He tossed them rapidly, consistently, and energetically. Mishi was able to dodge most of them, but the plates that hit her struck her chest and head and left her somewhat dazed. Kenzin joined her, holding a couple of butterfly swords with short, single edged blades. His arrival gave time her to pull herself back together. Mishi exhaled deeply and pulled out a couple weapons that looked like sickles, with their hook-like blades—Kamas. Mishi flanked Jubei from the right and Kenzin from the left. Jubei shadow dashed away, blur-like, unearthly. Kenzin and Mishi went looking for him in the hallway while he hung, unmoving, from the ceiling above the doorway that lead to the dining room.

When Kenzin and Mishi went to check the living room, Jubei dashed to the kitchen to go check on Malcolm.

Malcolm was alive, but he had lost a lot of blood and his pallor worried Jubei. He crouched beside him and whispered for him to pray. Malcolm was too weak to speak but Jubei knew that Malcolm would be grateful to know that even in this moment, Jubei thought of their Lord.

Jubei carefully opened the drawer and from it he took a butcher knife. He had a suspicious feeling and suddenly swerved aside, and a Kama nicked his neck and ended up stuck in the wall. Mishi hurled her other Kama at Jubei's legs but he jumped up in time and the weapon passed beneath him. Hanging from the ceiling lamp, Jubei tossed the butcher knife at Mishi and shrieked as she fell over. When she lifted herself up, Jubei smirked. He could see the handle of his knife protruding from her shoulder.

Jubei dropped to the floor and took cover behind the island just as dozens of Shuriken came at him like shooting stars. They missed him and lodged into the cabinets.

Kenzin jumped on top of the island and just as he stabbed down at Jubei, Jubei rolled out of Kenzin's reach.

Mishi had swiftly moved around the island and retrieved her Kamas. She hurled one and it struck Jubei's thigh. He yanked it out and hurled the bloodied weapon at Kenzin who deflected it.

Mishi went out a kitchen window, while Kenzin went through the window above the kitchen sink, leaving Jubei caught in between. Jubei stepped to the side as Kenzin stabbed at him. Jubei spun kicked Mishi in the face and her head slammed into the wall.

Kenzin slashed at Jubei, but he swerved and then ducked and spun around Kenzin. With titanium hands, Kenzin back fisted Jubei down the hallway. He landed at the front door. Kenzin balled his fist and launched his fist at Jubei. Kenzin's fist hit Jubei in the chest. Jubei went flying through the front door and onto the porch. Jubei tried to stand up but Mishi kicked his face.

Kenzin reattached his hand.

Jubei tried to stand up but Mishi kicked him back to the ground. Between clenched teeth she warned him, "You can't defeat us, Jubei. You are going to die." She kicked him once more and then lifted him up, only to punch him, over and over, in the head. Jubei staggered. Mishi spin kicked his face and he dropped. "We have been trained to know what you know and to kill the way you kill." She cut across Jubei's chest and then stabbed him in the waist. "You will die slowly." She readied to stab down at him. Jubei blew a powder into her eyes and while she frantically rubbed her eyes, Jubei got back up and kicked her head. She spun around. He grabbed Mishi by the back of the neck and punched her in the back, and then lifted her up high and slammed her down, hard. He kneeled beside her and began to pummel her face, knocking out several of her teeth, making her bloody features unrecognizable. From within she summoned enough strength to cut Jubei across the face and kicked him away. Slowly she stood up and meekly swung her Kamas at Jubei.

Kenzin launched both his fists at Jubei, however, Jubei ducked, and they struck Mishi instead. Kenzin jumped high and as he readied to perform a flying side kick, Jubei caught him by the leg. With his free leg Kenzin kicked Jubei and backflipped onto his feet. Jubei staggered. Kenzin spun around with a wheel kick to the side of Jubei's head. Jubei dropped to the ground.

While Jubei struggled back to his feet, Kenzin replaced his hands with sword attachments. Once more he attacked Jubei who managed to dodge Kenzin and spun around, kicking Mishi across her gnarled face. Blood splattered. She lost more teeth. Jubei grabbed Mishi's Kamas and sliced the back of her knees. She slumped onto her face. Jubei slashed at her brachial arteries and then across her femoral arteries, moving so fast that it was over before Kenzin could realize that Jubei had rendered his sister invalid. Jubei waited for Kenzin to charge at him and then back vaulted over Mishi, just as Kenzin swung his sword; it came down on Mishi neck and her head rolled. Kenzin was mortified. He had murdered his own sister. He teared up. His face reddened and distorted with rage. He bellowed and hurled himself at Jubei. The clanking of metal echoed. Jubei and Kenzin battled around the yard, blocking and deflecting each other's attacks.

The men found their way back into the house, in the living room. And in close quarters, it was all hand attacks and strikes with the blades.

Coming up behind Kenzin, Jubei drove the Kamas into his shoulders, twisted them around and then yanked them back out, cutting an arm off. Blood gushed. Still, Kenzin tried to fight back. Jubei cut off Kenzin's other arm. Kenzin desperately tried to kick Jubei, but Jubei blocked the lame attack and cut off Kenzin's other leg, right above the knee.

As Jubei readied to bury the Kamas into Kenzin's head, he felt a hand on his shoulder, and a man's voice said, "Jubei, don't." Instinctively, Jubei flipped the man over and began to bring the Kamas down on him when he realized it was Malcolm.

Malcolm had his eyes shut tight in anticipation of his own death. Jubei dropped to his knees. The floor was covered in blood, everyone's blood. Jubei felt ill. He released the Kamas and cried. Malcolm placed his hand on Jubei's. He was too weak to press it, but Jubei was grateful. Malcolm was breathing heavily. Jubei tried to help him into a more comfortable position and again instructed Malcolm put pressure on his wound. Then he turned his attention back to Kenzin, who was still alive, but barely. Kenzin turned his head so as not to see Jubei final blow. Instead, Jubei went to him and tended to his wounds.

Jubei pricked his ear. He could hear helicopters and they seemed to be approaching. It wasn't long before Narrow Gate agents swarmed the property. EMT's hurried to treat Malcolm and Kenzin who were hardly clinging to life.

Navaro encountered Jubei, bloodied and bruised, on the front porch, holding a small shopping bag from which he pulled out a tiny velvet box. Opened it. An oval-shaped diamond ring glittered against the charcoal velvet. It would have looked magnificent on Paty's delicate hand. Malcolm was right. She would have loved it. Indeed, she would have loved anything Jubei would have given her. She was in love with him. Well, she had been in love with him. Jubei closed the jewelry box and put it in his pocket. Paty was gone. The children were gone. Navaro caught Jubei in her arms as he faltered.

An hour later

Kenzin and Malcolm had been airlifted to the Narrow Gate secret medical facility. The agents had removed the bodies and were finishing up to eliminate any evidence of the violence that had transpired.

Jubei and Navaro stood in the living room, before the Japanese message that was scrolled on the wall in Paty's blood.

"This is a message for me. It says that my mother was taken back to Japan to be punished by the man who stole my father's destiny. I must go to Japan, Navaro. I must end this."

Three hours earlier

Marcus and Mara's laughter echoed through the house as they played Nintendo Wii in the den. In the kitchen, the women were preparing dinner.

Paty glanced at the clock. "What time did they say they would be back?"

"Six o'clock," Matsumi said. She smiled at Paty. "You've brought happiness into my son's life."

Paty blushed with pleasure. "He brought me a lot of happiness too. I feel like I've known him forever."

Matsumi nodded and said, "You do have a deep connection." She rinsed her hands and joined Paty at the table to help her peel the potatoes.

"I have never wanted the life of a ninja for my son," Matsumi said, without looking up. "Not after his real father was killed. I even tried to escape with him when he was still a child. I wanted for us to come to America, to live freely, to live a good life. But that was not what happened."

"How does one become a ninja?" Paty asked.

"They are chosen at infancy. The babies are taken from their mothers and placed in a pool. Those that do not drown are fit to be a ninja. The sorting process is as cruel as the life these babies grow up to live."

Paty lowered her gaze. This was not what she had really wanted to talk about with Matsumi. A smile crossed Paty's face as she thought of what she really wanted to ask.

Matsumi noticed the change and looked at her questioningly.

Paty jumped at the opportunity and asked, "So, what's up with you and my dad?"

Matsumi smiled coyly. She put down the potato peeler. "Your father is a very good man. And I care for him, deeply." Her face lit up as she spoke. Paty knew that look well. It was the same smile she look that she has when she talks about Jubei. "You're in love with my dad, aren't you?"

Matsumi opened her mouth to answer, but was interrupted by a crashing. The door busted open and Kenzin and Mishi appeared as if they had crept out of shadows. The women were stunned and did not scream. They were led into the living room. Marcus and Mara were pushed into the couch. You could hear footsteps could in the hallway and it was hard to believe it could get any worse.

Paty looked at Matsumi. She was pale. Her mouth dropped. Her eyes widened in horror at the sight of the man who had entered the room.

"Ukyo," Matsumi said in a whisper.

Flanked by Kenzin and Mishi, Ukyo stared at Matsumi blankly and said, "My love, you are gorgeous, for a dead woman." He turned his attention turned to Paty, looked her over. He grabbed the young woman and forced her to his feet. "So, this is Jubei's great love. You're a beauty, like Jubei's first love." He grinned and asked Paty, "Did you know that Jubei killed her, simply because I ordered him to?"

Paty was afraid. But she could not allow this man to think that he had poisoned Jubei's very soul. No. Jubei's soul had been saved. "He's not the same man he used to be," Paty said defiantly. "He walks with the Lord, now."

Ukyo chuckled derisively. "Misguided girl. A ninja cannot be anything other than a ninja. Jubei might appear to be one of you, but the demon within him is merely dormant. When confronted with the right situation, it will awaken and he will remember who he is. *What* he is. And your death, dear girl, your death will be the perfect catalyst."

"God have mercy on your soul," Paty said.

Ukyo stroked his wife's cheek.

Matsumi pleaded. "Spare this family, Ukyo. They have

done nothing to you. If there is even a trace of decency left in you, spare them. Please."

"I am going to spare them for I have come for you. I am taking you back to Japan and you are going to wish that you had burned on that stake." With the side of his hand, Ukyo chopped Matsumi's neck and knocked her out.

The children clung to each other, petrified.

Ukyo turned back to Paty and caressed her face. She flinched. "What a shame," he said.

"Kenzin. Make it quick for them. And then, wait until Jubei sees what his past has cost this family, before you kill him." He picked up Matsumi's limp body and said, "I will deal with my beloved wife, myself." He carried her down the hall and out the door. Although the helicopter waiting for him outside was loud, Ukyo could hear the screams coming from inside the house.

Three hours later, present time

"I'm sorry," Navaro said to Jubei. "If only we would have gotten here in time." She put her arm around him while he cried, and they sat in silence.

He thought of the woman he loved, who would never be his wife; the pretty ring she would never wear; the life together he would never know. He clenched his fists; murmured, "I believed I could live this Christian life. Those I loved most are dead, because of the life I led. I know now that I'm cursed to live as a killer. I cannot be anything else. I'm going to Japan, Navaro. I'm going to strike Ukyo down, and anyone, anything that stands in my way. Their souls will cry out to God, but he does not hear those in hell."

Navaro's cell phone rang. She excused herself and stepped away. She spoke briefly and then hung up. Upon returning, she told Jubei that Malcolm was awake and he asked to see him."

Aboard the helicopter, Jubei said nothing throughout the long flight. He thought of the Christian love he had experienced with the pastor's family, which had been just that, an experience. And he was left with this passion that Paty had inspired, but it no longer felt good, or right. It coursed through him unlike any poison he had known. He could not slow its course. It consumed him. Corroded. Strangulated. Without an outlet, Jubei was forced to endure its seething toxicity.

Jubei's face was placid, but, considering the circumstances, his sang-froid betrayed his mask and Navaro watched him apprehensively from the corner of her eye.

They landed on a private medical facility where an administrator greeted Jubei and Navaro, and escorted them to Malcolm's room. Navaro waited outside the door.

Malcolm was awake, but laid there a ravaged man. His body had been injured but that would heal.

The sight of Jubei brought a smile to the pastor's face.

Jubei kept at a distance from the bed. His head hung. His eyes were downcast. "I nearly killed you."

"But you didn't. I know that in that moment you did not know it was me."

"I'm sorry if I frightened you," Jubei said.

"You saved my life."

"But I did not save the children. Paty."

"They were dead by the time we got home."

"They are dead because of me."

"Jubei, look at me."

Jubei looked up and the pastor was looking back at him with such kindness. Understanding. Love. "What happened today, Jubei, was not your fault. It was not your fault."

Jubei nodded, but it was hard to believe that was true.

Malcolm cleared his throat and asked, "And Matsumi, is she dead?"

"Not yet. Ukyo has taken my mother back to Japan. He is going to kill her, and, knowing him, he will do it slowly. Methodically. He will take delight in killing her."

Malcolm turned his head for a moment. What he was hearing was too much to bear.

"I have to go." Jubei turned to leave.

"Wait," the pastor called out. "I know what you are going to do."

Jubei paused, but he kept facing the door. He was too ashamed to face this good man who only wanted to see the goodness in him. Jubei knew there was none left. It had been eradicated by the massacre of those he loved. And although he was glad to find that the pastor was still the man he was before his family was butchered, Jubei could also not understand how that was possible.

"I understand you must save your mother. And I know that you have to bring this all to an end. Jubei, I can see why you cannot live a Godly life until you put this to rest, but Jubei, please, don't fall away."

"It's too late, Malcolm."

"Listen. You spared Kenzin's life, even after he killed people you love, and even if he would not have spared yours. God, my son, He may be using you to put an end to this evil for good. But this doesn't mean that you have to kill. Be like Daniel in the lion's den, but you don't need to become a lion to overcome it." Malcolm reached for his bible on the nightstand. "I want to show you something that will help you battle evil without segregating you from God's love." Malcolm flipped through the pages and handed the open bible to Jubei. "Read Romans 8:31-39."

Jubei was hesitant.

Malcolm encouraged him.

Jubei took a deep breath and began to read out loud: *"With all this in mind what are we to say? If God is on our side, who is against us? He did not spare his own son, but gave him up for us all; how can he fail to lavish every gift upon us? Who will bring a charge against those who God has Chosen? No God, who acquits! Who will pronounce judgment? Not Christ, who died, or rather rose again; not Christ who is at God's right hand and pleads our cause! Then what can separate us from the love of Christ? Can affliction or hardship? Can persecution, hunger, nakedness, or sword? We are being done to death for your sake all day long, as scripture says; we have been treated like lambs to the slaughter and yet, throughout it all, overwhelming victory is ours through him who loved us. For I am convinced that neither death nor life, neither angels or demons, neither the present or the future, nor any super human powers, neither height nor depth, nor anything else in all creation, will be able to separate us from the love of God that is in Christ Jesus our Lord."* Romans 8:31-39

"Do you understand that scripture?" Malcolm asked.

"Yes. But what difference does that make? I can never be anything other than what Ukyo has made me."

Malcolm waved Jubei over, closer, and, when Jubei leaned in Malcolm slapped the back of his head. "What do you mean, what difference does it make? Have you forgotten what you left behind in the water that day you were baptized? The difference is *you*, Jubei. You're no longer the killer you were. Now you're a child of God, and the Lord will fight this battle with you."

Malcolm reached for a pen and then asked Jubei to open his hand.

Jubei gave his hand to Malcolm and he wrote something on Jubei's palm and closed it into a fist, which he clasped with both his hands. He looked up at Jubei and said, "In your hand you hold a weapon. Read what I have written before going into battle. And remember, Jubei, that no matter what happens, you are my family and I love you."

Malcolm was exhausted and could barely keep his eyes opened. He told Jubei that he needed to close them for just a minute. Jubei stayed with the pastor until he was sure that he was asleep.

Navaro awaited Jubei in the hallway. "I'm going with you," she said.

"No," Jubei said sternly. "What I am going to do will turn your stomach. Ukyo took everything from me, and I have nothing left to lose. I will kill every last one of them. I am going to exterminate the ninjas."

"I can help you," she said.

"You'll just be in my way, and besides, I don't want another friend to die."

Jubei began walking away.

Navaro grabbed his arm. "Please, let me help."

Jubei turned and before she realized what was happening, he had placed her in a paralyzing arm lock. Pain shot through her arm. She grimaced and cried out.

Jubei was unmoved. "This pain is nothing compared to what the Yagyu will subject you to. If you really want to help me, stay the hell out of my way." He pushed Navaro aside and walked down the long white hallway.

A police officer was guarding the door to one of the rooms. Kenzin, Jubei thought. He went outside and around the hospital, to where Kenzin's room should be, and went up to the window. Kenzin had an intubation tube in his mouth and was hooked up to several machines. He was awake. Upon seeing Jubei his eyes widened. Without arms and unable to call for help, he could only watch helplessly as Jubei lifted himself in through the open window.

Jubei walked slowly to Kenzin's bedside and observed the fear in his enemy's eyes. Jubei leaned and held a knife to Kenzin's throat. Jubei said nothing and just stood there with the cold blade pressed against Kenzin's throat. He could hear Kenzin's heartbeat accelerate on the monitor and enjoyed watching the rising panic on Kenzin's face. Suddenly, Kenzin flatlined and an alert went off.

Jubei had vanished by the time the guard and the staff entered. Kenzin's face was frozen in a terrified grimace. The medical team moved in and went through the motions to revive Kenzin. The effort was in vain.

Chapter Sixteen:
Facing the Demon

Three days later

In a private cottage in the Yujima Mountains, Jubei set his travel bag on the bed, opened it, and was considering unpacking when he noticed the bible inside his bag. He was perplexed. He thought he had left it at home. He had made a conscious decision not to bring the bible on this trip, not with what Jubei was planning on doing to the Yagyu clan. Indeed, this was no place for a bible. He put it in a dresser drawer, away from sight.

Jubei could make out the rusty tang of old blood, his blood, which had long ago stained these hardwood floors after some brutal mission. He knew this Tamuramaro safe house well. His ninja uniform hung in the closet, where he had left it, and in the corner of the closet was a large trunk, filled with weapons. He opened the trunk and took out a sword, removed it from its sheath and admired its blade. Before he realized what he was doing, he turned around and sliced a table in half. He flipped the sheath up in the air and spun around, caught the sheath and slid the sword into it. He glanced at the table he had split in half. He knew he needed to go outside, and take in some fresh air, so as not to destroy everything within the cottage. Jubei dropped the sword beside the broken table, grabbed an axe, and went out to chop some wood. While splitting each log he imagined an enemy being sliced down. He chopped and chopped and chopped some more. No matter how much he chopped he felt the need to chop some more. He must have spent hours outside, swinging the heavy axe over and over, because when he could no longer raise the axe, the sun had set and stars illuminated his path back to the cottage. He only hauled in the logs he would need for that night.

Jubei stacked the logs into the fireplace and lit it. He sat in front of the fire and watched it kindle. Its warmth made him think of Paty. He would love to sit with her, his arms wrapped around her, reminiscing about their first date at the movies and how nervous he had been. She would have teased him. They would have kissed. The children would peek at them from around the corner and giggle. Malcolm would scold them and they would run up the stairs and laugh out loud. Their laughter would echo through the house. That year with Malcolm and his family was the highlight of his life. Jubei opened his left hand. On his palm he could still make out Malcolm's writing that Jubei had tried to scrub off for days. But there it was, plain to read, Eph 6:10-17. That was Ephesians. And whatever did chapter six, verses ten through seventeen say? He drew a blank. Jubei longed for those days when he had the Lord in his heart. Once more he longed for his quiet time with Him. He went to the dresser, retrieved the bible, and returned to the fireplace where he settled held the holy book against his chest for a while, hoping that it would make him feel better, if only a little bit. It did not. Jubei had set himself up for disappointment, again, just like he had fooled himself into believing that his life would be like that always. Happy. Fulfilled. He felt like he had been fooled. He had allowed them all to delude him but had only himself to blame.

Exasperated, Jubei threw the bible into the fire and a flame burst toward Jubei, and he got into a defensive stance, but just as he was about to be burned, the flame deviated and swerved into the corner, where it metamorphosed into Ukyo, who stood there, arms crossed, glaring at Jubei. "You've lost some speed," he said. "You better get in touch with your innermost strength if you want to kill your father."

Jubei said to himself, "This isn't real."

Ukyo laughed derisively. "I'm as real as the nails you helped put in Christ's flesh."

Jubei rubbed his eyes and when he opened them Paty stood where Ukyo had been. "Avenge me, my love," she said in her sweetest voice. Kill Ukyo. Kill them all."

Jubei balled his fist. "Demon," he said between clenched teeth. He sprinted to the broken table and grabbed his sword, unsheathing it as he turned. The demon was nowhere to be seen.

"Show yourself!" Jubei shouted.

Paty reappeared surrounded in fire with black eyes. Her eyes were coyly downcast. "Why do you pull your sword against me, my love?" the demon asked in Paty's singsong voice. "I know you love me, Jubei. And I've loved you even after you confessed the unspeakable horror you had inflicted on Maki and her entire family. It seems that those you love die. Even when I knew that your past would eventually kill my family, I still loved you." The demon reached for Jubei and gently caressed the side of his face. Its hand felt like hers, and it was hard to believe this wasn't Paty. "I had it all wrong," she continued, "and you were right. The only way to live in peace is to kill Ukyo. You must kill him otherwise he will surely kill you. It's what the Lord wants. Why else would

He bless you with your magnificent talent for bringing lives to an end?" The demon teared up. "My love, I hate that our life together was over before it could begin. You know that I would have said *yes*. The ring, it was perfect. And I'll never be able to wear it because you failed to kill Ukyo when you had the chance."

Jubei tried to look away, but the demon turned Jubei's face back to confront him with Paty.

"Why didn't you kill him when you had the chance, Jubei? I would still be here."

The demon split in two forms that metamorphosed into Marcus and Mara. Together the children said, "We would still be here too. Avenge us, Jubei. We won't be able to rest unless you bring death to Ukyo and the Yagyu."

The children vanished and Paty stood in their stead. She began walking towards him, moving in that swaying way of hers that mesmerized him. Jubei did not back away. He thought he could hear another voice in the background, a familiar voice, but he couldn't make it out. He felt faint; lost his grip on the sword.

The demon cradled Jubei's face and was leaning in to kiss him when Jubei heard the other voice again—this time succinctly. "This is not my daughter Jubei. This demon is not your love. Paty was a woman of God and would never have asked you to commit an act that would put your soul at risk. She was a woman of God like you are a man of God. So, fight this demon as a man of God."

The demon kissed Jubei. Its lips felt as soft as Paty's. He wavered.

Malcolm's voice snapped him back. "Ephesians, Jubei. Chapter six, verses ten through seventeen."

And it all came back to Jubei.

Ephesians 6:10: Finally be strong in the lord and in his mighty power.

Jubei palm punched the demon into the wall. Jubei picked up the sword and held it in front of him, ready for battle.

The demon stood up. "Have it your way. When I'm done with you, your will will be tattered and your soul shall be mine." The demon took on Jubei's form. A flaming sword materialized in its hand.

Ephesians 6:11-13: 11Put on the full armor of God so that you can take your stand against the devil's schemes. 12For our struggle is not against the flesh and blood but against the rulers, against the authorities, against the powers of darkness. 13Therefore put on the full armor of God, so that when the day of evil comes, you may be able to stand your ground, and after you have done everything to stand.

Before Jubei could anticipate the demon's move, it slashed Jubei twice across the chest. Jubei staggered. Blood sprayed the wall. His cuts were deep.

The demon raised the sword, preparing for a straight downward to slash and Jubei deflected the sword, but the demon's strength forced Jubei to his knees. For extra support, to absorb the demon's attack, Jubei put his other hand against the blunt edge of the sword, and swiftly cut the demon across the leg. Jubei rolled underneath the demon, briskly got back to his feet and slashed the demon across the back. The demon staggered forward, regained his footing, turned and stabbed Jubei in the stomach. Jubei dropped to the floor. The demon kicked Jubei into the wall and, as Jubei tumbled to the ground, the demon was on him before he could make a move. The demon lifted Jubei up by the neck. In turn, Jubei chopped the demon repeatedly in the collarbone, and then shoved his fingers into its eyes. It released Jubei. Jubei did a dive roll and grabbed his sword, stood up and faced the badly battered demon.

Ephesians 6: 14-16:14Stand firm, then with the belt of truth buckled around your waist, with the breast plate of righteousness in place, 15and with your feet fitted with readiness that comes from the gospel of peace. 16In addition to all this, take up the shield of faith, with which you can extinguish all the flaming arrows of the evil one.

The demon charged at Jubei with an upward slash, followed by a spinning slash. Jubei deflected both attacks and slid across the hardwood floor. The demon slashed once more and cut Jubei across the cheek. The demon swung his sword and cut through Jubei's blade. It cut Jubei again and again; all well placed cuts intended to maximize suffering.

The demon swung down. Jubei backflip kicked the sword from the demon's hand. Jubei spun around and kicked its face, dropped to his knees and leg swept the demon, knocking it on its back. However, the demon stood up right away, held out its hand and set the sword afloat, projecting it onto Jubei, who stepped aside in time and caught the sword by the handle. But before Jubei could wield the sword, the demon punched him in the stomach and Jubei doubled over in pain. The demon delivered several more punches to Jubei's stomach until Jubei's hold on the sword weakened. Then the demon repossessed the sword and smacked Jubei across the face with the blade's flat edge, hurling Jubei across the ravaged room.

Jubei had been evading the demon's attacks as best he could, but it was proving to be far too swift and powerful, and it felt like the demon was just getting started.

"You cannot win this battle," the demon said. "Give in to me and the punishment will stop. One way or the other, your soul shall be mine."

The demon lifted Jubei up with an upper cut. It grabbed Jubei's ankle and swung him into the floor, and walls, leaving the entire cabin splattered with Jubei's blood. Jubei was on his hands and knees, dazed and coughing up blood. The demon kicked him in the stomach. Jubei rolled over in agonizing pain.

"You will not win this battle, Jubei."

Ephesians 6:17:17 Take the helmet of salvation and the sword of the spirit, which is the word of God…

In the fireplace, the bible had turned into ash, nevertheless, the word of God was omnipresent. And in its soothing truth, he perceived that he had thus improperly fought this battle.

18 And pray in the spirit on all occasions with all kinds of prayers and requests.

The demon balled his fist and charged at Jubei and in its eyes Jubei could tell that he was intent on finishing him off. Jubei knelt down and put his forehead to the floor. In despair he cried out, "Lord, I am lost and I am weak and I need you in this battle against a demon. My soul is filled with rage. My heart is blackened. I thirst to kill and I long to slaughter my enemies. My Lord, I need you more than ever."

The demon howled in pain and the darkness in its eyes flickered. Jubei kept praying and every word pierced the demon. It twisted and fell and rolled in agony. Never before had Jubei heard such despair and he teared up, kept praying. "Guide me through the valley of the shadow of death. I do not dwell here any longer and the demon endeavors to drag me into the darkness. Lord, you said you would never leave me nor forsake me, and I know you won't leave me now. Please, help me, God. Help me have mercy on Ukyo for what he has done to those I love. Help me bring an end to all of this, once and for all, but not in the manner that I had set out to, but in the manner you want me to. Guide me to end this, Lord, to stop my father's evil without losing myself. I cannot do this alone. Please God, fight by my side."

The demon was getting desperate. He dropped to his knees and began to whisper lies, half-truths and manipulations into Jubei's ear to confuse and distract Jubei while he prayed. Jubei continued to pray. No matter what the demon said and tried to show him. Jubei kept his head to the floor and his eyes shut tight. He prayed.

The demon took the sword and began to cut into Jubei's flesh and Jubei prayed. The sword eventually broke across Jubei's back. Jubei prayed.

The ground shook. The battle lasted throughout the night. The demon threw all it had at Jubei. Jubei prayed. He prayed and prayed and cried out to the Lord. The demon dragged Jubei to the gates of Hell, but Jubei prayed his way back. He was wounded and he bled, but it only reinforced his will to overcome.

"Lord, I am your son. You took my sins and with your blood you have cleansed me . With you there is no enemy I cannot face. I will put on the full armor of God and I will fight for your glory. You are my true father, and in Jesus' name I rebuke this demon. I drive him from my soul. The devil will not have a foothold. In the name of Jesus, leave me be, you murderous, treacherous demon. You have no power here. Get out! You are not welcomed and you will not dwell in me any longer. In the name of Jesus, get out!"

The demon screamed violently as it was being forced out of the cabin. Powerless. Defeated. It was gone. In the fireplace the fire simmered down. Jubei remained with his head on the floor and kept praying until the morning sun shone through the dusty window and filled Jubei with hope. "In Jesus' name I pray, amen."

The fire had burned itself out and Jubei was alone. And with the exception of the shattered table, the cabin was as it had been when he had dropped his bag on the bed the day before.

Jubei's sword was intact and in its sheath. His recent wounds were gone. Although the hardwood floor was still stained with the rusty color of old blood, there wasn't a trace of fresh blood to be found on any surface.

With some effort, Jubei got back on his feet, opened the door and went outside where the air was fresh. The sun warmed his skin, and the sky was clear. Jubei knew what needed to be done.

Yagyu Palace

Ukyo entered the court, escorted by ninjas, and sat in his chair, surrounded with guards. Servants danced and sung in unison. In the background, three wooden crosses were being erected.

A ninja approached Ukyo and bowed humbly before him. "I have news from America," he said. "Kenzin and Mishi have been defeated. Both are dead."

Ukyo nodded nonchalantly. "Well, they served their purpose. And I suppose you're going to inform me that Jubei is headed here?"

"Yes, my lord."

"Make sure he does not get here alive."

The ninja excused himself to go carry out Ukyo's command.

At the drawbridge, Jubei humbly knelt before the ninjas on guard duty. The ninjas glanced at one another in confusion. Two of the men cautiously searched Jubei.

Jubei allowed them to restrain him with chains and demanded to be taken to see Ukyo.

Apprehensive Yagyu men, women, and children, watched in awe as Jubei was paraded through their village. This was the closest they had ever been to this angel of death that had haunted their nightmares and their imagination. It was as if they helplessly expected that he would suddenly slaughter them all. But as Jubei was led through the parted crowd, all they could see in Jubei was a chained man.

The Courtyard

Matsumi was dragged into the courtyard and forced to her knees at Ukyo's feet. Her dress was tattered; her back exposed and bloodied.

Once more the doors opened and utter silence fell upon the court, as Jubei was escorted in. His chains clanked. Ukyo raised an eyebrow. Matsumi was distraught at the sight of her son in this place. Still, she smiled at him despite her tears.

Jubei was impassive. His stony gaze was fixed on Ukyo. When he reached Ukyo, Jubei was kicked behind the knee and forced to kneel, but he had not felt the kick and merely went through the physical motion. His gaze remained on Ukyo.

"So, my son, you return and allow yourself to get caught. Truly, you have slipped."

"I didn't slip when I eliminated Kenzin and Mishi, and besides, you are not my father. I am well aware of who you really are."

Ukyo glanced disdainfully at Matsumi. "Well, you know the truth, and, in this case, the truth shall not set you free."

"Release my mother and deal with me."

Ukyo scoffed. "You're in no position to demand anything."

The three crosses had been hoisted and were held in place. "You're a Christian now, aren't you? A man of Jesus? Then you can appreciate that you will die like Him. They say that Christ experienced one of the cruelest deaths in the world's history. Soon enough you will know if this claim has been exaggerated or if it is accurate."

"No one has to die Ukyo."

Ukyo slapped Jubei with the back of his hand. "Oh, you and your treacherous whore of a mother are going to die." Ukyo punched Jubei in the head and, still chained, all Jubei could do was allow himself to be punished by Ukyo. Jubei's mouth bled profusely. Matsumi struggled futilely. She was too weak to help her son.

"I see that this Christian faith of yours has made you weak. Weakness is a path to death." Ukyo signaled the guards and they dragged the weakened Jubei to the foot of one of the crosses.

"One cross is for you, Jubei. Another is for you, my beloved. And you both might be curious as to whom the third cross is intended for." Ukyo nodded to a servant that had been awaiting his orders. He momentarily left the room and returned with an older man whose hair was spiked and graying hair on the sides. Jubei had not seen him before, however, Matsumi shouted, "Hanzo!"

The man was visibly moved at the sight of her. "Matsumi!" he called out.

Both struggled to get to each other while Ukyo smirked at the unfolding drama.

"Jubei, meet your biological father. Whatever it was that your mother told you, she bent the truth to suit her reality. I did challenge this man for leadership of the clan, and I defeated him. Nevertheless, as you can see, I did not kill your father."

Jubei was bewildered.

Ukyo went over to Hanzo and put his arm around him. "Indeed, I did not kill you, my adoptive brother. Some things are worse than death, aren't they, Hanzo?" He turned to Jubei. "You see, Jubei, your father's deepest torment derived from being powerless at saving his own family, for had he even contacted either Matsumi or you, he knows too well that I would have put you both to death as a man of my word. So this father of yours, he had to step into the shadows and be subjected to witness, from afar, his loving wife become mine, and his precious son be raised to become the sort of man that is able to kill every living being in this very room; a man that strikes fear even among his brethren; a man whose name alone congeals the blood of his enemies. In truth, it is thanks to Jubei's skill as a killer that the Tamuramaro rose to power and amassed a vast fortune. And I have had the pleasure of enjoying the fruits of the Tamuramaro's prosperity, as well as the honor of destroying this clan at the zenith of its prosperity. With the Yagyu clan now restored and victorious, I figured that this is the ideal time for a long overdue family reunion." He turned his attention back to his adoptive brother. "You should be proud of your son, Jubei, the most powerful ninja in the world."

Ukyo signaled his ninjas to take Jubei and Hanzo to their crosses, on which they would be crucified, out of spite for Jubei's newfound faith.

Unexpectedly, Jubei pushed the men escorting him. He had managed to free himself from the chains during Ukyo's self-serving monologue. He pointed defiantly at the man he had once called *father*. "I challenge you, Ukyo. I cannot allow you to condemn my family and I challenge you for control of the clan."

"Jubei, no!" Matsumi pleaded.

Ukyo looked at Jubei in disbelief.

Right away Jubei was surrounded by ninjas armed with a multitude of weapons, including a spear-like wooden shaft, tipped with a metal blade—a Naginata.

Jubei shouted. "I only want Ukyo. No one else needs to get hurt. Back away, now."

Ukyo returned to his chair from where he watched a couple of ninjas brandishing swords charge at Jubei. Jubei moved out of the way of the first ninja and then ducked beneath second ninja's sword as he swung at Jubei's head. Once more the first ninja swung at Jubei, who moved to the side and disarmed the ninja from behind, and took possession of the ninja's sword in time to parry the other ninja's attack.

Jubei spun around, kicking the first ninja in the face. The ninja dropped. Easily, Jubei disarmed the second ninja and threw him on his back, knocking the wind out of him.

Another ninja sprang into the air and swung down at Jubei, who swerved in time. Jubei grabbed the ninja by the neck, while he was still in the air, and slammed him down. Hard. He tried to get back up but could not even roll onto his side. His spine had been dislocated. He would not walk again.

Jubei warned the ninjas who were tentatively moving in on him. "Just back away. I don't want to hurt anyone else."

Jubei dropped both swords and, while watching the ninjas in the corner of his eye, he turned his attention to Ukyo. "Are you afraid to face me alone?"

Hanzo and Matsumi struggled to free themselves from their restraints, but couldn't.

Ukyo shouted, "Kill him!" And at once the ninjas moved in. Jubei grabbed both swords from the ground and cut down the ninjas, one by one, as they attacked.

Jubei was sliced across the back and fell into a dive roll, rolling back to his feet. He jumped up and split kicked two ninjas who closed in from either side.

A ninja armed with a Naginata swung down. Jubei swerved. The heavy blade struck the floor. Jubei stepped on the blade to hold the Naginata in place, and kicked the man in the stomach.

Then Jubei threw both his swords at a couple of ninjas who were both hit in the shoulder. Jubei took the Naginata and, twirling it around, he deflected several attacks.

Jubei twirled the Naginata over his head, around his back, and brought it to rest at his side. The ninjas stopped in their tracks, in unison, standing in place for an instant, their faces frozen and gaze faraway. Suddenly their clothes split and dropped to their feet. Thereafter the men fell to the ground, naked, stunned, and wounded, but all of them alive.

"I could have killed every single one of you, but I don't want to. Whereas Ukyo doesn't care whether you live or die. Think about what you're doing."

From the sidelines, other ninjas moved in like a second wave. Jubei sighed.

One hurled a sequence of Shuriken, most of which Jubei managed to deflect, but a few metal stars struck his chest and Jubei staggered backwards.

Another ninja hurled Kamas at Jubei. Jubei dropped the Naginata and caught the Kamas in mid-air, quickly hurling them at an attacking ninja. He struck him in the kneecap. The man howling in agony, the man fell. Jubei pulled the Shurikens from his wounds and tossed them at three other ninjas, hitting their hands. He evaded another attack with a dive roll, jumped in the air and landed, straight up, on top of a ninja's shoulders. He stomped on the man's head and knocked him out.

Jubei grabbed a sword from the ground, and deflected a ninjas attack. Jubei was trying to make his way to Ukyo. Jubei rolled to the side and deflected another attack with the sword. Two ninjas moved in on Jubei. Jubei remained in place just long enough so that when he dashed out of the way the ninjas killed each other.

Jubei was heading up the stairs, as he fought off some ninjas, when, abruptly, several chains wrapped around his neck and yanked him down into an awaiting mob of ninjas.

After several minutes of trying to free himself, Hanzo was beginning to wiggle out of his chains.

Dragged by the chain, Jubei was choking. He grabbed for

a weapon and with it he cut through the chain. He did not have a moment to catch his breath. He had to fight on.

Jubei grabbed smoke bombs from a fallen ninja and dropped one. Smoke filled the air around him and he seemed to disappear in it.

Jubei grabbed a ninja from the crowd, pulled him into the smoke, and once more he was gone. The disconcerted men looked around, standing there like lost children.

Ukyo yelled out, "Fan out and find him!"

As ordered, the ninjas dispersed to search the court in a coordinated fan-like pattern.

Disguised in a Yagyu uniform, Jubei appeared behind Ukyo and put a knife to his throat. Ukyo dropped a smoke bomb and leaped onto a balcony overlooking his throne. Jubei dropped the knife, grabbed a sword and went after Ukyo.

Jubei landed on the balcony, which led into the grand dining room. He held the sword out in front of him, remaining vigilant as he expected Ukyo would appear from within the shadows.

Ukyo broke through a table, from beneath it, and shot a spring-loaded chain that had been concealed in his sleeves. The chain struck Jubei in the chest and would have crushed an average man's chest, and, although the blow was extraordinary, the body armor Jubei was wearing underneath the uniform absorbed the bulk of the impact. Still, Jubei was flung into the wall. He shook his head, rubbed at his chest, and slowly stood up.

Ukyo untied his sword and sheath from his waist.

"So, you want to challenge me?" said Ukyo. "Very well. Now you will see why I am the lord of ninjas."

Jubei raised his sword and they both men ran at each other, leaped upwards, but Ukyo was swifter than Jubei had expected and, while in the air, Ukyo kicked Jubei's chest and sent him crashing through a few tables. Jubei rolled back to his feet. Ukyo appeared behind Jubei and Jubei spun around in time to deflect his attack. Ukyo thrust his sword handle and hit Jubei's cheekbone. Jubei staggered back. Ukyo smacked Jubei's chin with the sheath, simultaneously side kicking him. Jubei rolled backwards, onto his feet.

Ukyo shot another chain at Jubei, which he evaded. In turn Jubei kicked Ukyo in the chest. He backflipped to his feet. Jubei moved in again, kicking the side of Ukyo's knee. As Ukyo went down, he palm punched Jubei's stomach. Right away Ukyo pulled out a knife and stabbed Jubei in the stomach. Jubei staggered as he kicked the knife from Ukyo's hand. Ukyo grabbed Jubei's legs and pulled them out from under him. Jubei hit the floor headfirst. Ukyo got on top of Jubei and punched his face, and when Ukyo finally got off, he lifted Jubei over his head and threw him across the room. In the air Jubei twisted and landed on his hands and knees.

Ukyo unsheathed his sword and said between clenched teeth, "Enough games."

Ukyo charged at Jubei and swung his sword. Jubei just barely dodged the blade. Ukyo was relentless, and, although Jubei did his best to evade the attacks, he was cut a few times.

Jubei kicked up one of the tables. Ukyo sliced through it. Jubei threw another table but Ukyo sliced through it as well. Jubei picked up his sword. Ukyo swung at him and he parried his attack. Sparks flew as their blades made contact.

Jubei stepped back, swung, and cut Ukyo across the face. Ukyo put his hand against the wound and Jubei kicked him in the chest, sending him airborne through the dining room and onto the balcony.

Below, ninjas gathered to watch the battle, which would be legendary, no matter who would emerge the victor. Jubei and Ukyo swung and parried and swung and parried, neither gaining an advantage on the other.

Jubei leaped and backflipped from the railing of the balcony. Ukyo followed.

Finally, Hanzo broke loose from his chain. He rushed to free Matsumi, whose guard had joined the other ninjas watching the ongoing sword duel. He freed Matsumi and she fell into his arms. Matsumi caressed Hanzo's face.

"Hanzo?" she asked.

Hanzo hugged Matsumi and held her as though this was last time he would ever be able to hold her in his arms. They could not speak to each other. Their son was in danger. Like the others they turned their attention to the battle.

Sniper ninjas had taken strategic positions and aimed at Jubei. Fired. Jubei felt the onslaught and deflected dozens of their arrows.

From behind Jubei, Ukyo stab down at Jubei, but Jubei swerved out of the way just as another arrow cut though the air, directly aimed at his heart. Jubei caught the arrow in mid-air, spun around and stuck the arrow into Ukyo's shoulder. Ukyo staggered. Jubei hit him in the stomach with the blunt end of the Naginata. Ukyo keeled over. Jubei raised his leg high up and brought it down heavily onto Ukyo's neck.

One arrow hit Jubei's leg and then another his neck, not fatally wounding him but the pain was excruciating. A third arrow penetrated his shoulder. Dozens more arrows came down upon him but he managed to deflect the arrows back at the snipers who were hit with their own arrows, but did not die from the injuries.

Ukyo was in his fighting stance. Jubei dropped the Naginata. Ukyo threw the first kick, which Jubei blocked. Ukyo followed up with a roundhouse kick that Jubei blocked as well. Ukyo waved his hands tauntingly and then palm punched Jubei in the chest. Jubei staggered. Ukyo palm punched him again and knocked him off his feet. Jubei landed on his hands and kicked upwards at Ukyo's face. Jubei spun around three times and kicked Ukyo in his face every single time. When Jubei finally landed he punched Ukyo in the face. Ukyo fell back, rolled onto his feet and dropped a smoke bomb.

When the smoke had cleared, Ukyo was gone.

Jubei got into a defensive stance and, unsure as to what direction Ukyo would be coming from, he peered over his shoulder. Ukyo sprang from the ground and kicked Jubei in the face, before vanishing again.

Ukyo was dropping down on Jubei as spikes sprung from the soles of his shoes. He readied to stomp Jubei's head, but Jubei had vanished by the time Ukyo landed where Jubei had been standing. Ukyo chuckled, and said, "I have taught you well."

Ukyo turned and Jubei was standing beside him. Jubei grabbed Ukyo by the neck, lifted him, and choked slammed him. He immediately picked Ukyo up and tossed him high in the air. Jubei jumped up after him, and, while in mid-air, Jubei struck Ukyo in the chest with a flying side kick that hurled Ukyo into his throne, smashing it to pieces.

With some difficulty Ukyo scrambled back to his feet. He took a deep breath and charged Jubei, throwing punches and different hand strikes at him. Jubei managed to block the last couple of hand strikes, and then he came back at Ukyo with palm punch, but Ukyo deflected Jubei's attack before he could strike his chest, grabbed Jubei's arm and twisted it until it snapped. Jubei cried out. Ukyo used Jubei's moment of weakness to aim his fist at Jubei's nose, to deliver a fatal punch that would drive Jubei's nasal cavity back into his brain. However, before Ukyo could even deliver the punch, Jubei poked Ukyo in the eye. Ukyo screamed and began to furiously kick and punch at the air. Jubei had easily dodged each attack, which only further infuriated Ukyo.

As Ukyo staggered about, Jubei delivered a near fatal

kick to his chest, breaking a couple of Ukyo's ribs and sent him crashing, face down, into the shattered fragments of his own throne.

Jubei walked over to where Ukyo was moaning softly. He stood over the man he had once called *father*, and stoically addressed him. "For years you have tormented my mother, a kind and loving woman you coerced to be your wife while blackmailing her true love, my real father, to remain in the shadows of our lives, this farce, an unnecessary tragedy you had masterminded for the mere purpose of stroking your own demented ego for reasons that you alone could ever be able to rationalize. And now you lay here broken, having lost a woman that I know you have loved despite yourself. And in this very moment she is reunited with the man whose life you coveted and usurped, only to have him in turn witness you forfeit it all. And the irony of it, Ukyo, is that you have proudly raised me to be a monster, like you, and, as that monster, I should not spare your life." Jubei crouched beside Ukyo, and Ukyo flinched, bracing himself for the inevitable fatal blow. "However, I choose not to be that monster but a man of God. And as a man of God I choose to forgive you."

The ninjas were stunned. They watched in awe as Jubei pushed himself back to his feet and slowly limped over to his parents where he collapsed in Hanzo's arms.

Ukyo rolled onto his side, grabbed a sword, and in a desperate last burst of energy he ran at Jubei with his sword raised above his head, hollering, already a victor in his own mind. The reunited family was taken aback and before either one of them could react, two ninjas intercepted Ukyo and shoved him to the ground.

Ukyo raised his head and stared back at Jubei with such hatred that it choked him up as he spoke. "I will be awaiting you in hell, Jubei."

Both ninjas raised their swords. One ran it through

Ukyo. The other decapitated him. The headed rolled a few times and then stopped, face upwards, eyes wide open and glazed over.

Both men sheathed their swords, turned towards Jubei and knelt down. The large court filled with the sound of ninjas and servants following their example, kneeling respectfully before, Jubei, the new lord of the ninjas.

A week later

Discharged from the hospital, Malcolm was in his room, reading his bible while awaiting his ride. A knock at the door distracted him and he raised his eyes. Jubei peeked in and Malcolm's face lit up. He eagerly waved Jubei in.

Jubei walked in with a slight limp. His right arm was in a cast and his neck was stitched up. Malcolm hurried over to Jubei and hugged him tightly. "Praise God, you're in one piece, my ninja friend."

"I have a surprise for you," said Jubei, and, as though on cue, Matsumi walked in, smiling. She hugged Malcolm. He was overjoyed they were both alive. Hanzo entered and Malcolm looked at him curiously.

"This is Hanzo," Jubei said. "He is my father."

Malcolm's mouth dropped open. He didn't know what to say.

Jubei laughed. "It's a long story. I'll tell you all about it later."

Hanzo bowed to Malcolm, and Malcolm returned the respectful gesture.

Days later

The mourners dispersed. Matsumi and Hanzo went to the car ahead of Jubei and Malcolm while both men hugged in the cemetery. They did not exchange comforting words. Their love and grief resounded in the tightness of their breath, the tremor in their jaw. Malcolm patted Jubei on the back and then took a long last look at the tombstones of Marcus, Mara, and Paty, which were flanked with large flower arrangements on stands—white lilies, red roses, and white larkspur—which had been their favorites. Malcolm nodded at Jubei and headed toward the car.

Jubei kneeled at the foot of Paty's tombstone. He murmured, "I miss you. I will miss you, everyday, for the rest of my life. But I want you to know that I have kept my word, Paty. I was loyal to my faith. And yet I brought my mother home, and my father as well. He was here just a moment ago. I know it's hard to believe, but all these years he was alive. Oh, Paty. I don't know what happens now. I don't know what I'm supposed to do without you, my love. All I know is that I will continue to follow the Lord and keep you in my heart, always."

Jubei stood up. He felt a presence and turned. Navaro was standing at a respectful distance. "I've been praying for you, Jubei," she said. "I now understand why you left me behind. And I'm glad you would not allow me to come along. I would not have been here today."

Jubei smiled gratefully and hobbled towards Navaro.

She smirked. "And judging by the looks of you, your father kicked your butt too, huh?"

Jubei paused. "Ukyo wasn't my father," he said sternly. "I discovered that, my entire life, Ukyo masqueraded as my father but my real father is still alive. And he is here." Jubei pointed to Hanzo in the distance. "I know it's complicated. But now my parents are reunited and Ukyo is no longer a threat."

"So, you killed him."

"I did not have to. His own evil brought death onto him."

"What will you do now?"

Jubei shrugged.

"Are you going to return to Japan to rebuild your clan?"

"My father will do that in my stead, and, from now on, our clan will be helping people, like my father had originally intended us to."

"You know, your skills could help the Narrow Gate lead people to safety. Malcolm's already agreed to help us. Our world is progressively degenerating. God is no longer even a thought in most people's lives. How I wish I could say that your days of fighting are over, but I sense they're just beginning, for all of us. Please, Jubei. The soldiers of the Lord are dwindling and more than ever He needs you."

Jubei took a step back. Navaro's words were nauseating, but their veracity resonated in his soul. He glanced at Paty's tombstone. What she would have done?

He turned back to Navaro, and said, candidly, "Count me in."